The Temptress
— — — —
Lament for a Lousy Lover
— — — —
The Stripper
— — — —

Three Novels by
Carter Brown

INTRODUCTION BY GEORGE KELLEY

Stark House Press • Eureka California

THE TEMPTRESS / LAMENT FOR A LOUSY LOVER /
THE STRIPPER

Published by Stark House Press
1315 H Street
Eureka, CA 95501, USA
griffinskye3@sbcglobal.net
www.starkhousepress.com

THE TEMPTRESS
Originally published and copyright © 1960 by Horwitz Publications,
Sydney, Australia. Reprinted in the U.S. by Signet Books, New York, 1960.

LAMENT FOR A LOUSY LOVER
Originally published and copyright © 1960 by Horwitz Publications,
Sydney, Australia. Reprinted in the U.S. by Signet Books, New York, 1960.

THE STRIPPER
Originally published and copyright © 1961 by Horwitz Publications,
Sydney, Australia. Reprinted in the U.S. by Signet Books, New York, 1961.

Reprinted by permission of the Estate of Alan G. Yates, and licensed via
The Carter Brown Foundation Pty Ltd, Australia. All rights reserved
under International and Pan-American Copyright Conventions.

"How 'Carter Brown' Sold 100 Million Books" copyright © 2023
by George Kelley

ISBN: 979-8-88601-023-7

Text design by Mark Shepard, shepgraphics.com
Cover design by Jeff Vorzimmer, ¡caliente!design, Austin, Texas
Cover art by Robert McGuiness
Proofreading by Bill Kelly

PUBLISHER'S NOTE
This is a work of fiction. Names, characters, places and incidents are
either the products of the author's imagination or used fictionally, and
any resemblance to actual persons, living or dead, events or locales, is
entirely coincidental.

Without limiting the rights under copyright reserved above, no part of
this publication may be reproduced, stored, or introduced into a retrieval
system or transmitted in any form or by any means (electronic,
mechanical, photocopying, recording or otherwise) without the prior
written permission of both the copyright owner and the above publisher
of the book.

First Stark House Press Edition: April 2023

THE TEMPTRESS
In which Lieutenant Al Wheeler must solve the murder of the private detective
♦ who was tailing the rich woman's daughter and her jazzed-up boyfriend
♦ who might have been involved in a shady blackmail racket
♦ who certainly had something to do with the kinky uncle

LAMENT FOR A LOUSY LOVER
In which Lieutenant Al Wheeler is paired with sexy Mavis Seidlitz to solve
♦ the murder of the TV western actor who gets in the way of a real bullet
♦ the mystery of the producer's missing diamond ring
♦ the dilemma of the doomsaying astrologer who has been set up to take the fall

THE STRIPPER
In which Lieutenant Al Wheeler fails to prevent a high-rise suicide that leads him to
♦ a suspicious lonely hearts club run by a couple right out of an ancient daguerreotype
♦ a shy florist with a penchant for loud showgirls
♦ and the star of the show, the voluptuous stripper known as Deadpan Doris

Contents

7
How "Carter Brown"
Sold 100 Million Books
by George Kelley

11
The Temptress
by Carter Brown

109
Lament for a Lousy Lover
by Carter Brown

201
The Stripper
by Carter Brown

289
Carter Brown
Bibliography

How "Carter Brown" Sold 100 Million Books

By George Kelley

"For Victor Weybright at Signet (NAL), who along with Stanley Horwitz, helped bring Carter Brown to a global audience, success was assured. 'I should not be surprised if, during the ten years of our arrangement with Horwitz Publications, the copies sold dwarf the figures of Erle Stanley Gardiner, Erskine Caldwell or Mickey Spillane...He writes with humour and a playful sense of fantasy, and succeeded in inventing a mythical USA with more verisimilitude than is revealed in the writing of many famous American realists'."

www.carterbrownonline.com/carter-brown

Alan Geoffrey Yates, an Englishman born in 1923, served in the Royal Navy during World War II. Once the War ended, Yates married a girl in Sydney, Australia, he had fallen in love with during shore leave. Over the next few years, the couple traveled back and forth between England and Australia. Yates tried several jobs but found a prime opportunity in Sydney working for Qantas Airlines in their publicity department writing for their in-house magazines. To supplement his income, Yates started using his free time writing for the Australian pulp magazines. He found success with Horwitz Publications, selling them Westerns, then horror stories, then science fiction stories using various pen names.

Yates's editors at Horwitz then suggested he try writing a detective story. Yates did and Horwitz bought it. Horwitz supplied the "by Peter Carter-Brown" beneath the title. Shortly thereafter, the hyphen and then the "Peter" were soon dropped and "Carter Brown" emerged.

While Yates continued to sell his work to Horwitz, there was a growing interest in Carter Brown in the United States.

"Signet evidently knew of the Australian Carter Brown books

that Alan G. Yates had been writing for Horwitz Publications since 1951– at the rate of a novel a month plus two novelettes – and they decided to give CB a try at snaring a share of the Shell Scott readership [Shell Scott, Richard S. Prather's popular California private eye character, whose adventures, like Al Wheeler's, invariably involved gorgeous women]. Victor Weybright, head of NAL, quoted by Yates in his autobiography, has a more succinct explanation: 'With Carter Brown, I thought we might be selling dime novels for a quarter. " –Art Scott, "carter brown: The Books and the Covers". *Paperback Parade 104* p. 22

The first "carter brown" (the lower-case font was Horwitz's logo design that Signet used from 1958 to 1972 when Signet switched from painted covers to photo covers) published in America was *The Body*. The paperback book was in stores and on newsstands July 1958. It featured the most popular Carter Brown lead character, Al Wheeler. Barye Phillips was chosen to do the covers for the initial run of Carter Brown in the U.S.

"Something else appealed to Brad Cummings, Yates's first editor at NAL. 'We especially like the Carter Brown pace. With very few exceptions, the reader is pulled along relentlessly …to the end. Alan includes enough atmosphere, movement and violent incident to make the reader feel he is getting a full meal.' E. L Doctorow, described by Barack Obama as "one of America's greatest novelists", was also to become a Carter Brown editor at one point."

www.carterbrownonline.com/carter-brown

THE TEMPTRESS

"She's a saucy seductress worth three million dollars—a good catch … for a killer."

That blurb captures the essence of The Temptress as Al Wheeler finds himself dealing with a rich, spoiled teenager who attracts the Wrong Kind of male attention. The story opens with a murder of a sleazy private investigator who had intimate photographs of the temptress in action. The temptress's millionaire mother hired the private investigator with the advice of her suspicious brother-in-law. Al Wheeler probes the complex family situation and discovers secrets that lead to the killer.

LAMENT FOR A LOUSY LOVER

"... and one wonders if he [Lt. Al Wheeler] and Mavis will ever wind up in the same book."

Anthony Boucher, *New York Times*, August 30, 1959

This quote appears on the Dedication Page of *Lament for a Lousy Lover* and suggests that the iconic Anthony Boucher, one of the few major book reviewers who liked Carter Brown mysteries and reviewed them in print, inspired the team-up of Al Wheeler and the ditzy private investigator, Mavis Seidlitz.

Mavis, on location for the filming of a hit TV western series, is hired to keep a couple of feuding starlets from killing each other. However, the star is murdered and Al Wheeler shows up to investigate the case. Mavis and Wheeler take turns narrating the story chapter by chapter in their own distinctive voices. Clever and funny!

THE STRIPPER

The Stripper is notable because it is the first Carter Brown paperback with a Robert McGinnis painting on the cover. McGinnis produced 100 original paintings for the covers of 120 Signet paperback editions of Carter Brown mysteries over 12 years. Those images were, in turn, also used on a great many UK and foreign language editions.

> "Robert McGinnis tells the story that, three years into Carter Brown's run with Signet, the sales figures were below expectation, and sagging; they were considering killing the series. To give CB a last chance, they decided to revamp the look of the covers by bringing in a new artist with a new approach. Robert McGinnis's first covers, for Dell, had appeared within a few months of Barye Phillips' *The Body* in 1958. By August 1961, when his first Carter Brown hit the racks, he had painted about 150 paperback covers, principally for Dell and Fawcett, and was clearly the hottest young artist in the business; he was then 35. It was very likely his work on Dell's Mike Shayne series that brought him to Signet's attention. His first Shayne cover was T*he Private Practice of Michael Shayne* in December, 1958; he eventually painted more than 80 covers for the series in an unbroken run until photo covers took over in 1971. More than twenty McGinnis Shayne titles had been published by the time he painted his first Carter Brown; Signet knew his talents well when they hired him. —Art Scott, "carter brown: The Books and the Covers". *Paperback Parade 104* p. 28-29

In the early 1980s, Yates worked with The Rocky Horror Show creators Richard O'Brien and Richard Hartley on a musical of The Stripper with Al Wheeler as its star which has been performed in both Australia and the UK.

Carter Brown continued to be a profitable and popular series until the end of the 1970s when cultural changes, recession, and reading tastes impacted sales.

> "At his peak in America, he was selling 350,000 copies a book and in Australia we were doing 30,000-40,000 a book....so you can see how he built up to 100 million copies. Yates was bigger than big…it was difficult to find a country he wasn't published in."
>
> — LYLE MOORE, HORWITZ
> www.carterbrownonline.com/carter-brown

—December 2022

George Kelley, a retired college professor, has more degrees than a thermometer: MLS, MA, MBA, and PhD. While working as a business consultant in the 1970s, George would visit used bookstores all around the U.S. after his consulting gigs. Over the years, his paperback collection grew so large it had to be housed in his basement because of the weight. Diane, George's patient wife finally told him: "There are so many books in this basement I can't get to the washer or dryer any more. You have to make a choice: books or clean clothes." So George picked clean clothes and donated 30,000 books to the State University of New York at Buffalo's Special Libraries (you can check out what happened next at: library.buffalo.edu/specialcollections/rarebooks/kelley/). Currently, George blogs daily about books, music CDs, and movies at georgekelley.org. George tries to read a book every day.

The Temptress
- - - -
Carter Brown

1

He lay face down on a sagging bed in one of the cabins belonging to a cheap motel which the proprietor with a sardonic sense of humor had called The Travelers' Rest. A shaft of sunlight through the dust-hazed window lit one side of his face and he didn't even look surprised.

Maybe there are some nice ways to die but having the back of your skull beaten into a gray-flecked, blood-soaked pulp isn't one of them.

I lit a cigarette, waiting until Doc Murphy straightened his back with a faint grunt of relief and looked at me, his face a couple of shades paler than usual.

"The proverbial blunt instrument as we already know, Wheeler," he said gruffly. "Did quite a job on him, whoever it was, didn't they?"

It was a question without need of an answer. I followed him into the bathroom and watched him run the cold tap, washing his hands with professional thoroughness.

"Any one of the blows, administered with the force they were, would have killed him," he said bleakly.

"Including the first one?"

"Exactly right, Lieutenant," he nodded. "He was hit a dozen times, maybe more." He shuddered slightly as he looked at the dirty gray towel on the rack beside the washbasin, then used his pocket handkerchief to dry his hands.

"You're looking for a maniac, Wheeler!"

"Yeah," I said absently. "You all through, Doc?"

"Sure—he's all yours!"

It was my turn to grimace as I walked back into the other room. The two crime lab boys I'd borrowed from Homicide had finished up and were already on their way back to town, taking the rusty hammer along with them, wrapped carefully in a nice clean cloth. The hammer had been on the floor alongside the bed, its business end encrusted with a mixture of hair and dried blood.

The shaft of sunlight still lit the side of his face, and when I turned the body over gently onto its back, the whole face had the same look of not being even surprised. The wide-open eyes looked at me with a calm, even remote, expression.

A guy in his early forties, with thinning brown hair and a sharp pointed nose—a small, lightweight guy who wouldn't have gone heavier than 140 on the scales, stripped. He was fully dressed in a crumpled tan wash-and-wear suit; with a cheap white no-iron shirt and clumsily knotted necktie underneath. On his feet were dirty, scuffed, brown suede shoes. He didn't look like he'd been a success.

I went through his pockets systematically and came up with a handkerchief, car keys, a handful of small change, and a billfold. I emptied the contents of the billfold out onto the cigarette-burned top of the dressing table. A hundred dollars in fives and tens, a New York State private detective's license made out to Albert H. Marvin, a driver's license, and a couple of receipted bills—one from a motel in Santa Monica, dated three days before, and one from this motel.

Doc Murphy made a rasping sound in his throat as he peered over my shoulder.

"Private eye, huh?" he said. "Long way from home, too."

"I'll trade you the investigation for the autopsy, if you want," I said coldly.

"Natural curiosity, Lieutenant," Murphy said cheerfully. "I figure he's been dead somewhere between eight to ten hours."

I checked my watch. "That brings it between midnight and two A.M. this morning."

The door swung open suddenly and Sergeant Polnik came lumbering in.

"I got a ride in the meat wagon, Lieutenant," he said breathlessly. "The Sheriff—" Then he got his first look at the guy on the bed and blinked rapidly. "Cheez!"

"What about the Sheriff?" I asked patiently.

"He said for you to get back to his office right away, only sooner," Polnik explained. "He was hopping mad like it was election year and you was running for Sheriff!"

"I'd like that," I said wistfully. "Sit around the County Sheriff's office all day making his secretary!"

"I never figured Miss Jackson was a girl like that?" Polnik sounded surprised.

"She isn't," I told him, "but I can dream, can't I?"

The boys from the meat wagon in their neat white coats filed through the doorway and the room got crowded suddenly.

"I only got here around a half-hour back," I said. "What's with Lavers—he's lost his mind again?"

"I wouldn't know, Lieutenant." Polnik shrugged helplessly. "But he sure wants you back in town in a hurry. Said for me to take over here."

"You can give me a ride in that miniature rocket of yours," Murphy interrupted. "Maybe prove my theory about guys that drive these foreign bugs?"

"Sports cars to you," I told him. "What theory?"

"They're all suffering from a guilt complex and it drives 'em into compulsive masochism," he said, his eyes gleaming enthusiastically. "Why else would they want to squeeze themselves into those bucket seats?"

Polnik stared down at the contents of Albert H. Marvin's billfold and grunted, "So he was a private eye, huh, Lieutenant?"

"The doc already said that," I grunted right back.

"Maybe he got hot? Knew too much about somebody so they knocked him off to shut him up?" Polnik theorized out loud. "What do I do, Lieutenant?"

I resisted the obvious answer, knowing he'd rather do anything but work. So I told him to go question the proprietor who had called in and reported the murder in the first place, then question the guests staying at the motel and find out if anyone had checked out this morning before the body was discovered.

Polnik's Cro-Magnon forehead corrugated deeply while he tried to memorize the instructions—I guessed I should have known better than try to tell him three things at the one time. That corpse must have unnerved me more than I'd realized.

I got back to the Sheriff's office just after eleven. His secretary, Annabelle Jackson—the blonde who's got everything but won't give one single inch—swiveled around in her chair and looked at me with an excited expression on her face.

"The Sheriff's been asking if you got back yet every five minutes, on the minute, for the last hour," she said breathlessly. "You'd better get in there fast!"

"So what's the panic?" I asked. "What's more important than a murder yet?"

"A quarter-billion dollars, I guess," she said, wide-eyed and still breathless.

"In fives and tens—and he wants me to help count it?"

"I mean the person who's in there with him right now is worth that much," Annabelle said. Her voice held a reverent tone as she breathed the name, "Mrs. Geoffrey Summers."

"She knocked over Fort Knox?" I said. "It's not our problem—that's to hell and gone over the county line."

"I don't know how you got so dumb without even trying," she said fiercely. "You can't just stand there and tell me you've never heard of Mrs. Geoffrey Summers?"

"I never even heard of Mrs. Geoffrey Summers," I admitted freely.

Annabelle took a sudden deep breath, not caring that she strained her blouse about as far as orlon cares to go, and that's a long, long way with a girl built the way she's built.

"Mrs. Summers is the New York socialite," she said rapidly. "Always makes the 'Ten Best Dressed' list every year. Her husband died three years back making her a widow and—"

"Leaving her a quarter-billion dollars along with the black weeds?" I finished for her. "I have the picture. If she was under fifty, I'd marry her, but even that much money is no consolation for spending the rest of my nights alongside a battle-ax—it can give a guy nightmares, I tell you!"

"Go on into the office, Al," Annabelle said sweetly. "You could be surprised."

The first surprise I got when I stepped into Sheriff Lavers' office was all the people in there already. Lavers is fat enough to make a crowd all by himself—add another three people and it's like a sellout at the ball game.

"What kept you?" Lavers asked with the open friendliness of a cornered cougar.

"Friction," I said. "The four wheels got to make continuous contact with the freeway and all that jazz."

"I hoped you'd show your usual disregard for the state speed limit," he said sourly. "I should have figured this was just business for you, not pleasure!"

With a quarter-billion dollars sitting right there in the room, I should worry about the County Sheriff. I gave the three visitors a lynx-eyed once-over, seeing if my years of training as a cop could help me spot the big money. I narrowed the candidates down to two right away—the third visitor was a man. I never heard of a guy yet calling himself "Mrs." Summers, even if they do tell me Greenwich Village is quite a place.

Lavers had a hunted look in his eyes as he turned toward the visitors. "This is Lieutenant Wheeler," he said. "Attached to my office from the Homicide Department on an indefinite basis, and an officer with considerable experience."

He studiously avoided looking at me while he made the build-up and I figured he must be in real trouble to make polite noises about and in front of me.

"Lieutenant," he continued quickly, "I'd like you to meet Mrs. Geoffrey Summers, who has a big problem."

"How do you do, Lieutenant," Mrs. Summers said with a slight touch of impatience in her voice.

So the money was the blonde and not the brunette. An elegant blonde somewhere in her late thirties and I dug Annabelle's crack about me being surprised. Mrs. Summers was a slim, attractive blonde, and I wouldn't have minded spending some of my nights close to her if she was only worth two bits.

"Miss Brent, her attorney," Lavers continued.

"Lieutenant." The brunette nodded with a pleasant smile on her face. She could give her client between five and ten years, and the charcoal suit she wore would have looked businesslike if it hadn't been for the generous curves underneath.

"Mr. Hillary Summers," Lavers completed the introductions. "Mrs. Summers' brother-in-law."

Hillary Summers nodded vaguely and went back to what he'd been doing before—looking at nothing with his eyes open. He was a tall, lean guy, around forty, with black hair graying at the temples, and the kind of sensitive face a lot of women get instincts about—the kind of instincts they prefer to call maternal.

"Mrs. Summers," Lavers cleared his throat aggressively, "would you mind repeating to the Lieutenant your reasons for this visit?"

"Surely," she said.

She twisted her body slightly in the chair so she looked at me directly. Her eyes were a clear, deep blue and completely impersonal—she was talking to the hired help.

"This concerns my daughter Angela," she said crisply. "It's perfectly simple, Lieutenant. I have requested the Sheriff to take the correct and lawful action over the matter, but for some obscure reason he seems reluctant to do so."

"You just don't know who's a communist these days," I said sympathetically.

Miss Brent's lips twitched for a fraction of a second—about the same time it took for Mrs. Summers' face to get that bleak look.

"You find this amusing, Lieutenant?" she asked icily.

"No," I said. "Please go on."

"I live, of course, in New York," she said, wrapping up California in six words and dropping it neatly into the nearest paper towel disposal unit. "Angela spent a year at finishing school in Switzerland, returning six weeks ago. She's always been a wayward child and I'm afraid the year in Europe didn't change her. I lead a busy life of my own, and perhaps I didn't devote enough time to her after she got back."

She shrugged her shoulders gracefully. "To come to the point, Lieutenant, a week ago, she ran away with some nightclub singer from Greenwich Village called Rickie Willis. It's not only embarrassing, it's absurd! I hired a private detective to trace them, and at last he's found them. They are right here in Pine City, Lieutenant."

"That is," Miss Brent added pleasantly, "in the area Sheriff Lavers' jurisdiction."

"Exactly," Mrs. Summers nodded. "So now I wish the Sheriff to take action—against this nightclub singer."

"For what—kidnaping?"

"I doubt if my daughter would agree that was the word," she said acidly. "They both need to be taught a sharp lesson, and I intend to see they get it!"

"How—exactly?" I asked.

"My daughter is seventeen and a half," she snapped. "I want you to arrest this man on a charge of statutory rape!"

I stared at her for a moment, then stared at Lavers, who rolled his eyes upward in an obvious appeal to the pagan god of county sheriffs to smite the woman where she sat.

"I understand the age of consent in California is eighteen," Mrs. Summers went on briskly. "Therefore, intimate relations with a minor is technically rape whether she was agreeable or not."

"That's right," I said. "But how will you prove it if your daughter won't testify?"

"I doubt if that will be a problem," she said acidly. "They're naturally registered as man and wife where they're staying, and I'm sure there won't be any difficulty in establishing the facts."

I lit a cigarette slowly and glanced at the female lawyer who shook her head slightly.

"This is not my advice, Lieutenant," she said evenly. "But Mrs. Summers is determined on this course of action."

"Isn't there also something called the Mann Act?" Mrs. Summers said coldly. "A federal law against transporting a minor across a state border for immoral purposes?"

"The FBI office is just four blocks down—" Lavers said in a hopeful rush of words that were chopped out in mid-sentence.

"I shall certainly see them if necessary," she told him. "But at this moment I want you, Sheriff Lavers, to take action against the man who's raped my daughter!"

"I side with Miss Brent," Hillary Summers said suddenly, in a soft, deep-timbred voice. "But my sister-in-law is determined this is the way to handle it. I've tried to impress her with the volume of publicity such an action will bring in its wake." He shuddered slightly. "The Press will have a field day with it—the daughter of Mrs. Geoffrey Summers, leader of New York society!"

"My daughter means more to me than the risk of cheap newspaper sensationalism!" Mrs. Summers snapped. "This is the only way to bring her to her senses!"

"You say this private detective you hired knows where they are now?" I asked her.

"He called me yesterday morning," she said, "and the three of us got on a plane right away. They're at a motel about fifteen miles south of here. A place called The Travelers' Rest, or some equally ridiculous name."

After five seconds had ticked away, she shifted irritably in her chair. "Really, Lieutenant! Must you stare at me like that?"

"This private detective you hired to find them," I said in a numbed voice. "His name was Marvin—Albert H. Marvin?"

"Why, yes. How did you know that?"

"Because I just got back from viewing his corpse," I told her. "Somebody pulped his skull with a hammer last night and I never saw anyone quite so dead as Albert H. Marvin in my whole life before!"

It was her turn to stare at me like that while the color ebbed slowly from her face and her mouth opened and framed words her paralyzed vocal cords wouldn't voice. Then her eyes glazed quickly and I caught her as she fell forward out of the chair.

2

I got back to the motel just after noon and found Polnik in the manager's office. The manager was a stringy, gray-haired character who looked like he'd been cheating the mortician for the last ten years. He wore a faded blue shirt and a pair of crumpled gray pants and needed a shave from sometime yesterday morning.

"This is Mr. Jones, Lieutenant," Polnik told me. "He owns the place."

"How long you going to be fooling around here, Lieutenant?" Jones asked in a sour voice. "I got better things to do than stick around here all day answering fool questions."

"You could always try charging us rent," I told him. "Send the tab into the Sheriff's office." I looked at Polnik. "What did you find out?"

"Six of the cabins are rented," Polnik said. "I questioned all of the people in them and they don't know from nothing, never heard any unusual noise last night or anything like that. I got a list of their names and addresses."

"Anybody check out this morning early?"

"Yeah," he said, with a pleased expression on his face. "A couple—name of Smith!"

"Smith?"

"Smith?" I repeated, and looked at the motel owner inquiringly.

"We get more Smiths!" he grunted. "Strictly one-night rentals and they're always gone in the early morning, some of 'em before sunup even."

"What did these Smiths look like?"

"Young," Jones said laconically. "The guy was around twenty-five at most—acted tough like he'd been around and seen it all before."

He spat with methodical precision through the open window into the dust outside.

"The girl was real young—only a kid. Not that I got to see much of her, just a glimpse when she went by the office. She had black hair that needed a comb, and a mean look on her face like she was mad at something—I figured maybe she was one of these bootniks. She was wearing a man's shirt and a pair of jeans—tight jeans."

His eyes flickered for a moment, remembering. "Kids got no self-respect these days—just bums the lot of 'em —don't matter where they come from!"

"What time did they leave?" I asked patiently.

"I was up around seven and they were gone then," he said.

"What were they driving?"

"Looked like a new sedan," he said. "A drive-yourself, I'd guess."

"You remember the make—the license plates maybe?"

"I want to make like a cop in this business, Lieutenant, and I don't got no business," he said grimly. "Most of my trade come in to buy a night's privacy and no questions asked."

"Which cabin did you give them?"

"Seven."

"Marvin had nine," Polnik grunted. "What's with these Smiths?"

"Save it till later," I told him. Explaining the Smiths to the Sergeant would be a cinch—like explaining nuclear fission to a Pilgrim Father.

"When did they get here?" I asked Jones.

"Monday night around eight," he said. "They went straight to the cabin and like I told you, I only ever saw the girl the one time. They booked for two nights and the guy was out most of yesterday but the girl wasn't with him. I went to bed around ten last night and he still wasn't back."

"When did Marvin arrive?"

"Monday night—maybe an hour after the Smiths checked in. He paid for one night, then yesterday morning he paid another night."

"Where's his car now?"

"Didn't have one," Jones sniffed. "Came in a cab."

"To a motel?" I said. "Didn't you figure that was kind of strange?"

"I been running this place the last ten years," he said simply. "There ain't nothing strange under the sun for me anymore. If a guy checked in riding a camel I wouldn't be surprised!"

"Did the Smiths tell you they were leaving this morning?"

"No," he shook his head. "They just went."

"Did you talk to Marvin at all while he was here?"

"No. Only to give him a receipt for his money, that's all."

"Thanks," I said wearily. "You've been a great help."

"You going to get the hell out of here now?" he asked hopefully.

"You have my word, Mr. Jones," I assured him. "As soon as I possibly can!"

We took a look at the cabin the Smiths had rented and it was like the one Marvin had, but stripped clean with nothing left to show their stay—not even a squeezed-out tube of toothpaste. It looked like one hell of a case for clues.

I shoehorned Polnik into the passenger's seat of the Austin Healey and drove back into town again, taking time out at a diner for lunch on the way, wondering if Lavers would agree this was just the time for me to take my vacation.

It was around three when I got back inside his office—he was alone this time, chewing on a cigar with an air of morose expectancy like a cannibal sampling his first lean missionary.

"They weren't there," he said as soon as he saw me.

"Check," I agreed. "They were there—for two days, but they vanished around sunup this morning."

"It figures," he said. "No clues, of course?"

"They left in a sedan, the owner says," I told him. "A self-drive it looked like. With the things he doesn't see, this guy should be a cop!"

"The afternoon papers have got the story of the murder," Lavers said gloomily. "They don't have the tie-in with Mrs. Summers and her daughter yet, but they will!"

"You heard from the lab about the hammer?" I asked, and slid into one of the vacant visitor's chairs, facing him.

"No fingerprints." He chewed on the cigar some more. "I've asked New York for information on Marvin."

"How about Mrs. Summers?" I asked.

"She's staying at the Starlight Hotel—along with Miss Brent and her brother-in-law. You remember the news of Marvin's murder knocked her for a loop, but I've got a nasty feeling she'll recover fast and come howling after our blood again any minute!"

"You got to admire her maternal instincts," I said. "It's not every mother gets so all-fired anxious to prove her daughter's been raped—technically!"

"A lovely woman, Mrs. Summers," Lavers growled. "Reminds me of my mother-in-law. The first time she stopped nagging in fifty years, they called a mortician right away. She died with her mouth wide open. This doesn't get us anyplace, Wheeler, does it?"

"No, sir," I agreed.

"Don't you have any of your usual brilliant, free-wheeling ideas?"

"Yes, sir, Sheriff!" I said eagerly. "Is it O.K. with you if I take my vacation starting now?"

"Oh, sure," he snarled. "Just don't bother to come back—there won't be any reason for it!"

The desk clerk at the Starlight wore his usual supercilious look when he saw me.

"I'm afraid our rates would be a little too high for you, Lieutenant," he sniffed. "We do have a vacancy for a bellhop—do you hop?"

"You're kidding me again, Charlie," I said reproachfully. "I've come about the drains—or maybe it's just the hotel altogether—but people are complaining in the street and perfume sales are soaring throughout the city."

"You want to see one of our guests?" Charlie said with a faint shudder of distaste. "Flatfooted policemen treading all over our beautiful carpets! Which one?"

"You have more than one?" I said disbelievingly.

"One hundred and twenty-three, to be precise!"

"You must have the biggest con game on the West Coast right here in Pine City," I said. "I want to see Miss Brent."

"She's in eight-oh-three," Charlie grunted. "If you wait a moment I'll call her and find out if she wants to see you."

"A room in this fleabag she may have," I said gently. "A choice about seeing me she hasn't."

"So all right already!" Charlie shrugged his shoulders with elaborate disdain. "The service elevator is at your disposal."

"I'll dispose with it right away," I told him. "Don't take any outdated credit cards, Charlie."

When I got there I found it wasn't a room, it was a suite—that figured with Mrs. Geoffrey Summers paying the tab one way or another. I knocked on the door and while I waited I daydreamed about getting Mrs. Summers mad at Charlie so she'd buy the hotel just for the pleasure of firing him—then rent me the place for a dollar a year. I'd have Lavers as doorman, dressed like a boy scout right down to the khaki shorts—Polnik as desk clerk—and I'd run a permanent harem in the penthouse suite with Annabelle Jackson as chief lady-who's-never-kept-waiting....

"If it's amnesia, Lieutenant," a pleasant voice said, "be a doll and go have it on the next floor up."

My eyes started work again and the female lawyer, Miss Brent, came sharply into focus. She looked different from the way she'd looked in Lavers' office, one hell of a lot different. Her midnight-colored hair with the neat center part had somehow escaped the severe hairdo, and made a soft frame for her pixie face. The flecked hazel eyes held a warmer, nonlegal look, and her lips were somehow softer, the lower lip stopping just short of a pout.

She'd discarded the efficient-looking charcoal suit for a black silk shirt that clung to the classic contours of her sharp-thrusting breasts, and a pair of mushroom wool-knit pants that fitted tight down to her ankles, creasing only where she creased.

"Any guy who'd waste time with amnesia when he could be talking to you would be crazy," I told her.

"Well, that's nice," she said in that voice with the husky overtone which did peculiar things to my spinal column. "You didn't come all the way over here just to tell me that, Lieutenant?"

"I figured we might talk a little?"

"A cozy chat?" Her lips curved in a mocking smile. "This is a new technique for a law officer, isn't it? I mean, you *are* working, Lieutenant, this is official business?"

"It started out that way," I said honestly. "Now you've got me confused."

"Maybe you'd better come in," she said, "and see my subpoenas."

I followed her into the living room of the suite and those wool-knit pants looked even tighter, rear view. She sat down in one of the armchairs and I sat opposite her.

"What's on your mind, Lieutenant?" she asked casually.

I told her what I'd found out when I went back to the motel—the "Smiths" who were Angela Summers and her singer boyfriend, Rickie Willis, for sure. That they'd checked out early in the morning, and the way I saw it we didn't have much chance of finding them—they could be in Mexico by now.

"You'd have circulated a description of them and so on, Lieutenant?" she said. "Isn't there a good chance they'll be picked up?"

"I wouldn't put money on it," I said. "If they murdered Marvin, would they head for any place other than Mexico?"

"You think they killed him?"

"I can't think of any better suspects right now." She relaxed in the chair, leaning her head back easily, but her eyes had lost that soft look and were guardedly watchful.

"This isn't why you came to see me, is it?" she said.

"No," I agreed. "I figured you'd like to know what's happened since Mrs. Summers passed out in the Sheriff's office this morning. Call it curiosity—a cop's curiosity—I hoped you might fill me in on the detail and background."

"You mean Lyn?"

"If that's Mrs. Geoffrey Summers, yes."

"Lyn's her Christian name," Miss Brent said. "She's also my client, Lieutenant, in case you've forgotten."

"Her interest in her daughter didn't sound motherly—or maybe I've got an old-fashioned approach," I said. "What's it all about?"

She lit a cigarette and looked at me for maybe five seconds before she answered.

"I guess it can't do any harm," she said finally. "Lyn is a widow, as you probably know. Her husband died three years back—they were a devoted couple and when he died something went out of her life forever—"

"The pocket handkerchief is brand-new," I said anxiously. "You don't mind if I drop my tears on the carpet?"

"Not unless I have to swim out of here!" She grinned slowly. "I guess it did sound corny, at that—sorry. But it's true—the only thing she had left was Angela and I guess her daughter became an obsession with her. She's watched over the kid like a hawk and Angela's always needed watching—a wild one, Lieutenant! She was thrown out of four of the best private schools in the country by the time she was sixteen. The finishing school in Switzerland was a kind of last resort. Then she was thrown out of that."

"So she came back home, met Rickie Willis, and took off with him for parts, unknown," I said.

"Lyn had plans for her," Miss Brent said evenly. "College in the fall—her coming-out party. The same kind of plans all mothers have maybe, except Lyn's would be on a much grander scale. High society is a delicate organism, Lieutenant, but with wealth and prestige, Lyn could put Angela any place she wanted. She had the whole social season planned for her coming out—and after. The way she saw it, Angela would have a year, maybe a couple, in college—it wasn't terribly important how long. What was important was Angela's social success as the glittering daughter of Mrs. Geoffrey Summers, and her taking of New York society by storm. The high point being her marriage in the next two, three years to the right kind of eligible bachelor—an English title if it was old enough—a career diplomat maybe."

"And the way it turned out, it was a Greenwich Village nightclub singer," I said. "I can understand Mrs. Geoffrey Summers blowing her stack, but this statutory rape bit is carrying it to an extreme, isn't it?"

She smiled again, suddenly. "You don't understand the morality of the very rich, Lieutenant, that's your trouble!"

"Call me Al," I told her. "Don't let a client stand in the way of friendship."

"All right, Al," she said. "My name is Ilona, and a client of mine can stand in the way of anything, if necessary."

"You were telling me about the very rich, Ilona," I said. "To a guy who never had more than a thousand bucks at one time, it's fascinating."

"Angela has some money in her own right," Ilona said. "About three million dollars, but she doesn't get it until she's twenty-one. Right now she's still a minor under her mother's control, legally, and practically she has the two hundred dollars a month allowance Lyn gives her and nothing else. Lyn is desperate, Al. This is her last throw—if she loses, she knows she's lost her daughter for good. So she thinks the only way to make Angela listen to reason is to scare her so bad, she'll never even argue with her mother again."

"What about the publicity—the sensationalism?" I asked.

Ilona shrugged her shoulders and I marveled at the taut lift of her breasts under the silk shirt.

"It's a calculated risk. Lyn's own position is untouchable, and she thinks it will only be a seven-day sensation at the worst. Six months from now, the memory of the story will give Angela a certain glamor even, in high society. There are only two unforgivable sins with the international set, Al. One is to marry beneath your social position and the other, which is worse, is to lose your money!"

I lit myself a cigarette and thought about it for a while—it made sense in a mad kind of way, like a United Nations debate.

"I'll buy that," I said. "So when she got definite news of her runaway daughter and boyfriend, she came hotfoot in pursuit bringing her lovely lawyer along for the ride. But why bring brother-in-law, too?"

"Hillary? He's taken the place of the man in the family ever since his brother's death. He advises Lyn on finance, handling the estate, and so on. In a crisis like this, I guess she thought Hillary should be along."

"She didn't take his advice, according to what he said this morning."

"Or mine for that matter," Ilona agreed. "Lyn can be a very determined woman when she wants. Imagine how frustrating it is to have more than enough money to buy anything that money can buy—then be faced with a situation where money is useless!"

"The only place I know where money's useless is Las Vegas," I said. "A weekend playing craps can be that kind of frustration."

"So," she smiled easily, "does that give you enough background and detail?"

"Almost," I said. "How about this private eye, Marvin? Did you hire him for Mrs. Summers, or was that her own idea?"

"It was Hillary's idea," she said. "He knew Marvin, said he was capable and discreet. I never even met him, and I'm almost sure Lyn didn't, either."

"Thanks a lot," I told her and got to my feet again. "You've been a big help."

"My pleasure." She stood up and walked to the door with me. "I thought Pine City was going to be dull, but now I'm not so sure."

"I guarantee you'll be proved wrong," I assured her. "How's Mrs. Summers feeling now? She took the news about the murder pretty hard."

"She's still upset—or she was when I last saw her a couple of hours back," Ilona said. "I persuaded her to take a sedative and I hope she's sleeping now. You won't disturb her, will you?"

"I wouldn't dream of it," I said hastily. "If this morning was a demonstration of her usual relaxed approach, it would be me who got disturbed!"

Ilona smiled faintly. "You have to make allowances, Al—she was emotionally off balance."

"This afternoon she could've fallen overboard," I said. "I'm no headshrinker to throw her a lifeline."

3

I got back to my apartment around six that evening and put a Peggy Lee record on the hi-fi machine because if anyone could soothe me right then it was Peggy. We're on a first names basis—natch—even if it is a strictly one-way deal. I know her from way back and she wouldn't know me from Hot Springs, Arkansas.

After I'd left Ilona Brent at the Starlight Hotel, I'd spent a couple of hours back at the office without getting anyplace. The Sheriff had tossed a description of Angela Summers and Rickie Willis all over the country but nobody had found them yet. He kept on asking me didn't I have any ideas and I kept telling him that's right I didn't until the atmosphere got more explosive than Cape Canaveral and it looked like a good time for me to get the hell out of there, so I got.

I made a nice mellow drink to go along with Peggy's nice mellow voice and settled back in a chair to try and relax. If this was being a cop, I figured my old man was right and I should have gotten into a respectable racket like organizing a numbers game around the kindergarten set.

Halfway through the second drink the buzzer sounded, the squawking noise of a middle-aged spinster caught bending by a myopic Hollywood talent scout. I walked to the front door hoping this was the answer to my woman-less week and outside was a breathless blonde who'd just lost all her clothes in a hurricane and was seeking shelter for the next couple of months. Then I opened the door and there was a loud pinging noise as my dream sharply disintegrated.

Standing in the corridor was a guy around thirty with a nervous look on his face.

"Whatever you're selling, friend," I told him, "I either got it or don't want it."

"You're Lieutenant Wheeler?" he asked politely.

"Yeah," I said. "But it's still no sale."

"You're the officer in charge of the investigation into the private detective's murder out at that motel?"

"I could be his twin brother," I said cautiously. "Are you a process server?"

"My name's Willis," he said. "Ray Willis—I'm Rickie's brother."

"You know where he is—where the two of them are?" I asked rapidly.

"Sure," he said. "That's what I came to see you about."

The world was suddenly a beautiful place where undeserving cops get paid off anyway—like a Las Vegas in the sky. I grabbed hold of his arm in case he'd just disappear in a faint puff of smoke, then pulled him gently inside the apartment. I let go of him when we got into the living room and offered him a drink.

"Thanks, Lieutenant," he said gratefully. "I could sure use one."

I made him a drink, revitalized my own, then took another look at him. He was a nice-looking guy in a cheap kind of way with thick glossy black hair and a thin mustache. His eyes were heavy-lidded and never kept still, like an appliance salesman always looking for the nearest exit once he's got the signature on the dotted line and the customer hasn't had time to read the fine print yet. His clothes were expensive but he was a razor-sharp dresser and it put your teeth on edge just looking at him for more than five seconds at one time.

"We heard about it on the radio," he said, then gulped down half the contents of his glass. "So we flew right back to Pine City."

"Where from—Tijuana?"

"Mexico?" He shook his head blankly. "Nevada, Lieutenant."

"Where's your brother and the girl now?"

"In a downtown hotel," he said nervously. "Not booked in under their right name, of course. I figured the best thing was to see you first and find out what happened."

"This guy Marvin got himself murdered two cabins down from the one they had last night at the motel," I snarled. "That's what happened—didn't they mention that minor detail on the radio?"

He drained the glass before he answered. "Well, sure they did, Lieutenant. But Rickie and Angela never had nothing to do with it, and that's the truth."

"Then they don't have a thing to worry about," I said. "You'd better take me to them."

"O.K.," he nodded. "I just didn't want to get them involved with the newspaper guys and everything right off—that's why I didn't take them straight to the sheriff's office."

"What are you—their keeper?"

His mouth twitched into a semblance of a grin. "Well, I'm Rickie's older brother, Lieutenant, and I guess he kind of looks to me for advice when he's in any trouble."

"O.K.," I said. "Let's go find out just how much trouble he's got."

The hotel was four blocks, and at the same time a million light-years, away from the Starlight. Some guy with the same type humor as that motel keeper had called it the Grand. A seedy-looking dump with the paint job faded and peeling—a last resort for crapped-out traveling salesmen and out-of-work, aging actresses. The kind of joint where they'd rent you a room by the hour.

Ray Willis shrugged apologetically as we got out of the car and walked across the sidewalk into the lobby.

"They're short of folding money, Lieutenant," he said softly. "This is all they can afford."

The furnishings were shabby, dusty—matching the desk clerk who didn't look like he was getting his fair share of the wages of sin. It figured. In this kind of decay there could be neither vice nor pleasure in sin—only habit could keep it going. We rode the wheezing elevator to the third floor, then Willis led the way down the corridor to a room marked 301, and knocked twice.

A younger edition of himself opened the door abruptly and stared sullenly at us.

"Rickie," Ray Willis said quickly, "I brought the Lieutenant along with me."

Rickie Willis took a good look at me and his eyes said he didn't care much for what he saw. It was a mutual feeling—he was tougher as well as younger than his brother. His black hair was chopped into a bristling crewcut and he was a real blunt dresser compared to Ray—he wore a tired, almost shapeless sports coat in large red-flecked checks, and a pair of creased cotton pants. The green knitted shirt underneath was open at the neck far enough to show the black wiry hair that sprouted on his chest like he gave it a hormone shot before breakfast every day.

"You tell him we didn't have nothing to do with it, man?" he asked in a thick-timbred voice.

"I figured you should tell him that, Rickie," Ray said in a soothing voice. "Ask us in, will you?"

"Uh—sure," Rickie said. "Hey, Angel!" he called over his shoulder. "You decent? We got company—cops no less!"

He waited a couple of seconds, got no answer, shrugged his wide shoulders under that refugee-from-vaudeville coat, and opened the door wider. I walked past him into the room with Ray following me, and Rickie closed the door behind us.

The two single beds proved the wages or sin were a lumpy mattress if nothing more. There was a square yard of carpet, frayed at the edges, on the floor between the two beds; a beat-up dressing table with two dirty glasses and a near-new fifth of bourbon on the top completed the furnishings. The girl was standing directly under the harsh light from the naked lightbulb, a cigarette dangling from the corner of her mouth, watching me with a bland expression on her face.

She was a brunette with a bird's-nest hairdo sitting like an inverted cone on top of her head. Her eyes were enormous, matching the color of her hair, and they had a veiled, negative look in them as she watched me.

Nobody would call her pretty even, but there was something about that oval face with the high cheekbones, small tip-tilted nose, and soft moist mouth with the almost ridiculous kewpie-doll heart shape, that did things to you. Then you looked at her body and knew right away that the face was the teaser—the hook. The figure was perfection you'd never believed possible before—not even in the girdle ads.

She wore a crew-necked orlon sweater in a bright lemon color which must have been three sizes too small, the way it molded the swelling, pointed perfection of her arrogant breasts—close enough to prove beyond doubt that she wore nothing at all underneath. Along with the orlon sweater, she wore black stretch-nylon tights that were stretched to the limit, giving her that bare look that nakedness can't ever match. If she wore anything underneath those tights, I didn't believe it because nobody's come up with a fabric lighter than air yet.

"Angela," Ray's voice broke the silence, "this is Lieutenant Wheeler."

"Don't spoil his dreams, Ray," she said in a mock-serious, little girl's voice. "He's not finished yet."

Somehow my throat was dry and I had to clear my voice before I could speak. "You're Angela Summers?" I asked the obvious question.

"Little orphan Angela, that's me," she said, mimicking my flat, official voice. "I thought the *Dragnet* technique was old hat now, Lieutenant—or hasn't anyone told you yet?" Her voice tried hard to be tough but even on her, all that education couldn't have been entirely wasted, and some of the cultured accents kept coming through.

"You want to play this cute, we can go down to the Sheriff's office and start over," I told her.

"Take it easy, Angela!" Ray said in an agonized voice. "You got enough troubles already."

She walked over to the nearest bed and the springs chimed harshly as she plumped down onto it. Then she crossed her legs daintily, hugging one knee with both hands while she looked up at me with an expression that was an equal mixture of polite expectancy and open derision.

"Yes, Lieutenant?" she asked in a demure voice.

Rickie Willis slouched across to the dressing table, sloshed neat bourbon into one of the dirty glasses, then carried it across to the bed and sat down beside the girl. "We never had nothing to do with the septic eye getting himself liquidated!" he said fiercely. "Man, we never knew he was for real even—no contact. You dig?"

"Why don't we get original and take it from the beginning—from when you lit out of New York a week back?" I suggested wearily.

Rickie shrugged again and I wondered if that wool-knit shirt was fazing some skin allergy or maybe it was just the hair on his chest limbering up.

"It was a drag, man!" he muttered. "We ride the railroad to Chi and give the jazz joints a quick going over but that was Dullsville—and a pad under the El! Who can sleep in a joint that's jumping all night? So next day we fade onto the rails again to L.A."

"We stayed in a downtown hotel in Los Angeles for two days, Lieutenant," Angela said sweetly. "Then we got tired of it, so Rickie got a drive-yourself car and we just drifted around—spent the next night at a motel in Santa Monica. About then we realized we were almost out of money, so we came into Pine City to see Ray. We thought he could help us."

"You stayed two nights at the motel and checked out early this morning," I said. "Marvin picked you up at Santa Monica and followed you into Pine City—he got into that motel just one hour after you did. And you never saw him, not even once, during the whole three days?"

"Maybe we did," Angela said innocently. "How do we know? We didn't know who he was anyway." She put her hand on Rickie's thigh and squeezed it affectionately. "We didn't exactly have much time for other people, Lieutenant. I'm sure you know what I mean."

I looked at Ray Willis because if I looked at those stretched nylon tights any longer I was going to bust a blood vessel, and who needs a coronary when we got taxes already?

"Where do you fit?" I asked him.

"The first I knew about it was when Rickie called me yesterday morning, Lieutenant," he said anxiously. "After he told me what it was all about, I suggested he'd better come and see me so we could talk. He came over to my apartment around four or five yesterday afternoon and stayed late—maybe midnight when he left."

"You sure of the times?" I asked.

He glanced at his brother for a moment, then shook his head. "Not real sure, Lieutenant, no. Maybe it was ten-thirty, eleven. We never had a reason to check."

"So you see now, Lieutenant," Angela said in the same sweet but crisp voice. "We know nothing about the poor man's murder!"

"I'd like to believe that," I told her. "Along with the long line of coincidence that's shaped up into circumstantial evidence already!"

"That's plain stupid!" Angela said coldly. "A sad little man peeping through keyholes for a living—why should we bother to kill him? What harm could he do us?"

"He located you for your mother," I said. "She was in the office this morning raising all kinds of hell because we wouldn't go right out and book your boyfriend for statutory rape."

For a split second she wasn't going to believe it, then her mouth curled slowly.

"Dear, darling Mom!" she said softly. "The girl with the new approach. If she wasn't all twisted up inside with a brain like an overripe peach crawling with maggots, she should have known if anyone had a justifiable plea for rape it would be Rickie, not me!"

"It's a technical offense," I explained. "Eighteen is the age of consent in California, and you're not eighteen yet."

She pulled a face at Rickie, then her fingers darted inside his shirt suddenly and plucked a hair from his chest, making him yelp sharply.

"You big, masterful brute, you!" she said fondly. "Taking advantage of a little kid like me!"

"Her own daughter!" Ray Willis said solemnly. "Can you imagine that? What kind of a woman is she?"

"The usual kind—as far as I could see," I snarled at him. "Where's the phone?"

"Down the hall—you need a dime," Rickie grunted. "What's with the phone?"

"I'll call the Sheriff's office and have them send a car," I said. "We wouldn't all fit in mine."

"Are you arresting us, Lieutenant?" Angela gave me the wide-eyed look.

"No," I told her. "Just taking you in for further questioning—once your mother sees you, she might change her mind about that statutory rape bit."

"Oh, I think she will, Lieutenant," Angela smiled confidently. "In fact, I don't think she has a choice."

"How's that?" I said cautiously.

"Well"—her shoulders moved gracefully under the orlon sweater and the twin peaks moved in unison with them— "I don't think you can prosecute a husband on those grounds, can you?"

"Husband!" I pointed at Rickie disbelievingly. "Him?"

"We were married at eleven this morning," she said easily. "Why else do you think we flew to Nevada?"

I turned my head slowly and glared at Ray Willis. "Your advice?" I asked in a choked voice.

His eyes cringed for a moment, then he got that righteous look on his face again.

"What else could I tell them, Lieutenant?" He gestured pleadingly with both hands held palm up. "The way things were between them I didn't figure it was right them not being married!"

4

Polnik brought the car and his eyes bugged when he saw Angela in all her stretched-nylon glory. He only got one look as she climbed into the back of the car but that was enough—the red lights had to look after themselves all the way back to the office.

When we got there, I left him with them in the outer office while I disappeared into the inner sanctum and gave the Sheriff a fast rundown on what had happened.

Lavers had been home when I called in and from the look on his face, his dinner was still there on the table, untouched.

"They got married in Nevada this morning," he repeated slowly when I'd finished telling him. "Oh, brother! Won't Mrs. Geoffrey Summers love that!"

"She'll have to dream up a new gimmick," I agreed. "Is the marriage legal, I wonder?"

"In Nevada anything's legal so long as you buy a license first," he grunted. "I called her mother as soon as I got back to the office—she'll be here any minute."

"What do you figure on doing with the newlyweds?" I asked him. "We don't have a thing to hold them on, Sheriff."

"Material witnesses," he grunted, but he didn't sound very sure.

"You can hold them for twenty-four hours maybe," I said. "Don't forget Momma Summers will have her tame lawyer along."

He glared at me, his face reddening rapidly. "Don't you have one little piece of evidence, Wheeler? Just something small—not conclusive even—we can use?"

"Not one," I said cheerfully. "But remember, Sheriff, the darkest hour is before the dawn—or haven't you ever left a warm bed to go home?"

"This isn't the time to make lousy jokes, Wheeler!" he grated. "If we don't pin this murder on somebody fast, I'll be laughed out of office on every front page throughout the whole country!" He bared his teeth at me. "And I'll make sure you come along for the ride!"

"You know something, Sheriff?" I said wistfully. "It's not the money that keeps me going, it's your faith."

"I'd better take a look at them," he rasped, and eased his paunch out from behind the desk so it drooped sharply with no visible means of support.

We got back into the outer office and Lavers nodded curtly to the Willis brothers when I introduced him, then took his first look at Angela. I waited for the steam to erupt out of the top of his head. He gurgled helplessly for a few seconds, then swung round toward me, his face an ugly, mottled color.

Wheeler!" he thundered. "Why the hell didn't you wait for her to get dressed before you brought her back to the office?"

"I am dressed, you dirty old man," Angela said calmly, "and don't look at me like that again—my husband doesn't care for it!"

The only thing that saved Lavers from a ruptured ulcer right then was the arrival of Mrs. Geoffrey Summers, her lawyer, and her brother-in-law. Mrs. Summers swept into the office to the sound of invisible trumpets with the other two following in her wake like respectful courtiers. She stopped a couple of feet away from the chair her daughter occupied and surveyed her with a clinical eye.

"You look disgusting!" she observed coldly. "Prancing around in your underwear—don't you have any modesty at all?"

"Heck, Mom!" Angela grinned at her nastily, burlesquing the junior high drawl. "You know how it is after you've been stat-raped—the little things in life don't seem so important anymore."

Mrs. Summer's face lost color fast. She opened her mouth to say something else, then changed her mind and closed it with a snap.

"Well, Sheriff?" She lanced him with a steely gaze. "You have no further excuses to procrastinate now—you've got the man responsible right here in your office. Arrest him!"

"For gosh sakes, Mom," Angela accentuated the maddening drawl even further. "Don't get so excited—you haven't even heard my big news yet."

Mrs. Summers ignored her daughter icily while she waited for Lavers to do something dramatic. From the look on his face the only hope she had right then was a sudden and spectacular heart seizure.

"It's about Rickie and me," Angela said brightly, "and I just know you'll want to be the first to congratulate us, Mom. I mean, golly! Gee willikins! and all that kind of jazz, we got married this morning."

For a while there I figured Mrs. Geoffrey Summers had gone into a trance. Her eyes closed slowly and she just stood there, her whole body rigid.

"It's not true?" she whispered finally. "It can't be."

"I got the marriage certificate right here in my pocket," Rickie Willis said sullenly. "You can X-ray it, if you want!"

"Look at it this way, Mom," Angela simpered. "You haven't lost a daughter—you've gained a son. Rickie!"

"Yeah?" he queried.

"Give your new mom a great big kiss!" she said happily. "I just know you two will get along fine together—be a couple of real pals—natch!"

Mrs. Summers had her eyes open again and I saw them start to glaze over—and for the second time since we'd met I stepped forward and caught her just before she hit the floor. It was getting monotonous. I eased her into an armchair, and Ilona Brent took over from there.

Hillary Summers walked over to where Rickie stood, his face pale and drawn.

"Let me see that certificate," he said curtly.

"Who're you?" Rickie growled at him.

"He's your Uncle Hillary, sweetie," Angela said. "Don't speak rudely to him, he may bust out crying. He's the sensitive type—does a lot of social work among the high school set and I guess that's what makes him sensitive."

Rickie fumbled in his pocket, then pulled out a folded document and handed it to Summers. After he'd glanced through it rapidly, Hillary took it across to Ilona.

"Is this the real thing?" he asked jerkily.

Ilona studied it for a moment, then shook her head doubtfully. "I'm not certain—it would have to be checked," she said. "At any rate, she would have had to lie about her age—you have to be eighteen in Nevada the same as here to get married without consent."

"Then it's not binding?" Hillary said.

"I don't know off hand. It depends on the Nevada law—whether it actually says such a marriage is illegal."

Lavers gave a rasping cough which drew attention to himself, and it was about time. "I'm not concerned with the legality of their marriage!" he snarled. "I'm concerned with a murder—or have you all forgotten that already?"

"You've had both of them in your hands for the last two hours or so," Ilona said sharply. "Haven't you finished questioning them yet?"

"I haven't even started," Lavers grunted. "Now the touching family reunion is over, I'd like the three of you to get out of my office and let me get on with my job."

Mrs. Summers must have had the recuperative powers of an ox. Suddenly she sat bolt upright in the chair, pushing Ilona's helping hand away from her impatiently.

"I think that is an excellent idea," she said briskly. "We shouldn't discourage Sheriff Lavers from doing his duty—it's taken him all this time to make up his mind to start already. We'll leave now."

Ilona hesitated for a moment. "You'll want me to represent Angela, of course?"

"I want no such thing!" Mrs. Summers said curtly. "She got herself into this mess, she can get herself out." She stood up, adjusting the blue mink wrap around her shoulders. "It must be obvious to you, Ilona, as well as me. Once he"—she nodded in Rickie's direction briefly—"knew Marvin had found them, he had to do something desperate, so he killed Marvin to keep him quiet. Then in panic he rushed Angela off to Nevada and married her. It worked both ways, don't you see? Anyone knows a wife can't testify against her husband, and she made it harder for us to get rid of him, too."

"You out of your mind?" Rickie blinked at her. "What's the deal? The way you talk to Angie, I'd figure you'd be glad to get rid of her this way."

"If you think," she hissed at him venomously, "that you will blackmail me for one red cent even, you're badly mistaken, Mr. Whatever-your-name-is! I don't have to raise my little finger to be rid of you because the courts will do that for me. You'll go to the gas chamber for murdering that unfortunate little private detective, and inside a year from now, Angela will be a widow!"

Rickie looked at his brother numbly. "What's with this broad?" he mumbled. "I don't dig her jive, man. How come she keeps spilling acid over my face all the time?"

"She's sick, Rickie," Ray said in a consciously pious voice. "Sick up here." He tapped the side of his head with one finger. "You should feel sorry for her, she needs help."

A volcanic rumble came from Lavers. "So help me, Wheeler!" he said in a rising voice. "If you don't get the three of them out of here in the next ten seconds I'll book them for obstructing justice!"

"Really, Sheriff!" Ilona laughed shortly. "You couldn't possibly—"

"All right then!" Lavers bellowed. "Obstructing traffic! Trespass! You got five seconds left!"

Polnik opened the door for them, that goggle-eyed expression still fixed on his face.

"I think it would be better if we left," Hillary said, and took Mrs. Summers' arm, leading her toward the door. Ilona followed them, with Lavers waiting at the boil until the door closed behind them. Polnik stared at him blankly.

"Get a female officer to look after this girl!" Lavers told him. "You'd better come into my office, Wheeler, and bring that—" he stared at Rickie for a moment, "—husband with you!"

Two hours later we were no further than when we'd started. Both Angela and Rickie stuck to their original story, which was simple enough. They hadn't known who Marvin was, they'd never noticed him around anyplace, including the motel. Rickie had gone to his older brother for advice because he was worried about what Angela's mother might do about her running away with him. He knew—I quote—she hated Angela's guts and would do anything to break them up. His brother had given him good advice if obvious—marry the girl—so that's what he did.

Ray Willis had backed up his story with that phony do-good look on his face that made the back of my hand twitch every time I saw it.

Lavers lit a cigar but his heart wasn't in it and the smoke only limped across the desk toward me.

"What have we got?" he said miserably. "Nothing!"

"No word from New York on Marvin yet?"

"Nor Rickie Willis either," he grunted. "Maybe we should get the girl back and go through it one more time."

"I had you figured for a lot of things, Sheriff," I said wonderingly, "but never a masochist."

"You got any better ideas?"

"Big brother," I said. "He's out of character—he must have an angle."

"Like what?" the Sheriff asked bleakly.

"There I give up," I admitted. "He plays piano in a downtown club—

he says—has a room there."

"It figures," Laver said. "The other one is a singer—why shouldn't Ray play the piano?"

"No reason," I said. "I might go watch him play for a while—I could get lucky and see the piano lid drop at the wrong time, maybe take off all his fingers at the wrist. I'd like that."

"Get the girl back in here," Lavers said tiredly. "Let's get this over with so I can go home and cut my throat."

The woman officer brought Angela back in and sat beside her silently. She was a redhead in the full flush of first or maybe second girlhood, but under that heavy blue uniform you couldn't tell.

Angela's mouth drooped at the corners and the bottom lip had a definite pout.

"What is this?" she demanded angrily. "The third degree or something?"

"Don't tempt me!" Lavers muttered. "No, Miss—"

"Mrs. Willis," she corrected him coldly.

"Mrs. Willis—we just want to ask you some more questions, that's all."

"Don't you ever run out of questions?" she snapped. "Are you getting payola for this or something?"

"Answer the jackpot question, Angela, and we can all go home," I said.

"How many times do I have to say it?" she said stormily. "I don't know who killed him—I never even met him!"

"He was hired to find you and Willis," Lavers said in a tired voice. "He caught up with you in Santa Monica, we know—maybe in L.A. even? He stayed right on your tail into Pine City, had a cabin two down from yours. Yesterday morning he called your mother in New York and told her where you were and—"

"Hold it!" Angela said. "When did dear old Mom get here?"

"She got a plane right after his call," I said.

"With Hillary—and the Brent woman?"

"I guess so."

Lavers snorted impatiently. "Don't sidetrack the question, Mrs. Willis! The only reason Marvin had for being in that motel was you and your husband! You're the only two people who could have any possible motive for killing him, and—"

"You're wrong, Sheriff," she said softly, "but so wrong!"

"The guy that owns the motel maybe didn't like the color of Marvin's socks, so he beat in his head?" Lavers asked with heavy sarcasm.

"You are three suspects short," she said. "If they flew over right after Marvin called yesterday morning they would have been here by late afternoon at least, wouldn't they?"

"Sure, but—"

"Have you checked them out yet, Sheriff?" she asked tensely. "How do their alibis stack up? And I do mean dear old Mom, and Uncle Hillary—bless his sensitive little hands—and not forgetting the legal eagle with the cute feathers!"

"What possible reason could any of them have for murdering Marvin!" Lavers growled.

"That's for you to find out!" Angela said tartly. "But they could have—they were right here in this little hick town of yours, weren't they?"

Lavers buried his face in his hands for a suffering moment. "Get her out of here before I lose what's left of my mind!" he groaned. "I can't take any more tonight."

"No reason to hold them, sir?" I asked politely.

"Not yet—but make sure they stay right where we can find them and don't get any bright ideas about taking a long trip suddenly."

"Yes, sir," I said. "Anything else?"

He took his hands away from his face for a moment to scowl at me. "Wheeler, I'm getting to be an old man fast, but I've always treated you right, haven't I?"

"There are two ways of looking at it, Sheriff," I said thoughtfully. "From my point of view the answer's no—but then I guess we have to consider your point of view?"

"Did I ever ask you a favor?"

"Not since yesterday that I remember."

"Then I'm asking one small favor from you now, Wheeler. If you haven't come up with anything by morning—turn yourself in and confess?"

"Can you guarantee a promotion if I play ball?" I asked eagerly.

"I can guarantee some new faces around this office if we don't get some results in the next twenty-four hours," he said. "If you've got any spare time, Wheeler, you might try thinking up some new routines for us."

"Routines?" I said blankly.

"I was thinking a song and dance act would be better seen than starving to death," he said gloatingly. "And I've seen you go through a dozen different routines right here in this office!"

5

Ray Willis sat beside me in the Healey without saying anything and it looked like another routine that was getting monotonous.

"The club's in the next block?" I asked him as we crossed an intersection.

"About halfway down, Lieutenant," he said coldly. "I appreciate you taking the trouble to drive me."

"It was nothing, Ray," I said warmly. "I guess you got a long night ahead of you, playing piano and all. I just figured if I could help you out a little, I should. You helped your brother, giving him that good advice—so now I help you. We all help each other and it makes the world go round and never mind the squares."

"Here," he grated.

I stopped the Healey at the curb and looked across the sidewalk at the plain wooden door with two big brass rings attached to the center panel.

"This is the most discreet nightclub I ever did see, Ray," I told him. "No neon, even?"

"It's a key club, Lieutenant."

He eased himself out of the car quickly. "Thanks again for the ride. Good night."

"Not so fast!" I got out my side and walked around to join him on the sidewalk. "You don't think I'm going home now without even hearing you play the piano?"

He forced a smile onto his lips while his eyes held a warm, murderous gaze. "Well, that would be real nice, Lieutenant, but I'm afraid it's not possible. Like I said, it's a key club—private, you know? Each member has his own key and they're only allowed to bring guests three nights a week, and this just isn't one of those nights. I'm sorry."

"Don't be." I patted his shoulder encouragingly. "It so happens I'm the owner of one of the most exclusive credit cards in the whole country—gets me in any place."

"Yeah?" he said dismally.

"Sure." I smiled happily. "So there's no problem about me getting in with you, Ray. I'll just produce my credit card. *Cop-carte blanche*, they call it."

He turned toward the door and fished a key out of his pocket. Ray was a tryer but he knew when it was smart to quit. We went inside where there was subdued light, thick carpet, and a tinkling piano somewhere in the background.

"That's a break, Ray," I said. "They got somebody pinch-hitting for you tonight."

A stunning blonde in sequined black bra and tights suddenly materialized in front of us. She had the longest legs I'd ever seen outside of my dreams; encased in black mesh nylons, they were the sexiest legs I'd ever seen, too.

"Good evening, Mr. Willis," she said in a husky voice. "May I take your hat?"

"Yeah," he said morosely.

"You can take mine, too," I told her earnestly. "Wear it in good health."

She smiled warmly at me. "Welcome to Club Double Zero, sir. Any friend of Mr. Willis is always welcome. I'll take good care of your hat."

A beefy character in a tight dinner jacket pushed his way through the drapes that separated us from the rest of the club, and the small foyer got suddenly crowded.

"Hey!" he said anxiously. "Where you been all night, Ray? I told you last week that redhead—Tina—was a lush. Boy! You should have seen her earlier tonight—started to tear the joint apart, chair by chair. Before we gave her the rush she hauled off and gave Old Man Denby a black eye. Was he mad! Yelling his head off the place wasn't run right and what the hell did the owner mean by not even being here when there was trouble. You'd better talk to him, Ray, he—"

"Shut up!" Ray snarled at him.

"I said something?" The beefy guy looked bewildered. "We got big trouble you don't want to know about it?"

"Why would it worry the piano player?" I asked mildly.

He stared at me for a moment. "Piano player?" He wheezed suddenly and his whole body shook in undulating spasms. "Yeah—that's rich, I like that! Why would it worry the piano player! Ray, how's about introducing me to your friend?"

"This is Lieutenant Wheeler," Ray said slowly, with icicles forming over each word. "From the County Sheriff's office."

The beefy character stopped laughing—like that. I watched the apple in his throat leap up and down like a demented elevator until I got tired of it.

"You made a boo-boo, pal?" I asked gently.

"Excuse me," he said jerkily. "I just remembered a couple of things I got to—" He fumbled his way blindly through the drapes and disappeared again.

I lit a cigarette leisurely, then looked at Ray's set face.

"Fancy piano player," I said cheerfully.

"So I've got a piece of the club," he said tightly. He held up his hand with the thumb and forefinger almost touching. "A very little piece, Lieutenant. Is that a crime?"

"Who was the fat guy with the sense of humor?"

"That's Joe Diment, the club manager."

"The way he talked, I figured you had all the pieces, Ray," I said.

"That Joe," he whispered. "The loud-mouthed bum!"

"I can't wait to see your piano, Ray," I said. "Why don't we go on in?"

He hesitated for a moment, then shrugged his shoulders helplessly. "Maybe we'd better go into my office," he said.

"You play your piano in an office?" I queried.

"O.K.! O.K.!" He clenched his teeth. "The piano playing bit is just a hobby—I own the club!"

"You see, Ray?" I said encouragingly. "Right there you were honest and it didn't hurt one little bit, did it? Why should I care anyway?"

He pushed the drapes aside and I followed him into the main room of the club. The lights were even more subdued inside than they were in the foyer. A bar, with the impressive lineup of brands discreetly displayed by indirect light, ran almost the length of one wall. There was a small dance floor right next to the tinkling piano, and the rest of the place was taken up with tables and the people who sat around them.

The Double Zero looked like it was doing good business—I never saw so many middle-aged guys and young dolls in one place before. I counted three cigarette girls as we walked across the room, all of them wearing the same kind of sequined outfit the hatcheck girl wore, except the colors were different. There was one brunette in a white bra and tights that made me feel like a real Marlboro man and I didn't care if the tattooing did hurt.

In the far corner was an ornate, heavy-timbered staircase, and just beside it, a door with nothing on it to indicate whether a lady had guessed right or not. Ray opened the door and I followed him inside into an office, which proved I'd guessed wrong.

Joe Diment, the guy with the beef and misplaced sense of humor, was standing at the bar beside the king-sized executive desk. He put his glass down quickly on the bar top as we came in.

"I needed something for my nerves, Ray," he said quickly. "After shooting off my mouth like that. Cheez! How stupid can I get?"

"You already demonstrated that," Ray told him.

He walked across the room to the bar, and stopped a couple of feet away from Diment, facing him.

"Hell! I'm sorry, Ray." Diment sounded nervous. "But how was I to know?"

"Never mind!"

"Well, O.K." Diment tried to smile. "I hate to bother you again, Ray, but that Denby guy is still squawking his head off upstairs—he's still sore about that redhead. I can't do nothing with him—he figures for the kind of dough he's paying we ought to spot a lush before she can get close enough to black his eye when he's only looking for what he already paid—"

Ray backhanded him across the mouth with brutal force and Diment rocked back on his heels, his eyes closed tight.

"That big mouth of yours, Joe," Ray whispered. "It'll be the death of you one of these days!"

Then he backhanded him twice more with careful deliberation. I watched the tears flow down the beefy guy's face, mingling with the blood that trickled from his cut upper lip.

"Get out of here, Joe," Ray told him. "My insides start heaving, just looking at you."

Diment opened his eyes again slowly. "I finish the drink first, Ray?" he asked in a cracked voice.

Ray picked up the glass and threw the contents into his face. Diment whimpered softly as the liquor splashed against his eyeballs, and he groped for his pocket handkerchief with clawing fingers.

"Now you finished your drink, Joe," Ray told him. "You can go, huh?"

The fat boy stumbled past me toward the door, dabbing his eyes gently with the fine linen handkerchief as he went. A moment later the door closed behind him gently, and I wondered if he was heading straight for the employment agency.

Willis stood with his back toward me without moving for a little while; then he moved into the bar and set up a couple of glasses.

"Drink, Lieutenant?" he asked without any inflection in his voice at all.

"Scotch on the rocks, a little soda," I said.

I moved over to a comfortable-looking armchair close to the desk and relaxed into it while he made the drinks, then brought them across to the desk with him He sat behind the desk and raised his glass. "Let's drink to that credit card of yours, Lieutenant. It sure gets you into the most intimate situations!"

"What could you expect—with that big, fat double-zero right on your front door?" I asked him. "What's upstairs?"

"Living space," he said. "I've got a couple of rooms. Diment and a couple of the other guys got a room up here, too."

"I'll use my credit card if you want," I said. "Maybe I could be a help, Ray? Smooth-talk Old Man Denby for you—the guy who paid for a redhead and got a black eye instead. You remember him, don't you—the guy Joe Diment couldn't forget?"

He lit a cigarette then looked at me with bleak eyes. "O.K.," he snapped in a crisp voice. "You've got the ball—what now?"

"I like you better this way," I told him sincerely. "Being your real self, Ray, slapping guys around and throwing liquor in their faces. It goes better with high-class pandering than that boy scout act you've been pulling down at the Sheriff's office all evening."

"So?"

"So this club of yours doesn't interest me that much," I said. "It's inside the city limits and I work for the county sheriff's office. The city vice detail would be most interested, naturally, but me—I'm interested in finding out who killed this Marvin guy."

"I wish I could help, Lieutenant," he said flatly. "But I've already told you what I know, and that isn't much."

I tasted the drink and like I'd expected, it was very good Scotch.

"Where were you last night around midnight?" I asked.

"Right here in the club," he said promptly.

"Can you prove that?"

"If I have to—there were plenty of people around who saw me. You don't think I knocked off the peeper!"

"It's an interesting thought," I said. "You have a record, Ray?"

"No."

"I can check it with no trouble," I told him.

"The answer's still no."

"How about the kid brother?"

He finished his drink in one quick gulp, then lowered the glass carefully onto the desktop like he expected it to disintegrate in his hand.

"This I can also check—we're waiting for an answer from New York right now," I added.

"Rickie did two years a while back," Ray said thinly. "He was only a kid, just got himself in with the wrong gang."

"How long back?"

"Three years maybe?"

"That makes him twenty-two at the time," I said cleverly. "But maybe he took a long time growing?"

"So he made a mistake, got caught, and served his time," Ray said. "You going to hold it against him the rest of his life?"

"I don't know yet," I snarled. "I'm getting tired of sitting around all night with a two-bit bordello-keeper and getting no place. I want the truth out of you, Willis, the real reason why your kid brother came to see you last night, and this is your last chance to tell it!"

He rubbed his chin nervously, the stubby fingers gouging into the flesh.

"He was worried sick," he said quickly. "Didn't know what to do. He met this Summers kid in the Village joint where he was working. She was all over him like a rash and—"

"They were both on the make and maybe they deserved each other," I interrupted him. "You're not telling me a thing I don't know already."

"I'm trying to tell you the way it was," he said sourly. "It was her idea they should take off and Rickie figured that was just fine—he knew all about her mother and all the dough in the family. Looked like a real good deal—he'd have his kicks with the broad and when he got tired of her, he'd do a deal with her old lady. Rickie figured she'd pay plenty to buy him off and avoid any scandal."

"He didn't know how Mrs. Summers felt about her daughter?" I said doubtfully. "All that refined hate?"

"Rickie found that out later," Ray said with a grimace. "He started remembering the Mann Act and the rest, and got real worried. They were running out of money fast, too, and when he mentioned it to the kid he got another shock—she's not worth a dime until she turns twenty-one."

"That motel looked the right kind of place to get disenchanted," I said. "What else?"

"She told him not to worry about money—if things got real tough she could always get plenty. When he asked her where from, she just laughed and told him never to mind, the guy was loaded and she had him in a corner. After that she clammed up and wouldn't say any more about it. Rickie figured maybe she was just dreaming and came over here to see me."

"Looking for help from Big Brother," I said. "So you gave him advice instead of money, which is a hell of a lot cheaper—told him to marry the girl."

"I figured that was the best way out."

"You went with them to Nevada?"

"Sure. Rickie needed someone along to handle the detail—he's too much of a dreamer, out of touch, you know—a musician."

"Yeah," I said. "I can see he'd need a piano player along."

"So that's the whole story, Lieutenant."

"You're sure?"

"I gave it to you straight, with nothing left out," he said coldly. "If you want, I can invent some fancy detail."

"I'll accept that without reservation," I told him, "which is more than I can say about the rest of your story."

I stood up and lit a cigarette before I started toward the door. Ray Willis got to his feet slowly, his face tense. "What now, Lieutenant?" he asked harshly. "You call in that vice detail?"

"Check," I said. "Whatever made you think I wouldn't?"

"You lousy—"

"That credit card of mine carries its own responsibilities," I said easily. "If you start now, you got the chance to play piano for the last time in the Double Zero."

He came around the desk fast, mouthing obscenities in a kind of mechanical frenzy, his arms outstretched in front of him, the fingers hooking toward my throat. I let him get within reaching distance, then stiff-armed him with the heel of my hand hitting the bridge of his nose. He staggered backward and thudded against the desk.

"You're not looking at this the right way," I said reproachfully. "Now you don't have any more problems, like Old Man Denby!"

For a moment he just looked at me, the hate flaring in his eyes, then his right hand dived inside his coat and came out holding a gun. I got so nervous my reflexes popped and I'd jumped him before I knew it. I guess I was lucky—I'd never have made it if I'd stopped to think first. The side of my hand chopped down on his wrist and the gun slid from his fingers to the carpet.

I grabbed the lapels of his coat, pulling him close to me.

"Ray," I said with great restraint. "Don't ever do that again."

Then I backhanded him across the mouth, the way he'd hit Joe Diment, and he had the exact same reaction rocking back on his heels with his eyes closed tight.

"You got a violent temper, Ray," I told him. "Watch it, why don't you, or you'll be smashing skulls with a hammer before you know it."

He opened his eyes slowly and stared at me while he moistened his split lower lip with his tongue.

"I'll get you, Wheeler," he said hoarsely, "if it's the last thing I ever do!"

"You're sick, Ray." I mimicked the pious voice he'd used about Mrs. Summers. "Sick up here." I tapped the side of my head with one finger. "I feel sorry for you—you need help."

6

I got back to my apartment just after eleven and put the flip side of the Peggy Lee record on the hi-fi machine, feeling her warm voice and immaculate sense of rhythm soothe my nerve ends while I made a drink.

The drink was about shot when the buzzer squawked suddenly, breaking up the mood I'd been working on with Peggy's help. I went to answer it, trying to convince myself that Ray Willis had been kidding with his "I'll get you, Wheeler, if it's the last thing I ever do" jazz. Still, and all, I felt better after I'd opened the door and saw my visitor couldn't be Willis because nobody could change their sex that fast—whoever heard of surgery While-U-Wait?

There was a faintly embarrassed expression on Ilona Brent's pixie face as she stood there.

"I hope I didn't drag you out of bed, Al?" she asked hesitantly.

"I don't mind," I said gallantly. "If it'll make you feel better, I'll let you drag me right back."

"Could I talk to you for a few minutes?"

"Any time," I assured her. "Come right on in."

When we got into the living room, I helped her remove the arctic fox stole and the atmosphere rapidly turned tropical. She wore a backless black faille dress, supported by a narrow halter strap. I looked at the creamy-white perfection of her shoulders, then finger-traced the line of her spine down to the small of her back where there was dress again.

She shivered suddenly. "Don't do that!"

"How could I help it?" I asked brokenly. "You thrust your beautiful—and naked—spinal column right in front of my eyes with no warning, no red lights, no howling sirens. It would unnerve a doctor, never mind a cop!"

She turned to face me, a slight smile on her lips, and I got the second shock. The dress was partially frontless, as well as backless, cut low enough to reveal the beginnings of the sharp swell of her full breasts and the deep cleavage between.

"Talk about me unnerving you!" she said in a slightly breathless voice. "That all-seeing stare of yours makes me feel I wasted my time worrying about dressing at all."

"That's positive thinking," I said approvingly. "Tell me some more."

She sat down in the nearest armchair, crossing her legs with that delightfully intimate rustling sound you don't get to hear so much anymore. I figure the percentage increase in lonelyhearts clubs is in direct ratio to the increased popularity of Bermuda shorts. The only mystery left about a dame wearing Bermuda shorts is why the hell she won't diet and take some of that weight off her thighs.

"I thought maybe we could have a cozy chat like we did before, Al," she said. "Kind of unofficial?"

"Have it any way you like, honey," I told her. "I'm just happy to sit here and watch."

"Will you please be serious for a moment?" she sighed.

"You figure I'm joking?"

"I had a busy time tonight after we left the Sheriff's office," she said. "It worries me, so I have to tell somebody about it and I couldn't think of anyone else but you."

"Make a great song title," I said. "Why don't you dream up some lyrics while I make us a drink. What would you like?"

"A whisky sour," she said promptly. "Don't tell me this is a problem because I just know you grow your own lemons in California!"

"In an apartment?" I queried.

"Sure," she said confidently. "They grow out of the bedroom wallpaper."

"I couldn't think of anyone else but you," I said out loud, getting back to that song title. "You—with your mind on the ball—those legs maybe five feet tall—growing lemons out of the wall—"

She shuddered. "That is a lyric?"

"Well," I said defensively, "just the verse maybe—the introduction. You figure out a chorus, huh?"

I got the lemon juice from the delicatessen-bought plastic bottle in the ice box, like any other Californian, then made the whisky sour for Ilona, along with the same old Scotch on the rocks and a dash of soda for me.

When I got back into the living room, Ilona had a dedicated look on her face which in my experience of dames means one of two things: either she's going to take off her clothes—or else try and convert me to one of those screwball religions that grow out of the wallpaper along with the lemons on the West Coast.

I put the glass into her unresisting hand, then sat opposite her, cradling my own drink in both hands while I tried to figure an angle where I could see past the black faille curtain that descended two inches above her knees.

"I couldn't think of anyone else but you," she said dreamily, "to give all my subpoenas to—"

"It was strictly my mistake!" I said hurriedly. "Why don't we forget the whole deal?"

"You'll listen to my problems?" she asked in a kidding-on-the-square voice.

"Anything but more lyrics," I agreed.

"I had visitors around ten tonight," she said. "Angela and Rickie Willis—they came straight to the hotel after they left the Sheriff's office. Angela didn't waste any time coming straight to the point— she wanted to know if I'd represent them legally. I told her I could only do that if her mother agreed, so she said she'd go see her mother right away—leaving me alone with her intellectual playmate!" Ilona made an expressive face. "I don't even speak the same language as that moron!"

"It's basically English," I said. "Rickie's is just a little more basic than most people's."

"Anyway," Ilona continued, "a long half-hour later, Angela came back all excited, with a flushed face and an air of triumph. She waved a roll of bills at me and said it was a retainer, also I needn't worry about my fees, there was plenty more where that came from. I told her to keep the money and I'd talk it over with Lyn—her mother. Then she told Rickie they were now staying at the Starlight and didn't have to go back to the crummy hotel they'd been staying at up until then—she'd just gotten them a room two floors down where they could be nice and private."

"Ever-loving Mom sure pulled a switch," I said.

"That's what I thought," Ilona nodded. "So I went along to her suite and saw her. When I told her about Angela she looked at me like I was crazy and said she'd never even seen her, let alone given her any money. So that left me all confused and I'm still feeling the same way!"

"One of them has to be lying," I said cleverly.

"My instinctive choice would be Angela," she said. "But where would she get all that money except from Lyn?"

"How about Hillary?"

She shook her head slowly. "I can't see him giving her a wad like that because she just walked in and asked for it. And there's something else."

"Like what?"

"Like that marriage certificate," she said. "I had a good look at it after they'd gone. It's a fake—not even a good one."

"You're sure?"

Ilona looked at me icily. "Next question?"

"Yeah—sorry." I finished my drink and waited a couple of seconds while she emptied her glass. "So why the fake marriage—just to fool Momma?"

"I guess so," she said. "Like I said, Al, I was getting tired of being confused all by myself."

I made fresh drinks and when I got back to the living room, she'd gotten up from the chair and was looking at my hi-fi rig.

"You're a hi-fi buff?" she asked as I gave her the new drink.

"In a mild kind of way," I said. "Not real gone addiction—I still like hearing music better than the sound of termites eating through concrete and all that jazz."

"Play some music," she said softly.

I took Julie London's *Calendar Girl* album out of the rack and put it on the machine. Julie is the girl for late nights and low lights—and the fidelity of my five speakers match the fidelity of her voice.

"That's nice!" Ilona said a couple of minutes later.

"Very relaxed," I said. "You don't get to appreciate it fully, standing up. Why don't we relax on the couch and listen?"

"I know there's a good answer to that question someplace," she said thoughtfully. "Right now I just can't think of it."

She kind of drifted across the room to the couch and sat down and I heard that intoxicating whisper again as she crossed her legs. I sat down beside her, close but not too close because the night was young and I didn't want to turn it into an aging, sleepless night alone just because

I got impetuous—that's a cute word meaning to grab with both hands.

"Do you think they did it, Al?" she asked suddenly. "I mean, with that fake marriage, how can we believe anything they say?"

I leaned my head against the back of the couch, missing her shoulder by a half-inch. "I'm relaxed," I said reprovingly, "and Julie's relaxed. What's with you, you got to be different?"

"Please!" she said tensely. "I have to know! Do you think Angela and Rickie killed that little man in the motel?"

"They're prime suspects," I said. "But there's no proof, not yet anyway."

"Proof or not, you must have made up your own mind, Al?" she persisted. "Do you *think* they did it?"

"How could I sit around thinking and be a cop at the same time?" I said. "Thinking is for intellectuals—the boys who figure out how to rig quiz shows and sell more shark fin soup by making it a status symbol."

"My God!" she said hopelessly. "Now I get philosophy—the barefoot boy on the beat. Flat feet gave him a whole new outlook on life! He never knew what he was missing until he got a larger size pair of boots."

"It finally penetrated Angela's pointed little head that they are the two chief suspects," I said. "She was but intrigued to realize her mother, uncle, and their legal aid were in town the night Marvin was murdered. She said I should check on your alibis first and quit bothering her. What do you think?"

"I think she's a nasty little—" Ilona sighed deeply. "But thinking is out, I forgot. Alibis? I don't know—we got into the hotel and then the three of us had dinner around eight in Lyn's suite. Hilary left around nine-fifteen and went back to his own suite as far as I know. I stuck around talking with Lyn for maybe another quarter-hour then went back to my own suite and went to bed."

"Maybe that Angela has something," I said. "None of you have an alibi?"

"None of us have a motive either," she said easily. "Lyn hired a private detective to find her runaway daughter and Hillary recommended a man he knew. Why would either of them want to kill him once he'd done the job they'd paid him for?"

"Maybe he had a West Side address in New York?" I said hopefully. "And they couldn't bear the shame and humiliation of knowing him?"

"*I'll remember April*," Julie London's intimate voice whispered out of the five speakers.

Ilona lay her head against my shoulder and sighed deeply without saying anything.

"This Rickie Willis," I said. "Did you know he's an ex-con?"

"Well," she said dreamily, "what the hell?"

"I thought you were the one all worried and confused."

"I thought you were the one all relaxed," she countered. "Julie's relaxed—I'm all relaxed. Why do you have to get tensions now?"

"It's my sense of timing," I admitted. "It's been shot to hell ever since that night I knocked on the door of a blonde's apartment and as soon as it opened, said, 'Baby love me tonight!'—then thrust a bunch of roses into the arms of her truck-jockey husband."

She gurgled with lazy laughter for a few moments. "Maybe you should put me on a permanent retainer basis, Al. You must need a lawyer nearly all the time."

Then her head turned toward me slowly, the hazel-flecked eyes molten and melting, her soft mouth open. I kissed her with the dynamite technique of the short fuse and long explosion, my arm sliding around her bare shoulder and my finger tracing the downward curve of her spine again. She shuddered, pressing herself harder against me, as her fingers dug cruelly into my chest.

A long time later she gently disengaged herself from my arms and stood up. Her midnight-colored hair made a tousled frame for the pixie face as she looked down at me for a moment.

"Too many lights in here," she said unsteadily. "You're nothing but a spendthrift, Wheeler."

She moved around the room, switching off the lights until the only illumination came from the shaded lamp on the corner bracket set above the hi-fi machine. As she walked back toward the couch, her fingers fumbled with the halter strap, and two seconds later the black faille dress slid down over her hips with a gentle rustling sound to her ankles. Underneath she wore a strapless black satin bra and hall-slip, and her fingers were busily unfastening the bra as she stepped neatly out of the dress. By the time she got back to the couch she was naked except for the black satin panties which had generous inserts of fine lace.

The soft light gave a luminous sheen to the pearly-whiteness of her full, taut breasts as she leaned down toward me.

"I doubt if this is legal, but I'm sure there's a precedent," she whispered.

"This must be the avant-American look all the girls are wearing this season?" I said admiringly.

She grabbed two fistfuls of my shirt and hauled me to my feet. "I hate couches," she said simply. "They always give me a feeling of insecurity."

I put one arm around her shoulders and the other under her thighs, lifting her into my arms. She purred contentedly as I carried her toward the bedroom.

"*That September*," Julie sang intimately, "*in the rain.*"

7

Mr. Jones, the motel manager, didn't look any better next morning when I saw him for the second time. His need for a shave had gotten twenty-four hours greater, the blue shirt a little more faded, the gray pants a couple of extra creases in the wrong places.

"You keep on coming out here for no good reason and I'll start charging you rent, Lieutenant," he said sourly.

"I want to take another look at both those cabins," I told him. "It's too early in the morning to argue and you look obscene in strong sunlight—so just give me the keys and I'll go look, huh?"

He grunted and spat at a nearby gray, trashcan-wise cat that dodged disdainfully, its fur bristling.

"O.K.," he grunted. "But make it fast will you, Lieutenant? Cops around the place are no good for my business."

I took the keys from his reluctant fingers. "It's you that's no good for your business," I said thoughtfully. "You look like an awful warning to any young guy about to embark on a night of vice. Why don't you get smart and get yourself a job with a temperance outfit playing a reformed alcoholic—you'd make a fortune!"

There was no percentage in waiting for his answer, so I didn't. I spent the next hour going over both the cabins again, inch by inch—I didn't have a fine-tooth comb with me because my teeth aren't the combing kind—but I did a real job on both cabins and came up with a double zero again to match the name of Ray Willis' key club.

Mr. Jones was in his office, his chair tilted back and both feet on the desk when I came in. I dropped the keys between his ankles.

"You find anything you couldn't find yesterday, Lieutenant?" he asked.

"Not a thing," I said. "It doesn't figure—not with Marvin, anyway. I never saw a guy travel so light—not even a spare shirt."

"He had a bag," Jones said. "Cheapskate beat-up suitcase—canvas kind."

"Why didn't you tell me that before?" I snarled. "Where is it?"

"You never asked me," Jones said, shrugging his thin shoulders. "I got it here—but there's nothing in it worth anything." He planted his feet back on the floor and leaned down behind his desk for a moment. He lifted a shabby mustard-colored bag and put it down in front of him. "Look for yourself," he said calmly.

Right then I was so mad I couldn't say a word—and for Wheeler, that's going some. I stared at him hard enough to curl him at the edges, and he didn't even blink.

I snapped open the clasps and lifted the lid of the suitcase. Dirty socks, underwear, shaving things. In the bottom a fresh shirt—or at least it had come from a laundry and was folded around a shirt board; it was badly frayed and gray at the collar.

"Sure there's nothing here you can use?" I said to Jones acidly as I tossed the contents one by one onto the desk. When I lifted the shirt, a large envelope that had been tucked inside it slid out. I saw Jones jump. "Guess you overlooked something, huh?"

It was addressed to Albert H. Marvin, at a West Side address in New York; at the top of the lefthand corner was the return address of the motel. It had not been through the mails, and it figured that it was something Marvin himself was mailing to his home address.

I slit it open with my thumbnail and shook out the contents. Seven or eight photographs fluttered down on the scarred wooden desktop, and when I shook the envelope a second time, a bunch of negatives followed.

"Hey!" Jones said hoarsely. His feet hit the floor with a crash as he craned his neck forward for a closer look. "Ain't they something!"

Look at them any way at all—and Jones sure did—they were something all right, with the same graphic intimacy of French postcards except the protagonists weren't anonymous. You could recognize Angela and Rickie in every one of them. I scooped up the pictures and negatives and put them back into the envelope.

"You don't have to be in such a hurry, Lieutenant!" Jones said plaintively. "I hardly got a good look at any of 'em. How about—"

"You're a dirty-minded old man," I said, stating an obvious truth. "Keep going this way and you'll never make one of the better-class cemeteries. No self-respecting embalmer would touch you even now, not even wearing rubber gloves!"

"What a dame!" he said coarsely. "What a figure! Hey, Lieutenant—you get a good look at her—"

"Have you got a camera?" I asked him suddenly.

"Why, sure." He scratched his head slowly. "But what—"

"We never found any camera in Marvin's room," I said in a hard voice. "With that fur-lined sewer of a mind you got, maybe you sneaked over to their cabin, nights, and took those pictures?"

"You're crazy!" he snarled. "I wouldn't—"

"That's it!" I snapped my fingers excitedly. "Sure—and Marvin caught you at it that night and scared the hell out of you so you killed him with the hammer, then dragged his body back to his own cabin. You got the pictures developed fast the next morning and you'd taken his bag so you could plant them in it and make it look like *his* dirty work."

"It was him!" Jones yelped. "That's his handwriting on the envelope! Look at his name in my register if you don't believe me!"

"You mean you wrote his signature in your book and the handwriting matches the writing here?" I asked coldly. "It all adds up—why else would you be fool enough to pinch that bag?"

He gibbered for a moment without being able to get any words out, then cleared his throat desperately and spat again, missing the open window by a minimum of two clear feet.

"I'll be back," I told him in my best "youdunit" voice as I pocketed the envelope. "Just don't try leaving town, huh, Jones?"

I drove back into town figuring I'd already done my good deed for the day—at least I'd given Jones something else to think about besides sex.

When I got back to the office, the ever-present Annabelle Jackson was present, wearing a shirt dress in charcoal-gray linen. It had sleeves that came right down to her wrists and should have given her a covered-up look, but didn't. The kind of figure Annabelle has would get through to you even in a Hawaiian muumuu.

"Hush ma mouth," I said admiringly. "You-all is pretty as a picture this morning, magnolia blossom, honeychile, sweet memory of my ole Kentucky home."

"I'd love to hush that ole running-off mouth of yours—you aging Casanova," she said calmly. "With three beautiful women involved in this case, I wonder you have time to even see little ole me!"

"It comes from living a clean life, thinking clean thoughts, and cirrhosis of the liver," I explained. "My virility increases in direct proportion as my life expectancy decreases. Just one question before I go see the master?"

"No!" she said violently.

"Does your underwear whisper when you move?" I asked interestedly.

"You're disgusting!" Annabelle said, her face a sudden flaming red. "And it most definitely does not!"

"Aren't you worried you'll catch cold?" I said sympathetically, then ducked into the Sheriff's office before she threw something.

Lavers scowled at me as I closed the door and headed toward the nearest vacant chair.

"Where the hell have you been all morning?" he demanded.

"The motel," I said.

"Why waste your time out there when you're supposed to be catching a murderer?"

I figured maybe it was a good question because I couldn't figure out an answer, so I let it ride. Lavers rammed a cigar into his face and I watched, fascinated, while he lit it.

"How many cigars a day do you smoke, Sheriff?" I asked him.

"I don't know," he grunted. "Eight—nine. Why?"

"I bet you were a bottle-fed baby," I said. "The psychologists figure it shows a subconscious yearning for the warmth and safety found only at a mother's—"

"Wheeler!" He gobbled in fury for a moment. "Don't you ever get your mind off sex?"

"Sir!" I said reproachfully. "We were talking of your mother."

Lavers closed his eyes for a short while, giving me a chance to light a virile cigarette.

"All right," he said finally. "What did you find at the motel that's new?"

I took the envelope out of my pocket and pushed it across the desk toward him. While he goggled at the pictures, I gave him a rundown on the events since I'd left the office the night before. My visit to the Double Zero Club with Ray Willis—the facts that Ilona Brent had told me. The more I talked, the more I got the feeling he wasn't appreciating my efforts. When I'd run out of talk and just sat there, his beady eyes bored into mine with the ruthless speed of an electric drill.

"Of course," he said gently, "I'm only the county sheriff and I know I don't count for much around here. But I think you just might have had the courtesy to tell me what had happened before you sent the city vice detail into the Club!"

"You're so right, sir!" I said warmly. "And don't think for even one moment that I wouldn't have."

"Now you've lost me again!"

"If I'd sent the vice detail around to see Ray Willis, I'd have called you first, Sheriff," I explained.

His mouth sagged open and the cigar spilled out from between his teeth onto the desk. It was starting to burn a hole in his desk pad before he grabbed at it.

"You mean you didn't call them?"

"That's right, sir."

"He's running a bordello with a private key club as a front," Lavers said in a hushed voice. "He pulled a gun on you as well—but you didn't bother calling the vice detail." He looked at me almost apologetically, "I wouldn't want to embarrass you, Wheeler, or anything like that, but under the circumstances I feel the question is necessary. Why didn't you call the vice detail about Willis?"

"I didn't want them fooling around with one of my murder suspects," I said truthfully. "You can't trust these city cops in a deal like that—first thing you know they'd have booked him or something stupid. I don't want Ray Willis slapped in a cell—I want him out in the open—for now, anyway."

"So he's free to commit another murder, if he is the murderer!" Lavers exploded. "And you're supposed to be a law enforcement officer. My God! I'm compounding the felony just sitting here listening to you!"

"Yes, sir," I agreed. "If it's any help, I'm working on those song and dance routines."

"What the hell?" he said hopelessly and relaxed back in his chair, taking cover behind a cloud of black smoke. "You think you have any kind of lead on the killer?"

"No leads, only complications," I said cheerfully. "That marriage certificate is a fake according to Ilona Brent—but I can't see that that means much more to us than discrediting the three of them—Angela and both Willis brothers. Or do we detect here the faint odor of red herring?"

"I don't have any answers," Lavers said. "Let's hear some more of your questions."

"Those pictures," I said. "Marvin must have used a camera to get them—he must have used his own developing equipment too. What happened to them? They weren't in the cabin. They weren't in his suitcase—which, by the way, Sheriff, I left right where I found it. It can be picked up any time."

"Fine, Lieutenant," Lavers said with broad sarcasm. "And let me know when you trade in that form-fitting capsule of a car for something big enough to squeeze a suitcase into. It'll save the county a fortune in extra trips!"

"But why did he take the pictures anyway?" I went on, generously forgiving his insensitive attitude toward my Healey. "If it was for his client—Mrs. Summers—then why didn't he mail them to her, instead of himself?"

"Blackmail?"

"That's what it looks like, Sheriff," I agreed. "But who? Angela and Rickie?—Mrs. Summers?"

"I heard from New York this morning," Lavers said. "They check out Ray Willis' statement about his brother having a record. Rickie did two years for burglary, then a year on parole. He's clean now."

He sorted the papers in front of him. "They gave me a rundown on Marvin—he sounds like a real nice citizen."

"How's that?" I asked.

"He lost his private detective's license six months back," Lavers said. "Mixed up in a call-girl racket—pandering at very high prices with maybe a little blackmail on the side. They didn't have enough to indict him, apparently, but enough to get the D.A.'s office to can his license."

"That's very interesting," I said. "For no good reason it makes me remember little Angela's suggestion we should look into the alibis of her family. Maybe Marvin was trying to blackmail Mrs. Summers—either directly, or through her brother-in-law. Could be the reason for planning to send the pictures to himself in New York—for safety."

"Could be," Lavers grunted. "Or maybe he was trying to lean on one—or both—of the Willis brothers? Either of them could have killed him with no trouble at all, by the look of their record."

"I guess I should go out and ask some more questions," I said. "You mind if I take those pictures with me? They might help get some answers."

"O.K.," Lavers said reluctantly. "But you'd better leave the negatives here."

I took the envelope, minus the negatives, and put it into my inside coat pocket.

"Before you go—answer me just one question," the Sheriff said grimly.

"The vice detail, sir?" I anticipated him. "I suggest we leave sleeping cops lie—to coin a brand-new phrase."

"You sure you didn't make some kind of a deal with Ray Willis?" he asked suspiciously.

"Fifty per cent of a bordello?" I said dreamily. "It sounds like the wandering boy's dream of home, Sheriff. A regular unearned income every week and the freedom of the house.... Just call me Polly Wheeler! And I'd like you to know, sir, that any time you visit with us we'll gladly discount your tab fifteen per cent—for cash."

"Get out of here," he muttered morosely. "You're undermining my moral fibers!"

8

"Miss Angela Summers?" The desk clerk at the Starlight said with a gleam in his watery eyes. "She's in six-seventeen—and Mr. Willis has six-eighteen, adjoining. Miss Summers insisted they have adjoining rooms. The maid tells me that six-eighteen is practically undisturbed."

"Gosh, Charlie!" I said admiringly. "You guys in the hotel business sure see life. I'll bet you've been to a burlesque show, even?"

"No need," Charlie said happily, "not after seeing Miss Angela Summers. That Willis is a lucky guy—I'd sure trade my nights with him anytime."

"I wouldn't bet on it," I said. "You know if they're in?"

"Miss Summers is in—Mr. Willis is out," he said promptly. "Please remember, Lieutenant, the management frowns on attempted rape—it's a house rule."

"Then how come you're still working here?" I demanded. "No dame under forty-five ever gets past the desk without being deflowered by your X-ray eyes."

"It's a hobby, Lieutenant," he said smugly, "you know—like home movies?"

A couple of minutes later I knocked on the door of 617, and a muffled voice called out for me to come in. The door was shut but not locked, so I went inside the room and right away I figured that Charlie wasn't far out when he mentioned the house rule.

Angela Summers lay on the couch, her hands clasped behind her head, looking at the ceiling. She wore a gingham blouse in bronze check which was buttoned right up to the neck, giving her a demure look. The hem of the blouse came down as far as the tops of her thighs and underneath were a pair of white, fine silk-knit panties. Her long tanned legs were crossed at the ankles and her feet were bare, the toenails painted a mottled robin's-egg blue to match her fingernails.

She turned her head slowly and looked at me, the bird's-nest hairdo still the same inverted cone on top of her head. The big dark eyes looked at and through me with complete lack of interest.

"I figured it was Rickie," she said casually.

"I'll go outside again and wait till you get dressed, if you want?" I suggested.

"I'm dressed—aren't I?" She looked down at herself idly. "Sure—I'm wearing pants, so you don't need to take off!"

She swung her legs down off the couch, then stood up, stretching her arms above her head so that the pointed breasts thrust firmly against the thin blouse.

"I could use a drink," she said, and walked leisurely across to the bureau and picked up the bottle that stood there.

"You want a drink, Lieutenant What's-your-name?"

"No, thanks," I told her. "And the name's Wheeler."

She poured bourbon into a glass and brought it back with her to the couch and sat down again, patting the empty space beside her.

"Why don't you take a load off your feet?" she asked in a bored voice. "You look like you're going to make with more questions."

I sat on the couch beside her, trying not to look at those beautifully sculptured legs the whole time.

"So make with the questions," she said. "Be my guest."

"Who faked the marriage certificate?" I asked gently.

"Who said it was faked?" she countered.

"You can take my word for it," I said. "Don't get cute."

She drank some of the bourbon slowly, watching me out of the corner of her eyes.

"Ray found out ever-loving Mom had arrived in town," she said finally. "We had to do *something!*"

"Why?"

"What's the matter with you—out to lunch?" she asked scornfully. "You know she wanted to pull that stat-rape caper. We figured she'd try and pull something like that—so we needed some kind of defense against her."

"Whose idea was the marriage certificate?"

"Ray's." She smiled, showing sparkling white teeth. "That Ray—he's the ginchiest, a real abominable snowman!"

"He's abominable, all right," I agreed.

"Don't be a drag!" she said coldly. "He's the nicest guy I know, next to Rickie."

"I hope you don't know Ray as well as you know his brother," I said.

"I'm not in orbit with that crack," she said with a question mark in her voice.

I took out the envelope and handed it to her. She pulled out the photos and looked through them with avid interest.

"Vavoom!" she said breathlessly. "And away we go!"

"They were found in Marvin's suitcase," I told her. "They just turned up today."

"He was a lousy grub!" she said. "Sneaking around the windows with his dirty little camera like this! Like there's no privacy even in your own pad anymore!"

"Did you know he'd taken any pictures?"

"Of course not," she said. "What are you going to do with them, Lieutenant?"

"They're evidence," I said. "If you and Rickie had known about them, they'd have given you an excellent motive for murdering Marvin."

"We didn't know about them," she said hotly. "And we didn't murder Marvin. Why are you trying so damned hard to pin it on us, Lieutenant? Ever-loving Mom promise you a big fat bonus or something?"

"Yeah," I said nastily. "If I can hang the rap on you, I get to keep the pictures!"

She hauled off and slapped me across the mouth with the palm of her hand, and it hurt. The palm of my own hand itched until I had to do something about it, so I got to my feet and walked across to the bureau.

"I'll have that drink you offered me," I said. "Don't you have any Scotch around the place?"

"You're a kook!" she said wonderingly. "Why didn't you slap me right back?"

"Don't think I wasn't tempted," I told her. "I guess I'll have to settle for bourbon, seeing it's an emergency." I made the drink and lit a cigarette to go with it.

"I'm—sorry," she said in a slightly hesitant voice. "I guess I asked for that crack."

"Marvin lost his license six months back," I said, watching her face in the bureau mirror. "He was mixed up in a call-girl racket—pandering, with a little blackmail on the side."

"You think he was going to try and blackmail us with these photos?" she asked.

"What good would it do him to blackmail you?" I said. "You don't have any money—or you didn't until last night."

"What do you mean?"

"You called on Ilona Brent," I said. "Left Rickie with her while you went to see your mother—you said. When you returned a half-hour later, you had what Ilona called a triumphant look on your face—and a fistful of money."

"Ever-loving Mom got soft and I made a touch," she said, then giggled suddenly.

"You never saw your mother," I said patiently. "She didn't even know you'd been inside the hotel."

"She was lying," Angela said without any conviction in her voice.

"You know she wasn't," I said, the patience bit wearing a little thin. "Anyway—we were talking of Marvin. Your mother hired him on your uncle's advice, did you know that? Hillary said he'd had dealings with Marvin before and he was a reliable operator."

"No," she whispered, "I didn't know that."

I sipped at the bourbon, then turned around to face her.

"The way things are now, Angela," I told her, "you might make eighteen O.K. but your chances of ever seeing nineteen are real lousy! Couple the circumstantial evidence with those pix as a motive and I could put you into court right now, with a seventy-thirty chance that a jury would find you guilty!"

She bit down on her lower lip until two pinpoints of blood showed. "But I didn't kill him!" she said dully.

"You made a couple of cracks about Hillary," I said idly. "Something about him doing a lot of social work among the high school set? At the time I figured it was probably just one of your sweet girlish gags you throw at people all the time—but now I'm not so sure. I get curious about his relationship to the late Albie Marvin—was Marvin his panderer, maybe? I get curious why, after a half-hour alone with him last night, you come back with a flushed face and a wad of folding money. Maybe it's just the kind of mind I've got?"

"That's for sure!" she said quickly.

"Is it?" I looked at her for a few seconds, seeing the deep scarlet flush across her face slowly. "How many times do I have to say it, Angela? This is a murder rap you're facing. You're so close to it right now, you can reach out and touch it!"

"What do you want me to do?" she asked hoarsely.

"Tell me about Hillary," I said.

She drained her glass, then held it out toward me. "I need another drink."

I took the glass from her hand and went across to the bureau again, keeping my back turned toward her while I made the drink in slow time.

"I don't know about Marvin pandering for him," she said in a toneless voice. "I guess it could be. Hillary sure does have a thing about the high school set—I found that out before I went to Switzerland."

I took the fresh drink over to her, and sat at the far end of the couch. She lifted the glass to her mouth, tilted her head back, and drank the contents in one long gulp.

"He seduced me," she said casually. "Two months after my sixteenth birthday—a kind of late birthday present, maybe. I wasn't exactly innocent when it happened, but it was my first big deal. Do you have a cigarette, Lieutenant?"

I gave her the cigarette and lit it for her, and one for myself.

"It got to be a habit for a while," she went on. "I didn't really mind. Hillary is a gentle guy—and ever-loving Mom was crazy about him—had been even before Father died, I think. I guess I got a kick out of him choosing me for his bed instead of her. Then came the inevitable—she walked in on us one day unexpectedly. Maybe she'd gotten suspicious, I don't know, but she sure caught us at the right moment. You should have seen her! I thought she'd end up in a funny farm, the way she screamed and threw herself around. At one stage, she picked up an icepick from the bar and tried to cut his heart out with it! But that was it—vavoom!—Switzerland for little Angela!"

She drew hard on the cigarette, inhaling deeply. "So I guess dear old Hillary's always had a soft spot for me ever since that time. He's been useful—ever-loving Mom kept me on a tight allowance all the time, so when I needed cash I'd tell Hillary and he'd always come across with a respectable amount, like last night."

"A real nice guy!" I said with my teeth on edge. "Compared to him, Ray Willis is a gentleman!"

"Don't get mad at Hillary, Lieutenant"—she pouted her lower lip. "He's no different from any other man, after all!"

"I don't know too many forty-year-old guys who go around seducing sixteen-year-old girls," I said. "Do you?"

"They would if they had the chance," she said calmly. "You aren't forty yet—somewhere in your mid-thirties I'd bet, huh?"

"But I never made a pass at the high school set," I said. "Not since I left high school, anyway."

"How about a nearly-eighteen-year-old?" she asked in a soft, wicked voice. "If you had the opportunity?"

"Look," I said hastily. "Let's not—"

She laughed slowly—a harsh sound caught deep inside her throat. "What's the matter—chicken, Lieutenant?" I watched as her fingers undid the buttons of her blouse, one by one, then came up on my feet with a nervous reflex. She stood up simultaneously, sliding her shoulders out of the blouse in a sensual movement, letting it slide down her back to the floor.

There was no bra underneath, so she was naked from the waist up. She took a deep breath which lifted her high, pointed breasts in a slow, lilting motion.

"Do I make you nervous, Lieutenant?" she said huskily. "I didn't mean to!"

She grabbed my right hand and cupped it around her left breast, squeezing my fingers hard.

"What's wrong, Lieutenant?" Her eyes searched my face for a moment. "You have some special kick, maybe? I'll put the blouse back on if you like and you can rip it off."

"What makes you think you're so special?" I said coldly, pulling my hand away. "I should be excited about taking candy from a kid—I'm not Hilary!"

A dull film shrouded her eyes as she still stared at me. "I should have known it was too late," she said venomously. "I guess ever-loving Mom beat me to the punch?"

The door opened suddenly and Rickie Willis came into the room. "Hey, Angie! I—" He stopped suddenly.

I saw the gleam in her eyes a fraction of a second before her hand exploded against the side of my face.

"Leave me alone, you dirty maniac!" she screamed hysterically. "Don't touch me!"

She ran into Rickie's arms, clinging to him fiercely with her head against his chest while she sobbed convulsively.

"Keep him away from me, lover!" she moaned. "Don't let him touch me again! He's a maniac—he tore off my clothes, and all the time he kept on telling me what he was going to do when he'd finished! I thought you'd never get back, lover!"

Rickie Willis stared at me, his face darkening rapidly.

"Cop!" he said thickly. "Dirty, stinking cop! They're all the same—the lousy—" He pushed Angela away from him violently so that she staggered and fell to the floor.

She rolled over on one elbow, watching me with a malevolent sparkle in her eyes. "Get him, Rick!" she whispered. "Get him good!"

He walked toward me slowly, his arms hanging down at his sides, the fingers clenching and unclenching spasmodically. To say he looked like a gorilla would be insulting evolution.

"I'll tear your guts out, you dirty, stinking cop!" he growled. "Laying your filthy paws on her, thinking just because you got a tin badge she's got to smile and say nothing about it!"

"You've got a lousy line of dialogue, Rickie," I told him. "Along with a limited vocabulary and a nonexistent brain. I don't want any part of her—she was trying me on for size. Maybe she wanted to keep in shape until you got back."

"Don't try and crawl out of it, copper!" he snarled. "You got it coming, man, and you're going to get it good!"

He was almost close enough to take a swing at me, and obviously in no mood for sweet reason. I was in no mood for a punch in the nose, either. I pulled the thirty-eight out from its belt holster and rammed the barrel hard into his navel.

"Take one punch at this dirty, stinking cop," I snarled at him, "and you'll get a dirty, stinking piece of lead right through your belly!"

He stopped right where he was and blinked at me a couple of times. "You wouldn't?" he said doubtfully. "Not with Angie as a witness."

"Try me?" I said softly, and rammed the gun an inch further into the softness of his stomach.

"He's only bluffing, Rickie!" Angela said shrilly. "Get him!"

Rickie licked his lips slowly. "He'd do it!" he said in a flat voice. "You can tell about this kind of deal—when a guy's kidding or he isn't." He turned his head and looked at her. "Sorry, honey, but there's nothing can be done—you dig?"

"You squirrel!" she said contemptuously. "You're chicken!"

"You must have some kind of a brain under all that hair, Rickie," I said. "Primeval as it may be. What was she wearing when you went out?"

"Huh?" He squinted at me blankly.

"Angela, you lamebrain," I said tersely. "What clothes was she wearing when you left?"

"A shirt," he said. His head turned slowly until he was looking at Angela, still sitting on the floor. He scratched his head, deliberating for a while. "And those white pants she's wearing now."

"I'm the guy who tore off all her clothes while you were gone," I explained carefully. "That means I ripped off her shirt—right? She's still wearing the pants!"

"Yeah," he said grudgingly.

I pointed at the blouse on the floor. "There it is, Rickie-boy. Take a good look. If there's one button missing you can hold the gun and belt me over the head with it."

"Don't listen to his lies, lover," Angela hissed. "He's just trying a snow-job."

Rickie stooped down and picked up the blouse carefully, then examined it with minute tenacity, checking off the buttons one by one. When he was finally satisfied, he tossed the blouse onto the couch, then walked stiff-legged over to the bureau, his hand reaching for the bourbon bottle.

Angela got quickly to her feet and ran across the room, throwing her arms around his chest and hugging herself against his back.

"You don't believe *him*, lover?" she asked softly.

He shrugged himself free of her enveloping arms, then turned around to face her, the drink in his hand.

"If I didn't know you better, baby," he said softly, "I'd figure you planned the whole deal so I'd stop a slug from the Lieutenant's gun."

"Rickie!" Her eyes dilated and she pressed the back of her hand against her mouth tightly. "You don't think I made it up?"

"Right now I'm not sure, baby," he said in an expressionless voice. "I got to think about it—figure it out, huh?"

He put the flat of his hand over her face in a casual gesture, then the thick fingers tightened into a hard painful grip as he pulled her toward him—like the start of a pitcher's windup—then pushed her away, letting go his grip on her face at the last moment when his arm was fully extended.

It was a miniature study in controlled violence. Angela almost flew across the room until her back hit the opposite wall with a sharp explosive sound. She crumpled onto the floor and lay there making faint whimpering sounds, her face gray as she tried desperately to get some air back into her lungs.

"Don't crowd me, doll," Rickie said mildly. "How can I figure it out when you're all over me the whole time?"

I started to walk toward her and Rickie grabbed my arm with a heavy, restraining hand.

"She'll be O.K., Lieutenant," he said. "She's a real tough baby under that delicate skin! And she had it coming."

"Whatever you say, Rickie," I agreed politely, turning toward him, showing him a man-to-man understanding of woman troubles on my face.

At the same time I pivoted up on the balls of my feet and let him have my right fist just under the heart with all my weight behind it. I used that arm like a piston, giving him two more in quick succession, and by the time he got the third one he was wrapped around my arm like a pretzel. I cuffed his shoulder with the heel of my left hand so he toppled sideways and dropped onto the couch, out cold.

"And you had that coming, Rickie-boy," I said unnecessarily.

Angela had managed to get up on her hands and knees by the time I got to her. I put my arm around her shoulders and helped her shuffle across to the bathroom. Once we were inside, she shook her head violently and gestured mutely for me to get the hell out.

It was another emergency, so I had a little more of the bourbon, figuring if I hung around Angela Summers long enough, I'd develop a taste for it. Two, three minutes dragged by with Rickie still out cold on the couch, then Angela came back into the room, walking slowly, but looking a little better.

She opened a bureau drawer and took out a sweater and the black stretch nylon pants, pulling the sweater down over her head first, then stepping into the pants and wriggling them up over her hips.

"You know something, Lieutenant?" she said in a thin voice. "I spent a whole year in that Swiss finishing school and it was all wasted—they didn't even tell me how to take care of a situation like this!"

"Even Emily Post would need to think twice," I said politely. "You want me to stick around for when Rickie wakes up?"

"I think it would be better if you weren't here when he does," she said. "But thanks for the offer."

"Just one more question before I vavoom!" I said. "Where were you yesterday when you weren't in Nevada?"

"We went to Ray's club," she said tiredly. "We sat around and killed a bottle and cooked up the marriage-in-Nevada deal when Ray produced that phony certificate."

I walked to the door and opened it, then looked back at her. "You're sure you can handle him when he wakes up?"

"Sure." She nodded her head irritably. "I guess this is a big day in my life, Lieutenant. If I'm not getting a college education, at least I'll graduate from the school of H.K. Hard knocks, that is!"

"Sure," I said sympathetically, "and like Rickie said—you had it coming!"

9

I knocked on the door of the suite two floors up, and a different world away from 617. Hillary Summers opened the door and looked at me with an expression of mild surprise on his face.

"Lieutenant Wheeler, isn't it?" he asked pleasantly.

"That's right," I said. "I wanted to talk with you, Mr. Summers."

"Sure." He opened the door wider. "Come right in, won't you?"

We got settled in the living room, sitting opposite each other, with Hillary trying a little too hard to look perfectly relaxed.

"What can I do for you, Lieutenant?"

"You could tell me something about Marvin," I suggested.

"I don't think I can help much there." He shook his head regretfully. "I hardly knew the man."

"But you advised your sister-in-law to hire him?" I said.

"That's true," he nodded quickly. "I employed him to do a couple of small jobs for me and he was efficient, so naturally when Lyn talked of hiring a private detective to find Angela and the Willis boy, I suggested Marvin for the job. But I can't say I knew him at all, Lieutenant, not in the real sense of the word."

"Did you know he lost his license six months back?"

"No, I didn't!"

"He was mixed up in some call-girl racket—pandering with a little blackmail on the side," I added.

Hillary shrugged his shoulders awkwardly. "I had no idea. I would never have dreamed of recommending him to Lyn if I'd known."

I took my time about lighting a cigarette, watching his lean, sensitive fingers drum a soundless tattoo on his knee.

"Angela Summers came to see you last night?" I asked abruptly.

"Why do you ask?"

"She left Rickie Willis in Miss Brent's suite, then paid you a visit—although she told Miss Brent she was visiting with her mother."

He brushed the dark, gray-flecked hair back from his forehead with a curiously boyish gesture. "Well, yes, she did drop in and visit with me for a few minutes, Lieutenant. She wanted to leave the sordid hotel where she was staying and move in here—she asked me if I would make the arrangements for her, so I called the manager right away and fixed it."

"And gave her some money?"

"After all"—he smiled wanly—"she is my niece."

I took the envelope containing the photos out of my inside pocket and handed it to him.

"We found this among Marvin's things," I said.

He took the pictures out of the envelope and leafed through them slowly, staring at each one in turn.

"This is infamous!" he croaked, the blood draining from his face. "I'm surprised you haven't destroyed them already!"

"They're evidence, Mr. Summers," I said. "Maybe they provide a motive for Marvin's murder."

"You can't possibly think Angela had anything to do with it?" he said hotly. "Maybe the Willis boy—but Angela!"

"I think anyone could have killed him," I said, "including you, Mr. Summers."

"What!"

"I understand from Miss Brent you both had dinner in Mrs. Geoffrey Summers' suite that night?"

"That's true."

"You left around nine-fifteen?"

"I know it was sometime after nine—why?"

"What did you do then?"

"I came back in here and went to bed."

"I don't suppose there's anyone who can substantiate your story?"

"I don't think that's amusing, Lieutenant!" he said in a bleak voice.

"So you don't have an alibi for the time of the murder?"

"Are you implying I need one?" he asked incredulously.

"Yeah," I said simply.

He got out of the chair and started to pace up and down the room, his hands thrust deep into the pockets of his beautifully cut Italian silk suit.

"This is ridiculous!" he said finally. "I have no intention of allowing you to walk all over me, Lieutenant. If you wish to continue this interview, I insist that Miss Brent be present, as my legal representative!"

"That's O.K. by me," I said. "You want her to hear Angela's story of your close relationship, I don't mind."

He stopped pacing suddenly and swung around toward me, a haggard look in his eyes.

"What do you mean?" he whispered.

"She just told me the whole story," I said flatly. "How you seduced her a couple of months after her sixteenth birthday—how her mother caught the two of you later and bundled her off to that school in Switzerland."

He sank back into the chair and buried his face in his hands. "She—she threw herself at me!" he muttered.

"It's bad enough the way it is now," I said contemptuously. "Don't make it worse!"

"I need a drink," he said thickly. "You'll excuse me." He got up again and went over to the small bar set in one corner of the room and opened it up, displaying a half-dozen bottles.

"That's how you got to know Marvin in the first place?" I asked. "He was your panderer—around the high school set?"

"You can't prove that," he said dully.

"Maybe," I said. "I don't know yet—we can try."

He made himself a drink and gulped it down quickly, then replenished the glass right away.

"Why would Marvin bother taking those photos?" I went on. "There's only one logical reason and that's because he was going to use them for blackmail. But who was he going to blackmail, Mr. Summers? Not Angela or Rickie Willis—they didn't have any money. Not Angela's mother because she wouldn't have given a damn—in fact they could have helped her bring her charge of statutory rape against Rickie. That leaves just you!"

He swallowed most of the second drink quickly, then looked at me with savage, impotent hate in his eyes. "You're out of your mind!" he snarled.

"And you have no alibi for the time Marvin was murdered," I said. "If you drove out to the motel or some other meeting place to see him that night, there'll be somebody, someplace, who saw you—and I'll find them, Mr. Summers."

I got up out of the chair and walked toward the door. "And when I find them," I added. "I'll book you for first-degree murder and you'll wind up in the gas chamber."

"Get out!" he said thickly. "You hear me? Get out!"

"I was just going," I said reasonably. "If you get tired thinking about the gas chamber, Mr. Summers, you can always think about the sensation Angela's going to be in court when she gives evidence about her intimate relationship with you. You're going to be front page news on a worldwide basis then!"

I stepped out into the corridor, closing the door behind me gently just as the phone started to ring inside. I walked along the corridor to the next suite and knocked on the door, beginning to appreciate the problems of a traveling salesman.

A badly dyed blonde in a maid's uniform opened the door and looked at me haughtily, like I wasn't what she expected to be calling on a quarter-billion dollars.

"I'd like to see Mrs. Summers," I said.

"I'm sorry." She looked down her sharp nose at me. "Mrs. Summers is resting and doesn't wish to be disturbed."

"Don't we all?" I sighed regretfully. "I'm Lieutenant Wheeler—from the sheriff's office—I think she'll see me."

She glared at me for a moment, then said reluctantly, "I'll find out." The door closed in my face abruptly.

It looked like that was another vacuum cleaner I hadn't sold today. I checked my watch and saw it was just after five—it had been a long afternoon and that steak sandwich I'd had for lunch was only a memory. Then the door opened again and the maid was back, complete with glare.

"Mrs. Summers said for you to wait in the living room," she said shortly.

I followed her inside and she gestured with one finger toward a stiff-backed chair.

"You're kidding!" I told her cheerfully, and gave her a cosmopolitan, man-about-town, slap across the bottom as I walked past her toward the couch.

She squealed indignantly. "You—you *beast!*"

"How come you never married?" I asked interestedly as I settled down onto the couch.

Her curiosity fought a short, sharp battle with her outraged virginity, and won. "How did you know I wasn't married?" she asked sharply.

"One look," I said happily, "and it figures!"

She marched out of the room, her back stiff with frustrated fury, and I relaxed against the cushions of the couch. Maybe ten minutes later, Mrs. Geoffrey Summers came into the room.

She wore a negligee in a rich white satin, hand-embroidered, I guessed, in gold thread. The same tall, slim blonde—all elegance and fine steel—with icy-cold, deep blue eyes. I stood up as she came into the room, and she made a small, impatient gesture with one hand, telling me to sit down again.

"Is this visit of some importance, Lieutenant?" she asked crisply. "Or just a routine call?"

"I wouldn't say it was routine," I told her. "Did you bring the maid with you from the East Coast?"

She closed her eyes and shuddered delicately. "I wouldn't employ her to wash dishes at home! She's the best I could get from a local agency, and the best proof anyone could have that traveling in the less civilized areas of this country is something to be done only after adequate preparation, or preferably not at all!"

"I figure no nose could be that pointed unless it's been pressed against a million keyholes," I said.

Mrs. Summers straightened her already straight back another half-inch. "Vera!"

"Yes, ma'am?" The maid came into the room, looking at her inquiringly.

"I won't need you anymore today," Mrs. Summers said. "You can go now."

"Yes, ma'am," the maid said regretfully, and gave me a dirty look as she walked toward the door.

Mrs. Summers waited until the door had closed behind the maid, then sat down opposite me in an armchair, the white satin whispering richly as she crossed her legs.

"Now," she said briskly, "what do you have to tell me that's so confidential we can't risk the maid hearing it, Lieutenant? That you've arrested Rickie Willis, I hope?"

I went into the routine that was getting monotonous again, wondering if I should use a phony French accent to go along with the postcards. She took the envelope out of my hand, extracted the pictures, and looked at them with an icily remote expression on her face. Ten seconds later she handed them back to me.

"Well?" she asked calmly.

I told her how I'd come by the pictures, how I figured Marvin had intended to use them for blackmail.

"I don't see how, Lieutenant," she said. "Angela had no money at all to pay him—and I wouldn't have given him a penny for them."

"Not even to use as proof of statutory rape against Rickie Willis?" I prodded.

"There was plenty of other evidence," she snapped. "As I told you before in that grubby little office of yours. You have a short memory, Lieutenant!"

"One of my minor faults," I assured her. "I'm with you—he couldn't have blackmailed either Angela or you with them."

"So why did he bother?" she asked in a bored voice.

"Hillary might have paid big money for the negatives," I suggested.

"Hillary?" She raised her eyebrows fractionally. "What on earth for?"

"Angela told me the whole story an hour back," I said. "How he seduced her when she was sixteen years old—how you found out about it. Marvin lost his detective's license six months back because he was pandering for a call-girl service, suspected of blackmail, too. Chances are he was Hillary's panderer, too."

"Do you think all this intimate knowledge of yours makes you one of the family now, Lieutenant?" she asked in a dry, hard voice.

I tried to give an elegant shudder. "I wouldn't wish that on Rickie Willis, even!" I told her truthfully.

She made a hissing sound deep in her throat as she came out of the chair with her hand raised ready. I jumped to my feet and caught hold of her wrist, twisting it down, around behind her back so she was forced against me, hard enough for me to feel the soft curve of her breasts against my chest.

"You slap me, honey," I grinned at her bleakly, "and I'll slap you right back, quarter-billion dollars and all."

"Let go of me!" she panted, and tried to wrestle her arm free.

I never kissed that much money in my whole life before and I wasn't going to miss the opportunity now. I gave her wrist a gentle tug which forced her even harder against me, so I felt her fast heartbeat hammering against my chest. She reacted violently when our lips touched, jerking her head to one side. I grabbed the back of her neck with my free hand, making a clamp of my fingers so she couldn't move her head any more than an inch either way.

She froze then, letting me kiss her with a rising violence, standing immobile like a statue until I finally quit in despair, letting go of her wrist.

She looked at me stonily while she gently massaged her wrist. "I suppose I can't really blame you for thinking I'm no different from the rest of the family," she said in a strained voice.

"You're a very attractive woman, Mrs. Summers," I said sincerely. "Even if your emotional reactions are all deep-frozen."

I saw the sudden warmth come into her eyes and didn't believe it for a few seconds.

"Call me Lyn," she said suddenly. "It's ridiculous having a man who's just kissed you still saying 'Mrs. Summers.' You must have a Christian name—I refuse to say 'Lieutenant' anymore. What is it?—something horribly smalltown I imagine, like Elmer?"

"Al," I said wonderingly. "I guess it's no improvement?"

"Not much," she snapped. "Do you want a drink?"

"Always."

"There's some cognac in the kitchen—make mine over the rocks," she said briskly.

Mine not to reason why. I went out to the kitchen, found the cognac, and made the drinks. When I got back to the living room she was sitting on the couch waiting for me.

She took the glass from my hand and looked at me obliquely for a moment. "What do we drink to, Al? Your masculine virility, I suppose?"

"Coupled with your feminine curves," I said. "Or maybe I should put that some other way?"

"It'll do," she said, and sipped the cognac sparingly. "I imagine Angela was with Hilary last night when she was supposed to be with me?"

"That's right," I agreed. "Tell me something—why do you hate her so much? You must have worked at it for a hell of a long time."

She rocked her glass gently, watching the ice cubes knock against the rim. "I was eighteen when I married Geoffrey," she said in a low voice. "By the time I was twenty, Angela had been born, and I was too old for him. He just wasn't interested in girls over nineteen, so from then until his death, I had to watch him getting older and his playmates getting younger each year. Oh, everyone thought our marriage was successful enough and there was one good reason for not divorcing him—Angela. I didn't want her name sullied by the exposure of her father's philanderings with high school and college girls!"

"If you hated him, it figures," I said. "But why hate Angela?"

"Because she's her father all over again," she said tautly. "I didn't want to believe it at first, I closed my eyes to it, pretended I was imagining the things that happened from the time she reached fourteen, on. When the principals of all those exclusive private schools tried to tell me—so discreetly—what was the trouble, I refused to believe them. Then came the episode with Hillary and I had to believe it!"

"Maybe that was more his fault than hers," I said tentatively.

Lyn shook her head determinedly. "I should have guessed that Hillary was cast in the same rotten mold as his brother—but I saw them, Al! If anyone had been seduced, it wasn't Angela. After that I sent her to school in Switzerland and she lasted there a year before they threw her out. When she came home I threatened and pleaded with her not to see Hillary—so inside six weeks she'd run away with that dreadful Rickie!"

She turned her head toward me and I saw the iceberg had finally melted, as the tears glittered in her eyes.

"I don't *hate* her!" she whispered hopelessly. "She's my child, how could I ever hate her? But when she ran away, I thought I had only one hope left—to frighten her so much, she'd reform. That's why I talked statutory rape and the rest of it. I would never have gone through with it, Al, you have to believe that!"

"The night Marvin was murdered," I said. "The three of you—Ilona Brent, Hillary, and yourself had dinner in here?"

"Yes," she nodded.

"Hillary left first, around nine-fifteen?"

"It would have been around that time, anyway," she said.

"And you didn't see him again until next morning? He went back to his own suite, to go to bed?"

"Yes, but I saw him again, about twenty minutes later. I needed something to make me sleep and I'd run out of tranquilizers, so I went and asked him for some."

"He was there all right?" I asked gloomily.

"Of course. He gave me some pills and I came back here."

"That was all that happened?"

"I don't remember anything else."

"Was he in his pajamas?"

"No, he was still dressed. I wasn't in there more than five minutes and most of that time I was waiting until he'd finished with his phone call."

"What phone call?" I yelped.

"It rang just after I got into his suite," she said casually. "He spent about three minutes talking to whoever it was, while I waited."

"He didn't say who it was?"

"No, I think he was annoyed I was there—he was very guarded about what he said, just grunted most of the time."

"Can you remember any part of the conversation, other than the grunts?" I asked her hopefully. "Anything at all—it doesn't matter how disjointed?"

"Well—" she thought about it for a moment. "The only coherent thing I remember him saying was, 'Eleven o'clock—I'll be there,' or something like that."

"Nothing else?"

"I'm sorry," she smiled faintly. "Nothing else, Al. Does it help at all?"

"Could have been Marvin calling, and Hillary made a date to see him," I said. "But you couldn't offer it as evidence in a courtroom."

"You really think it was Hillary who killed him, and not that dreadful Willis boy?"

"Hillary had plenty of motive," I said. "Willis hasn't."

She finished her drink and offered me the empty glass. "What's the time, Al?" she asked indifferently.

"Five of six." I took the glass out of her hand.

"Don't they blow a siren or something when it's time for you to finish work?"

"Didn't you hear it?" I said. "The whistle just blew."

"I'm glad you heard it, anyway," she murmured. "I was beginning to wonder."

"I'll go make fresh drinks," I said brightly. "Even if I am disenchanted with the glasses."

"What's wrong with them?"

"I expected solid gold goblets, no less!"

"They might be all right for the Miami crowd, darling," she said with a grin. "But in my set they'd be considered ostentatious."

I went into the kitchen again and made the fresh drinks, then took them back with me to the living room. The night looked like it had fallen with a sudden thump—the room was nearly dark. When I'd left a minute before, the sun had been shining through the windows. It was no trick really to use my deductive powers and realize the room was near-dark because the shades had been pulled down and the drapes drawn across the windows.

Lyn Summers had vanished from the couch and while my eyes were still getting used to the near-dark, I couldn't see where the hell she'd gone. I parked the drinks carefully on a side table and went to sit on the couch again, then didn't. It wouldn't have felt right to crush all that beautiful satin and hand-embroidered gold thread. The adrenalin started to pump through my veins as I stood there looking at Lyn's negligee, getting a sharp mental image of how she must look without it.

There was a soft click, and a table lamp on the other side of the room glowed suddenly with a warm, diffused light. Lyn stood beside it, looking at me with an almost anxious expression on her face.

"You did say you heard the whistle blow, Al?" she asked nervously.

"Like a clarion call!" I said.

She came toward me slowly, the lamplight making intricate, everchanging patterns on her moving flanks, displaying her durable body in loving detail; the small, pink-tipped breasts that would never sag, the soft swell of her hips merging into the rounded firmness of her thighs. I took her into my arms when she got close and felt her body tremble slightly as it pressed against mine.

"You're scared?" I said softly.

"I'm thirty-eight years old," she said in a small, bewildered voice, "and right now I'm more nervous than I was twenty years ago, on my wedding night!"

"Hey!" I nibbled her ear lobe gently. "What's with this mixing sex and sentiment—a new kick?"

Her body relaxed suddenly as she laughed in a throaty gurgling sound. "I guess sentiment's considered ostentatious in the cops and robbers set," she said.

I ran my hands down the smooth back, following the indented curve of her waist, over the lithe, eager firmness of her flanks, and she stopped laughing in one sharp intake of breath.

It was a little after eight when I walked across the hotel lobby up to the desk, with the keen eyes of Charlie, the desk clerk, watching me the whole time.

"You been here so long, we should charge you rent!" he said. "Been on a high society kick, Lieutenant?"

I shook my head. "It's the drains again, Charlie. I've checked all over the hotel—but the real bad smell is coming from behind this desk. How do you figure that?"

Charlie's eyes gleamed as he looked me up and down carefully, then shuddered.

"I don't want to get personal, Lieutenant—but that suit! One of the County Sheriff's cast-offs, maybe?"

"Well, sure it is," I said defensively. "But I had it taken in a couple of feet around the waist already."

"I'm glad to hear it did belong to the Sheriff one time," he said happily. "When I first saw it, I figured you were on relief!"

He turned away to welcome a new guest—a tycoon-executive type with a bristling white mustache and bloodshot eyes.

"Good evening, sir," Charlie said deferentially. "Welcome to the Starlight Hotel!"

"Just one more thing!" I said loudly. "You tell the manager from me if he doesn't get that ceiling fixed tomorrow, I'm checking out. Took me a half-hour with a scrubbing brush to get that stuff off my face this morning."

The tycoon-executive looked at me curiously. "Plaster?" he asked gruffly.

"Plaster, I wouldn't mind," I said bitterly. "Blood! The guy on the next floor up blew his brains out last night and that damned ceiling was still leaking at nine this morning."

"Suicide?" His eyes bulged alarmingly, and the bristle went out of his mustache in one *poof.*

"I guess you couldn't blame the poor guy," I said "Had a busted leg and couldn't move out of his room. After two weeks eating nothing else but the hotel food, I figure blowing your brains out would be a ball!"

I turned and walked away from the desk quickly, but not quick enough to avoid hearing Charlie's soothing voice.

"He tries to be funny, sir," he said, pitching his voice loud enough to make sure I couldn't dodge it. "Used to be a professional comedian once, but he hasn't worked since they stopped making silent movies. I expect you noted the professional touches—the coat four sizes too big and the baggy pants? We try and help out where we can—he's just finished a job cleaning out the trashcans. I guess that's why he's so excited."

I revolved through the revolving door out onto the sidewalk, figuring I must be losing my grip—Charlie was always getting the last fifty words lately. The Healey was parked way down the street, and I started to walk toward it slowly, lighting a cigarette as I went. There was another interesting problem—did I smoke virile cigarettes because I was virile—or did smoking virile cigarettes make me virile? Either way I was just lucky, I guessed.

The sound hit my eardrums with almost physical force—a thin wailing scream of absolute terror. I came to a sudden stop wondering for a split second where the hell it had come from. Then the snooty-looking redhead in a white mink jacket walking in front of me let out a wild yell and pointed upward.

I jerked my head back and saw what looked like a great white bird, with flailing wings, hurtling down out of the sky toward me. It increased in size with fantastic rapidity, then hit the sidewalk six feet from the redhead, with a horrible splitting noise, like someone had dropped an overripe orange.

I went past the redhead who was still screaming her lungs out, and saw the nude body of a man spread-eagled on its back across the sidewalk. An even wilder scream from the redhead made my head jerk around to see what was wrong. She stared at me blankly through glazed eyes, gesturing frantically at herself.

Then she took a second look at the dark, glistening wet stains splashed across the front of her jacket, befouling the white mink. Her knees gave way suddenly and she fainted on the sidewalk.

I got one quick look at the naked body pulped against the concrete before I went back to do something for the redhead. Just one quick look, but it was enough to see that the fear-distorted face, with its wide-open mouth and staring eyes, was recognizable.

It belonged to Hillary Summers.

10

The three of us stood grouped around the bedroom window, looking down onto the sidewalk where Summers' body had landed thirty minutes before.

"Eight floors," Lavers grunted. "It sure is a hell of a long way down. I never know how they get the nerve to jump—it's the worst way to do it!"

"Maybe he didn't jump," I said.

"You mean, Lieutenant," Sergeant Polnik said eagerly, "like—maybe he tripped?"

"Well," I rode herd on my baser instincts, "he was an athletic character, at that!"

"Most of the time, Wheeler," Lavers said heavily, "you appall me, but

I can understand you only too well!"

"Thank you, sir," I said enthusiastically. "Do you wish to split the fees with my analyst?"

"But this one time I don't figure you out at all!" he growled. "You spend all day working up a case against Hillary Summers—you do your damnedest to frighten all hell out of him with it—to scare him into making a mistake. This, by your own mouth, as you told it ten minutes back. Right?"

"Right," I agreed.

"So he goes and makes the mistake," Lavers roared. "You scared him even better than you knew. You scared him so much he figured he had three strikes against him already—so he jumped out the window. You've proved your case and it's finished—you've done a good, fast job on something that could've turned real nasty if we hadn't gotten a fast result. Fine! Even I'll admit it was a nice piece of work. So then what do you do? You start yakking about maybe he was pushed—that we've got another murder yet!"

"It's just a feeling I've got," I mumbled.

"An inspired cop!" he howled despairingly. "Did you bring your violin along—or are you using the Ouija board this time?"

"I didn't know this guy too well," I said. "But maybe I got an insight this afternoon when he was bleeding there for a while. You saw him, Sheriff. A guy who's a multimillionaire—a lean, sensitive character who had a big guilty secret to hide from everyone else. He was an oddball with young girls making his kicks—so in every other way he'd make himself look as normal as he could."

"Psychology yet!" Lavers snarled.

"It figures," I said patiently. "Summers wore nice, conservative and expensive, suits—the kind you'd expect a guy in his position to wear. I'll bet he never got drunk, picked up a ticket for speeding, shouted at waiters, complained about room service.... He was always trying to hide behind a mask of respectability, hoping people would take him at face value the whole time—because this was the only way he could keep his nasty little secret. He had, for sweet Sigmund Freud's sake!—a guilt complex. If Hillary Summers was going to suicide, he'd have done it in a quiet, gentlemanly way, like maybe cutting his wrists in a hot bath. But even if he got around to jumping out the window, he wouldn't have jumped naked—it would've been like admitting he chased teenage girls into bed!"

"Why don't you take your brain someplace and get it washed?" the Sheriff asked disgustedly. "By me, the case is closed—Summers murdered Marvin—and that's the way it'll be unless you can prove different."

"All right," I said, breathing heavily. "So why don't you take your blood pressure out of here and let me get started?"

Lavers glowered at me for a few seconds, then rammed a cigar into his face with brutal disregard for his front teeth.

"All right!"—he bit off the words along with the end of the cigar. "I'll give you twenty-four hours, Wheeler, to come up with some proof that he was murdered. But not a minute more."

"Thank you," I said coldly.

"Be my guest," he said sourly, then stamped out of the bedroom. A few seconds later I heard the front door of the suite slam behind him.

Polnik looked at me wistfully. "Some case, huh, Lieutenant? All those gorgeous society dames mixed up in it. I bet you had yourself a ball— I, uh, guess there just ain't room for a sergeant?"

"Polnik," I said sadly. "I haven't treated you right in this case, have I?"

"Cheez!" he said emotionally. "You don't have to worry about me, Lieutenant. Maybe I'll get lucky next time around—but I sure would've liked to get close to the brunette again. You know, Lieutenant, the one who wears those black stockings right up to her waist?"

"Angela Summers," I said. "And they're stretch-nylon tights."

"If they stretch real good maybe I can get a pair to fit my old lady?" Polnik said thoughtfully. "Like maybe she'd look different?"

"Vavoom!" I agreed enthusiastically.

"My throat gets me the same way sometimes," he said "You want a cough drop, Lieutenant?"

"I want you to catch up on what you've been missing, Sergeant," I said briskly. "Get into that diamond-studded satin lingeried world you've been missing out on!"

"Cheez!" Polnik nearly choked with emotion. "You figure maybe I'll get to rub shoulders with them mink and chihuahuas and all?"

"Sure," I said. "Just watch it you don't get bitten."

"What do I do?" he asked happily.

"Check on Angela Summers and Rickie Willis first," I said slowly, giving each word time to penetrate the rocklike skull. "I want to know where they were when Hillary went out the window. I was on the sidewalk when he came down and it was eight-ten exactly."

"Got it!" Polnik snapped.

"Then check on Ilona Brent and find out where she was," I told him. "I'll take care of Mrs. Summers myself."

"O.K., Lieutenant. Anything else?"

"That'll keep you busy, Sergeant," I assured him. "I'll check with you in the office tomorrow morning around nine."

"You, Lieutenant?" he stared at me with his mouth open. "Inside the office at nine in the morning?"

"I didn't say I'd be there," I said pointedly. "I expect you to be there, so I can check with you. Maybe I'll use one of the newer things like this kid inventor, Alexander Graham Bell, has just come up with."

"Some kind of code, huh?" Polnik looked worried. "I sure hope you can make it easy, Lieutenant—they tossed me out of the vice detail because the numbers racket got me kind of confused once the numbers came into doubles."

"I'll make it simple," I told him. "Hadn't you better get started? Champagne in a sterling silver slipper goes flat awful fast!"

"I'm gone already!" he said gleefully, and he was.

I took a last look around the bedroom before I left the suite. Hillary's clothes were in an untidy heap on a chair, and that didn't figure. He'd been a neat character and habit doesn't die any quicker than its owner. It was the third argument against suicide, along with him being naked, and the sound of his scream as he came down. I guessed a guy might change his mind too late, after he'd jumped, but the way I heard it, it sounded like he was screaming from the first moment he started to fall.

I went out of his suite, along to Lyn Summers' door, and tapped on it gently. The door opened maybe six inches, then she saw who it was and it opened wider.

"Come on in, Al," she said. "I was just getting dressed."

After I got inside the living room and closed the front door behind me, I looked at her and saw she wasn't kidding. She wore a cream-colored bra made of heavy silk lace, and a pair of white, fine silk-knit panties, which made me wonder how often Angela had raided her mother's wardrobe.

"Come and talk to me in the bedroom so I can finish dressing," she said briefly, and led the way.

I leaned against the bureau watching, as she sat on the bed and pulled on a pair of nylons.

"You were obviously right about Hillary," she said coolly.

"Were you in here when it happened?"

"Yes," she nodded. "I was lying on the bed—" her mouth quirked at the corners momentarily "—resting!"

"Did you hear anything?"

"Nothing," she said flatly. "I wish I had—I might have been able to stop him."

She stood up and dropped the heavy satin slip over her head, smoothing it down over her hips until it sat smoothly, the bosom a froth of fine lace. Her eyes met mine for a moment, and that ice-cold impersonal look came back into them.

"Please stop leering at me!" she said sharply. "There's nothing I detest more than that lecherous, old goat look!"

"Can I help it?" I said mildly. "That beautiful figure of yours, and all that satin and lace and silk jazz, doing a tease job at the same time."

"You might remember that tired old joke, Lieutenant," she snapped. "The punch line goes something like, 'Sleeping together is no valid reason for social introduction.' It sums up exactly the way I feel!"

"It's your privilege," I said. "Where are you going?"

"I don't know—anywhere," she said tautly. "I think I'll go mad if I stay cooped up in here any longer—after poor Hillary killing himself! I'm going out somewhere where I can find bright lights and soft music and lots and lots of people."

"So long as they're the right kind of people?"

"Where would I find them on the West Coast?" she said derisively. "Marineland?"

"You want an escort?"

"I'll put it into words of one syllable for you," she said in a murderously sweet voice. "Once in maybe every two years, when I'm suffering some deep emotional stress, I have a sudden, overwhelming need for a man—any man—the nearest man! Then I'm cured for the next twelve months at least. This afternoon, you were that man, Lieutenant. Is that clear?"

"Like glass," I agreed. "Just before I go sob my heart out in the nearest bar—tell me something I forgot to ask you before."

She opened the closet door and lifted out a short evening gown, pale blue chiffon. It looked a simple little number.

"This isn't the question," I said. "But I'm strictly a rubberneck—how much did you pay for that?"

"This?" She slid the gown off its hanger and stepped into it easily. "I spend an average of sixty thousand a year on clothes," she said calmly. "It's hard to remember the individual price tags, Lieutenant, unless it's something like a floor-length mink for the opera. That's special."

"You got me hooked," I admitted. "How special?"

"The last one cost me twenty-eight thousand," she said. "I wish you'd stop being such an inverted snob—it's faintly nauseating!"

"I'll stop," I said politely. "I should be grateful."

"How's that?" She raised the elegant eyebrows a premeditated millimeter.

"You might remember that tired old adage, Mrs. Summers," I said brightly. "'A bitch in time saves nine'?"

"Most amusing!" she said thinly. "You can zip me up at the back before I go."

She turned her back toward me and I closed the zipper obediently.

"That question—I'd nearly forgotten," I said. "Did you pay Marvin, or did Hillary handle it?"

"I gave the thousand-dollar retainer to Hillary in the first place, to give to Marvin," she said.

"Was that the only payment made?"

"When he called me in New York to say he'd found them at the motel, he asked if I'd wire him another two thousand."

She slid her feet into evening shoes, then sat in front of the mirror, making last-minute adjustments to her hair and makeup. Then she fastened a sapphire and diamond pendant around her neck, and clipped on matching earrings.

"You sent him the money?" I asked.

"Of course. I was very pleased with his work in finding them so quickly. I wired him the money immediately—he would have gotten it in a few hours."

She stood up, draping a rich mink stole around her shoulders, then picked up her purse and walked toward the door.

"You could be useful, Lieutenant," she said as she reached the door. "You can ride down with me and call a cab."

"Don't be a piker, Lyn!" I said reproachfully, "Buy one, and have it sent up!"

The door slammed behind her, shifting the hotel's foundations a couple of feet. I waited maybe a minute, then left the suite. She wasn't anywhere in sight by the time I reached the lobby so maybe she had bought that cab.

I took the Healey from the curb and drove downtown at a pedestrian speed—I knew it was exactly that speed because a guy out walking his dog stayed level with me for three blocks. Maybe a half-hour later I parked outside the Double Zero Club. I was halfway across the sidewalk when I remembered it was a key club and the one thing I didn't have was a key.

While I was standing there wondering if anyone would open the door if I knocked, a guy walked past me and stuck a key into the door, solving all my problems. When he stepped into the small foyer I was right behind him, closer than a brother.

The stunning long-legged blonde in the black sequined bra and tights materialized from nowhere again, and took the guy's hat, then ushered him through the drapes into the main room.

"Can I take your hat, sir?" She smiled warmly at me, now it was my turn.

"Gee, thanks," I said earnestly. "Can I check my badge and handcuffs, too?"

Her smile faded fast as a look of recognition showed in her disturbingly brilliant eyes.

"Oh," she said flatly. "It's you again—the cop!"

"Wheeler," I smiled encouragingly at her. "Lieutenant Al Wheeler."

"How nice for you!"

"What's your name?" I persisted.

"Jerrie Cushman."

"Mr. Willis in his office?"

"I think so," she said. "I'll find out for you."

"I'll do it, thanks all the same," I said, and gave her my hat. "Take good care of it, honey. They don't make hats like that one anymore."

She turned it over in her hands fastidiously. "Not since the Alamo," she agreed in a shaken voice.

"If you need any help finding another job, look me up," I told her. "I'm in the phone book."

"I already have a job, thank you!" she said coldly.

Then her head started to shake slowly, in time with mine.

"I don't?" she said sadly.

"I got a feeling the place will be under new management soon, Jerrie," I said. "But—that's show biz!"

"But you wouldn't call it exactly legit?" She nodded gloomily.

I walked past her, and as she held the drapes open for me, she rubbed the back of her hand against the side of my face gently, and I could almost hear the static electricity leap into sudden life.

"In the book, you said?" Her voice was a husky, intimate whisper. "I'll have to remember you, Al."

"I'll remember you, honey," I said truthfully, taking a last look at her sequined bra and tights. "You're the girl with the most poured into the least."

11

The main room didn't look any different, and the cigarette girl in the white bra and tights still gave me that virile feeling as I walked past. I didn't bother to knock on the door beside the timbered staircase; I just turned the knob and went right on in.

Ray Willis and the beefy guy with all the brains, Joe Diment, were inside the office having a drink. They both looked up as I walked in, and from the expressions on their faces I was welcome like the boll weevil in Annabelle Jackson's home town. They both had one thing in common—a split lower lip.

"Hello, Lieutenant," Diment said unhappily and tried to smile, then winced painfully as his lower lip refused to stretch.

"What's with you, Wheeler?" Ray Willis said nastily. "Couldn't you sell your story to the vice squad? Or did you chicken out on your double-cross after all?"

"I tell you this more in sorrow than in anger, Ray," I said in a melancholy voice. "I was in no hurry to get the joint closed down—not till I learned you'd let me down. You said you were telling the truth and I believed you. It hurts, Ray"—I put my hand over my heart—"right here. But now I got to do it."

"What are you talking about, Lieutenant?" Diment asked, with three chins quivering on the answer.

"Ask the boss. He knows," I said.

"Hey, boss—" Diment began, but Willis cut him off.

"Don't just stand there, you fat slob!" he snarled. "Get the hell out of here—this is no damned business of yours!"

"Sure, I'm going," Diment said unhappily. "How come things change so fast around here? Two minutes back we're having a social drink like we're buddies." By that time he'd reached the door, and he looked over his shoulder at Willis. "Now I'm a big fat slob again! It's getting like I don't even know who I am anymore!"

"Get out!" Ray bared his teeth. "Before I split your top lip so they both match up!"

Diment leaped out of the office, pulling the door shut behind him.

Ray Willis looked at me and made a supreme effort, pulling a mask of contrite apology across his face.

"I heard about the Summers guy tonight, Lieutenant," he said. "Believe me it makes a difference to know the case is sewn up—now I can talk freely."

"No cover charge, Ray?" I queried. "Is that good for business?"

He smiled weakly. "I admit I lied last night about going to Nevada and those two kids getting married. It was just a gag in the beginning, and then it seemed like a good idea to stick with it when we heard about the murder and about Angela's mother's ideas about statutory rape and all that. You know how it is, Lieutenant—once it got started, I didn't have any choice. I had to go along with it, for the kid!"

"Your kid brother, Rickie?" I checked.

"Who else?" He lowered his voice a fraction. "He's the only folks I've got."

"Who wouldn't quit after scoring two like you and Rickie?" I agreed.

"I admit it was a stupid idea," he went on, shaking his head ruefully.

"I guess I knew that certificate wouldn't fool anyone for long—hell, it was just one of a bunch of them I had made up once for a party—you know, to give the boys a morning-after shock—" He looked like he was going to wink at me, but I wasn't having any, so he got solemn again. "I just hoped it would make the cops pause a little before they nailed a murder rap on a couple of innocent kids who incidentally had a tie-up with Marvin. After all, a boy and girl in love and about to get married don't go around knocking off guys. But they were in a jam, and Rickie was scared stupid, and if you could've seen the way the kid had his arm around Angela, like to protect her, and all the time counting on me, his big brother, to get him out of the mess. Well, I tell you, Lieutenant, it kind of churned me up inside!"

"It churns me up inside too, Ray," I said sincerely. "I may vomit at any time now."

"I guess if I hadn't been way out on that emotional limb," he went on doggedly, "I would've told you right away last night that the certificate was a fake." He shrugged his shoulders resignedly. "But there it is, Lieutenant. The ball's in your court. You still want to close me up, it's your privilege."

"That's very generous of you to admit it, Ray," I told him.

He lit a cigarette, his fingers fumbling with the lighter for a couple of seconds, while his eyes looked every way but at me while he waited for my reaction.

I let him wait.

Finally he couldn't stand it any longer. "You see, Lieutenant, I knew Rickie and Angie hadn't killed anyone, but I had to do all I could to keep things slowed down a little till a smart cop picked the guy who really did it," he said. "And you did, Lieutenant!"

"It was nothing, Ray," I said modestly. "I just waited till Summers leaned out the window, then gave him a shove!"

He smiled uncertainly, "You sure got a strong sense of humor, Lieutenant!" Then he took a deep breath. "Well, what do you say? Do you close me up or are you giving me a break and just forget it?"

I picked up the phone on his desk and dialed Police Headquarters.

"Give me Lieutenant Johnson, vice detail," I said when a voice answered.

"What?" Ray came out of his chair slowly, a look of complete disbelief on his face.

I smiled at him while I waited for Johnson to come on the line. Ray's face underwent a startling number of different expressions in a very short time, like he'd just graduated from the Actors Studio and was trying for an Oscar his first time out as a pro.

"You can't do this to me!" he said thickly. "You dirty, stinking, lousy cop!"

"I can tell you and Rickie are real close," I said. "You even talk the same way."

"I'm not letting you get away with it, Wheeler!" he bellowed suddenly. "I said before I'd get you if it was the last thing I ever did and—"

"Ah, shut up!" I told him. "I get sick in the stomach every time I listen to you run off at the mouth, Willis. The last time I was here, you pulled a gun on me, and I haven't forgotten that. The next time you even raise your voice a halftone, I'm going to smear you around the walls!"

He stood with mouth wide open, gaping at me for a moment, then he pushed past the desk, heading toward the door in a blind, stumbling trot. Maybe he'd left his guts outside and had gone to get them.

"Johnson," a crisp voice said in my ear.

"I thought you were dead," I said conversationally. "But you were just giving a rookie policewoman her last lesson in unarmed combat, huh?"

"Al Wheeler," he said, as a statement of fact. "What's wrong, you mislaid a blonde someplace?"

"If you find her, you can keep her, Bill," I said generously. "I've got a nice little setup here, all ready for your guiding hand."

"O.K.—give!"

"Just one string attached."

"I never got a straight deal out of you yet," he said in a resigned voice.

"The owner is a guy named Ray Willis—book him by all means but make sure he gets bail. I want him loose to commit even greater crimes."

"Whatever you say," Johnson agreed. "Now give me some detail, huh?"

I gave him the name and address of the club, the kind of place it really was.

"Private key club?" he said. "How long you had a key, Al?"

"Long enough," I said smugly. "One of the members is called Denby—known as Old Man Denby—he got a black eye from one of the girls a couple of nights back—so if you find him he should make a good witness."

"I'll find him," Johnson said confidently. "Inside the next hour that club's coming up with a real double zero."

"I'll tune in for the next installment," I assured him.

"See you around, Bill."

"Yeah," he said. "And thanks."

On my way out I stopped to collect my hat from Jerrie Cushman.

"Leaving so soon, Lieutenant?" she said, pouting prettily.

"It's a new trend," I said. "You have a coat? Put it on and go home."

"I'll get fired if I leave this early!" she said.

"You'll get fired anyway, honey," I said tiredly. "It's like that new trend I was telling you about. Everybody gets to be fired, but they get to hear about it downtown and then they got to get their fare home from a bail-bondsman."

"I read you loud and clear, Lieutenant!" she said quickly. "I get my coat and I'm gone like I was never here."

"It makes me sad—all those lovely sequins going to waste," I said. "But that's show-biz, huh, kid?"

"Right now I see it's no-biz," she said. "Thanks for the tip-off, Lieutenant. If I have trouble getting another job, I'll call you."

"Who cares about jobs?" I said. "Just call me. I have a hi-fi machine in my apartment with five speakers. I can make at least five different drinks without a recipe book. I am a most unusual and interesting character. I can show you life like you never lived it before."

"What else you got in your apartment?" she asked, poker-faced. "A trapeze?"

I drove straight home from the Double Zero, and got into the apartment around ten-thirty. The trouble with being married is that most times you want to be alone you got company waiting for you at home—and the trouble with being a bachelor is most times you want company you get to be alone. I stepped into the apartment and got the best of both worlds. Ilona Brent was sitting in an armchair, waiting for me.

She wore one of those businesslike suits again, with a white, heavy silk blouse underneath. The pixie face looked real cool—maybe cold even.

"How did you get in here?" I asked her.

"I told the janitor if I couldn't get some of my back alimony from you tonight, I'd be thrown out of my apartment," she said calmly. "So he let me in to wait for you."

"I bet that story built my credit rating," I said bleakly.

"He was very nice," Ilona said smiling sweetly. "He said what else could you expect from a lousy, flatfooted cop, and the next time your hi-fi outfit woke him up in the middle of the night, he'd just cut off the power to your apartment until the next morning."

"There's no gratitude," I said morosely. "Nobody has loyalties any more. Only last Christmas I gave him a quarter and this is what I get in return!"

"From the way he was talking, you may get fifty cents' worth yet!"

"Well," I brightened up fast. "This is wonderful—just the girl I wanted to see—I'll go make us a drink and we can talk—or something."

"I don't want a drink," she snapped. "Just the girl you wanted to see, huh? You spent about seven hours in the hotel today but you didn't get around to knocking on my door. Most of the time you were only a wall away, too!"

"Honey," I said in a long-suffering voice, "you know how it is—I'm a cop. Work all the hours around the clock—go where we have to with no choice!"

"You mean it was Lyn's decision you go to bed with her?" she almost snarled.

"With that kind of hearing you must be able to hear the termites as they chew their way through the building," I said in an awed voice.

"Are you implying I sat with my ear to the wall?" she gasped in fury.

"I just dropped in for a drink," I said feebly. "What I can't figure out yet is, how come we're having a fight like we've been married for years when you only came in to see if you could gouge some of the back alimony out of me—and we didn't even get married yet?"

For a long second she fought to keep a straight face, then she dissolved into a helpless wail of laughter. I sneaked out into the kitchen and made a couple of drinks. She'd quieted down to a convulsive giggle that erupted on a five-second frequency by the time I got back.

She took the glass out of my hand, nodding her thanks.

"Lyn told me about it—a confession of triumph," she said when she'd gotten her voice back. "I had to listen and smile, while all the time I wanted to tear out her liver—and it was all your fault!"

"Mine?"

"You should have had some will power and said no. Once she realized you meant it, she wouldn't have bothered you anymore."

"I bet you tell that to all the girls," I said gloomily. "But the song of love was kicked off her hit parade tonight. I got it all in words of one syllable to make sure I'd dig the message. That dame is sure different. She doesn't get a seven-year itch like ordinary people—she gets a two-year blight! Hits like lightning, quicker than taxes, and when it does she grabs a man—any man—the nearest man. This year it was Wheeler!"

"The funny thing is, I'm inclined to believe her," Ilona said, sipping her drink idly. "That makes me feel better—not much—just a little."

"I'm happy for you, honey," I said. "Did my faithful sergeant get around to see you before you left the hotel?"

"I knew there was something else I was mad about!" Ilona yelped. "That man is out of his mind—a schizophrenic! I was wearing a negligee when I opened the door, and I guess that was my first mistake. He just stood there—looking. He'd be there now if I hadn't lifted his chin so he *had* to look at my face. Then, when I sat down to answer his questions, he suddenly dived off his chair, skidded across the carpet, and grabbed hold of my foot!"

"He was kicked by a chorus girl when he was very young," I explained. "You dig?"

"It wasn't my foot he wanted!" she said indignantly. "It was my shoe—he wrenched it off, then kept on walking around the room asking me where was the champagne the whole time!"

"Down at the Sheriff's office we call him 'unorthodox,'" I said smugly. "Throws a suspect off-balance all the time."

Ilona's face sobered down suddenly. "How about Hillary?" she asked softly.

"He saw he didn't have a chance so he walked out the window," I said. "Next case, please."

"You don't believe that!" she said tensely.

"The County Sheriff does," I said. "With great reluctance he gave me twenty-four hours to prove him wrong."

"Hillary wasn't exactly my ideal pinup—"

"Not since you turned seventeen, anyway?"

This got only a puzzled look out of her, so I had to tell her about Hillary's passion for teenagers. "You never knew it?" I said.

"I never would have even guessed it." She sighed. "Well, he was still a very nice man in many ways."

"How many ways?" I murmured thoughtfully. "I wonder if any of them kept count."

Ilona glared at me. "If you're going to be frivolous all the time I might just as well shut up and not waste my time talking."

"It's only a difference of opinion, honey," I said placatingly. "I don't figure Hillary Summers could have qualified as a nice guy any way you looked at him. He was a weakling with a rare and nasty weakness—not that it entitled him to be pushed out an eighth-story window as the fall guy for the real killer."

"You really don't believe he did it, either!" she said happily. "So what are we arguing about?"

"Tell me something, legal eagle?" I said seriously. "Angela doesn't get any money in her own right until she's twenty-one. Could she make an agreement to give part of her inheritance to someone else when she comes of age?"

"Of course she could," Ilona said, "only she couldn't do it quite so directly as that. It's done all the time—people borrow against money they know is coming to them in the future. All she'd have to do would be make a proper contract with the party concerned, stating that she'd pay the amount within a reasonable time after she reached the age of twenty-one—say six months."

"Would a contract like that have to be notarized?"

"If it was a large sum. You think Angela's borrowed against her inheritance already?"

"No," I said. "I think she could've been blackmailed into signing away a hefty chunk of it. I'd like to know."

"Where would the contract have been signed? Do you have any idea?"

"Right here in Pine City, two days back," I said.

"I'll go to work on it first thing in the morning, if you like," she said enthusiastically. "It shouldn't be too hard to find the notary public who prepared the contract and witnessed the signatures."

"That would be wonderful," I told her. "Now let's relax and play legal fun-games or something. You be a cast-iron contract and I'll be a get-out clause trying to sneak into the contract—torts and caveats can be played wild and—Hey! Where are you going?"

"Back to the hotel, lover-man!" she said crisply. "The two-year-blight may be gone, but the memory lingers a little too close right now. Good night, Al." She opened the front door and stepped out into the night.

"I'll give you three caveats to my one tort?" I yelled hopefully, but the door was already closing behind her.

I guessed the guy who first said you can't win all the time was right—the slob!

12

Polnik sat beside me in the Healey, nudging me with his elbow occasionally to make sure I was real. He hadn't recovered from seeing me in the office at nine in the morning yet—maybe he never would. I wondered idly if it would make any difference.

"Where we going, Lieutenant?" he finally managed to ask.

"The motel," I said.

"That crummy joint?" he said in a bewildered voice. "When we could've gone to the Starlight Hotel? —and this early, maybe we'd have caught all the dames in their shirties."

"Shorties!" I gritted my teeth. "It sounds bad enough when you pronounce it right—it's one of those diminutives the world will never forgive Madison Avenue for."

"Is that a fact, Lieutenant?" Polnik said blankly. "I had the Russians figured as the bad guys—with all them spitniks and whoniks and whatever."

"You may well be right," I said hastily.

I parked the car in front of cabin number seven, and climbed out.

Polnik eased his bulk out inch by groaning inch, and when he'd finally made it, lumbered across to where I stood in front of the cabin.

"You figuring on buying it, or something, Lieutenant?"

"I was mourning the loss of a photographic genius, Marvin by name," I said. "How many windows does this cabin have, Polnik?"

"Just the one—you're looking through it right now," he added carefully.

"That's one hundred per cent correct. Take a look through the window and tell what you see, Watson."

"Watson?" Polnik tugged at his ear lobe nervously. "I'm Polnik, Lieutenant—you remember me?"

"I was thinking of that sergeant who used to work the narcotics detail one time," I apologized. "Look through the window!"

Polnik did as he was told, his forehead corrugated anxiously. He was a guy who never doubted that a job should be done right—only that he was capable of doing it at all.

"So what do you see?" I asked.

"The inside of the cabin, Lieutenant?"

"Fine—what else?"

"The bed, the bureau—that's about all there is in this crummy passion pit!"

"Where's the bed?" I encouraged him.

"Against the far wall, facing me like."

"Just suppose I was in the cabin right now—lying on the bed. What would I be doing?"

"Looking right at me!" he said triumphantly.

I lit a cigarette and let the smoke combat the strange, early morning air that was a newcomer to my lungs.

"So that's why we mourn the late Albie Marvin," I said. "He was a photographic genius. He got eight pictures of the two of them in the most intimate situations without being noticed—when all either one of them had to do was lift their head a fraction to see him, and his camera, peeking at them through the window."

"You sure he used this window?" Polnik asked.

"It's the only one in the cabin."

"Yeah." He thought about it for a moment. "Maybe he waited until it was dark so they couldn't see him?"

"And used a flash gun?"

I heard the heavy footsteps crunching behind me a turned around to greet Mr. Jones.

"You must like this place, Lieutenant?" he said sourly. "You keep on coming back!" He spat contemptuously, adding a fresh stain to the discolored concrete, six inches away from my right shoe.

"Miscalculation," he grunted insolently. "Sorry!"

"You know what I like about beating up an old man, Sergeant?" I said conversationally. "There's no chance of him hitting back."

"They break easy with them brittle bones," Polnik brooded. "But I guess that's because they're old, huh?"

"If you got any business here, state it, Lieutenant!" Jones said harshly. "Or else get off my property!"

"Number seven," I pointed at the cabin in front of us. "The one the young couple stayed in, right?"

"You know it!"

"Number nine." I pointed up the line. "That was Marvin's—right?"

"Some kind of game?" he asked stiffly.

"Right in the middle—number eight," I said. "Open it up for us, Mr. Jones, will you?"

"What for?"

"Because I asked you real polite!"

"You got no right—where's your warrant?" he blustered.

"O.K.," I sighed gently. "Sergeant, there's a health department ordinance that makes spitting an offense within a ten-yard radius of any building that is leased or rented to the general public. Put a pair of bracelets on Mr. Jones and sit him in the car—we'll take him back with us when we go, and book him when we get back into town. Meanwhile, you go and get the keys."

"Yes, sir, Lieutenant!" Polnik beamed.

"All right!" Jones grunted. "I'll get the keys."

I waited while Jones walked stiffly across to his office, with Polnik breathing heavily down his neck. They were back inside two minutes and Jones offered me the key.

"I'd prefer you to open up the cabin," I told him.

He grunted, then turned the key in the lock and pushed the door open. "After you," I said. Inside there was a bed with a bare mattress on top, a bureau to match the ones in the other cabins, and that was about all.

I eased Jones into the bathroom and followed him in. It looked like a beatnik dream of home—there was junk everywhere. Developing tanks, trays of hypo-fixing solution, trays that had dried with a hard brown acid crust. There was a built-in wooden bench along one wall which supported an enlarger. Beside it, stood an expensive-looking 35mm camera with an f/1.8 lens.

"Hobby, Mr. Jones?" I asked politely.

"Any law against it?" He spat into the acid-stained washbowl. "I told you I had a camera!"

"So you did," I agreed.

Back in the other room I took a close look at the dividing wall between the two cabins. You didn't see it till you got real close—the square piece of wood that slid back easily in a greased groove, exposing a circular hole, the exact circumference of the camera lens, I guessed. Whoever used the camera would know the exact distance between the lens and the center of the bed, so the focusing would be automatic. The square of wood could be slid back a fraction of an inch at a time, so the cameraman could peep in on the occupants of the next cabin, until he was sure they were too engrossed to notice the small hole in the wall. Then the camera lens would replace the human eye at the peephole, ready to maybe turn a passing fancy into a permanent record.

"Which do you like best, Mr. Jones?" I asked him. "The peeping, or taking the pictures?"

"Call the Sheriff and ask him to come right out," I told Polnik. "I want him to see this."

The motel proprietor leaned against the wall, his face suddenly ten years older—I wouldn't have believed he could do it and still stay alive.

Lavers came bustling into the cabin a half-hour later, and I showed him the setup with the hole in the wall and the rest of it.

"How did you figure it out?" he asked suspiciously.

"Like I said, Sheriff, it was obviously impossible for Marvin to have taken those pictures through the window—the other possibility that Rickie and Angela posed for the shots didn't seem likely. So it had to be this kind of rigged deal—and that meant Jones had to be in it.

"There were a couple of other pointers—the pictures turned up, but we never found any camera belonging to Marvin. When I checked his billfold there was a hundred bucks in it, but Mrs. Summers had wired him two thousand the morning of the day he was murdered. The murderer could have lifted it out of the billfold—but in that case why leave the hundred? It sounded more like he needed the money for a payoff. Who else could he be paying off in this place but the owner?"

Lavers wrinkled his nose disgustedly. "I don't like this case one little bit. You start figuring you're dealing with a bunch of ordinary people—except one of them's a murderer. Then you get closer to them and you touch nothing but dirt! A piano player who runs a bordello—a millionaire who buys the favors of high school girls—a woman who wants nothing more than to prove her daughter was raped in the legal sense of the word—and now we got an old man who spends the last days of his life peeping on unsuspecting couples who believed if he didn't give them much else for their money, at least he gave them privacy!"

"Maybe it wasn't a nice thing to do," Jones quavered. "But it ain't no crime!"

"Let's go back to your office, Mr. Jones," I said. "We haven't even started with you yet!"

He sat down heavily in his chair behind the desk as soon as we got inside his office, and stared at the desktop fixedly.

"You ain't got nothing on me!" he said sourly. "And I ain't saying nothing!"

"The photos inside that envelope in Marvin's bag," I said. "Who took them?"

"Marvin, of course!" He glowered at me. "Any fool could tell that—it was his writing on the envelope!"

"How did he take them?"

"I don't know."

"The only way possible was by using that setup of yours," I said. "He couldn't have gotten in there, never mind even known of it, unless you helped him. How much did he pay, Jones?"

"I don't know what you're talking about!"

The Sheriff leaned his hands on the desk, thrusting his neck forward until his face was only a few inches away from the old man's face.

"Listen good, Jones," he said in a low-pitched growl. "You cooperate and I can make it a little easier for you maybe—but if you don't cooperate, I promise you right now you'll die of old age in jail!"

The old man's head twitched suddenly as he stared blindly into Lavers' unblinking eyes.

"All right," he whispered. "What do you want to know?"

"Rickie Willis and Angela Summers arrived," I said. "Then Marvin followed them in by cab an hour later. Take it from there."

"Well, he checked in," Jones mumbled, "and then he asked me some questions—he knew the kids were here all right. He told me he was a private detective and he'd like my help—put fifty bucks on the desktop right in front of me.

"I told him sure I'd help, if I could. Then he tells me the girl is loaded and the kid's a bum who ran off with her. Now he's got them tabbed, he wanted some concrete kind of evidence that they'd been living together, and the only thing he could figure out was to get hold of a camera and bust in on them during the night."

"So you asked him what it would be worth to get a whole series of photos?" I said.

"You're a damned smart aleck!" he said spitefully. "Yeah—and he said a thousand." Jones laughed contemptuously. "What a sucker—overplaying his hand that way. I showed him the setup first and he was hot for it, so then I told him I wanted two thousand or no deal. He cussed me for a while, then he cooled off and said it was a deal. He gave me three hundred on account and said he'd call his client in New York in the morning and get her to wire him some money so he could pay me the rest."

"What was her name?"

"Summers—Mrs. Geoffrey Summers."

"Go on."

"We got the pictures early the next morning, around six, six-thirty." He chuckled evilly. "Hot morning sun always makes the young bucks restless—"

"You can skip the detail," I told him.

"I developed the negatives right after we'd finished, and Marvin was tickled to death when he saw them—he told me to make an extra set of prints. Then he went off to call New York for the dough.

"Later on I saw him talking hard to the boy, and right after that the kid took off in his automobile and didn't get back till around midnight, maybe even later, I'm not sure."

"What else?"

"Came evening and the extra set of prints was ready. I had them in an envelope for him, and he come in here to pick them up. He looked like the cat that's just swallowed the canary—said I did a great job."

"Did he say anything else?" Lavers barked.

"Sure," Jones nodded slowly. "Guess he felt so pleased at himself, he was so goddamned smart, that he just had to tell someone—and there was only me around to tell. Said he was going to clean up a fortune with those pictures—three ways at least."

"How did he figure that out?"

"The kid's mother hired him to find them in the first place—but she hired him through her brother-in-law who was sweet on the kid himself." Jones allowed himself the luxury of one, wheezing guffaw, but the look on Lavers' face shut him up again fast.

"So the kid's uncle tells him to put pressure on her to ditch the young bum—come back to New York and be nice to him again. 'So,' Marvin says, 'I showed the young bum the pictures this morning—threatened him I'd turn them over to the sheriff's office and tell them he was an ex-con at the same time. They'll have him on a rape rap, and maybe the FBI will hit him with a violation of the Mann Act.'

"I can see him now," Jones said reflectively. "Sitting just across the desk from me—right where you are now, Sheriff—laughing his fool head off. He figured he'd scared the hell out of the boy all ways—told him to take off right then and never come near the girl again or he'd spend the rest of his life in the pen.

"'So that got rid of the kid,' Marvin said, 'and the mother would be so pleased she'd pay big money.' And a few years from now, when the girl was all set to marry some society character, Marvin figured that would be the time to sell her mother a set of those prints at a very fancy price!"

"Big-mouth Marvin!" I said. "I wonder he lived so long?"

"He was only warming up!" the old man sneered, almost proudly. "I never met a guy with so many angles before—it was like an education."

"You get a close look inside the back of his head?" Lavers asked in a harsh voice. "That was an education, too."

Jones shrugged indifferently. "Next on his list was the girl—he was hot for her. He figured with the Willis kid gone for good, he was going to move in with her that night. He'd show her the pictures, tell her the boyfriend had gone forever, and Uncle wanted her back in New York where he could visit with her on a regular basis again. She had no choice—she goes back to her family the next morning—but for the last night at the motel, she'd better be real nice to Marvin or the cops will get the pictures along with the information that Willis is an ex-con."

"Murder in degrees, we got already, Sheriff," I said. "How about a bronze star, or something, for people who murder guys like Marvin?"

"Let's hear the rest and get it finished with, Jones!" Lavers said. "My flesh is starting to crawl."

"'We got to take care of good old Uncle next'—that's what he said," Jones went on in his slow, grating voice. "'Watch this!' Marvin told me, then he lifted the phone and called a hotel in Pine City and asked for Hillary Summers. He told Summers he had the pictures, then described them in detail, but along with the pictures, he'd gotten himself a problem.

"The girl's mother wants the photos to use as evidence against the Willis boy, have him indicted for statutory rape. And after the boy's convicted, the mother is sure as hell gonna send the girl off into solitary somewhere—some rest home or something where she'll be out of circulation for a good long time—and Uncle wouldn't like that maybe?"

"The way you tell it, you old goat, we'll be here next week!" Lavers exploded. "So Marvin told Summers he'd sell the pictures to the highest bidder—right?"

"If you know already," the old man said in a surly voice, "why bother asking me?"

"How much did Summers bid?" I asked quickly.

"A hundred grand!" Jones said reverently. "That's what Marvin told me."

"How was it to be paid?"

"Certified bank check—he told Summers they could work out the details later the same night."

"What did you say?" Lavers asked almost politely.

"He told Summers to be here in the motel at eleven," Jones grunted. "Why don't you listen?"

"Did they meet at eleven?" I asked him.

"I wouldn't know," he said listlessly. "I got me a bottle of good liquor and got settled in one of the unrented cabins around nine-thirty—that's the last I remember until sunup next morning."

"Then how did you know Rickie Willis didn't get back until midnight?" I said irritably.

"One of the guests made a complaint in the morning, about him revving his motor in the middle of the night," Jones said triumphantly.

"We've heard enough," Lavers said. "Get him out to my car, Polnik. Don't let any more of him than you can help touch the upholstery!"

"Sure, Sheriff," Polnik grunted. He heaved the old man onto his feet and guided him out of the office.

"The air's a little cleaner, anyway," Lavers said, after the door closed behind them.

"Mr. Jones," I grinned at him. "One of the Jones boys!"

"Well, Wheeler?" There was a condescending note in the Sheriff's voice. "I guess that does it up real good!"

"Because that old peeper told us Marvin arranged a meeting with Summers?" I sneered. "What proof you got that Hillary even showed up?"

13

Ilona Brent smiled a welcome at me as I walked into her hotel suite. I ran the smile through my little gray computers and got only a "platonic-plus" reading.

"It's lunchtime," I said. "So I figured you might buy me lunch."

She wore a white orlon sweater, over a pair of tight, gray cotton slacks, and somehow it gave her that healthy, outdoor-sexy look you read about in English novels, where the heroine's always called Pamela.

"Lunch is a good idea, Al," Ilona said. "Why don't we eat here? I'll have room service bring it up. What do you feel like right now?"

"Are we still talking about food?"

"But definitely!"

"A thick, rare, and bloody steak," I said. "With a French salad on the side."

"Is that all?"

"For me, it's a big deal," I assured her.

She called room service, then made us a drink, still radiating an air of "Miss Efficiency, 1960," which was irritating to a disorganization man like myself. Then she sprang her big story, and I could dig the efficiency bit.

"I found him, Al," she said with elaborate casualness.

"How long was he lost?" I asked absently.

"Don't be a moron! The notary public—I found him!"

"Oh—him!" I was suddenly a lot more interested.

"You were right," she said quickly. "Seventy-five thousand dollars to Ray Willis, for services rendered, to be paid not later than six months after she reaches twenty-one."

"You sure worked fast, Ilona!" I congratulated her.

"I'm a pretty damned smart attorney," she said complacently.

"Or you will be—when you get out from under the Summers family," I said.

Her face flushed violently. "That's a stinking thing to say!"

"Why? Because it's true?"

The food arrived, saving her the trouble of finding an answer. We ate—and when we were finished, I gave her a quick rundown on the motel's special facilities for peeping and candid camera work, then old man Jones' story of Marvin's conniving blackmail schemes.

"It's fantastic, Al!" Ilona said breathlessly. "You wouldn't believe one man could be so—evil!"

"There was plenty of it around he could draw on," I said soberly. "Do you still want to help?"

"Of course I do," she said determinedly. "I told you last night I knew Hillary never killed Marvin."

"You could end up wishing he had!" I warned her.

"I'll take my chances on that," she said defiantly.

"O.K.," I grinned bleakly, "so now we're in business."

She leaned her elbow on the table, her chin cupped in her hand, staring at me earnestly; and I wondered uneasily if she was about twenty years too young for the caper I had in mind.

"Shoot!" she said suddenly. "Lay out the plan of campaign, General!"

"Let's start with Hillary. If he didn't commit suicide, he must have been murdered because he knew who killed Marvin—and the killer was scared Hillary might crack under pressure and talk."

"I'm still with you," Ilona nodded gravely.

"Right now, the killer is feeling safe and secure—the Sheriff's office thinks Hillary's death was suicide and blame him for the murder. That makes it too late for questions, clues, and all that kind of jazz. The only way we can get him now is to put a bomb under his tail, and hope he'll jump before he has time to think."

"A brilliant thesis, General!" She gave me an exaggerated salute.

"Keep listening," I said drily. "You could change your mind fast. At the same time we plant the bomb, we've got to make it look like it can be deloused without much trouble or risk on his part. You dig?"

I was suddenly dazzled by the warm, shining glow in her eyes.

"I truly admire you, Al!" she said in a hushed voice. "It must take an awful lot of cold courage to set yourself up as a clay pigeon."

"Not me, honey." I shook my head sadly. "You!"

"*Me!*"

"Sorry," I apologized, "but the casting is perfect—nobody else can play the bit."

"My hero!" she said bitterly. "Here I am, thinking all kinds of noble thoughts about you, while all the time you're setting me up as a—" Her spine straightened with a sudden jerk. "Hey! They shoot clay pigeons!"

"You can gracefully decline," I said mildly. "Nobody's going to think badly of you—like they used to tell the paratroops the moment before they booted them out of the plane."

"Maybe I'll think about it," she said cautiously. "Tell me exactly what your sneaking, cowardly mind has cooked up."

"Your story goes something like this," I said. "Yesterday morning Hillary came to you, as the family's attorney, gave you a sealed envelope, and said to do nothing with it unless he suddenly died during the next seven days. If that happened, you were to open the envelope."

"It sounds grisly," Ilona shivered.

"You opened the envelope this morning. Inside was another sealed envelope and a list of instructions. First, you had to call the four people listed, and tell them in accordance with his wishes that the second envelope would be opened exactly twenty-four hours after his death and the contents read aloud to them at the Travelers' Rest Motel."

"Now I know you're crazy!" she said.

"Who's going to shoot at a clay pigeon sitting on the County Sheriff's desk? It has to be someplace where the killer figures he's got more than a sporting chance."

"I'm ahead of you, Al!" she said brightly. "I'm supposed to open the envelope at eight-ten tonight, but a couple of hours before, you'll have a truckload of Sheriff's men well-hidden all around the—"

"You blew the bit again," I said sorrowfully, "not a chance! The killer would smell it a mile away. There's going to be just you and the four others—and me. No one but you will know I'm there, I hope."

"You make it sound irresistible," Ilona said dully, "like typhoid!"

"At least one of them is going to ask why you didn't give the sealed envelope to the police right away," I warned her. "You say Hillary's instructions called for the strictest secrecy, and as his attorney, you'll see his wishes carried out."

Ilona nodded dismally. "When do we start?"

"Right now," I said. "Call them before they make other plans for the evening."

"Who are they?"

"Lyn and Angela Summers, Rickie and Ray Willis."

"And one of them is a murderer?" she asked nervously.

"I don't have any other suspects—outside you and me," I said reasonably.

"Where would I find Ray Willis?"

"I'm not sure—his club's out of operation now. Ask Rickie, he'll know."

"What do we do after that—until eight o'clock tonight?"

"Make the calls first," I suggested. "We can worry about that later. Remember, you must make it sound real good! If anyone even thinks it could be a gag, we'll have blown the bit. Then we can sit around here the rest of the afternoon with egg all over our faces."

"I'll make it good!" she said determinedly.

"That's my girl," I said. "Probably all of them will want to see the envelopes and instruction list, so you'll have to brush them off fast and hard—don't give them a chance to bounce back."

"I'll say I couldn't possibly give any one of them an unfair advantage over the other three?" Ilona suggested.

"Fine! Go to it."

She called Mrs. Geoffrey Summers first, and hung up on her three minutes later while Lyn was still asking questions. Angela was next, then Rickie, who told her she could contact his brother at the Central Hotel, in the heart of downtown Pine City. It was another fleabag along with the Grand, I remembered.

Ilona was an expert by the time Ray Willis answered the phone. She gave him the facts neatly leaving nothing out, then replaced the receiver before he'd even got around to framing the first question.

"That was great!" I told her. "You did fine."

"I'm glad it's over, anyway." She flopped onto the couch. "I'm positive they all took it seriously. What do we do now?"

"Why don't I make us a drink?"

"Fine," she said. "What then?"

"We'll just sit around and drink some more," I said. "If we're right, and one of those four people is the real murderer, he, or she, thinks you've got a sealed letter exposing him—so figure it out for yourself."

"I'm not too sure I want to," she said cautiously. "You spell it out for me?"

I made the drinks and walked them back toward the couch. "He knows at a little after eight tonight you'll be at the motel, ready to open the envelope. So he's got from now until then to make sure it doesn't get opened."

Ilona closed her eyes and shivered violently. "You mean he's going to come here looking for it! Stay close to me, Al!"

Then she gave a sudden shriek and opened her eyes wide.

"Is that close enough?" I asked innocently.

Around four-thirty, there was a sudden, loud knocking on the door which made Ilona leap convulsively.

"Take it easy," I whispered. "I'll be in the bedroom—play it cool, and if it looks like it's getting rough, I'll be in."

"Don't hesitate, Al!" she said fervently. "If somebody bats an eyelash even, I want you to come running."

I catfooted into the bedroom, nearly closing the door, leaving a thin crack through which I could see most of the living room. Ilona opened the door, and I heard Rickie Willis' gruff voice.

They came into my line of vision as Ilona brought him across to the couch, then sat down.

"Won't you sit down?" she said politely.

Rickie scratched the top of his crewcut and gave her a hostile stare. "I didn't come here to play no games, sister," he said thickly. "I want that envelope you got."

"Envelope?" Ilona repeated weakly.

"Don't play it dumb," he rasped. "You called Angie and me and told us all about it a couple hours back. I want it!"

"What for?"

"I got my reasons!"

Ilona shook her head dubiously. "I can't give it to you, Rickie. Hillary Summers made some specific instructions as to how it should be handled, and I have to do it that way because I'm his attorney. I'm sure you understand."

"Hillary Summers!" he snarled. "The nut! He was crazy—you must have known that! He could've put anything in that letter—any crazy thing at all!"

"Well"— Ilona's voice had a false note of brightness—"we'll all know at ten after eight tonight, won't we?"

"No!" He leaned down until his savage, brooding face was only a few inches away from hers. "Because you're going to give it to me now, and

I'm burning it!"

"Why?"

"I told you—don't tell me you've lost your marbles, too!" he said disgustedly. "That nut, Hillary, could've written anything at all. Like it wasn't him that knocked off the septic eye—like it was somebody else maybe."

"Why would he say you did it, if you didn't?" llona's voice shook slightly.

"Me?"

He straightened up again, a look of blank amazement on his face. "Man! Somebody send for the little men in the big white coats!" His head shook slowly. "You need help, lady! Why in hell would I knock off the septic eye? He didn't worry me."

"Then why do you want Hillary's letter if you're sure it doesn't accuse you of the murder?" Ilona asked.

Rickie dug a crumpled pack of cigarettes out of his leather jacket, stuck one into his mouth, and lit it, dragging the smoke down into his lungs impatiently.

"I don't wanna get tough with you, lady," he said thickly, "not unless I got to. So maybe give it to you slow—just one more time. I want that letter because Hillary was out of his mind—he was crazy for Angie all the time—and when Angie took off with me, he flipped! Now, you dig? So before he makes like an elevator out an eighth-floor window, he writes a letter and gives it to you, huh? What better way's he got to get his revenge against Angie? Say it was her killed the septic eye, not him! A dead man always bugs people—they'll believe it!"

"I see," Ilona said faintly.

"That's where you're wrong again, sister!" he snarled. "Not you, not anybody else either, gets to see that letter, because I'm putting a match to it right now!"

There was a second knock on the door, and Rickie moved his shoulders uneasily under the leather jacket.

"Go find out who that is," he said. "Tell 'em to go away!"

Ilona got up from the couch and went to the door. A moment later she backed away from it as Ray Willis followed her into the room, a gun in his hand.

Behind him came Angela, wearing the black, stretch-nylon pants with the vivid yellow sweater again. The bird's-nest hairdo was a little more groomed than usual, and her big, dark eyes held a look of excited anticipation.

Rickie's mouth dropped open as he saw the two of them. "What goes on?" he asked sullenly. "Who asked you to the party? I can handle this on my own!"

"I got to your room just after you left," Ray snapped. "She told me where you'd gone. Why didn't you stay out of it, you dumb ox?"

"Lay off, Ray!" Rickie scowled at his brother, his shoulders moving again under the jacket. "You're not so smart—letting that dumb lieutenant close you up!"

Angela sauntered past Ray toward Rickie, moving with a feline, animal grace that went a long way toward explaining, if not excusing, Hillary Summers. She put her elbow on Rickie's shoulder, leaning her body against him provocatively as she looked at Ilona.

"Did she give you the letter yet, honey?" she asked in a childish drawl.

Rickie's mouth turned down at the corners. "Not yet."

"See?" Ray sneered. "I told you, kid, you don't have the know-how to handle a thing like this right."

"Ah, why don't you go—"

"Don't get mad at Ray, lover-man," Angela giggled excitedly. "Let's get the letter from her."

"That's what I've been trying to do!" Rickie took a deep breath. "What a dame! Yack, yack, yack! I think I'm blowing my stack listening to her questions! I'm trying to keep it polite because I don't want to get rough and—"

"Tell us some other time," Ray said curtly. "Let's get what we came for and get out of here."

Angela held out her hand to Ilona. "The letter please, Counselor."

"I can't give it to you," Ilona said doggedly. "I've got to obey Hillary's instructions, and—"

"Did he instruct you, too?" Angela giggled again. "He had a lot of cute tricks, didn't he?"

"Shut up!" Rickie growled.

"I didn't know he went for older women." Angela's voice had a shrill sound to it. "Did you enjoy the preliminary routine, Miss Brent? I always figured it was monotonous, but Hillary used to get a big bang out of it. You know, first, he'd make you take—"

She stopped suddenly as Rickie's fist drove into her ribs with brutal precision. The pain sharpened her face into hard, drawn lines so she looked twenty years older.

"I said for you to shut up!" Rickie slurred the words thickly, meshing them together in an indistinct growl. "All the time you keep talking about that slob—all the time! Why do you keep on, huh? The bum is dead all right, isn't he? It was you lined him up, all hot and eager, in front of that window and then gave him a shove, wasn't it?"

He stopped suddenly, gaping at her, his eyes almost pleading.

"You stupid moron!" Ray said bitterly. "You know what you've done?"

"Yeah," Rickie shrugged petulantly. "It's her fault, the teasing bitch! She gets me so mad all the time I dunno what I'm saying."

"Now we've got to do something about her," Ray said sharply, nodding toward Ilona.

Angela took a deep, shuddering breath, still massaging her ribs with her left hand. "What, Ray?" The excited anticipation bubbled in her voice. "What are you going to do? Can I help, please, Ray, please?"

He shook his head wearily. "Sometimes I wonder how I ever got mixed up with you two weirdos—I must have been out of my mind!"

"Yeah—seventy-five grand's worth!" Rickie sneered.

Ray walked slowly toward Ilona, who shrank back as he got close. He moved his arm up even more slowly, until the barrel of his gun was touching her forehead.

"We don't have any more time to kid around, lady," he said in a deceptively mild voice. "The letter?"

She swallowed twice before she could speak, "It's—it's in the bedroom."

"Then we'll go get it," he said.

"It's all right," she said frantically. "I know where it is, I'll get it! There's no need for you to come too."

"Uh-uh," he said, shaking his head. "You might be thinking of doing something cute—like throwing it out the window, maybe?"

"Of course not!" Ilona quavered. "I just thought—"

"Bad habit!" Ray shook his head reprovingly. "Buy yourself a load of grief that way. Let's go get it now, huh?"

"It's in the second drawer of the bureau—under an evening purse!" she said desperately.

"Now you're being smart," Ray said with a grin. "Get it, Rickie!"

I moved back against the wall, so when Rickie opened the door it would cover me. His footsteps thumped heavily across the room, getting louder all the time, until the door swung open suddenly.

He moved straight across the room toward the bureau, kicking the door shut behind him with unnecessary force—maybe he imagined it was his brother's face.

I moved out from the wall with the thirty-eight in my hand, and a second later he saw my reflection in the bureau mirror. He stopped abruptly, standing very still, his eyes watching my reflection with the absolute concentration of a cornered animal.

"No noise, Rickie," I said softly. "Turn around."

He turned to face me, his arms dangling loosely at his sides. I checked with my free hand and found he wasn't carrying a gun.

"O.K.," I said. "Let's go and join the party. I'm going to be right behind you, Rickie-boy, so if you get any fancy ideas about brother Ray getting in a fast shot, just remember he's got to shoot through you!"

"I hear you—cop!" he said tightly.

He opened the door again and stepped out into the living room, with me right behind him.

"You get it?" Ray turned his head to look, and saw the two of us.

"Drop the gun, Ray!" I said sharply. "You got just two seconds!"

He opened his fingers and the gun dropped to the carpet.

"How did he get in there?" he snarled at Rickie.

"He was already there—he must've been there all the time," Rickie said.

"You mean you never even cased the apartment when you first got inside?" Ray almost screamed. "Why, you stupid, dumb—"

"Don't keep on calling me them names!" Rickie growled. "I get tired, all the time you calling me names!"

Ray closed his eyes in anguish for a couple of seconds, then opened them slowly. "What's the use?" he said limply. "You let him con us all the way down the line." He looked at me dully. "No letter, huh?"

"No letter, Ray," I agreed.

"Strictly a come-on?"

"Yeah."

Angela cleared her throat gently, then smiled at me. "Hi, Lieutenant!"

"You lined him up in front of the window then gave him a shove?" I repeated Rickie's words gently.

Her smile broadened. "It seemed like the best thing to do at the time. You see, Hillary had a date with Marvin that night, at the motel, but he was late. Marvin figured he wasn't going to show up, so he came to the cabin and showed me those pictures. I was all through, he told me, he'd scared Rickie so hard I'd never see him again. And in the morning he was giving me back to dear old Mom. She'd take me back to New York, where Hillary was going to make sure he kept me in line!"

Her smile started to get a fixed look about it. "Not much of a future for a girl, was it? But Marvin was only starting, I found that out quickly. He was going to spend the rest of the night with me, he said, and if I objected he'd give the pictures to the police and have Rickie arrested for rape. With his prison record, Rickie wouldn't stand a chance, he said, he'd go to jail for the rest of his life!"

"So you killed him?" I said.

She nodded, almost casually. "I couldn't bear him to touch me—a dirty little man with cruel, filthy eyes. I knew he was going to hurt me—he'd get his kicks that way. Then I remembered the old hammer I'd seen in the bottom drawer of the bureau. I told him I wanted to pick up a couple of things and then I'd go to his cabin with him—that would be better in case Rickie came back. So I got this real sexy nylon gown I have and carried the hammer with it, right into his cabin. I pretended I was getting excited about the idea of spending the night with Marvin, and the little monster believed it. I told him to turn around and not peek for a moment while I took off my clothes."

She giggled again, helplessly. "He looked so funny, standing there solemnly gazing at the wall, having fantasies about what he was going to do with me—and all the time the hammer was lifting higher ... higher ... higher ..."

The whites of her eyes showed briefly, then she collapsed in a limp heap onto the floor. I stepped toward her, moving in front of Ray Willis deliberately, being careful not to look at him.

Ilona was down on her hands and knees beside Angela, trying to do something for her. My spine did a tango as I heard the sudden, furtive moment behind me. I gave him one more second, then turned around.

Ray was coming up off his knees, with the gun he'd grabbed off the floor in his hand.

"I said I'd get you, Wheeler!" he snarled, as the gun barrel swung toward me in a short arc.

I pulled the trigger of the thirty-eight three times, watching the triumphant grin on his face dissolve suddenly as the slugs hammered through flesh and bone to lodge in his brain. He slid sideways to the floor and was dead by the time he reached it.

Rickie hadn't moved; there was a secretive look in his eyes as he stared down at his brother's body, almost a look of satisfaction.

Ilona was staring at me blankly, her eyes quick-frozen.

"How's Angela?" I asked curtly, hoping it would snap her out of it.

"Angela?" she repeated slowly. Then her eyes came alive again. "She's all right, I think, Al. She must have just passed out with the emotional pressure, or something."

I moved over to the phone, keeping a watchful eye on Rickie while I called the Sheriff's office.

When I'd finished, Ilona got to her feet and looked at me. "I don't know what it is, but she won't come round—her breathing seems normal."

"I told them to bring a doctor," I said. "I could use a drink—how about making us one?"

"Yes, sir!" she breathed heavily. "What about him?" She nodded toward Rickie.

"Why not?" I shrugged.

She started to make the drinks, then looked at me again. "Did you know it was Angela all the time?"

"I wasn't sure until Hillary went out that window," I said. "I guess you couldn't blame Angela too much for using sex to get what she wanted, not after the kind of introduction she'd had. You remember you told me she visited with you that night, then went off to see her mother, but didn't? When she came back, she was waving a wad of notes around— and her face was flushed, with a kind of triumphant look?"

"She went to see Hillary of course," Ilona nodded. "The money came from him and … oh, I see."

"Sure you do," I said. "Hillary was the kind of guy who would have been too embarrassed to kill himself unless he looked his best! So it figured that Thursday night when he went out the window was just a carbon copy of Wednesday night when she got the money from him—except with a different ending."

"Lieutenant," Rickie was mumbling, "I didn't have nothing to do with killing the septic eye—that's honest!"

"I'll believe it," I told him. "My guess is Hillary showed up late for his meeting with Marvin—just about the time Angela was leaving Marvin's cabin. Being Hillary, he wouldn't help her, but he didn't want her in jail either. So he did nothing, just kept his mouth shut."

I looked at Rickie again. "When you came back, she told you what had happened?"

"Yeah," he nodded. "She had the pictures and we burned 'em. We didn't know there was more of them—figured they were the only ones he had!"

"Early next morning you went to see big brother, Ray, to get him to help," I said. "He cooked up that stupid Nevada story and faked a marriage certificate for you—at a price. That made me wonder when I heard about it—it wasn't even a serious attempt to alibi you. Angela must have had one hell of a guilty conscience to pay that kind of money for the punk service Ray gave her!"

"'Get smart!' he said." Rickie looked at his brother's body again. "All the time he'd keep on at me I was a stupe, a moron, a dumb one!" A slow smile crept across his face. "Me—I'm the dumb one all right—I'm the one that's still alive!"

Angela moaned softly, then slowly sat up, staring at me with her enormous dark eyes a complete blank.

"You feeling better, Angela?" I asked her.

Her lips moved rapidly but no sound came from them.

"Angela!" Ilona said sharply. "Are you all right?"

Slowly the head turned in the direction of Ilona's voice, then she stared at her for maybe ten long seconds without saying anything, while Ilona cringed away from the blank, staring eyes.

"Hey, Angie!" Rickie said uneasily. "Say something, huh, baby? You giving me the creeps, just sitting there, doing nothing. Wassa matter, baby? You sick or something?"

Her lips writhed, then suddenly she spoke, her voice a harsh, discordant croak.

"Mom?" The blank eyes looked around the room slowly. "I want my mom!"

"All passengers for Flight Six-Thirteen, Los Angeles, Chicago, and New York, should proceed to Gate Six immediately!" The metallic voice boomed through the airport lounge.

"That's us," Ilona said in a small voice.

"I shall go now," Lyn Summers said in a precise voice. "Be careful you don't miss the plane, Ilona!"

"I'll be there," Ilona said easily.

Mrs. Geoffrey Summers adjusted the collar of her white chinchilla jacket a little closer around her neck, and moved toward the gate. Her ice-cold eyes looked at me, then through me, for the last time. Then she was gone.

"She could have spoken one word anyway," Ilona said. "The last thirty minutes she's been with us, you didn't even exist!"

"Why do you bother going back to New York with her?" I asked. "You don't owe her a thing."

"Hillary dead—her daughter a murderess," Ilona said softly. "She needs somebody to look after her now!"

"With the kind of money she has, she could buy the Waldorf-Astoria and turn it into a private residence," I said. "Then she'd have so many servants, she could—"

"There's no one now except me she can even talk to, Al," Ilona said. "Draw your own moral—the things that money—"

"And all that jazz!" I finished the tag. "O.K. I'll miss you."

"I'll miss you, Al." She smiled. "It was fun in a kind of unorthodox way!"

"Last call for Flight Six-Thirteen," the loudspeakers blared.

"I must go!" she said. "Did you hear any more about Angela?"

"A catatonic trance, the doc said. When the load gets too great, the mind refuses to carry it anymore, then—nothing."

"It's horrible!" she whispered. "What will they do to her?"

"Plead insanity, put her into a sanitarium," I said. "You never can tell about those things—maybe one day she'll be cured."

"I hope so!" She kissed my cheek suddenly. "I have my bruises in ever-loving memory!" Then she ran toward the gate at a fast clip, just making it on board the plane.

After the plane had left, I went back to the Healey and drove into town. It looked like it was going to be a lonely night. I debated visiting with Sheriff and Mrs. Lavers—then remembered the look on his face when I told him he'd been wrong about Hillary, and decided against the visit. That way, I was still alive, if lonely.

It was about nine-thirty when I parked outside the apartment building and I hadn't been home that early in years. I met the janitor in the lobby, and watched his gray hair bristle when he saw me.

"Cheater!" he mumbled loudly.

I thumbed the elevator button, then looked at him. "What did you say?"

"They got special rules for cheating cops so they don't go to jail like other folks?" he asked belligerently.

"Don't tell me," I said. "You just lost your mind—I'll help you look for it."

"Least you could do is pay the alimony!" he snarled.

The elevator arrived and the door slid open. I stepped forward, still watching him curiously.

"How many wives have you got!" he exploded.

The sliding door wiped him off, leaving me wondering. I was still wondering when I opened the front door of the apartment and walked in. Now it was my turn for the funny farm. The lights were on, the hi-fi machine was oozing music through the five speakers....

"Cigarette?" a husky voice asked.

A stunning blonde wearing a black-sequined bra and tights sauntered out to meet me.

"Jerrie Cushman!" I said slowly.

"You said for me to call you, Lieutenant," she said demurely. "I called and called, but you weren't answering, so I thought I'd come over and wait for you to get home."

"How did you get into the apartment?"

She dimpled. "I hope you don't get mad at me, Lieutenant. I told the janitor I was your ex-wife and if I didn't get to see you tonight—"

"—and pick up some of the back alimony, you'd be thrown out of your own apartment!" I finished for her.

"I thought it was original!" She shrugged her beautiful, honey-tanned shoulders. "He took a lot of convincing. Asked me how many wives you had—so naturally I told him just the one, me. Then he got all sympathetic and kept shaking his head and saying, 'You poor little thing, you don't know ...'   Is he a screwball?"

"I'm working on it," I said. "But you helped a lot, Jerrie, believe me!"

I followed her into the living room where the lights were subdued, the music soft, and two tall drinks stood waiting on top of a small table in front of the couch.

"I thought I'd make things comfy, Lieutenant," Jerrie murmured.

"Al's the name," I said absently. "Comfy?"

"I need the job," she said in a mocking voice. "Sit down, honey. Cigarette?"

"No, thanks," I said happily as I sat down on the couch.

"I have the drinks ready." She sat down, but on my lap instead of the couch. "Is there anything else I can do for you?"

"I know show-biz is a tough racket, Jerrie," I said, patting her thigh sympathetically. "But I'm just an easy-going cop—have your drink first!"

THE END

Lament for a Lousy Lover
- - - -
Carter Brown

"… and one wonders if he [Lt. Al Wheeler] and Mavis will ever wind up in the same book."

Anthony Boucher, *New York Times*
August 30, 1959

1

Mavis Seidlitz

Well, I've met some broadminded broads in my time but this Amber Lacy was so far out—right at the end of the strip and I don't mean Sunset—she embarrassed even me and I'm not a girl who blushes easy. It was the kind of situation dear old Aunt Gabbie never mentions in her newspaper column—I guess they won't let her talk about sin even if she is syndicated.

So I just stood in the open doorway of the trailer trying hard to think up some conversation, with my face getting redder all the time. Amber didn't move a muscle as she reclined on the bunk, wearing nothing but a sweet smile and a cloud of perfume; but Lee Banning beside her sure reacted fast, scrambling onto his feet and glaring at me ferociously.

"Why in hell didn't you knock first?" he snarled.

"I did," I said simply, "three times. I have news for you, Mr. Banning—your wife is on the prowl and she's getting closer all the time!"

"Yeah?" He paled suddenly. "If she finds me here—" He didn't wait to spell out the rest. One sudden dive took him past me and out the door—faster than an agent who's just heard he can get 10 per cent of Brigitte Bardot if he hustles.

"Shut the door, sweetie." Amber's smile was starting to wither around the edges. "There's one hell of a draft!"

I pushed the door shut behind me and looked at her scornfully. "What's the matter with you, you got to grab the married ones all the time?"

"You've done your job, sweetie," she said tersely. "No need to worry that dumb blonde head of yours about my motives. Just get the hell out of here, will you?"

I guessed she was right—about me having done my job. That was what Mr. Bliss, the producer, hired me for in the first place. To keep the peace was the way he put it because he's a gentleman, at least I think he's a gentleman because he hasn't made a pass at me yet but we've only been on location a couple of days so he's got plenty of time left. What he really meant was to keep Amber Lacy away from all the men around the unit and the married men in particular and especially Lee Banning because he's not only married but he's the star of the series, too.

When you've got a television series like *Dead Shot* I guess you worry about it the way Mr. Bliss worries—never out of the first half of the top ten ratings and going into its fifth year and all. So when Mr. Bliss came into my office and told me all about how he was going to make a real big one out of the opening show for the fifth year of production and take the whole unit out on location near Pine City, I could see right away he had problems. Then he told me Amber Lacy was going to do the guest bit and I knew even his problems had problems—Amber has a reputation up and down the Strip of being a man-eating tigress with a liking for happily leg-roped guys as a kind of hors d'oeuvre.

Well, I wasn't too enthusiastic about taking the job. Playing chaperone to Amber was like trying to preach togetherness to a bunch of rattlesnakes right after you fell into their nest, but a girl has to eat and the confidential consultant business had been pretty slow lately, like it was a big day at the office if the janitor showed.

About five seconds after I'd closed the door of Amber's trailer and started back toward my own, I ran full tilt into Peggy Banning and it was me who bounced off because I'm built that way while Peggy is a stringy blonde with sharp muscular angles instead of curves. I figure Lee Banning married her for some good reason but she sure keeps it well hidden. She glared at me with her sallow face flushed like uncooked hamburger and I could tell right away she was mad about something.

"Where is he?" she panted. "Where's that two-timing, four-flushing bum of mine? If he's with that oversexed, pneumatic piece of well-worn upholstery that dares to call herself an actress, I'll cut his heart out—and hers!"

"Why, Peggy honey!" I said consolingly. "If you mean Amber Lacy, you've got it all wrong. I just left her trailer and she's there all by her hot little self."

"Yeah?" She still glared at me murderously. "Then where's that lousy little rat who's laughingly known as my husband?"

"I'm sure I don't know," I said truthfully. "Maybe he's hidden out someplace learning his lines."

"I know the kind of lines he's practicing O.K.," she snapped. "All it needs is for me to catch him at it—just once!" She drew her index finger across her throat and made a nasty, ripping sound out of the corner of her mouth.

"You wouldn't do that, Peggy honey?" I said reproachfully. "After all, a good man is hard to find!"

"Sure," she said sourly, "and that no-good husband of mine is even harder!"

She took off in the general direction of Amber Lacy's trailer and I felt real glad I'd gotten there first or maybe Mr. Bliss would've had a double murder on his hands. The way it was now the worst thing that could happen would be Amber catching cold because of the draft from people opening the door all the time, and perfume just doesn't keep out the cold the way wool does.

Thinking about Mr. Bliss, I figured I'd better go tell him what had happened to prove I was earning the money he paid me. So I walked along to his trailer which was right at the other end of the unit location and on the way I met the unlikely twins. That was my own name for them, Mr. Ivorsen and Mr. Toro, because they were always together and they looked about as much alike as King Kong and Woody Woodpecker—and how unlikely a twosome can you get?

Mr. Kent Ivorsen had a piece of the show, Lee Banning told me—when I asked him which episode he got mad at me for some reason. Anyway, Mr. Ivorsen was one of the backers, I guess—a little guy always neatly dressed like he was going to a funeral and always awfully polite like the mortician who's just dropped in with a measuring tape. Mr. Toro was a great big mountain of muscle and always looked like he needed a shave and he was so polite he never said anything—he just grunted.

"Good morning, Miss Seidlitz." Mr. Ivorsen lifted his hat and there was more than a glint of eighteen karat gold in his smile. "A lovely morning."

"It certainly is." I smiled right back and twitched my hip out of reach of his wandering hand. I mean, he might have a piece of the show already but he certainly didn't have a piece of *me* yet.

"How are you, Mr. Toro?" I asked brightly, craning my neck to look up into his face. But I was wasting my time and talent as usual—all I got back was a deep-throated grunt from somewhere inside the five o'clock shadow.

"Mrs. Banning was looking for her husband a few minutes back," Ivorsen said, his hand regretfully patting the air where my hip had been a moment before. "She seemed very angry—there's nothing wrong is there? Nothing that will affect the schedule, I mean? You know Lucian Bliss is shooting the big scene right after lunch—I wouldn't want anything to interrupt that, would we?"

"There's nothing to worry about, Mr. Ivorsen," I said firmly. "It's all been taken care of."

"I am happy to hear it," he said sadly. Then he moved so fast the quickness of his hand deceived the confidential consultant and I was being patted right where a girl prefers to choose who does the patting.

"You are a credit to the enterprise, Miss Seidlitz." His washed-out blue eyes regarded me with mournful approval for a moment. "We can continue our walk, Toro, in a happier frame of mind now."

"Ugh!" Toro said. I figured if he ever got tired playing Mr. Ivorsen's twin he could make a steady living playing a Sioux in the *Dead Shot* series.

"Thank you, Miss Seidlitz." Ivorsen inclined his head courteously while that absent-minded hand of his goosed me gently in an aw-revore but not goodbye. Then the twins continued their stroll, both of them in perfect step so that Mr. Toro minced along like an overweight ballet boy as he shortened his stride to keep pace with Mr. Ivorsen's short legs.

When I reached Mr. Bliss's trailer I knocked on the door three times without getting any answer but then I heard him talking inside so I opened the door and walked in anyway because I know he's absent-minded like Kent Ivorsen sometimes. There's a Hollywood story about the time he dictated the first three paragraphs of a letter to his chair while he sat on his secretary—well, that's the way she told it.

He was talking O.K. but this time it wasn't to a chair. The other guy in the trailer with him was Drew Fenelk and if anybody with a phony name like that asked me out to dinner I'd check his credit rating first. I didn't like Fenelk from the first time I met him. He was one of those smooth characters who figure Apollo would bust out crying if he got a glimpse of their magnificent profile. (You remember Apollo—he made a couple of Tarzan movies before a hot-tempered husband busted his nose and ruined his acting career.)

Mr. Bliss is a real nice man most of the time but like all great men he has his wilder moments. Fenelk is one of them and a strong belief in astrology is another. Fenelk is his personal astrologer and I guess Bliss figured this spectacular was so important to him that he brought his astrologer along with him on location so he could get hip to what the stars foretold for the next day's shooting.

"If you don't believe in me anymore, Lucian," Drew Fenelk said in a pained voice as I came into the trailer, "then say so and I'll go back to L. A."

"Have a good trip," I said enthusiastically, "and don't do anything Sagittarius wouldn't!"

"Oh, my God!" Fenelk said wearily. "Here comes Little Mavis Moron!"

"Shut up, Mavis," Mr. Bliss said absently. "I'm busy right now."

"We don't need to go through it all again," Fenelk said curtly. "The moon enters the Scorpio sign at two-thirty this afternoon—you're a Leo subject and the Scorpio sign is hostile. Banning is a Scorpio too, remember—and the Lacy woman is an Aquarius, another hostile sign."

"I know, but—" Mr. Bliss said almost apologetically.

"You know the current phase of your own personal horoscope," Fenelk continued relentlessly. "The conjunction is bad, very bad. If you insist on being reckless, Lucian, I can only foresee disaster!"

"O.K., O.K.," poor Mr. Bliss muttered. "You know I always listen to you,

Drew. But I can't postpone the takes this afternoon. Everything's all set—even the weather's right. This location deal has cost a fortune already—I just can't afford not to go ahead and get the climax in the can!"

Fenelk shrugged his shoulders disdainfully. "Very well. But remember I warned you. Disaster! It's right here." He tapped a complicated-looking chart with his finger. "You can see for yourself—as plain as—" he glanced at me for a moment—"as the obvious fact that Mavis is a woman. All you have to do is look through that revealing blouse to find out, and you only have to look at this chart here to see disaster written across it in blood!"

I was glad to see my sheer nylon blouse and peekaboo lace slip weren't a waste of money—even if it was only Fenelk.

"Let's skip the dramatics, huh, Drew?" Mr. Bliss sounded like he was getting impatient. "I pay writers for that kind of dialogue."

"For the last time," Fenelk almost snarled, "I'm not dreaming up some fantasy—it's all here." He tapped the chart with his index finger again. "Danger, disaster, and death!"

"So now I get rubbed out if I don't play ball? Oh, brother!" Mr. Bliss breathed heavily but not the same way that means a girl's reached the point of no return, and any moment now she'll have no secrets left except maybe her social security number.

"Not death for you, Lucian," Fenelk said softly, "but close to you, bringing disaster in its wake."

"Well," I said philosophically, "you can't have a death without a wake, can you? One of my girlfriends cried for three whole days after her husband got his."

"It must have been true love," Fenelk said bleakly.

"On the fourth day she sobered up and realized what had happened," I told him happily, "then she didn't stop laughing for a week!"

The stargazer gave me a venomous look, like I was a smudge on his natal chart or something, then ignored me.

"Hell!" Mr. Bliss exploded suddenly. "I don't have any choice about this, Drew. Buying that goddamned diamond ring set me back forty thousand, cash! Sure, it's going to make us a million in publicity but that's still in the future. Here I am with Banning bitching about a new contract and threatening to walk out if he doesn't get it right away—and this special show way over its budget already before it's hardly gotten started!"

Drew Fenelk shrugged his shoulders carefully so that any responsibility still clinging to him dropped on the floor right there and then. He took time out to reassure himself I was a dame and it only took a fraction of a second and one more eagle-eyed glance right through my blouse. If the lace slip left anything to his imagination, he was busy imagining as he walked past me and out of the trailer.

The door made a distinct and final click as it shut behind him, and Mr. Bliss said something under his breath I was glad I didn't hear, then ran both hands through his hair like he was figuring on pulling it out by the roots.

"You wanted to see me about something, Mavis?" he asked in a dull voice.

"It's not important," I told him because I could see he was in no mood for trifles like Lee Banning's trifling with Amber Lacy. Then my girlish curiosity got the better of me and I had to ask.

"That diamond ring you mentioned," I said breathlessly. "You really paid forty thousand dollars for it?"

"Sure," he nodded. "It was worth every cent."

"Gosh!" I said, impressed. "Who's the lucky girl?"

"Girl?" He blinked at me for a moment, then grinned suddenly. "You got it wrong, honey. This ring belonged to the real life Shep Morrow—he won it in a poker game from a railroad tycoon."

"You mean the Shep Morrow that Lee Banning plays in the series?" I asked, wide-eyed. "I never knew he was real—I figured he was something dreamed up by your writers."

"He was real O.K.," Mr. Bliss grunted. "But not so well known as Wyatt Earp and the others—or he wasn't until we started making the *Dead Shot* series."

"And this is the very same ring he won in that poker game?" I asked disbelievingly.

"It's authentic all right," Mr. Bliss said. "I had that ring checked the way the FBI checks a visiting hatchet man from behind the Iron Curtain!"

"It seems like a waste," I said wistfully. "What does Lee Banning need with a rock like that on his pinky?"

"It matches the rocks in his head," Mr. Bliss said, smiling sourly, "except it sparkles a hell of a lot more."

Then he glared down at the chart Drew Fenelk had left on the table and I sensed the interview was over, though if he'd been his usual amiable self he'd have told me to get the hell out of his trailer. I felt real sorry for him with all those financial worries and all—for a guy who's been married three times the alimony should be enough.

"Don't let that phony, Fenelk, get you down, Mr. Bliss," I said comfortingly. "Him and his disaster and death and all that jazz—he's just a kook from outer space."

I knew right away from the frozen expression on his face that I'd said the right thing and he was back to normal.

"Mavis," he said with his usual executive crispness, "get the hell out of here!"

"I guess I couldn't get one itty-bitty peek at that chunk of ice before I go?" I asked hopefully.

"The hell—" Mr. Bliss shouted, with the veins in his neck standing out like freeways on a contour map of Los Angeles, "—get out of here!"

2

Mavis Seidlitz

Right after lunch I went back to Amber Lacy's trailer and pretended I was trying to be helpful while she got dressed for the afternoon's shooting, but I was really checking up to make sure Lee Banning hadn't sneaked into the woodwork while I wasn't looking. Amber wasn't real delirious to see me but like she said, she'd gotten used to me being around the trailer all the time like the plague.

I'm a girl who's always trying to improve her mind mainly because there's nothing can be done to improve my figure—I mean in all modesty it's perfect already—but sometimes I get confused like when Mr. Bliss says television's a funny thing except for domestic comedies. But when I watched Amber getting dressed for the big scene I could see what he meant.

Everybody knows the traditions of the Old West—all about the ranches and the horses and the two-gun marshals and three-gun baddies and four-flushing saloonkeepers and the saloon girls, who just stand around in their short, tinsely dresses waiting for the cowpokes to buy them a drink. Like it has nothing to do with the word that scares sponsors so bad (*S-E-X*), it's just tradition. I figured it was only coincidence that Mr. Bliss had used that tradition in every *Dead Shot* episode to date—and from the look of Amber Lacy, the special season opener wasn't going to be any exception, even if they were using real scenery in this one instead of an old Tom Mix set.

In the big scene they were shooting that afternoon, Amber Lacy played a saloon girl who'd been kidnaped by the villain and locked in a deserted shack beside a deserted mine shaft right in the middle of the desert. She tried to get away but he caught up with her after a couple of miles of tough going through the cactus and brought her back to the shack. I guess everybody knows what cactus will do to a tinsely dress and they'd figure it would be ripped right up to here—and it was, believe me!

The dress was made out of white satin with a V neckline that plunged right to the edge of a censor's indecision, then fitted tight around Amber's waist before it flared out to a hemline that stopped four inches above her knees. The wardrobe department had done a real job on it, better than cactus even. There was a two-inch strip of satin that still hung close to her knees, but the rest of the hemline ended somewhere around the top of her thighs.

It figured the viewers would get a nice close-up view of her black silk stockings that somehow missed the cactus, along with the genu-wine diamint-studded garters and just a tantalizing glimpse of the wardrobe department's idea of what Grandmother wore under all that gingham jazz. What with the shape of Amber's legs, I had to admit grudgingly to myself that the end result was as nice a piece of tradition as you could get in a foreign movie even.

Amber snapped the last garter into place, took another look at herself in the mirror, and smiled placidly at her own reflection—I guess everybody smiles when they see their own true love. While she was still paying homage the door of the trailer flew open and in stormed Peggy Banning.

"If you had any manners, you'd knock!" Amber said coldly, turning away from the mirror reluctantly.

Peggy Banning was breathing quickly, her face all flushed like she'd been chasing her husband again and like always he'd gotten away from her.

"This is the last time I'll say this," she snarled at Amber. "Lay off my husband or I'll cut your throat!"

"Why, sweetie," Amber purred, "you're all upset. Why don't you be sensible and just quit while you're so far behind?"

"I mean it," Peggy said hotly. "If you don't leave him alone I'll kill you!"

Amber yawned widely right in her face. "I get so bored with the old tired routine—everyone does the outraged wife bit exactly the same. For your information, darling, the big event hasn't happened yet."

"I'm telling you," Peggy repeated dully, "for the last time—"

"I know," Amber snapped, "and if you'd had any brains and kept your big mouth shut I would've dumped Lee along with the rest of the garbage—he's no prize except maybe for those cute muscles. But now you've put it into the big league, I guess I'll have to go on and make a score, just for the hell of it. See what your big mouth's done?"

Peggy started toward her with both hands raised ready to scratch her eyes out and it wasn't that I cared much about Amber's face either way but I figured Mr. Bliss would get awful mad at me if I let it happen so I didn't. I grabbed Peggy's wrists and twisted her arms behind her back into a full nelson, then gave her the rush out of the trailer. She was the kind of a girl who needed a little friendly advice so I told her if she tried it again I'd break off one of her arms and use it to beat her brains out.

When I got back inside the trailer, Amber was smoking a cigarette like nothing had happened and didn't even say thanks and before I even had a chance to give her a piece of my mind which was red hot and sizzling, the door of the trailer burst open again. There was one difference—this time it wasn't Peggy Banning back to get her arm twisted right off—it was Jason Kemp, the actor who played the chief baddie in the show.

He was a very masculine character, somewhere close to forty, built like an athlete with none of it running to fat. His black hair was cropped short and his eyes were midnight blue so when he looked directly at me I felt kind of limp inside—like I'd agree before he asked the question. Dressed the way he was, all in black with a Colt .45 on each hip, he was the guy to scare hell out of a girl for the first five minutes in a dimly lit room, but later on she'd spend the rest of the night dreaming about it. What I mean is Jason Kemp was a real sex cymbal!

"What the hell do you want?" Amber asked tersely.

"A little conversation," he said in a deep vibrant voice that kinked my spine like one of those fiendish all-over girdles you see in the color advertisements. Then he looked straight at me almost as if he didn't notice the fast rise and fall of the peekaboo lace and grunted, "In private!"

"I'll wait outside," I said reluctantly and started to edge my way toward the door.

"No, you don't!" Amber snapped. "You stay right here, Mavis. For once in your sordid life you can be useful—I'm not being left alone with this educated primitive."

"Gosh!" I said, shaken right down to my—well, never mind. "Don't tell me there's a man left alive who can still scare Amber Lacy?"

"Make it fast, Jason," she snarled. "I'm busy."

"It won't take long," he said coldly. "Banning's riding me to death. He's at Bliss all the time to get me tossed out of the show altogether." He smiled bleakly. "For a while there I wondered why—until I had a confidential talk with his wife ten minutes back."

"I don't know what you mean," Amber said stiffly.

Jason grinned at her in a friendly kind of way that made me shiver inside.

"I figure you do, doll," he said softly. "You've got Banning lined up for your collection and until the scalp's hanging in your boudoir, you just don't want an ex-husband around offering him advice—even if he won't take it."

"I never knew you two were married," I said excitedly, with my female curiosity twitching so hard my hips did a cha-cha under the tight linen skirt.

"Who admits to a dreadful mistake like that?" Amber said sullenly. "It only lasted four days."

Jason grinned at me suddenly. "You want to know Amber's dreadful secret?" he asked casually and the beast knew I'd just die if he didn't tell. "It was me who walked out, not her."

"You only beat me to the door by a split second!" Amber said furiously. "You—"

"I found out she was a commie," Jason said solemnly.

"Gosh!" I said blankly. "I never figured Amber had time for politics."

"That was the only explanation I could figure out," Jason said blandly. "How else could you explain the butler wearing my pajamas?"

"Don't listen to the lying slob!" Amber said thickly. "It was all a mistake anyway. The butler—"

"—did it, like always." Jason interrupted her in a crisp voice. "Listen good, Amber. I don't give a damn about Banning's scalp. Have it and welcome—wear it in good health. But tell him to lay off me and stop whispering in Bliss's ear or he'll regret it—and so will you."

"Are you threatening me?" she asked in a choked voice.

"You could call it that," he said evenly. "So don't forget to tell Banning, huh?"

He walked across to the door, opened it, then looked back at her for a moment.

"You might remember I'm not the kind of guy to kid around with over a deal like this—tell Banning that, too." Then he stepped out of the trailer, closing the door behind him gently.

"Who does he think he is?" Amber stormed petulantly. "Daring to threaten me like that!"

"To think you were once Mrs. Kemp," I said wistfully. "It must have been an exciting four whole days!"

The deserted shack and mine shaft where they were shooting the big scene that afternoon were situated about a mile from the trailer camp. I figured I'd walk over there because I needed the exercise and I politely refused Mr. Ivorsen's offer of a free ride in his Cadillac because I didn't need that much exercise.

When I got there I saw that Mr. Bliss as producer of the series wasn't taking any chances with this opener so he was using the best director he knew—himself. Everything was set up ready and waiting with cameras, microphones, cranes, booms, cables, and confusion. You couldn't miss seeing Mr. Bliss all the same—he was sitting in a chair with his name stenciled across the back in large letters. I went over and started to tell him about Jason Kemp but he wouldn't listen. He told me to save it until later.

Out of the corner of my eye I saw Mr. Ivorsen and Mr. Toro coming toward us so I moved away fast from Mr. Bliss because past experience told me Mr. Ivorsen would never dream of suggesting I save it for later. Then, what with looking over my shoulder all the time to keep tabs on Mr. Ivorsen, I couldn't look where I was going and a couple of seconds later I bumped into something painfully solid which turned out to be Drew Fenelk. He looked down at me like I was an allergy, then closed his eyes like he hoped somebody would slug me with a virus while he wasn't looking.

"I figured you'd be on your way back to Los Angeles by now, Mr. Fenelk," I said brightly to make conversation.

He opened his eyes and looked at me coldly. "Lucian will need me," he said in a hollow voice. "I am not the kind of man who deserts a friend!"

"If you change your mind, you sure picked the right place," I said, looking at the shack and the mine shaft. "Everything's deserted around here already."

"Mavis." He stared at me for a moment. "Tell me something in confidence. Did you ever go to school?"

"Well, of course I did!" I said, smiling at him for asking such a silly question. "For years and years."

"When did you leave—which grade?"

"What's a grade?" I asked cautiously.

Fenelk didn't answer—I guess because right then about six people were all shouting, "Quiet!" at the top of their voices. Mr. Bliss was starting the first rehearsal of the scene they were going to shoot.

After they'd rehearsed it six times, he said he was ready for a take and everyone looked hopeful like they figured with luck it wouldn't take more than ten takes to put the scene in the can (that's a polite word in Hollywood).

Well, it seemed an awful lot of fuss and bother to me, but Mr. Bliss sure took it seriously. I mean, it was only a simple little scene. After the villain has caught the saloon girl running through the cactus and dragged her back to the deserted shack, he's so busy chasing her around inside it gives Shep Morrow (that's really Lee Banning, remember?) and his sidekick a chance to sneak up on the shack. Then Shep shouts for the villain to come out with his hands up. Then—I bet you guessed—the sneaky villain comes out O.K. but he pushes the saloon girl in front of him, and like everyone knows, no self-respecting western hero would risk putting a slug through a saloon girl's bodice.

So while Shep and his buddy are looking around for an umpire, the sneaky villain shoots the sidekick (but you find out later it's nothing serious, like it's just a scratch across the heart or something) and then he shoots the hero in the shoulder. Right then the saloon girl courageously bites the villain's hand forcing him to let go of her so the hero gets the chance to give the villain the cup-de-grass, which is French for the business.

Mr. Bliss gave the high-sign and the cameras moved in for a close-up of Lee Banning as the hero with a determined look on his face and that gorgeous diamond ring flashing on his finger. Then the next shot showed a young guy named Mel Parker, who plays Lee's sidekick in the series, and the next shot after that showed the two of them sneaking up on the shack.

Amber let out a couple of girlish shrieks from inside the shack to let everyone know they were still playing tag in there, then Lee shouted for the villain to come out with his hands held high.

I got real breathless watching and wondering to myself if it was real and I was the saloon girl, what would I do? But I couldn't kid myself—I knew what I'd do all right if it was me in there playing tag with Jason Kemp. I'd tell Banning and his sidekick to get the hell out of there and mind their own damned business.

The door of the shack opened and out came Jason with a gun in one hand and Amber in the other, a nasty sneer on his face as a bonus. The cameras got another close-up of the worried looks on both Lee's and Mel Parker's faces, then Jason fired a couple of quick shots which sent Mel sprawling backward onto the ground.

My heart beat a little faster when I saw the triumphant grin on Jason's face as he aimed his gun at Lee, then pulled the trigger. Right after that, Amber sank her teeth into his hand and from where I stood, it sure looked as if she enjoyed doing it. Jason yelped very realistically while Amber broke away from him and ran gracefully into the camera, making sure the lens got the full impact of her shapely legs and the busty bounce of her low-cut bodice.

"Cut!" Mr. Bliss screamed suddenly.

Amber stopped running and for a moment there, the bounce was out of sync. She glared venomously at him and snapped, "What was wrong with that?"

Mr. Bliss didn't even bother to answer her, he was too busy walking across to where Lee Banning was stretched out on the ground.

"Four years you've been with this series already!" he yelled as he walked. "And you don't know better than to lie down when you've been shot? In the shoulder, it says in the script, that's all. You got to make a production out of it? Damn it to hell, Lee, you know a hero only staggers a little when he's hit—even if it's real serious like a lung or something—but he never falls down! You want the whole five million audience to figure Shep Morrow's chicken?"

I guessed Lee Banning just didn't care to hear Mr. Bliss's views on how a hero should act because he still lay right where he'd fallen on his face and didn't even answer.

"Lee!" Mr. Bliss's face reddened like it was about to burst into flame. "You hear me?"

Banning still didn't answer and Mr. Bliss exploded, saying a few short sharp words about Lee's ancestry, and at the same time he stuck his foot under Lee's ribs and rolled him over onto his back.

"Why don't you tell the bum it's all over and he can come out now?" Jason Kemp suggested coldly.

Mr. Bliss didn't seem to hear him—he just kept on staring down at Lee, his eyes getting wider and wider all the time. Then I figured he'd decided to show Lee how he wanted it done because he staggered back a couple of paces until his knees buckled suddenly and he dropped to the ground and lay there.

"Danger," Drew Fenelk said in a low voice beside me, "and disaster—then death!"

"Huh?" I frowned at him.

He walked quickly toward the two prostrate men without even taking time out to give me an answer, so I had to run to catch up with him. When he was about six feet away from them, Fenelk stopped suddenly so I bounced into him again.

"I warned him," he said in a low voice. "You were there, Mavis, you heard me?"

"Please?" I asked anxiously. "What the heck are you talking about?"

"That!" he said grimly.

I followed the direction of his pointing finger and found myself looking straight down at Lee Banning. He wore a blue shirt I remembered and it took me around five whole seconds to figure out why the front of it was now bright red.

3

Al Wheeler

"I'm Lieutenant Wheeler," I said with no enthusiasm at all, "from the County Sheriff's office."

"My name is Lucian Bliss," the tall, overweight character with the thick gray hair said. "I'm the producer of *Dead Shot*." His eyes had a glazed look like someone had just asked him what's television.

"Somebody called in about a cadaver," I said patiently. "Did anybody get shot?"

"Anybody?" he gurgled. "It was *Lee Banning!*"

"I thought that happened every week," I said politely.

"There must be fifty thousand cops in California," he said bitterly, "and I had to get you!"

From the look on his face he wasn't going to be much use to me, not for a while anyway. I left him with his grief and walked over to where Doc Murphy was down on his knees beside the body.

"*Dead Shot!*" Murphy said happily. "One of my wife's favorite shows. How many times have I prayed this would happen!"

"Maybe it's the start of a whole new trend," I agreed. "Canned westerns with live bullets?"

The doc looked down distastefully at the gory front of Banning's shirt. "Whoever shot him knew what he was doing by the look of it. Right through the heart—as they say at spy executions."

"You can tell just by looking?" I asked, disbelievingly.

"So wait till the autopsy corroborates it," Murphy growled, trying to sound hurt. "Maybe I should show this to my wife. For five years now I've been trying to convince her what an unholy mess a real high-caliber slug makes."

"You're wasting your time with legal homicides, Doc," I said sincerely. "You should be in television—heading up an organization like 'Ghoul Productions.' I got you a slogan already— 'The story may be fiction but the blood is real.' How about that?"

A deep grunt at my elbow announced the arrival of Sergeant Polnik. I turned around real slow because it looked like it was going to be a hard day and Polnik's face is the kind you edge up on slowly.

"Lieutenant?" The primeval chunk of flesh contorted painfully and the voice held a problem somewhere in the sandblasted overtones. "There's a screwball dame back there keeps on bothering me."

"Tell her to put her glasses back on," I suggested. "That should fix it O.K."

"She says she was a partner in a private eye outfit once and now she's a confidential consultant and she wants to help out." He shuddered violently. "She won't go away, Lieutenant, and she keeps on talking like my old lady but faster even—she's driving me nuts!"

"Bring her right over," Murphy suggested with a Machiavellian twitch of his bushy eyebrows. "Give her a close-up look at the cadaver—that should do it up good."

"She saw it already," Polnik said morosely. "She was watching when it happened. But she knows Jason Kemp didn't do it even if he did shoot Banning."

"How's that again?" I asked nervously.

"Somebody else put real bullets instead of blanks into his gun," Polnik said, glassy-eyed. "Maybe it was Peggy because she's been real jealous about how Amber's been leading her husband around by the nose—or maybe it was Mr. Ivorsen because any guy who'd goose a dame when she wasn't looking couldn't be trusted. And what about Mr. Toro who never says nothing?—and don't forget that Drew Fenelk, the phony, he forecast the whole thing right there in Mr. Bliss's trailer and how about that?"

"Yeah," I echoed feebly. "How about that, Doc?"

Murphy had completely forgotten his corpse and just stared numbly up at Polnik, his mouth wide open. I made a conscious effort and felt my own teeth click sharply together.

"She said all that?" I asked.

"That's only the beginning." Polnik shuddered again. "I'm a sick man, Lieutenant, my stomach's acting up like a stripper's G-string or something—I can't take it anymore."

"What's her name?"

"Alka Seltzer?" Polnik muttered thickly.

"Leave your stomach out of this," I snarled.

"Honest, Lieutenant." A hurt look showed on his face while his forehead corrugated painfully. "Or something like that—hey!—I got it—Seidlitz!"

"If you're trying to be cute—" I said ominously.

"Mavis Seidlitz," Polnik finished triumphantly. "That's it, so help me, Lieutenant, Mavis Seidlitz."

"That's me!" a bright voice said somewhere in back of my left shoulder blade.

I turned around real slow, the same way I'd turned to face the sergeant, because I knew right then that the hard day had caught up fast. Facing me with a look of eager expectancy on her face, was a blonde—the genuine, corn-colored kind of blonde who's a big relief from the blue and green streaked kind you meet all over these days.

She had bright blue eyes that were more ingenuous than innocent, a cute uptilted nose, and lips that were warm and full, inviting and generous. She wore a see-through nylon blouse and underneath a slip which sprayed lace carelessly around the twin peaks of her high full breasts and across the deep valley in between. Her waist was ridiculously small, emphasized by a wide cinch belt which grabbed the top of a tight skirt. The skirt fitted her hourglass hips as intimately as the nylons that sheathed her long shapely legs and trim ankles.

It was like somebody made Old Mother Nature a sucker bet she couldn't produce the perfect physical specimen of woman in one try and *blam*—Mavis Seidlitz.

"You must be the lieutenant the sergeant told me about," she said eagerly.

"Wheeler," I gulped, watching the lace foam billow gently. "Al Wheeler."

"I'm Mavis Seidlitz," she said, then went right on without even pausing for breath. "I was telling your cute sergeant here all about the suspects in the case because I used to be a partner—the senior partner of course—in a private detective agency in L. A.—Rio Investigations—and I guess you've heard of it but Johnny Rio went to Detroit so I started in on my own as a confidential consultant. You can see I've had lots of experience and believe me, I knew right away that no good would come out of Amber Lacy chasing poor Lee Banning while his wife was chasing the both of them! That's Lee down there, Lieutenant—the one that's dead—you know? Well, like I was saying—"

"Hold it!" I said desperately. "Why don't we—"

"But I haven't even started yet."

She gave me a baffled look from under the downsweep of her deep-fringed eyelids. "You see, Lieutenant Trailer, I was in Mr. Bliss's wheeler this morning, and Drew Fenelk, the astrologer—say! I bet you're a Capricorn, I can tell just from looking—he forecast the whole deal in three words. Danger, disaster, and death. Like that! You can see from all that blood on poor Lee Banning's shirt he was absolutely right—and how about Mr. Ivorsen and Mr. Toro, huh? How about them?"

"Mr. Who and Who?" I asked weakly.

"Mr. Ivorsen and Mr. Toro," she repeated patiently, "the unlikely twins—that's my name for them but I just made it up as a joke—I don't think they're real twins but there's something funny about them or I guess they're like what Mr. Bliss says about domestic comedies in television, huh? Do you have a sense of humor, Lieutenant?"

"I mislaid it someplace just now," I said thickly, "along with my sanity."

"Well,"—she smiled brightly—"I wouldn't worry too much, Lieutenant, most of the guys I've ever known are just the same—always losing their sense of humor in the most unlikely places, you know, the tunnel of love, a free-form couch, a girls' dressing room? I mean, take a burlesque show for example—you ever hear any guy laugh when one of the girls is doing the funniest things with a couple of fringed tassels? But I was telling you about the suspects and you can take it from me, Lieutenant, that Jason Kemp didn't have anything to do with it and don't believe anything Amber tells you about him threatening her and Lee Banning because Lee was trying to get him in bad with Mr. Bliss!"

I looked appealingly at Polnik and Doc Murphy, but one quick glance told me I was wasting my time. The screwed-up expression on Polnik's face suggested that his stomach was giving him the kind of hell he usually got from his old lady—and the dazed eyes confirmed Murphy as either a somnambulist or the victim of sudden catatonia. What I needed was an inspiration to get me out from under, and suddenly I got it.

"I mean," Mavis Seidlitz continued remorselessly, "it just couldn't have been Jason Kemp—a guy like that, so virile and all—he wouldn't murder anybody. You can see—"

"Miss Seidlitz?" I meant it to sound polite but it came out like a dying foghorn. "Tell me something?"

"Wheeler," Murphy croaked, "you're a masochist!"

"Why, sure, Lieutenant." Mavis Seidlitz smiled warmly. "I mean, that's what I've been doing all along, isn't it? You have been listening—or would you like me to repeat it?"

"Just one question," I said swiftly. "Where is the men's room?"

She frowned slightly, then bit her luscious lower lip gently. "Gosh, I'm awful sorry, Lieutenant, but I don't know. You see, I've never been there."

"Do me a favor?" I pleaded. "Go find out from Mr. Bliss."

"O.K.," she said in a resolute voice like I was a four-star general who'd just told her now was the time to push the button. "You wait right here, Lieutenant, and I'll be back."

I waited until she was out of earshot, then snapped my fingers under Doc Murphy's nose a couple of times. He shook his head slowly and blinked at me.

"A little delicate work under the tongue with a scalpel," he said thoughtfully, "and she'd be fun to have around the house."

"When she comes back, I'm gone," I said, "and you don't know where."

"All right," he agreed reluctantly, "but for this you owe me and I'll work it out tonight—for sure, it'll come expensive!"

"Polnik!" I snarled at him because that's what sergeants are for in this kind of situation. "Find out who loaded Kemp's guns for the scene they were filming. Check the time they were loaded, where the slugs came from, and who else could have got at the guns before Kemp got them."

"Sure, Lieutenant," he grunted painfully. "But if it was that wackie, yacking blonde—I quit!"

A quick glance over my shoulder showed that Mavis Seidlitz was nowhere in sight and without wishing her any harm, I hoped some little thing might have delayed her, like breaking a leg. The nearest technician was twenty feet away, leaning against the base of a camera crane with a faraway look in his eye like the star getting shot dead on camera was strictly routine with him and the union would take care of it anyway.

"You know where I can find Miss Lacy?" I asked.

"She went back to the trailer camp, I guess," he yawned. "Threw a fit when Banning got killed. She was hot for him which maybe made the difference—or maybe you heard?"

"I heard," I agreed. "Where's this trailer camp?"

"About a mile further on into the valley," he said and yawned again. "Are you a real cop or just a private eye from one of the rival production units?"

"It's my brother's day off so he lent me his badge," I said.

He looked at me curiously for a moment then nodded. "It figures," he said simply.

I walked back to Murphy who was on his feet again rubbing his hands together briskly like a mortician who's just heard the dam broke.

"I guess that about wraps it up—as they say on television," he said snappily.

"Like I said before—you should be in the business," I told him. "A natural for *This Is Your Life* with the opening shot of you standing on a mound of cadavers with a close harmony quartet in the background giving out with 'Oh, What a Beautiful Morning.'"

"You're jealous," he said loftily. "I'm all through—you want the body or shall I have it taken away?"

"Why not?" I said and looked nervously over my shoulder, but there was still no sign of the blonde talking machine.

Polnik returned with a mournful expression on his face which said no dice before he did.

"The guy who looks after the guns is back at the trailer camp, Lieutenant," he announced dolefully. "So I don't get to talk to him."

"And that's where Amber Lacy is," I said. "So we've got two good reasons for going there."

I heard someone clear his throat and turned my head to see Bliss standing on the other side of me.

"I sent Mavis on a runaround routine—that's what you wanted, isn't it?" he asked.

"You're so right," I agreed fervently. "There's nothing more we can do here, so you can tell everyone to get back to the trailer camp and I'll see you there later—O.K.?"

"Whatever you say, Lieutenant," he said listlessly. "I still can't face the terrible reality of this thing—the initial shock was so great!"

At Doc Murphy's signal, the two guys in white coats brought their stretcher up and laid it alongside Banning's body.

"Where are you taking ... him?" Bliss swallowed hard.

"The county morgue," Murphy said cheerfully. "He'll do just fine there—air conditioning and all!"

"One thing before you remove the remains," Bliss said quickly. "I don't wish to appear a ghoul, you understand, but the enormous value forces me—"

He knelt down beside the body while he was speaking and lifted Banning's right hand gently. For a long moment he knelt there holding the corpse's hand, frozen in a macabre tableau, then he started to shake.

"This guy bugs me," Polnik growled huskily. "What's he waiting for—a duet?"

"It's gone!" Bliss said in a low whisper. "It's not on his finger anymore—who took it?"

"What's gone?" I asked irritably. "What the hell are you talking about?"

"The ring!" His voice shook in sympathy with the rest of him. "Shep Morrow's diamond ring—Lee was wearing it!"

"Is it valuable?"

"Valuable!" His haggard face stared up at me blankly. "I paid forty thousand for that ring—thank God it's insured!"

Ten minutes later we knew for sure the ring wasn't in Banning's clothing and hadn't slipped off his finger onto the ground beside or underneath where his body fell. It hadn't strayed—it had been stolen, and obviously before we arrived. That made it a nice easy problem—presumably anyone who was around at the time Banning was shot could have stolen the ring. I gave up and told Bliss we'd go back to the main camp and take it from there.

Murphy escorted the corpse to the meat wagon and I told Polnik to stick around and make sure everyone did go back to the camp, then to follow on himself. I made a break for my Austin Healey and got the motor started just as a dazzling blonde reappeared and broke into a bouncing trot toward the car.

The Healey screamed down the dirt road, laying rubber in twin tracks as it went. As I shifted up into third, I heard a faint, anxious shout on the wind.

"Lieutenant! Yoohoo—Lieutenant!" She sounded like she was real upset. "You're going the wrong way! I found the men's room. It's ..." and I never did find out because by then she was far behind me.

4

Al Wheeler

I knocked on the door of Amber Lacy's trailer and figured if she could talk the way Mavis Seidlitz talked, I'd quit the County Sheriff's office along with Polnik and go back to Homicide.

"Who is it?" a soft voice asked from inside the trailer.

"Lieutenant Wheeler, County Sheriff's office," I called. "Can I talk with you?"

"I guess so." The voice didn't sound enthusiastic.

When I got inside I saw she was sitting at a vanity table, a bottle of bourbon and a half-empty glass in front of her. She was still dressed for the western epic—like a saloon girl who's just had a rough time with a forty-niner out to make his score an even fifty.

The plunging neckline of her dress vied with the tattered remnants of its hem, which barely covered the tops of her thighs, for the focal point of interest. It was maybe the first time in my whole life I'd ever felt in need of a gun belt and spurs.

Amber Lacy looked at me like I was an old contract which expired six months back and nobody picked up the option.

"You're from the police?"

"Like I said—County Sheriff's office."

"A real backwoods boy!" She sniffed disdainfully. "You're wearing shoes—that's something."

"You're not wearing much of anything," I said appreciatively, "and that's really something!"

"Keep your mind on your work!" she said tartly. "Don't you have any sense of what's fitting—right after poor Lee's been murdered?"

"It was the fitting I appreciated," I told her, taking another look at that dress. "The way I hear it you could be the reason for Banning getting himself killed, and I'm beginning to understand why."

"What?" She looked at me sharply. "Are you accusing me of murdering Lee?"

"You were chasing him, and his wife didn't go for the idea," I said mildly. "Jason Kemp threatened both you and Banning, didn't he?"

"You've been talking to that loudmouthed Mavis Seidlitz!" she snapped. "Sure, why should I try and cover for Jason? He busted right in here just before we started shooting this afternoon and sounded off with some wild jazz about Lee trying to put him in bad with Lucian Bliss. Told me if I didn't get Lee to lay off, he'd do something violent about it himself."

"Why tell you?" I said doubtfully, "Why not tell Lee Banning?"

"Jason figures he's got an edge on me." She bared her teeth in a grimace which didn't even have a coincidental resemblance to a smile. "Because we were married one time."

"Just the once?" I asked innocently.

"You're cute," she snarled.

"There could be another reason," I said. "Kemp figured you had Banning right where you wanted him so he'd listen to anything you said, maybe."

"Maybe." She shrugged her beautiful creamy-white shoulders. "I wouldn't know."

"How about the jealous wife? You think she could have killed him?"

Amber shrugged again. "You're the detective—don't ask me."

"Did she ever make any threats?"

"A million! She was in here this afternoon, five minutes before Jason—it got so this place looked like the corner of Hollywood and Vine—leave her husband alone or she'd cut my throat. Maybe she would have done it right then, but Mavis for once in her stupid life got useful and tossed Peggy out of the trailer on her ear."

"Honest?" I exclaimed, doing a double take. "She doesn't look like that much muscle to me—except maybe in the head! Is there anyone else besides his wife who'd want Banning dead?"

"Honey," she said with the unconscious condescension of a twelve-year-old explaining the birds and bees to her younger brother, "Lee was the star of the series—naturally everybody would hate his guts."

"Who's everybody?"

"Mel Parker for one—he's played second fiddle in the series for three seasons now. But he's got some following—and with Lee gone, they might just do the rest of the series with him as the star."

"He's got enough ambition to murder his opposition?"

"Why don't you ask him?" she said flatly. "And while you're busy asking, maybe you should ask dear old Lucian Bliss about his troubles with Lee demanding a new contract and all."

"You're not what I'd call a help," I said glumly. "I had this thing figured as a neat and orthodox homicide—open and shut in a couple of hours—Kemp shot Banning deliberately, not accidentally, and that was all there was to it. Now, you got me real confused."

"You look like you confuse easy, Lieutenant!" she said acidly.

She tilted the bourbon bottle until the glass was full to the top, then drank with sober concentration.

"Are you holding a private wake—or you just drink every afternoon like it's routine?" I asked.

"I'm emotionally disturbed," she said in a brooding voice. "And you don't help any by watching. Get lost, why don't you?"

Right then I didn't have any better ideas so I walked out of the trailer in time to meet Polnik—ignoring the disappointed look on his face that I was out of Amber Lacy's trailer before he'd had time to get inside.

"They're all back, Lieutenant," he grunted, "like you said."

"I guess that includes Mavis Seidlitz?" I winced.

His face was suddenly a mottled color. "She's worried about you, Lieutenant, figures you must have a real problem by now."

"I've got a nasty feeling she's right," I agreed, "but we're talking about different problems. Did you find the guy who loaded those guns yet?"

"I sure did!" He smiled proudly. "They call him a prop man, Lieutenant, and it don't mean the front guy for a heist man like I figured when I first heard it."

"I know," I said hastily. "What about the guns?"

"He loaded them himself a couple of hours before they left for that old mine shaft," Polnik said gloomily. "He was out of his trailer for maybe an hour at least before they left, so he figures anybody could've gotten inside the trailer and switched the slugs."

"How come they have real slugs on hand as well as blanks, anyway?"

"He told me that. Sometimes they make a close-up of the hero in a gunfight and to make it look real good they fire a real slug into a door panel so it splinters close to the hero—but not too close. They use an expert and he's maybe only five feet away from the door, beside the camera," Polnik explained lengthily.

"That's great!" I said bitterly. "Anybody could have switched the bullets—anybody could have heisted that diamond ring off Banning's finger—and the way I'm hearing it so far, everybody had good reason to want him dead!"

"Maybe we should search them and find out who's got that ring," Polnik suggested hopefully. "I'll start right off with Amber Lacy,

Lieutenant—how about that?"

"It's a nice thought, Sergeant," I told him. "But with what she's wearing she couldn't conceal a subversive thought even. You know where I can find Kemp?"

"Sure." The sergeant pointed down the line of trailers. "The fifth one down on your left, Lieutenant. You want me along?"

"I want you to find the cameraman and make sure we get the piece of film showing Banning actually being shot," I said. "Give him a gentle nudge like if anything happens to that film we'll book him as an accessory before, after, and during the fact."

Polnik walked away with one last longing look at the closed door of Amber Lacy's trailer, and I started toward the one that housed Jason Kemp, but I didn't get there. Two guys appeared from behind another trailer and walked toward me rapidly. One was a slim little guy, immaculately dressed, and the other looked like Mr. America of 1932 who'd started running to fat in 1933 and just kept going. I had them tagged before they got within talking distance—Mavis's unlikely twins.

They stopped in front of me and the small guy smiled politely while his eyes X-rayed my skull.

"Lieutenant Wheeler?" His voice was neat and precise like the rest of him. "I am Kent Ivorsen. This is Mr. Toro."

"Something on your mind?" I asked.

"Ugh!" Toro grunted.

I looked at him for a moment, then back at Ivorsen. "Something on *your* mind, I meant," I said. "I don't expect miracles."

"I have a financial interest in the *Dead Shot* series," Ivorsen explained carefully. "So naturally I am most disturbed by the unfortunate death of its chief actor, Lieutenant. While I appreciate the necessity of your investigation, I'd like your assurance you won't interfere with our schedule—once we get it straightened out again."

"How will you overcome the basic problem now you don't have Banning anymore?" I asked, genuinely fascinated. "Use a voodoo expert to hex him into a zombie for the rest of the picture?"

"We've already overcome that problem," he said placidly. "Bliss doesn't see it my way yet, but he will. We'll do the obvious, Lieutenant— promote the second lead to the starring role and begin this one all over again, with a few script changes, of course. I expect you know Mel Parker has been playing the second lead all through the series so far?"

"Sure," I said. "There's only one possible problem—why don't you make sure first it wasn't him that killed Banning?"

"You think he did it?" Ivorsen blinked at me thoughtfully.

"No," I admitted, "but I don't have any reason to think he didn't, either."

He sighed gently, then held up his right hand and snapped his fingers once. Toro grunted and dug a cellophane-wrapped cigar out of his top pocket, carefully stripped off the wrapping, and placed the cigar between the first and second fingers of Ivorsen's hand. A couple of seconds later he struck a match and shielded the flame carefully until the cigar was lit to his boss's satisfaction.

"You don't reassure me, Lieutenant." Ivorsen shook his head reprovingly. "I must make clear to you that we can't afford to waste time. We're spending a great deal of money on this particular show and the more time it takes, the more it costs. I trust I do make myself clear?"

"Would you like me to limit the investigation," I said wonderingly, "like to a couple of hours in the morning —early?"

"The evenings would be better," he said seriously. "While the weather's right, we plan on making a very early start in the mornings, but any time after six in the evenings would be fine."

"I must make clear to you just one point, Mr. Ivorsen," I said gently. "I'm investigating a homicide and if I figure it's necessary for all of you to stand around with your hands in the air for the next week, that's what you'll do. I trust I do make myself clear?"

"You would be ill advised to make any unnecessary delays to our shooting schedule, Lieutenant," he said curtly. "I am not without influence."

"There's an easy way out of this," I said hopefully. "Help me find Banning's killer."

Ivorsen stared at me for a moment like I was a slab of raw steak offered for approval on a waiter's platter.

"You have any ideas who might have killed him?" I prodded.

"It certainly wasn't any member of our cast," he said deliberating. "If I had to make a choice at the moment, I'd settle for that faker, Drew Fenelk. He's been trying desperately hard to earn the liberal retainer paid him by a gullible producer. I hear he forecast danger, disaster, and death—if Mr. Bliss didn't take his advice. Maybe Fenelk felt an imperative need to make his forecast come true—take Fate into his own hands, so to speak."

"It's an interesting theory," I said. "I'll take a closer look at it."

"At once, if you please." Ivorsen smiled wanly at the man mountain beside him. "Come, Toro, we mustn't detain the Lieutenant from his work!"

"Ugh!" Toro grunted his agreement.

"Who knows?" Ivorsen smiled vaguely. "Maybe we will be able to help him find his murderer."

I leaned against the wall of Jason Kemp's trailer and lit a cigarette while he paced up and down. He looked tough and intelligent and that combination made him two up on me already.

"Somebody played it real cool," he growled. "Set me up for the patsy, Lieutenant, and I don't like it!"

"Maybe," I said without any enthusiasm. "But they were taking an awful chance, weren't they?"

"Why?" He stopped pacing for a moment and stared at me hard. "All they had to do was read the script—it was all written down there for anyone to see—I fired two shots at Parker, then one shot at Banning."

"So they reloaded your gun—the first two blanks, and the third a live slug—for Banning."

"Sure," he said. "What else?"

"They were taking an awful chance you'd even hit him—let alone kill him," I snapped. "But if it was you who reloaded the gun—then you'd be real careful you killed him."

He grinned at me wearily. "I don't want to boast, Lieutenant, but shooting is a hobby of mine—I've got a showcase full of cups and shields at home. I'm a marksman—a dead shot with a pistol. Ask anyone around the lot! Everybody in the business knows it—and whoever put the live slug in that gun knew I'd automatically aim accurately at Banning's chest as I pulled the trigger. Ask anyone!"

"Don't worry—I'll ask everyone," I said sourly.

"I don't get it," he said almost to himself. "I just don't get it—why me?"

"Maybe Banning had the same thought when that slug hit him," I suggested. "You threatened both Amber Lacy and Banning before the murder—in Amber's trailer. What was that about—exactly?"

"Banning had been trying to make trouble for me with Lucian Bliss," he said evenly. "Tried to get me thrown off the production—I only found out from his wife this morning that Amber was chasing him. I was married to her once,"—he grinned bleakly—"for four whole days! I figured Amber didn't want an ex-husband around and neither did Banning—that was why he was working on Bliss so hard."

"Why did it worry you that much?" I asked.

The grin slid from his face leaving the bleakness behind.

"I guess it's true, huh, Lieutenant. A cop is like a priest or a psychoanalyst. When you're in as deep as I am right now anyway, your only hope is to make a clean confession." His jaw set hard. "O.K.—I'm on the skids. It's as simple as that—not one movie in the last three years and strictly eating money from television. No guest billing, not even featured player—just my name in a list of other names at the end of the credits. This opening show Lucian's doing for *Dead Shot* this season is a real break—a lot of publicity, and I get the featured player treatment. It can make all the difference, Lieutenant. I can't afford anything to go wrong with it!"

"You make it sound like a motive for murder."

The grin came back as he shook his head slowly. "You're wrong—somebody set it up and me along with it. I'd like to know who, too."

"Maybe you can make a guess," I said.

Kemp thought for a long moment, then shook his head slowly. "No, I can't even do that. Amber isn't exactly a fan of mine but I doubt if she hates me that much—and her killing Banning doesn't make sense anyway."

"How about Mrs. Banning? She told you why her husband was gunning for you with Bliss—maybe she bet on you having a fight with Amber, one that would be remembered later."

"Peggy?" He considered it for a couple of seconds, then rejected it. "I don't see her being smart enough to plan this kind of deal—it needed a lot more brains than she's got. She isn't the subtle type, Lieutenant. If she was going to murder her husband, she'd have cut his throat in Amber's trailer so the blood messed up Amber's things!"

"If I've got a choice between the least obvious suspect and the most obvious," I said, "I'll take the most obvious. Right now that's you—and you're not even trying to give me an alternative. This I don't dig."

"Well, there's Kent Ivorsen," he said doubtfully. "But I can't see any motive because he's got big money tied up in the show. You know about him, of course?"

"Know what about him?"

"I thought everybody knew about Kent." He stared at me in genuine surprise.

"I'm just a hick from Nowheresville," I said, grating my teeth, "so fill me in on the detail!"

"Sure—Ivorsen's only been legit the last four or five years," Kemp said easily. "Before that he had quite a reputation in Florida as a strictly illegitimate operator—gambling mainly, the way I heard it—but a real tough boy. Then he quit suddenly, came to the West Coast and started investing his money in legit enterprises—like *Dead Shot*, for example."

"That explains the tame monster he carries around all the time," I said.

"Toro—the ex-bodyguard who's never gotten around to being an ex," Kemp agreed. "I've often wondered if Ivorsen keeps him because he's got an uneasy conscience or because it's just an ingrown habit with him."

"How about Mel Parker?" I went on doggedly. "Ivorsen just told me Parker's taking over where Banning left off so quick. Maybe Parker saw his big opportunity and took it."

"Maybe." Kemp didn't sound like he believed it. "I doubt if he'd have the guts."

"You think it needs guts to let somebody else do your killing without them even knowing it?" I asked mildly.

Kemp shrugged his broad shoulders. "Put it that way and I guess you're right—maybe I meant I don't see Parker having the brains for it, either."

"How about Bliss?"

"Lucian?" He laughed with genuine amusement. "He'd have to wait until the stars were right!"

"Maybe he did—Fenelk forecast the whole deal."

"Fenelk!" he said contemptuously. "A con man with a penny-ante pitch!"

"The way you tell it," I said thoughtfully, "nobody's got the brains or the guts for it—except you."

5

Mavis Seidlitz

I didn't get to see silly Lieutenant Wheeler again that afternoon which was just as well because I'd have given him a moment of truth like they say in the casting offices, I mean all the trouble and embarrassment what with the rude answers I kept getting and everything and at the last moment he didn't even wait to find out where it was.

Around six that night, Mr. Bliss told me he was having an important conference in a half-hour's time and he wanted me along with a notebook to take notes. It brightened me up a little—him wanting me along at an important conference—so I used the half-hour to have a quick shower and get dressed in the new dress I'd brought along with me.

It's kind of cute in black with a chalky white binding around the high neckline and right down the front, and it's got military buttons all the way down the front, too. It's the kind of dress that's hard to come by because at first glance it looks demure, and then it doesn't—when a man looks a second time you can see his imagination gets to work right away on those military buttons. I figure the designer had in mind the tired executive whose secretary has to keep up a businesslike front and at the same time show him her front isn't all business.

When I arrived on time at Mr. Bliss's trailer I saw there were a few people there already, including Mr. Ivorsen and Mr. Toro. I made real sure I didn't get to sit next to Mr. Ivorsen—I mean my shorthand makes me concentrate hard enough, without getting a lesson in touch-typing thrown in for free. So I sat between Jason Kemp on one side of me, and Mel Parker on the other.

Drew Fenelk was there already with Mr. Bliss and neither of them looked very happy. Then five minutes later Amber drifted in, wearing a blue silk shirt and a pair of skin-tight velvet pants and looking like the honeymoon was over but only just. Peggy Banning was missing and I figured she was too upset to worry much about what was going to happen to *Dead Shot* now that her husband had crossed the Great Divide.

Mr. Bliss looked at all of us like we were suffering from the same incurable disease and I got my notebook and pencil ready, remembering what they told me at secretarial school about always keeping alert otherwise you might be taken unawares and Gosh! that was nothing but the truth with so many guys like Mr. Ivorsen around these days.

"I know how we all feel for Mrs. Banning at this time," Mr. Bliss said, running his hands through his hair in a gesture of remembrance. "And I know the strain this dreadful tragedy imposes on all of us. But if the series is to continue we have to get to work on it right away or it'll fold up underneath everyone."

He took a deep breath and raised his eyes sorrowfully toward the ceiling of the trailer. "I like to think that Lee Banning is right here with us now in spirit, encouraging us, adding his enthusiasm and determination to the proud tradition of the show must go on!"

"It figures, Lucian," Amber said in a listless voice. "We all lose dough if it doesn't."

Mr. Bliss winced visibly. "Well, that's a practical way of looking at it—why don't we get right down to business?"

Drew Fenelk shook his head disapprovingly. "I tell you again, Lucian, now is not the time. Your conjunction is still bad—very bad. Leo moves into the house of Mars—"

"—and we waste valuable time listening to such nonsense," Mr. Ivorsen interrupted in a sad voice. "Get to the point, if you please, Lucian."

"Sure." Mr. Bliss carefully avoided seeing the look of hurt indignation on Drew Fenelk's face. "I guess it's obvious to everybody that with Lee Banning dead, we have to start over with a new leading character and a new script. I've got two writers working over the script right now and they'll have enough done for us to start a new shooting schedule in the morning. The more important issue is to create a new star with no time at our disposal—but I'm thankful to say we've overcome that problem. So I want you to meet the new star of *Dead Shot* —" As he paused for a moment, Mel Parker half rose out of his chair beside me.

"—Jason Kemp!" Mr. Bliss finished.

I guess the only sound after he'd made the announcement was the dull thud beside me as Mel Parker slid back into his chair.

"I appreciate the uproarious enthusiasm," Jason Kemp said drily. "It makes me feel good to be on the team!"

"Hey!" Parker said in a strangled voice. "How about me?"

"I'm sorry, Mel." Mr. Bliss gave him a warm sympathetic smile that was only strained around the edges. "You're doing fine in the second lead but it needs an older man to carry the role—a strong character to replace Lee—and you just don't have it yet!"

"But what the hell!" Parker exploded, getting up onto his feet angrily. "I've been with the series since the first damned episode! Four years, Lucian—you know my fan mail is two-thirds the size of Banning's and building the whole time. But you're going to pass me over for a has-been heavy who's on the skids right now!"

Mr. Bliss's face turned the color of that new nail polish I've been trying out the last couple of weeks.

"That's the decision, Mel," he grated. "So shut up and sit down!"

"Just one moment," Mr. Ivorsen said calmly, and everyone turned to look at him because it was the voice of authority speaking all right—it made me feel sixteen again and there was old Miss Thursteton saying in that awful voice, "Mavis, not in the locker room!"

Mr. Ivorsen snapped his fingers. "Toro!"

"Ugh!" Mr. Toro agreed, then took a cigar out of his breast pocket and carefully peeled off the wrapping. Mr. Ivorsen let us all wait breathlessly until he had the cigar going nicely, then he smiled at Mr. Bliss.

"This was not the decision we discussed earlier, Lucian," he said almost primly. "But naturally, you've been upset by the day's events. Sit down quietly for a moment and reflect."

"I'm sorry, Kent," Mr. Bliss said coldly. "But this is my final decision and I don't have to remind you as producer of the show, the casting is my responsibility alone."

"Our young friend is right, you know—" Mr. Ivorsen smiled and nodded benignly toward Mel Parker. "He is the logical choice for the starring role now Banning has departed—and he's my choice, too."

"I don't want to argue the point, Kent," Mr. Bliss said stiffly, "but on this question you don't have a choice."

Mr. Ivorsen's free hand searched around for something soothing until it finally discovered Amber Lacy's thigh and fondled it with absent-minded appreciation.

"Confidence is so hard to come by, Lucian," he said, shaking his head slowly. "I value it above all things—a priceless commodity. So when it disappears, I grieve deeply." The hand holding the cigar patted his chest slowly. "I feel it here, Lucian, right in the heart." The hand on Amber's thigh tightened as he gave it a final squeeze—probing with the sure touch of a Texas cattleman valuing steers on the hoof—before he let go and got to his feet.

"So this is goodbye, Lucian," he whispered. "I wish you well."

For a moment nobody spoke, then Drew Fenelk let out a strangled whinny almost in my ear. "Lucian! If you've ever valued my services, listen to me now! Make no decisions at all—the aspects are even worse than they were this afternoon. There is still danger and disaster"—his voice suddenly dropped to a bloodcurdling whisper—"and still more death to come!"

Mr. Bliss didn't look like he'd even heard him. He was concentrating on Ivorsen, with all the color drained from his face.

"Goodbye?" he gurgled. "You're joking, Kent?"

"When confidence is lost, there is nothing left." Mr. Ivorsen shrugged, bravely accepting the cruelest cuts of outrageous misfortune like the immortal bard said.

"I shall withdraw my financial support immediately," he added casually.

"But you can't do that!" Mr. Bliss snapped. "Not right now—you'll undermine the whole operation, this show, everything! Be reasonable, Kent!" There was a pleading, desperate note in his voice.

"Then restore my confidence, Lucian," Mr. Ivorsen told him politely. "Make the logical choice of Parker as Banning's successor!"

For a long moment there Mr. Bliss didn't speak, I guess because he couldn't. Finally the apple in his throat jumped convulsively a couple of times and he managed to nod.

"O.K.," he said hoarsely. "Parker steps into the lead."

"Don't I get a say in this?" poor Jason Kemp asked harshly.

"I'm sorry, Jason," Mr. Bliss gave him a stricken look. "I guess you don't!"

"I'm glad we're all in agreement." Mr. Ivorsen beamed at everyone as he sat down again and his hand dropped back onto Amber's thigh, only four inches higher this time. I figured Amber must be real tired or something because she didn't even open her eyes.

"This is wrong, Lucian!" Drew Fenelk shouted in a fury of absolute frustration. "You're only making it worse as you go on! As your friend and counselor, I—"

"—interest me greatly." Mr. Ivorsen had gotten back into his bad habit of taking half of someone else's sentence and using it for himself. "I regarded you first as a harmless faker when Lucian insisted that he bring you on location with the rest of the unit. But now I'm wondering if you are harmless—if you've somehow acquired a dangerous mania for your horoscopes and the rest of the nonsense."

"What do you mean?" Fenelk gurgled.

"A sudden thought occurred to me," Mr. Ivorsen said in an icy voice. "Lucian hasn't listened to you much lately, has he? Maybe you got desperate, Fenelk, and your forecasts became more and more alarming—danger, disaster, and death—but still Lucian wouldn't listen to you. Maybe it became an obsession, Fenelk? Maybe you decided to *make* your forecasts come true?"

Drew Fenelk stared at him blindly for a moment, then lunged toward him awkwardly. "You're a monster!" he whimpered. "A foul, filthy—"

"Toro!" Mr. Ivorsen snapped his fingers gently.

"Ugh!" Mr. Toro said thoughtfully and reached out with one massive hand, grabbed hold of Fenelk's lapels, then lifted him effortlessly into the air and carried him out of the trailer, ignoring the fine stream of invective that poured out of Fenelk's mouth like all the signs of the zodiac had gotten together to pelt curses at Mr. Ivorsen.

Amber opened one eye and looked around her beadily. "Is the conference all through?" she asked in a slurred voice. "Or should I go back to sleep?"

Mr. Bliss was looking at Kent Ivorsen with his mouth hanging wide open in amazement.

"Kent," he asked humbly, "you really think Drew could have murdered Lee Banning just to make his own predictions come true?"

"I feel almost sure of it," Mr. Ivorsen said gravely. "Why should anyone else want to kill him and sabotage the production which means income to us all?"

"But he'd have to be crazy to do that," Mr. Bliss said blankly.

"Do you have any proof he isn't?" Mr. Ivorsen asked interestedly.

"I never thought of that," Mr. Bliss said slowly, like he was talking more to himself. "Drew—a schizophrenic!"

"How do you spell that?" I asked eagerly, with my pencil poised ready, but I guess nobody listened because nobody told me.

"He'll have to be watched," Mr. Ivorsen said briskly. "I shall inform the police lieutenant in the morning of my suspicions and I have no doubt he's competent enough to make a thorough investigation. I think we should get back to our major problem, Lucian. We are agreed that

Parker is the man for the role?"

"I guess so," Mr. Bliss said grudgingly.

"Fine!" Ivorsen beamed at him. "Then I can safely leave the rest of the detail in your capable hands, Lucian." He squeezed Amber's thigh again, hard enough for her to open her eyes and glare at him.

"If you want my leg that bad, why don't you just break it off and take it with you?" she snarled at him.

"We all need some stimulus, Miss Lacy," he said warmly. "Why don't you come back to my trailer and have a little nightcap?"

"You mean wear it!" she sneered. "If you want some cozy grabbing games, go play them with the dumb broad over there!" She had the nerve to nod in my direction and it really burned me up—me—dumb!

"Miss Lacy—" The smile had been wiped clean from Kent Ivorsen's face in one quick wipe.

"Get lost!" she said contemptuously. "You little freak!"

He got to his feet slowly, his lips set in a thin line and a look in his eyes that sent cold shivers up and down my spine.

"You drunken bitch!" He hissed the words at her in a cold-blooded fury, then a second later there was a sound like an explosion as the back of his hand slapped the side of her face so hard she was knocked clean out of her chair onto the floor of the trailer. Mr. Ivorsen drew deeply on his cigar, then walked leisurely out of the trailer in a dense cloud of blue smoke.

"I guess that about wraps it up!" Mr. Bliss said weakly. "Mavis! See Amber gets back to her own trailer and she's O.K."

"Right away, Mr. Bliss," I said briskly. "How about my notes? Do you want them now?"

"No!" he snapped.

"Then what will I do with them?" I asked anxiously.

I could see from the tortured expression on his face that my notes were important to him because he was fighting some dreadful battle inside himself. Finally it was all too much for him—he just buried his face in his hands and whispered, "Mavis—get the hell out of here!"

By the time I'd gotten Amber on her feet, Mel Parker had already left and Mr. Bliss still had his face in his hands—taking a catnap maybe. Jason Kemp was standing in front of me, with a grin on his handsome face.

"Can you manage?" he murmured in that deep-timbred voice that kinked my spine every time I heard it.

"I guess so," I said regretfully, "but it was nice of you to ask all the same."

"Ivorsen picked the wrong girl, but he had the right idea," he said softly. "We certainly do need something stimulating. I want a few short and sharp words with Judas Bliss first—how about a drink in my trailer after you've taken care of Amber?"

"Gosh!" I gulped. "That would be fine."

"It could take me a little time to tell Bliss exactly what I think of him," he whispered. "Would you mind waiting in my trailer a little while if I'm not back by the time you get there?"

"It would be a pleasure," I said truthfully.

"Fine!" He smiled right at me and I saw his midnight-blue eyes crinkle when he smiled and it gave me that nervous empty feeling inside like Eve must have had when she first saw the new Adam.

By the time I'd gotten Amber outside the trailer, she'd passed out cold and one good sniff told me it was probably liquor more than Ivorsen's slap that had done it. I slung her over my shoulder and carried her back to her own trailer which wasn't far. After I dumped her onto the bunk she just lay there limp and I figured she wouldn't wake up until morning, so I stripped off her silk shirt and sandals. Then three fast falls helped me wrestle the tight velvet pants down to her ankles.

While I was trying to get my breath back, she opened one eye and looked at me with a hazy, out-of-focus stare.

"Who're you?" she croaked. "Undressing me?"

It made me real mad after all my efforts to make her sleep comfortable. "I'm Lieutenant Wheeler!" I snarled. "Remember me?"

"Oh, sure." She gave me a lopsided smile. "That's O. K. then—I thought you were Ivorsen!"

The eye shut suddenly as her head dropped back to the pillow and she started to snore gently. I guess that first snore was the last straw, like the old proverb says, and I was real hopping mad by then. One last vicious jerk brought the velvet pants clear of her ankles and that left her wearing a strapless bra and a pair of minute silk briefs.

I went over to the dressing table and checked in the mirror to see if I looked O.K. for my date with Jason Kemp. I borrowed Amber's lipstick for a small repair job, and then I had a flash of inspiration—the kind only a woman can get because men just don't have that basic fiendish feline streak in their make-up—the suckers!

With the lipstick still held firmly in my right hand, I tiptoed over to the bed and used it to write carefully across her bare midriff, "Ivorsen was here." I figured gleefully she'd have more than a hangover to worry about in the morning.

6

Mavis Seidlitz

On the way over to Jason Kemp's trailer I realized I was still carrying my notebook full of notes on the conference and somehow I had a feeling Mr. Bliss wouldn't want them tonight, and I certainly didn't want to give Jason any encouragement to sit down and read. I mean it's just not my idea of a romantic interlude ever since that time I went out with that poet who used to read his own poetry to me all the time—it didn't even rhyme—and the one time I couldn't stand it any longer and kissed him, he fainted.

So I detoured to my own trailer and left the notebook and pencil there, then walked down to Jason's trailer and knocked gently on the door. Nobody answered, so I pushed the door open and walked in and found he wasn't back yet—maybe he'd decided to give Mr. Bliss some long sharp words instead of short ones.

His trailer was about the same size as mine, which made it a little on the small side, and I didn't have much choice of where to sit—either the bunk or a straight chair on the floor—and I'm just not built to sit on floors or straight chairs. So I sat on the bunk and waited for Jason and while I waited I exercised my brain like it says you should in the slick magazines. Nothing frivolous about clothes or anything—real deep stuff like love and emotion and the things that break down a girl's resistance to the point of final surrender. I even got around to making a mental list that ran to five pages. Then I grouped them in order of importance—the guy who first invented the couch came top of the list.

Maybe fifteen minutes after I'd sat down on the bunk, I heard somebody's footsteps outside coming closer and closer, until they stopped at the door. In the couple of seconds before Jason stepped inside the trailer I put a quick mental match to my five-page list just to be on the safe side—you never can tell who's telepathic these days.

Then Jason was inside the trailer and I noted how carefully he made sure the door was closed real tight before he came across to the bunk.

"I'm sorry I took so long, Mavis," he said apologetically, "but we had to get Fenelk straightened out."

"You mean Mr. Toro left him all twisted up?" I asked brightly.

"Not exactly." He grinned and my spine knotted in ecstasy again. "He just dumped him back in his own trailer and locked the door on the outside. Fenelk got hysterical, so I went with Bliss and helped calm him down. He's O.K. now—his door isn't locked and now his ego's restored—but he's still predicting disaster and death all because he claims Lucian made a dreadful mistake in agreeing to Mel Parker taking Banning's place." Jason grinned bleakly. "I'll go along with that, naturally! Fenelk's also threatening Ivorsen with a ten-million-dollar suit for assault and personal injury to both his person and professional reputation. Offhand, I would say he is a guy with problems."

"I almost feel sorry for him," I said, "and I would if I was sure he's a genuine screwball and not just a clever phony. How do you feel about him?"

"If you'd seen him just now," Jason said soberly, "you'd be on Kent Ivorsen's side—Fenelk's really flipped his wig!"

He opened a cupboard and took out a bottle of Scotch and two glasses. "Anyway," he said, shrugging his powerful shoulders, "let's forget him. The idea was a little stimulus would do us both a lot of good, right?"

"Right," I agreed. "Make mine a small one, please."

"You won't get much stimulation from a small one, Mavis," he said reprovingly. "Let your hair down, honey, this is a party!"

"Oh," I said frigidly. "You didn't tell me you'd asked some other people along."

"Two people like us can make it a party, honey!" he said confidently.

I watched while he made the drinks and brought them over to the bunk. The glass he gave me didn't look like it held a small drink, not the way it was, full to the brim.

"Here's to a close and intimate friendship, Mavis!" Jason said softly and clinked his glass against mine which would have been real romantic only some of the Scotch spilled on my knees.

"Likewise!" I said sincerely and drank some of the whisky.

The taste reminded me of the mouthwash I swallowed once by mistake instead of gargling like it said on the label, but I managed not to pull a face because I know drinking is one of the hazards a romantic girl has to endure while she sits around waiting for the romancing to start.

"Ah!" Jason grunted happily. "This is what I need after a long hard day. One hell of a day—treachery in the morning, death in the afternoon; and for maybe a half-hour there tonight I was the new star of the *Dead Shot* series."

"I thought Mr. Ivorsen was real mean going on the way he did," I said indignantly. "I mean, that Mel Parker's O.K. I guess, but he's only a kid and Mr. Bliss was absolutely right when he said you'd make the best replacement for Banning because the part calls for a more mature and stronger character." I could feel myself warming up to the theme like I was dedicated or something. "A guy who's got that virile masculinity us girls go for, that's you, Jason! Well, you only got to make a comparison with Mel Parker to realize what I mean—how can he compete against a man who's tall, dark, and handsome, and mature along with it, huh? Tell me?"

"Why—Mavis, honey!" Jason looked at me warmly and for a moment I thought I saw something electric snapping in his eyes, but maybe it was just the lousy light inside the trailer. "Just love to hear you talk." He smiled down at me with a kind of quizzical look on his face. "The biggest thing an actor ever has going for him is his own ego. I could just sit here and listen to you talk nice things about me all night!"

"That wasn't the idea—exactly," I told him.

"To say nice things about me?" he queried.

"To just sit here and talk all night," I hinted delicately. Jason tilted his glass abruptly and emptied it fast like one of those anonymous alcoholics who won't tell their names to a bartender. Then he put the glass down and a moment later his arm slid around my shoulders—I only just had time to get rid of my own glass before his other arm slid around my waist. Like the girl on the beach who yearned for the lifeguard, I went with the tide.

Being kissed by Jason Kemp was a real experience and I enjoyed it. I mean being so close to a hunk of virile man like him isn't an opportunity a girl gets every day and I figured on making the most of it. The only trouble was when we got to where I figured the pace should slow down a little, all I had to fight with was a permanently kinked spine and a hollow feeling inside.

I guessed vaguely that Jason must have been in the Army sometime or maybe the Marines, because those military buttons were no trouble to him at all and by the time I'd gotten the will power to tell him to stop it was too late to worry—there was my cute new dress neatly draped over the back of the chair and there was me draped wildly all over the bunk. There was a big decision I had to make fast right there and then, but from the eager gleam in Jason's eye he figured it wasn't up to me at all. Then there was a slamming sound as the trailer door crashed open, followed by a high-pitched hysterical feminine voice demanding Jason should stand up so she could shoot him. It was kind of unnerving and I struggled up frantically into a sitting position to see who the heck it was because I've always thought I'd feel silly being shot in my underwear. From the look on Jason's face as he sat up on the bunk beside me he must have felt the same way.

Peggy Banning stood just inside the doorway, facing us with an enormous gun in her hand and from where I sat the barrel looked big enough to mount on a battleship.

"You killed him," Peggy said in a low brooding voice which sounded more frightening than her first hysterical yell. "You shot him down in cold blood because you were jealous—couldn't stand the comparison between Lee's success and your own failure!"

"You're wrong, Peggy," Jason said, watching her cautiously.

Her bottom lip curled. "Don't lie! Lee was right on top as an actor, starring in *Dead Shot*, while you've been on the skids so long the grease is running hot. He was even making your ex-wife while all you could do was stand around and watch!"

"You got it all wrong," Jason said evenly. "I killed Lee accidentally—the real killer substituted a live bullet for a blank in the gun."

"That's right," Peggy sneered, "crawl! Crawl on your belly and beg, Kemp! It won't do you any good. I'm going to kill you the way you murdered Lee, but you've got an advantage—you know what's coming."

I was getting a cramp sitting in the one position all the time so I wiggled a little and recrossed my legs and pulled my slip down over my thighs at the same time. It was a shame, Peggy being a woman I mean—otherwise my legs would have distracted her attention—but there it was and there she was with that gun and all. The more I tried to figure the whole situation, because I'm an expert in tactics which I learned from a Marine sergeant once along with unarmed combat, the more I figured it was up to me to do something because if Jason even twitched a little the odds were Peggy would put a .45 caliber bullet through him right where it would hurt most.

"Peggy, honey," I said softly, giving her a we're-all-girls-together smile. "You don't want to be hasty about this. Supposing Jason's right? I mean, you'd never forgive yourself for shooting him would you?—and the State wouldn't either."

"Shut up, you muscle-bound hustler!" she snarled at me.

"Muscle-bound!" I snarled right back. "Don't you dare call me that! Maybe my curves are a little generous—and let's face it, honey, you could use some yourself to take away from that angle-iron look—but I don't have muscles, only firmness!"

"Angle-iron look!" Peggy hissed. "Why, you overweight frowzy—"

"Frowzy!" I yelped. "You look like a string bean, honey, and your hair matches. All you need is a crew cut and the boys will be calling you 'Mac.'"

She'd made me so mad I forgot all about the gun and stood up ready for combat.

"*Mac!*" Peggy shook with uncontrolled fury. "You asked for it, Mavis, and you're going to get it—right now!"

I'd taken a couple of steps toward her while she was still talking, but then I froze on the spot as she twitched the gun in my direction so I looked straight down the barrel.

"They can only put me in the gas chamber once!" Peggy spat the words at me. "So it makes no difference if I kill both of you."

Well, I had to admit to myself she was right but it was no consolation—I figure sometime when the fun's gone out of romance I'll maybe get married and live quietly the next forty years, but Peggy sounded like she was going to ball up my schedule but good.

"Do me a favor, Peggy," Jason said in a hard voice. "Shoot me first?"

"How did you get to be a hero so quick?" she snapped.

"The way I see it," Jason grinned nastily, "you won't have a chance of killing both of us—whichever one is last on your schedule is going to jump your gun while you're busy shooting the first one. I've still got a few gentlemanly instincts left—so shoot me first and Mavis can jump you while you're doing it."

The gun twitched again so it pointed at Jason instead of me. It looked like it was now or never and I remembered a girlfriend once told me she who hesitates is lost which was nothing but the truth because a couple of weeks later she hesitated when she meant to say no fast, and now she's married with twins and a cost-of-living problem called George.

I rolled my eyes and staggered a little, then made a low, moaning sound like the call of a half-wild goose, before I pitched forward onto the floor praying Peggy would think I'd fainted. The floor was hard like a rock and I just knew I was going to bruise in a couple of awkward places. But the main thing was it brought Peggy's ankles within grabbing distance and I grabbed frantically, then jerked hard so she fell over backward and collected a couple of bruises for herself.

There was a dull thud as that damned cannon dropped out of her hand and bounced off my head. I staggered onto my feet with the walls of the trailer doing a mambo, while a streak of lightning shot past me and picked up the gun.

"Mavis!" Jason straightened up with the gun in his hand and beamed at me. "I could kiss you for that."

"No need," I gasped. "I've got the reaction already?" I shook my head a couple of times and the walls slowed down. I wished the music would slow down too but some budding Krupa was working up a solo drum-break. That was bad enough but when the way-out chanteuse started in with those wildcat improvisations it was murder!

"Peggy!" Jason roared suddenly. "Shut up!"

I looked down and saw who was to blame for the music session—Peggy was still flat on her back, her heels drumming wildly and hysterical shrieks issuing from her wide-open mouth like refugees from the

Metropolitan.

"She's hysterical," Jason deduced brilliantly.

"I can take care of it," I told him happily.

I hauled Peggy onto her feet which took care of the drumming heels, then slapped her face a couple of times—well, maybe I did put some beef into it but it was strictly therapeutic. It was so quiet after she suddenly stopped yelling that I made a mistake and let go of her. Her knees buckled and she collapsed onto the floor again out cold.

"Did you need to slap her so hard?" Jason asked in an awed voice. "I mean I figured the whole idea was to *stop* a murder."

"She's only fainted," I said, crossing my fingers and taking a close look to make sure she was still breathing. "I guess I'd better take her back to her trailer. First Amber and now Peggy—it's getting monotonous!"

"It was bad luck she came in when she did," Jason said in a wistful voice.

"I think it was good luck," I said truthfully. "If she'd arrived a couple of minutes later she might have killed the both of us with one bullet."

For some reason the look on his face got even more wistful.

"How about I take her back—and you wait right here for me?" he suggested hopefully.

"I don't think so, honey," I said sadly. "I'm leaving anyway. This interlude with Peggy wasn't what you'd call real romantic, was it? It kind of killed the mood, so I guess I'll just drop her off and go on back to my own trailer."

I reached out for my dress, but Jason picked it up first and I must say he told Peggy the truth when he said he had a few gentlemanly instincts left. The tender care he took in helping me get that dress back on reminded me of that great gentleman of history, Sir Walter Rally, who threw his best cloak in the mud so Queen Elizabeth wouldn't get damp and maybe catch cold while they had fun in the lousy English climate.

The only thing was I had to kind of revise my ideas about Jason having been in the Army sometime because he had all kinds of trouble doing up those military buttons, fumbling with each one, and then having to go back every time and check he'd really done up the one before in the right way. Finally I had to tell him I couldn't understand it because he'd had no trouble undoing them in the first place at all, but he was so busy fumbling he didn't even hear me—I think.

Peggy was still out cold when he eventually finished, so I hoisted her over my shoulder while Jason opened the trailer door for me.

"Change your mind and come back, honey, please!" he pleaded as I walked past. "Even if we only have a drink and talk a little?"

"I'll think about it," I promised, "but I don't honestly think I can make it because it's hip and hair night."

Jason stared at me blankly. "You're hip—this I dig—but hair?"

"Two hundred strokes of the brush for the hair—and exercise for the hips," I explained. "A girl has to keep in trim, honey, else she'll wind up married to some dull little guy whose idea of fun is asking awkward questions at a P.T.A. meeting!"

I went out of the trailer and humped Peggy back to her own trailer which, because of her husband's star treatment, was one of the most luxurious in the camp. It even ran to two separate beds instead of bunks. I dropped her on the nearest one—they weren't marked "His" and "Hers" and anyway I figured it didn't matter much now.

A couple of seconds after I'd put her on the bed she opened her eyes and looked at me dully.

"Take it easy, honey," I told her. "Everything's O.K. now. All you need is a good night's sleep."

"I must have been out of my mind!" she whispered. "After it happened I came straight back here and sat on the bed and thought about it. I guess I got myself so worked up about losing Lee, I didn't think straight anymore. I'm sorry, Mavis!"

"Think nothing of it," I said brightly. "I'm sorry I slapped you so hard."

"I had it coming," she said. "Tell Jason Kemp I'm sorry too, will you?"

"Sure." I nodded. "Why don't you take your things off and get into bed?"

"The funny thing," she said tonelessly. "I loved Lee—I was crazy about him. He wasn't even a nice guy, he was a louse, Mavis, nothing but a louse!"

"Don't think about it anymore," I said sympathetically. "Why don't you try and get some sleep?"

"He never grew up," she went on, ignoring my good suggestions. "He was a big kid but a nasty, arrogant kid. Lucian Bliss made him into a star from nothing and Lee showed his gratitude by demanding a new contract. No dame under seventy was safe when he was around—he was the most predatory man I ever knew. Every new woman was a challenge to his ego—"

A sudden, unearthly sound from somewhere outside stopped Peggy in midsentence. Her face paled quickly. "What was that?" she whispered.

"I don't know," I said nervously. "It sounded like a scream or something."

Then it came again and this time there was no doubt at all—it was a scream. A horrible, sickening sound like someone or something was in violent agony.

"Mavis!" Peggy reached out and grabbed my hand tightly.

I gulped and tried to smile at her. "Maybe it's nothing," I said, trying hard to stop my teeth chattering. "I'll go take a look and be right back."

I stumbled out of the door and stared frantically up and down the trailer line. The bright moonlight showed clearly there was no one outside and for a moment I wondered if we'd both imagined we heard the scream.

Then I heard a soft, shuffling sound from somewhere close around me. My blood seemed to freeze in my veins and I couldn't move a muscle. The shuffling sound continued, and it sounded as if it was coming closer to me the whole time. I managed to move my head, looking from side to side desperately to see what made the sound.

From behind the trailer next to Peggy's, the figure of a man appeared. It looked like a very old man, bent double and shuffling along slowly as he fought to drag the weight of his tired old body toward me. I still couldn't move from the spot where I stood, so I watched as he took a few dragging steps toward me, his arm raised in a curiously pleading gesture, before he sank gently to the ground.

It made me feel ashamed. I mean there was this poor old man looking for help and all I could do was just stand and watch him because some nightbird had scared the wits out of me. Mavis, I told myself as I ran toward him, it just shows how stupid you can get when you let your imagination run away with you!

I knelt down beside him as he lay still on the ground in a doubled-up position with his face turned away from me, and said, "Are you in pain?"

He didn't answer—in fact he didn't even move—and then I got real worried. I slipped one hand gently between the hard earth and the side of his face, then lifted his head toward me. For a timeless moment his wide-open, tortured eyes stared at me blankly, then I let go of his head in a convulsive reflex so it flopped back onto the ground again.

I stood up slowly, hearing a panic-stricken whimpering sound from somewhere close and it took a little while to realize it was me making the noise. An old man, I'd thought, a poor old man too tired to lift his head as he walked. When I'd lifted his head it had been a young man's eyes that stared back at me from Mel Parker's face.

I thought wildly there had to be a reason for him walking that way—bent double—shuffling along as though each separate step was an agonized effort. The horrible screaming sounds must have come from him and not any nightbird, I realized painfully.

The moon reappeared from behind a cloud as I knelt down beside him again and forced myself to look closely. A shaft of silver light spilled across the body and then I saw it—the knife buried almost to the hilt in his stomach. His right hand was still clenched around the two inches of naked blade that hadn't penetrated his flesh, and the fingers were stained with a glistening, dark-colored wetness.

Something glittered on the haft of the knife and I peered closer and saw it looked like some kind of badge. The moonlight strengthened rapidly and then I could see it clearly enough to pick out the detail of the silver ram that sat patiently against a background of tiny stars. I didn't have to be Drew Fenelk to recognize the zodiac sign of Aries.

Dimly I heard voices and the sound of running feet, then a strong hand caught hold of my elbow and helped me onto my feet again.

"Mavis!" Jason said urgently. "Are you O.K.?"

"I'm fine," I stammered. "It's Mel Parker—somebody stabbed him—I think he's dead!"

"All right," Jason said tensely. "You're sure you're O.K.?"

"Just fine," I repeated mechanically. "I—"

I stopped suddenly because it happened—the end of the world, I mean—they'd dropped the bomb and I guessed it was more powerful than they'd even realized. The end of everything including Mavis Seidlitz and somehow I didn't even care. I was too fascinated watching the moon swinging around and around in crazy circles, going faster all the time until it made me dizzy and I had to close my eyes. There was no relief even then—the crazy gyrating moon suddenly swooped down at me, blotting out everything else just as a disembodied voice from outer space announced, "It's the shock of finding him—better take her back to her trailer."

7

Al Wheeler

Some hip character once called it the witching hour when graveyards yawn and he knew what he was talking about—midnight. I yawned right along with the graveyards. The long day was turning into a longer night and I was beginning to feel like a piece of film being run backward through the projector.

It started out with a corpse in the afternoon, a lot of questions that got me no place, then a long unpleasant session with County Sheriff Lavers—and now we were back where we'd started. There was one difference, we had a fresh corpse.

Doc Murphy wiped his hands fastidiously and launched into a highly technical discourse on how—exactly—Parker had died. I listened sourly until he'd finished, wondered how it was for his wife nights when she felt romantic and he talked veins and arteries and all that jazz.

"So there you have it, Lieutenant!" Murphy said smugly. "The whole story."

"Just to make sure I've got it straight," I said, "he's dead because somebody shoved a shiv into his guts?"

"There is only one thing repels me more than your crudeness," Murphy said with immense dignity, "and that's your personality."

I sighed nostalgically for the lost charm of yesteryear.

"How long would it have taken him to die after he was knifed?"

Murphy grunted cautiously. "Theoretically death would have occurred within seconds, a minute at most. But you're talking about will power, Lieutenant, and that can't be measured scientifically."

"I knew a redhead once," I said reflectively. "You could measure her will power scientifically—in terms of resistance anyway."

A powerful flashlight beam hit me square in the eye, announcing the return of Sergeant Polnik.

"I just found something, Lieutenant," he said eagerly.

"A sure way to blind me?" I snarled.

"Sorry, Lieutenant." He switched off the beam, leaving me in a world of pitch darkness, punctuated by sudden dizzy flashes of light.

"There's a trail of blood leading to one of the trailers!"

The way he said it, it sounded like the title of a campfire song.

"Which trailer?" I opened my eyes and blinked a few times until I could see again without spots getting in the way.

"That one." He pointed triumphantly.

"Whose is it?" I asked the obvious question.

"I don't know," Polnik said sheepishly. "I guess I should go ask, huh, Lieutenant?"

"Never mind," I said. "We'll find out later. You know who found the body?"

"Guess," he said in a hollow-sounding voice.

"Oh, sure," I snarled irritably. "I'm right in the mood to play guessing games with a—no!"

I could feel Polnik brooding for a couple of seconds while he faced up to his problem. "Lieutenant—what's a no?"

"It's a like a prayer," I told him, "only I didn't finish it off like, 'No! Not Mavis Seidlitz!' Now you make my prayer come true, huh?"

"I wish I could, Lieutenant," his voice quavered. "She passed out right after she found it, they tell me, and now she's in her trailer resting."

"You meaning tuning-up," I said gloomily. "Getting into shape to give us a three-hour rundown on the suspects yet."

"I'm all through here," Murphy interrupted briskly. "Want anything before I go, Al—like an aspirin maybe?"

"If you're taking the cadaver with you, we'd better have the knife first," I said. "Look after it, Polnik, will you? Have one of the boys take it into Homicide for the crime lab. Then go talk to Mavis Seidlitz if you can get a word in edgewise and find out why she was the first one to find the body."

"That's an order, Lieutenant?" he croaked.

"Strictly in the line of duty," I said almost happily. "I'll teach you to appreciate your old lady yet!"

I walked across to where Lucian Bliss waited with Ivorsen and his faithful shadow, Toro. Bliss's face looked haggard and I could almost sympathize with him—if this kept up he wouldn't have any actors left.

I pointed out the trailer Polnik had already shown me and asked who owned it.

"Drew Fenelk," Bliss said in a tight voice.

"Is he in there now?" I asked.

"Yes, I think so." His voice sounded constrained in the kind of whisper used by the more distant relatives at a funeral.

"I'm sure of it," Ivorsen said coldly. "I have the key."

"You mean you've got him locked in there—why?"

"There are some things about Fenelk you should know, Lieutenant," Ivorsen said curtly. "As I remember, I told you of my suspicions this afternoon, but apparently you decided to ignore them."

"It was obviously my mistake," I said. "What else should I know about him?"

Ivorsen gave me a fast recount of the meeting they'd had earlier in the night to decide who was to replace Banning in the television series and how Fenelk had gotten hysterical to the point of physical violence, so Ivorsen was forced to have him removed by Toro and locked in his trailer.

"Had my wishes been respected," Ivorsen said heavily, giving Bliss a deathwatch beetle glance as an aside, "I have no doubt this second murder would never have happened."

"The trouble with genius is it takes so long to get recognition," I agreed. "So what happened?"

Bliss cleared his throat nervously. "Well, after the meeting was finished, Jason Kemp stayed behind to talk with me for maybe fifteen minutes. Then we heard a terrific noise coming from Fenelk's trailer so we went over to find out what was happening. He sounded as if he'd gone completely insane—kicking the walls of the trailer and smashing the furniture inside. Jason got the key from Mr. Toro and we went inside and found Drew was completely hysterical."

"The cunning of the professional faker, Lieutenant!" Ivorsen said sonorously. "A man like Fenelk, who lives by trickery, resorts to another trick to win his freedom!"

"It's a funny thing, Mr. Ivorsen," I said courteously, "but you sound more like daytime radio than nighttime television. Go on, Mr. Bliss."

"He said he felt I'd betrayed him at the meeting," Bliss continued in an unhappy voice. "I'd allowed him to be subjected to insults and ridicule and then physical violence—you can imagine the tirade I got, Lieutenant. But the one thing that obviously infuriated him the most was being locked inside his own trailer. After a while Kemp and myself managed to calm him down and I figured the easiest way out was to promise he wouldn't be locked in again—he seemed perfectly rational then."

"The mind apparently rational," Ivorsen said sadly. "But inside—something has already snapped—like that!" He snapped his fingers to emphasize the point and Toro automatically began peeling off the cellophane from a new cigar.

"You mean you think it was Fenelk who killed Parker?" I asked patiently.

"And Banning!" Ivorsen barked. "I explained this before, Lieutenant. It would have been better if you'd paid more attention then!"

"So Fenelk was hysterical," I said. "After what happened at that meeting, I wouldn't blame him, and it doesn't prove anything. Do you have any concrete proof to add to this theory, Mr. Ivorsen?"

"I presume you examined the murder weapon?" he asked coldly.

"The knife," I said. "Sure. It's significant?"

"There was an emblem in silver on the haft."

"A ram," I agreed.

"Denoting the zodiac sign of Aries, Lieutenant!" Ivorsen said triumphantly.

"You lost me again," I admitted.

"Fenelk is an astrologer," he snapped. "His personal sign is Aries—right, Bliss?"

"Right," Bliss mumbled.

"That doesn't make him unique," I objected. "For all we know it's also the personal sign of a dozen more people around here."

"But the knife is his—Lucian has seen it many times—right?" Ivorsen said.

"Right," Bliss said again, nodding. "One of his clients gave it to him after he'd predicted the right movement of some stock. Drew was proud of it almost like a kid—he was always waving it around."

"I guess I'd better go talk with him," I said.

"You'll need the key," Ivorsen said. "I took the precaution of locking him in again after the discovery of Parker's body. Toro!" He snapped his fingers, then held up his hand, palm open, and a moment later the key dropped into it.

Ivorsen smiled thinly as he handed me the key. "I told you we might find your murderer for you, Lieutenant."

"You not only told me, you keep on telling me," I said. "I am getting sick and tired of listening to you, Mr. Ivorsen, and I'd appreciate it if you'd do me a big favor and shut up!"

"Ugh!" Toro growled warningly.

"You could learn a lot from—whatever-it-is—" I told Ivorsen. "He says it all in one grunt."

"Don't trifle with me, Lieutenant," he said icily. "I have—"

"I know," I said wearily, "influence. So while I still have a badge I'd like to ask some questions—like who got to the body after Mavis Seidlitz found it?"

"There was a whole bunch of us," Bliss said. "You see, Lieutenant, Parker screamed a couple of times and it was the most horrible sound I've ever heard in my whole life! I guess it brought most of us outside to see what had happened."

"Did that include you?" I looked at Ivorsen.

"It did."

"You were in your trailer when it happened?"

"Yes." He bristled. "How much more valuable time are you going to waste questioning us when you should be questioning Fenelk, Lieutenant?"

"I said for you to shut up and speak when you're spoken to," I reminded him. "Anybody with you in the trailer?"

He took a deep, shuddering breath. "Yes, Mr. Toro was with me."

"Is that right?" I asked the man mountain.

"I told you already he was there!" Ivorsen snapped.

"Ugh!" Toro added.

"I'd like to hear it from him," I said. "In words."

"I'm afraid that's impossible, Lieutenant." Ivorsen smiled bleakly.

"He can tell me here or back at the Sheriff's office," I growled. "He's got a choice."

"You don't understand," he said. "Mr. Toro can't talk to you any place or at any time. He has no tongue."

"Ugh!" Toro nodded confirmation.

"I'm sorry," I mumbled.

"It doesn't worry him now," Ivorsen said good-humoredly. "He's gotten used to it after all this time—he wasn't twenty when it happened."

"How did it happen?" Bliss asked curiously.

"Mr. Toro was carving a successful career for himself as a stool pigeon but unfortunately he talked about the wrong people and they caught up with him."

Ivorsen paused for a moment, savoring every word. "They tore out his tongue by the roots."

"Ugh!" Toro grunted excitedly, then leaned forward and opened his mouth wide.

I unlocked the door of the trailer and motioned Bliss to go in first. Fenelk was sitting on the bunk, a dejected look on his classic profile.

"Drew," Bliss said quickly, "this is Lieutenant Wheeler, and he wants to ask you some questions."

Fenelk lifted his head and stared at me dully. "Questions?" he repeated in a high-pitched voice. "Is that all? You're sure he doesn't want to insult me or beat me up? Or maybe lock me up again in this trailer?"

Bliss looked at me with raised eyebrows, then shrugged his shoulders eloquently.

"Do you own a knife with a silver emblem on the hilt?" I asked Fenelk. "With a zodiac design—Aries, the ram?"

"It is one of my most prized possessions," he said gloomily, "or was, I should say."

"Was?"

"It was stolen from me sometime tonight." His voice was listless. "But it's not important by comparison to the other things that have happened to me, Lieutenant!" He shook his head in slow bewilderment. "It must be some kind of mass insanity—that's the only explanation I can think of—but what triggered it off I don't know."

"Tell me about it," I suggested.

It was a mistake to open the dam gates without having a fast exit planned. For the next ten minutes I just stood there while a ceaseless torrent of words flooded down on my head. This Fenelk was a kind of male Seidlitz without any of her compensating attributes.

"You certainly had a rough time," I said quickly when he momentarily paused for breath. "Did you hear Parker's screams?"

He shuddered violently. "I most certainly did, Lieutenant! They'll haunt me to my dying day—sounded as if they came from right outside."

"Did you go and see what the noise was about?"

He shuddered again, even more violently. "I'm an absolute physical coward, Lieutenant—I wouldn't have set foot outside this trailer if it had been my mother screaming out there! I stayed right where I was with my eyes shut and hoped whatever it was would go away."

"There's a trail of blood leading from just outside here to where Parker finally died," I said. "He was killed with your knife, Fenelk. How do you explain those two things?"

"Explain!" His voice jumped an octave. "There's a simple explanation, Lieutenant! I'm the victim of a murderous and bloody conspiracy—someone hates me and wants to destroy me for some paranoid reason I don't understand."

He glared balefully at Bliss. "And for some other reason I can't understand, my so-called friends, the people I trusted, have deserted me in my hour of need!"

"You have any idea who's behind this conspiracy?" I prodded.

"Ivorsen!" he shrieked in a frustrated falsetto. "Who else? He's the man who publicly insulted me—who told his brute of a bodyguard to manhandle me—who kept me locked in this trailer as if I were a common criminal or worse! I tell you, Lieutenant, that man's a maniac!"

"Why would he do all these things to you?"

Fenelk lowered his head again dejectedly. "I keep asking myself the same question," he muttered. "If he'd only tell me his birth date I could get a line on him from his natal chart, but he's too cunning to divulge the vital information—a typical paranoid reaction, I might add."

"You predicted the murders," I said. "There's a suggestion you could've given the stars a gentle nudge to make sure your predictions came true."

"I predicted danger, disaster, and death," he snapped, his mouth set in a prim line. "I did not predict who—or how many—would die. Astrology indicates the possibilities and sometimes the probabilities, Lieutenant, but never the absolute." His head jerked up suddenly and he stared at me, wide-eyed. "You mean, you think I murdered Banning and Parker just to prove my predictions were correct?" He laughed incredulously. "I'd have to be stark raving mad to do that!"

"That's the other half of the suggestion," I said helpfully.

I turned and walked out of the trailer with Bliss in back of me, and figured I hadn't exactly been a comfort to Fenelk.

"That you, Lieutenant?" A bulky figure was suddenly silhouetted in the bright moonlight beside me.

"It's me," I agreed reluctantly. "How come you got through with the Seidlitz dame so fast?"

"She won't talk to me," Polnik said happily. "She says she'll only talk to the Lieutenant because you're better looking and you're not married either."

Bliss chuckled gleefully. "That sounds like Mavis!" he said. "I guess you won't want me along, Lieutenant."

"No," I said bleakly, "there's no point in both of us losing our hearing."

Just before you go—where were you when Parker screamed?"

"In my trailer," he said evenly.

"Alone?"

"Alone."

"It would be nice," I said wistfully, "if just once somebody would come up with an alibi!"

"Sorry I can't oblige, Lieutenant," Bliss smiled. "Is that all?"

"For now," I said. "I might get back to you later."

"Fine." He walked away at an easy pace toward his trailer.

I lit a cigarette and scowled at Polnik. "I guess you fixed it so I have to go talk with the Seidlitz dame."

"It was her own idea—honest, Lieutenant!" he said quickly.

"In there," I said, jerking my thumb toward the door of the trailer behind us, "is a guy called Drew Fenelk. Maybe he's just a harmless nut who's had a raw deal—or maybe he's a homicidal maniac who'll make up his mind to go and keep on going. I want you to make sure he stays right where he is—inside that trailer."

"Sure thing, Lieutenant," Polnik said confidently. "I'll keep an eye on him."

"Keep two eyes on him," I suggested, "or else you might finish up in the morgue with the other two stiffs."

8

Al Wheeler

I knocked on the door and waited for a moment but there was no answer, so I walked in.

"Twenty-eight!" a clear, musical voice said breathlessly.

For a couple of seconds I didn't see her, then I looked down and there she was on the floor, stretched out on her back, her legs up in the air with the toes pointing at the ceiling. She wore a short, fingertip-length nightgown in pale blue silk, and a matching pair of briefs that had a lace trim. From where I stood, only her long, delectable legs, rising from the lace trim, were visible. It was almost enough for a man to dwell on in quiet contentment for the rest of his days.

"Twenty-nine!" she said firmly and her legs swayed alarmingly first to one side, and then the other.

"Miss Seidlitz?" I said loudly.

"Thirty!" The legs swayed again from one side to the other, then she let them drop and sat up expectantly.

"I know it's a stupid question," I said, "but why?"

"Why don't you call me Mavis?" she asked warmly. "That Miss Seidlitz jazz makes you sound stuffy and you don't look stuffy at all."

"Why?" I repeated firmly.

"Oh, it's my hip and hair night," she said eerily.

"Something like fox and hounds?" I ventured.

She came to her feet quickly in an epic bouncing movement. "Silly! I give my hair a real good brushing, then do my exercises—it keeps my hips from expanding too much—I figure they're just right as they are." She patted them complacently. "What do you think, Lieutenant?—and if you're going to call me Mavis, I can't keep on with this 'Lieutenant' jazz."

"Al," I said weakly. "And—yeah—I figure your hips are just about right."

She sat on the bunk and leaned back against the cushions, with her hands clasped behind her head so the breathtaking curves of her full breasts sprang into startling outline against the taut silk.

"Come and sit down, Al," she said invitingly.

I went across to the bunk and sat down gingerly beside her. She traced the outline of my jaw delicately with one finger.

"We could have a lot of fun getting to know each other better, Al," she said dreamily, "if I didn't have a romance going already."

"It's a beautiful thought," I said, "and I'd be happy to just sit there and think about it if it wasn't for a couple of unsolved murders."

"Gosh!" She blinked at me a couple of times. "You're a guy who's really got his mind on his job, aren't you, Al? I'm glad of that—I hate a guy who can't think of anything but sex almost as much as I hate a guy who can't ever think of it. I had to find out for sure if you were the right kind so I dreamed up a little test like the shortie nightgown and lace frills and all because I figured if you didn't make a pass in the first five minutes it absolutely proved you were the guy most wanted in my book—and maybe if my other romance doesn't work out the way it should—well, who knows?"

"I'll live in hopes," I snarled. "You don't mind if we talk a little about that corpse you discovered a couple of hours back?"

Her face sobered down suddenly. "Poor Mel," she said softly. "It was horrible."

"How come you got to him first?"

"Well, I was trying to cheer up Peggy Banning and we both heard it and it was ghastly so I went outside to take a look and I didn't see anything at first but then this little old man appeared, walking slowly toward me and all bent over. Well, I was scared, Al, I was—"

"Speechless?" I asked hopefully.

"—rooted to the spot," she said coldly. "Then he just collapsed onto the ground and I went over to help him and discovered it was Mel Parker—it was a dreadful shock and then when I saw that knife sticking out of his stomach!" She shuddered slightly but not delicately—she wasn't built that way.

"How come you were with Peggy Banning?" I asked idly.

"Well—I'd just carried her back from Jason's trailer," she said simply.

"Couldn't she use her own feet?"

"Of course not, silly!" Mavis gave me a pitying smile. "Not after I'd slapped her a little too hard and knocked her out cold!"

"You had a fight?"

"Well, kind of, I guess." A slight frown shadowed her eyes as she figured it out. "You see, Al, I had to slap her to stop the hysterics."

"Hysterics," I repeated slowly. "Brought on by her husband's death, huh?"

"Well—" The frown deepened rapidly. "I guess that had something to do with it but the main reason was she hadn't killed Jason the way she'd planned."

If my eyes widened any more I'd be able to see what went on in back of my head. I fumbled a cigarette out of a new pack and lit it gratefully.

Mavis ploughed on effortlessly until she'd given me the full story from the end of the meeting when she'd carried Amber Lacy back to her trailer after she'd been slugged by Ivorsen, through a little depressing detail of Jason Kemp's masculinity and finally the full detail of Peggy Banning's dramatic entrance and attempted murder.

"So you and Peggy can alibi each other," I said when she'd finished. "That's something—and Kemp was alone at the time of the murder, too."

She stiffened and looked at me coldly.

"You aren't suggesting that Jason could have killed Mel by any chance, Lieutenant Wheeler?"

"I'm only suggesting he had the opportunity like a few other people," I said soothingly.

"That's ridiculous!" she sniffed. "Jason couldn't kill anybody—he's too noble and generous and—"

"Virile?" I suggested.

"You've got a nasty, suspicious mind, Al Wheeler!" she snapped. "I don't think I like you anymore."

"Jason had a good motive," I said, warming to the theme. "From what I hear about that meeting, Bliss had him lined up to take Banning's place until Ivorsen killed the idea by insisting on Parker."

"Jason was disappointed," Mavis admitted grudgingly, "but it's ridiculous to think for a moment he'd murder Mel just to spite him!"

"That must have been one hell of a meeting," I reflected out loud. "I wish I'd been there to hear what really went on."

"If you're that interested," Mavis said coldly, "you can read my notes."

"Notes?"

"Mr. Bliss asked me to take a pad and pencil and make notes because it was a very important meeting." Mavis smiled happily and tried to look modest. "I'm not a stenographer or anything like that so I guess he asked me to do it because he figured it was so important that he could only trust somebody with a very high intelligence—like me!"

"Yeah," I said slowly. "How about that?"

"Only he got so excited he didn't remember to tell me what kind of notes he wanted," Mavis continued doubtfully. "So I just wrote it all down—everything that was said and everything that happened."

"In shorthand?"

"Well—kind of." She looked at me out of the corner of her eye. "It's my own special shorthand really. Instead of using all those silly little squiggles I just write the words down instead—it's so much quicker I wonder everybody doesn't do it."

She got up from the bunk and walked over to the dressing table—her hips moved with the controlled abandon that made all those exercises worthwhile. I stood up as she took a notebook from the dressing table and tossed it across to me.

"I don't think Mr. Bliss will want them now," she said, "so you're welcome to them, Al."

"Thanks, Mavis," I said sincerely, "thanks a lot!"

"Just one thing, Al Wheeler," she said determinedly as I headed for the door. "If you get sneaky and try to blame Jason for the murders—I'll never speak to you again!"

"Mavis!" I closed my eyes and fought hard against it. "Don't tempt me!"

Peggy Banning sat huddled in a heavy robe on the edge of one bed while I sat facing her on the other. Her face was drawn and white, and her hair looked like a bird sanctuary—she was obviously having a tough time.

"I guess you heard already I blew my stack and went after Kemp," she said listlessly.

"I heard. Where did you get the gun?"

"It belonged to Lee—a presentation from his fan club—he took it everywhere with him."

"Do you still have it?"

She shook her head slowly. "I guess Kemp's got it—I dropped the damn thing when Mavis jumped me and I remember vaguely he had it in his hand when I got the screaming meemies. What's the charge, Lieutenant? Attempted murder?"

"There won't be any charge," I told her, "not unless both Kemp and Mavis prefer one. For me, it's only hearsay and nobody got hurt."

She put her hands against her puffed cheeks gently, then smiled. "Only me—that Mavis sure packs a wallop! But thanks, Lieutenant—thanks a lot!"

"I'm more interested in why you were so sure it was Kemp who killed your husband," I said.

"I was halfway out of my mind, I guess," she answered candidly. "Not thinking straight anymore. I figured Jason couldn't stand the comparison at such close range. Lee was a successful actor right on top while Jason's been going down steadily for the last three years or so. And I've always thought Jason still carries a torch for Amber Lacy even though their marriage only lasted four days—and there was Lee making her without even trying and she liked it so much she couldn't leave him alone!"

The raw bitterness in her voice wasn't pleasant listening but whoever promised a cop he'd have a pleasant job in congenial surroundings, anyway?

"I was crazy for Lee—I guess that's pretty obvious, Lieutenant." Her voice softened as she spoke his name. "It must sound like a lament or something." She laughed briefly. "Lament for a lousy lover! But you don't want to hear any more of this?"

"Keep going," I told her. "Maybe it does you good to talk about it, and maybe it'll do me good to hear it—the more I know about Lee Banning, the better."

"I guess you're right—do you have a cigarette?"

After I'd given her the cigarette and a light, she inhaled deeply, appreciating the tobacco for a moment before she spoke again.

"He was a lousy lover even in the technical sense—like he held an overdue mortgage and all he wanted was immediate possession. I've met a few guys you could call a louse in my time, but Lee was something special—he came king-sized! I figure he was faithful to me for the first whole week of our marriage and after that he was back playing the field—one at a time in strict rotation!"

"There must be a lot of guys who'd like to see him dead on that basis," I said dismally.

"Not only on that basis," Peggy Banning said harshly. "He couldn't do anything right—he had to cheat everybody from the newsboy on the corner up! Look at the way he repaid Lucian Bliss for making him what he was!"

"How's that?" I said quickly.

Her face was turned toward mine but her eyes didn't see me—they had that slightly unnerving, out-of-focus stare of complete absorption with a mental image.

"Four years back, Lee was nothing," she said flatly. "One of a couple of thousand other brawny pieces of beefcake registered with Central Casting for extra work. He got his break when he had a walk-on bit in one of Lucian's private eye series—Lucian noticed him and talked to him the next day. He had the *Dead Shot* series in his mind, complete with a format and half a dozen scripts. What he badly needed was someone to play Shep Morrow—and he couldn't afford a name because he'd had to raise all the finance from outsiders like Ivorsen. None of his own money was in it—he didn't have any then. If he got a name to play the lead, the name would automatically demand a percentage and the only percentage left was Lucian's and that was small enough!"

She ground the butt of her cigarette under her heel on the floor, then shrugged. "Anyway—Lucian signed Lee to a seven-year contract starting at two hundred a week and escalating to a thousand as top from the third year on. You know what happened—*Dead Shot* was a sleeper—it could have gone on forever so long as Lee stayed with it.

"It worried Lee—Lucian making all that money while he was only making his l'il ole thousand a week! So before this season started he went to Lucian and demanded a new contract. He didn't want much on top of his thousand a week—only a twenty per cent piece of the ownership and fifty per cent of all the royalties from the Shep Morrow merchandising gimmicks—that was all! Lucian tried to be nice about it and explained the extra costs he was facing with this first show among other things.

"Lee told him the hell with his costs—either he signed the new contract or he'd walk out and leave him flat. For a whole week, every day Lucian would be at the house pleading with him to wait six months and then talk about a new contract but not on Lee's impossible terms. I pleaded with him—reminded him what Lucian had done for us both in three years and he laughed himself sick at the thought of owing somebody a debt they can't collect, like gratitude. At the end of the week, Lee said he'd wait exactly one month and if he didn't have the new contract by then, he'd walk out and he didn't give a damn if he never worked in a studio again!"

"I see what you mean," I said truthfully. "He was the kind of operator who'd never trust an honest deal because he couldn't see anything snide about it."

"I've talked too much, Lieutenant!" Her eyes came into focus suddenly and she looked embarrassed. "You only sat there being polite to the brand-new widow!"

"I was fascinated," I said. "So Lucian signed the new contract anyway?"

"No," she said, shaking her head positively. "There was still another ten days to go to Lee's deadline—from today." The corners of her lips turned down as she smiled slowly. "I wonder what kind of contract he's had to sign now!"

A sudden loud knocking on the door made us both jump.

"Who is it?" Peggy Banning asked sharply.

"Lucian," Bliss's voice called. "Is Lieutenant Wheeler with you?"

I went across to the door and opened it. "What do you want?" I grunted.

"I think you'd better come right away, Lieutenant!" Bliss said breathlessly. "Your sergeant's just had some trouble with Drew Fenelk!"

9

Al Wheeler

A look of relief showed on Polnik's face as I came into the trailer with Bliss close on my heels. Ivorsen and Toro were already inside, standing with their backs against the wall, their faces a studious blank. I figured I could take care of them later—what really worried me was Drew Fenelk stretched out on the floor and not moving. A third cadaver inside twenty-four hours was all I needed to send me hotfoot to the nearest funny farm for a nice new strait jacket I could call my own.

"What the hell happened?" I snarled at Polnik.

He scratched the end of his nose nervously and even the rasping sound had an embarrassed quality to it.

"Well," he mumbled, "like you said, I'm standing outside to make sure this Fenelk character don't take it on the lam, when Mr. Ivorsen and Mr.—" His forehead corrugated for a moment, then he gave up. "—the other guy with him came up and asked was it O.K. if they had a talk with Fenelk. So I figured it was O.K. so long as I stuck close to them."

A plaintive note of self-pity crept into his voice. "So I knocked on the door and when Fenelk opened it, I told him real polite that Mr. Ivorsen and his friend wanted a little confab with him. Then for no reason, the guy blows his stack and starts screaming something about everybody being nuts and now it's hit the cops too and he's not staying for any more persecution by Mr. Ivorsen, he's had enough already!"

"Get to the point—what the hell happened!" I yelped.

"I'm telling you what happened, Lieutenant, if you'll only listen," Polnik said with a betrayed look on his face. "Well—you told me the nut might feel like taking a powder and it was up to me to stop him—didn't you?"

"I did." I grated my teeth savagely. "All I want to know is *how* you stopped him!"

"He came out of the trailer like they just lifted the barrier at Santa Monica and a friend of the jockey told him he could win!" Polnik said with a poetic fervor that left me speechless with wonder.

"So what could I do?" he asked plaintively. "I give him the rush back into the trailer and the next thing is he grabs hold of a chair and comes at me swinging it over his head like to split my skull into two halves—all the way down the middle. So I didn't have no choice, Lieutenant—I had to slug him."

"What with?" I asked reluctantly.

Polnik clenched his Gargantuan paw into an immense fist, then stared at me blankly. "With this, Lieutenant, what else?"

"You mean he's just out cold?" I asked, feeling the relief seep through my tensed muscles in a sudden flood.

"Sure. I guess I hit him pretty hard," Polnik said defensively, "but with that chair and all, I didn't want to take no chances. But he's O.K. There's nothing broken, I mean."

"Is that all?" I said coldly. The relief was suddenly replaced by an overpowering fury. "Then why all the goddamned panic about rushing me back here? I figured you must have killed him at least the way everybody was acting up. What are you trying to do to me, Sergeant?—give me a coronary?"

"Sorry, Lieutenant." He looked sheepishly at the wall two feet above my head. "But there's more."

"Tell me," I whispered hoarsely.

"Well, after I slu—hit him, he dropped the chair and kind of went backward until he bounced off the wall onto the floor."

"Are you insisting on giving it to me the hard way—round by round?" I queried, feeling my lips curl back from my teeth as I spoke.

"No, sir!" Polnik ventured a quick look at my face, then shuddered visibly. "When he hit the floor he rolled over and over maybe six or seven times—and something dropped out of his breast pocket."

"Something dropped out of his pocket," I repeated slowly. "Let me guess—his jockey!"

"This!" Polnik yelped, then held out his hand in front of him and a moment later closed his eyes tight in case I cut it off at the wrist.

I stared down at the dazzling brilliance of the ring, cradled in Polnik's hand, which had the largest diamonds I'd ever seen in my whole life, outside of a Tiffany ad.

"It's my ring!" Bliss said excitedly. "The one Lee Banning wore when he was killed—the one that was stolen, Lieutenant!"

"I have to admit that I, too, was wrong, Lieutenant," Ivorsen said happily. "I should have realized that a professional con man like Fenelk would have a practical motive for murder."

"How much did you say it was worth?" I asked Bliss.

"Forty thousand," he said huskily.

Ivorsen walked across the trailer with Toro a step behind.

"Do you have a sense of humor, Lieutenant?" he asked blandly.

"If you say anything like, 'A funny thing happened to me tonight on my way to the trailer,' I'll strangle you with my bare hands!" I warned him.

"It won't take a moment," he said smugly.

With a sudden movement he lifted the diamond ring from Polnik's open palm and held it up in the air between his thumb and index finger. "Toro!" he snapped quickly.

"Ugh!" Toro took the ring from him and held it between his thumb and index finger.

"Like button, button, who's got the button?" I snarled.

"Ugh!" Toro's grunt had a different sound to it somehow, and I looked at him in time to see the first faint beads of sweat appear across his forehead. He grunted a second time on a note of triumph, and a moment later there was a small, splintering sound like someone had just cracked a walnut the hard way.

My eyes bulged as I watched fragments of the diamond ring spray out from between Toro's thumb and index finger and drift gently down to the floor.

"You had the value wrong, Lucian—" Ivorsen almost chuckled. "Not forty thousand but fifty bucks, maybe?"

"I—I don't understand," Bliss gurgled.

"Paste!" Ivorsen said crisply. "You're not a businessman, Lucian, you take chances without realizing it. But I am a businessman—that's why I had an imitation made within a few days of you making the purchase. I switched them without your knowledge because it was safer that way. If you were obviously convinced it was genuine, then nobody else would question it either—least of all a potential thief!"

"Where's the real diamond ring?" I asked.

"Right here!" Ivorsen fumbled in his pocket for a moment then held up the ring so the light did full justice to its dazzling brilliance.

"I could've collected insurance on a fake!" Bliss yelped suddenly. "That's a criminal fraud!"

"No, you couldn't, Lucian," Ivorsen said benignly. "The insurance company knew of the paste imitation I'd had made."

"And the guy who stole it?" Bliss stuttered. "When he came to get rid of it he'd maybe get fifty dollars as top price?"

"I doubt if it's resale value would have been that much," Ivorsen said dubiously. "Let's say—fifteen?"

There was a sudden thud as Bliss crumpled to the floor close to my feet.

"Poor Lucian!" Ivorsen's body shook with suppressed laughter. "He takes it all too seriously!"

Fenelk groaned painfully and opened his eyes, reminding me he still existed.

"Get him out of here and take him downtown," I told Polnik.

"Right away, Lieutenant," the sergeant said happily, then hoisted Fenelk onto his feet and propelled him toward the door.

"Book him, Lieutenant?" Polnik asked dutifully as he went past.

"Suspicion of larceny," I said.

"What's that you said, Lieutenant?" Ivorsen asked incredulously. "Larceny?—what about murder?"

"What about it?" I said coldly.

"But—but what more proof do you want? Your own sergeant found the ring in Fenelk's pocket! What more motive do you need for murder than a diamond ring worth forty grand?" A harsh, grating tone came into his voice. "Even if it was a paste imitation, Fenelk was convinced he'd stolen the real thing!"

"Sure," I said. "Would you mind getting the hell out of here, Ivorsen? I'm busy!"

He stood for a long moment glaring murderously at me, then his fingers snapped the command and the two of them walked quickly out of the trailer. Bliss gave a couple of interrogative grunts as a prelude to coming out of his faint, and I figured he could look after himself while I went and talked with Jason Kemp.

Kemp looked almost pleased to see me which was a pleasant change anyway. He invited me to sit down and I thought if I never saw another trailer in my whole life I'd be grateful. I perched on the only chair while Kemp lounged on the bunk.

"They're keeping you busy, Lieutenant?" he said amiably.

"You know how it is—actors!" I said.

His grin widened a little. "If I didn't before, I sure know now, after what's happened the last twenty-four hours!" His face sobered. "Lee Banning—then Mel Parker. It makes a guy wonder if there's some kind of jinx on the whole outfit!"

"Yeah," I said vaguely. "I talked with Mavis and she gave me a description—with details—of what happened tonight up to the time she carried Peggy Banning home."

"Crazy, mixed-up kid!" he said softly. "How is Peggy?—I hope she's O.K."

"She's fine," I said heartily. "We had a long talk—all about your motives for murdering Banning."

"What?" He straightened up quickly, dropping his feet to the floor. "What are you talking about?"

"Lee was on top and you were on your way down—fast," I said cheerfully. "Maybe you couldn't stand the comparison at such close range? Then—as Peggy put it so delicately—it must have been tough for a guy still carrying a torch for his ex-wife to see Lee Banning make her without even trying?"

His face slowly turned a beet-red color. "That conniving little bitch!" he said hoarsely. "I guess she's got a motive for me killing Parker all figured out, too?"

"No," I smiled. "I've got that one figured out all by myself. It's easy—Bliss wanted you to take over Banning's role but Ivorsen insisted it should be Parker. There was one sure way you could stop him taking over, wasn't there?"

Kemp stuck a cigarette into the corner of his mouth and lit it slowly.

"I was right here when it happened," he said carefully.

"Alone?"

"Well, sure—but Mavis hadn't been gone more than a few minutes!"

"A couple of minutes would've been long enough," I reminded him.

"Look, Lieutenant!" His hand stabbed the air emphasizing each point as he made it. "You got the story from Mavis, not from me. I invited her in for a drink after the meeting and we got along together just fine—like a house afire! Then Peggy came busting in with that gun in her hand right at the wrong moment, and when we'd gotten that taken care of, like Mavis said, the mood was busted anyway, and she had to put Peggy to bed—right?"

"That's the way I heard it from Mavis," I agreed.

"I couldn't know Peggy would come gunning for me, could I?"

"I guess not," I said.

"But according to your theory, I start out by inviting a dame back to my trailer for the usual reasons, then have to sweat out the threat of being killed myself by a hysterical dame with a loaded forty-five in her hand—and ten minutes after that's all over I suddenly make up my mind to murder Parker? I must be a lucky guy, Lieutenant! Somehow that knife just drops into my hand and around the next corner is Parker—being a nice guy he didn't want to give me any trouble finding him, so he came out to meet me!"

"The knife belonged to Drew Fenelk," I said. "He claimed it was stolen from him tonight. You could've easily taken it when you were in his trailer with Lucian Bliss. In this trailer camp it would be hard to miss Parker—he'd either be inside his trailer or within a hundred yards of it. There just ain't no place else to go around here."

Kemp was starting to get a hunted look on his face so maybe I wasn't wasting my time.

"I'm a cop," I said obviously, "and the thing I like best is a nice full confession or ten unimpeachable eyewitnesses who saw the whole thing. But in this case I'll settle for the circumstantial evidence, brother!"

"What do you mean?" He pulled a handkerchief out and patted his face with quick, nervous movements.

"The most hostile witness you can ever get in a courtroom is the widow of a murdered man," I said evenly. "Just imagine what Peggy Banning's evidence would make you in the eyes of a jury! She'd give you motive on two counts—jealousy of his career and his affair with your own ex-wife. But the strongest motive is your chance of taking over his job once he was dead—and the proof is that Bliss offered it to you the same day."

"But I didn't get it!" he blurted desperately.

"You're so right, Jason." I grinned encouragingly at him, "Parker got it—and he was murdered the same night."

The handkerchief was almost sodden but he kept on dabbing his face furiously with a compulsive movement.

"Lieutenant,"—his eyes pleaded frantically—"I know it sounds bad—the way you say it—but I didn't kill anybody. I swear it!"

"Maybe." I shrugged indifferently. "Like I told you before—if you didn't, then somebody's trying to frame you awful hard. It could be a good idea to sweat over figuring out who it might be. They must have a damned good reason to hate you that bad!"

"Yeah, sure!" he said eagerly. "I've been trying to think who it could be ever since I talked to you this afternoon—even before Mel—but right now it's got me beat."

I let him dab some more before I changed the subject. "When Bliss offered you Banning's job," I queried, "did he talk terms?"

"Sure." Kemp managed a weak smile. "I've been around this business too long to take somebody's word where money's concerned."

"What did he offer?"

"The same as Banning got—a thousand a week. He wanted me to sign a five-year contract and give him an option after the first twelve months."

"What does that mean exactly?"

He grinned again and made a better job of it this time. "It meant if he didn't want me anymore after the first year he could get out of the contract. But I didn't have the same right—once I signed, I'd be on the same money for the next five years."

"Would you have signed it?" I asked interestedly.

"You're goddamned right I would," he said forcefully. "Fifty thousand a year coming in steady after what I've been picking up the last three years is a fortune to me!"

"It's a fortune to me, too," I said, and that was nothing but the truth. "You knew Banning wanted a new contract?"

"I heard rumors." Kemp shrugged his shoulders. "Maybe he was being smart or just plain stupid—I wouldn't know."

"What do you know about the financial setup on this *Dead Shot* series?"

"I heard a few things," he said slowly. "What did you want to know?"

"How big a piece does Bliss own?"

"The smart boys tell it like fifteen per cent—twenty as absolute top," he said.

"The backers own the rest of it—the other eighty per cent?"

"Who else?" He became aware of the sodden handkerchief he still held clenched in his hand and he relaxed his fingers furtively so it dropped to the floor.

"How big a piece has Ivorsen got?"

"I couldn't be sure about that, Lieutenant," he said slowly. "Ivorsen is a smart operator and he plays it real close to his vest the whole time—but I'd say for sure he's got a two-thirds interest and maybe he's got it all."

"O.K." I got onto my feet. "That's all for now, Kemp. You keep thinking hard about who it could be—the character that set you up as the patsy, huh?"

"Sure thing, Lieutenant." His voice hardened suddenly. "You could be surprised—I'm thinking hard right now!"

"That's fine," I said politely as I opened the door. "Don't believe that old line about it's folly to be wise, hey?"

"But that's only in special circumstances, Lieutenant, isn't it?" The icy calm in his voice hit me with almost physical force. "Like—when ignorance is bliss?"

On the way back to where the Healey was parked, I checked my watch and saw it was 3:30 A.M. and wondered why the hell I was a cop, when all I had to do was ask my dear old uncle in Georgia to use his influence and get me into a chain gang when the next vacancy occurred.

The moon had quit for the night and I didn't blame it. A wide strip of darkness stretched ahead of me, flanked by the even darker silhouettes of the trailers on either side. I guess everybody has their own personal idea of hell and this was mine—a bleak dark road that stretched ahead of you endlessly with never a single light to break the monotony, so you just kept on walking throughout all eternity and never arrived any place.

A couple of minutes later I figured there were only a few—three at most—trailers to go and I knew the Healey was parked about fifty yards past the last trailer in line. The hell with the Sheriff's office, I decided, and the hell with the Sheriff too—I'd had enough for one day. I was going straight back to the apartment, an outsize Scotch on the rocks with the usual dash of soda, and then to bed. The vision shattered suddenly when someone grabbed my arm.

"In here, Lieutenant—quick!" an urgent voice whispered in my ear.

I felt my arm dragged fiercely and went along with it because I didn't have the energy to argue anymore. Whoever it was pulled me inside the trailer and closed the door quickly behind us. My imagination got too lively while I waited in the absolute dark, wondering if my host was the same character who'd knifed Parker and was busy right now debating where would be the best place to sink a shiv into Wheeler.

Then the lights came on and I blinked a couple of times until I saw my host and that made me blink some more.

"I had to talk to you, Lieutenant," Amber Lacy said in a tense voice. "I've been waiting for hours to catch you as you came by—I thought you'd never come!"

Somehow I'd forgotten just how beautiful Amber was and when I looked at her a second time I figured I must have been out of my mind— or getting senile.

She'd combed out her shining black hair so that it reached her shoulders in a series of gentle waves making a soft frame for the ivory-textured face. Her dark eyes watched me anxiously, while her mouth pouted unconsciously in an automatic reflex to any male who appeared on the scene. She wore a white cashmere sweater which was skintight from neck to waist and molded the outline of her high breasts close enough to prove she wore nothing underneath. Along with the sweater, she wore a pair of tight black velvet pants which stopped at mid-calf. There was nothing original about the outfit—it was slightly old-hat even, the standard requirement in every young man's fantasy of what the bachelor girl wears when she entertains, informally, in her own apartment. There was one thing that made the vital difference to the outfit, naturally, and that was Amber Lacy who not only wore it but was for real, too.

"Skip the travelogue, Lieutenant!" There was a trace of impatience in her voice. "You don't think I pulled you in here for that?"

"Don't knock it too hard," I pleaded. "Over the years it's given more people more fun than ice cream even!"

"I need a drink!" she said tautly. "Do you mind making it? In that cupboard there."

I opened the cupboard and found a fifth of a fifth of Scotch and an unopened bottle of bourbon. There was no soda, but you can't have everything as the guy said when his wife jumped off a bridge and only left him half her money.

Amber draped herself over the bunk and watched while I made the drinks. I took them over to her and she grabbed hold of the nearest glass without bothering with any minor pleasantries, and stayed right where she was, making it painfully obvious I could please myself where I sat, but not on the bunk.

I grabbed the nearest ankle and tossed her leg away so I had enough space to sit down next to her. She squealed indignantly and it didn't bother me any because I was the guest, what the hell.

"You've got the manners of a pig!" she said viciously.

"I know," I said, and stretched luxuriously. "That's why it feels so good to be home."

The frigid silence that followed lasted long enough for me to drink my Scotch. Then I looked up and saw she was watching me with smoldering eyes.

"You heard what happened to me at the big conference Lucian Bliss organized?" she asked frostily.

"You told Ivorsen to go paddle his trailer along the nearest freeway," I said, "so he hauled off and slugged you."

"You brute!" she said in a small, tearful voice. "Don't you have any of the finer feelings at all? A defenseless girl gets knocked unconscious by a subhuman animal and you think it's funny?"

"I don't think it's funny," I said and yawned heavily. "But the defenseless girl bit—now *that's* funny!"

"I want protection!" she stormed in a sudden fury. "Everyone around here is frightened to death if Ivorsen even looks at them. He hates me now—I know it, I saw it in his eyes just before he hit me. I'll bet he's planning his revenge right now—and when he does come for me I'll be all alone."

Her lower lip trembled pathetically. "All the others will pretend they didn't see it—or they didn't hear it. That's why you've got to give me police protection!"

"I could make you a deal," I said reflectively. "In the morning you go right up to him and insult him real good so he'll slug you again—then I'll book him on an assault rap, like that!"

She buried her face in her hands and started to weep—the polished technique where they start out silently and finish up bringing the walls down around your ears. All the time you know you've got a choice of offering sympathy so they'll stop, or listening to it get louder every minute.

"I'm all alone!" she sobbed passionately. "Nobody cares what happens to me—they don't care if I live or die, even!"

"Jason Kemp does," I said. "The way I hear it, he's still carrying a torch for you, honey."

The muffled sobbing sound stopped suddenly as she lifted her face and stared at me incredulously.

"Jason—carrying a torch for me?" She giggled uncontrollably. "He wouldn't even see it, not beside that great searchlight he carries for himself the whole time!"

She dissolved into more helpless laughter while I sat and watched, more or less patiently.

"Whoever told you that?" she asked when she finally stopped the guffaws.

"Peggy Banning."

"Oh—Peggy!" There was a sneer in her voice. "I bet she thinks that's why he killed Lee, huh?"

"That was the theory."

"She's a woman with a one-track mind," Amber said tartly. "I guess I have to be fair—with her mind she doesn't have the room for two tracks!"

"Listen!" I said. "You didn't really drag me in here just to put over that jazz about being scared of Ivorsen, did you?"

"I most certainly did!" Her eyes widened as she leaned toward me. "I'm not kidding, Lieuten—don't you have a name? Every time I say 'Lieutenant' I feel like I'm talking to a public institution!"

"Al Wheeler," I said. "You can call me, Al—for free."

"Al!" She leaned even closer so I'd get the full impact of her words. "Two people have been murdered—right here inside this location unit—and I'm sure it was Ivorsen who killed them! If you'd seen the look in his eyes when—" She closed her eyes and shuddered violently.

"I like him about as much as you do, honey," I said. "If you can think up a good reason why a guy who owns not less than two-thirds of a successful TV show should want to kill off his star first, and then his replacement—"

"Reasons—I don't know from reasons!" she said petulantly. "That's your job—you're the expert. All I know is I'm a girl and I'm alone!"

"You figure even if Ivorsen didn't knock off the other two, he'll make a start with you?"

"Look!" Her fist pummeled my chest desperately. "I'll be honest with you, Al—real honest! I don't think he really plans on murdering me, but I'm sure he's planning something horrible—like disfiguring me, leaving me scarred for life!"

"Yeah," I said. "Well," I said. "Well, it's a hard life all over, honey."

I dragged myself up off the bunk and walked toward the door wearily.

"Al!" she screamed wildly. "Aren't you going to do *anything* at all?"

My watch said it was four A.M. and I had to stifle a quick impulse to beat her brains out with the nearest bottle.

"I'll make you a deal," I said. "You want police protection—right?"

"Oh, Al!" She gave me a brilliant smile. "I knew all along you were only kidding when you said you wouldn't help me."

"So I'm a policeman," I said logically. "Ask me real nice and I'll stay the rest of the night."

Somewhere inside her head she flicked the switch and the brilliant smile faded faster than the friend you just asked for a loan. The ivory texture of her skin was suddenly diffused with a rich red color that looked mottled for a moment, then rapidly built to a hellfire crimson. She closed her eyes tight while her whole body shuddered—it looked like I'd blown the safety valve off that evil temper of hers and the results were still only gathering momentum.

It was worth the five minutes' sleep it would cost me to stay and watch. She shuddered again, more violently this time, then moaned softly from between clenched teeth. The crimson drained from her face even faster than it appeared. A slow, deep breath banished the shudders—her eyes opened wide and in back of them was July Fourth.

"You!" The way she said it, the word kind of exploded into the room.

"Me?" I said expectantly, and waited for fireworks to be displayed in glorious technicolor.

"You," she repeated, and suddenly her voice was soft and purring. "Are you married?"

"No," I said. "It's just the long hours on the job make me look that way."

She got up from the couch the way a panther rises from the ground—her joints didn't seem to move at all, she just uncoiled. I stood transfixed, while she glided toward me, the brilliant smile back in place, and I figured it was only my imagination made me think that this time I could see a lot more of her teeth. When she was maybe six inches away, she came to a pulsating stop and looked up into my face. So if a beautiful dame wants to kiss me, who am I to stop her?

I bent my head obligingly while her cool hands crept around my face, cradling my head with tender passion, while they gently tugged my lips closer to hers. The next moment she sank her sharp white teeth firmly into my lower lip.

Whatever the record is for a standing jump, I broke it right then by a minimum two feet. I hit the floor still yelping painfully while she stood with her hands on hips and a wicked grin on her face.

"Al Wheeler," she said huskily, "you just made yourself a deal—I've got police protection, and you've got me!" Then she clenched her right fist and sank it painfully in my solar plexus to clinch the deal.

There's a limit to any man's endurance and I'd passed it sometime back. I lunged for her with both hands but she dodged at the last moment, so I wound up with two fistfuls of cashmere sweater.

"Now you're getting hip, lover!" she said with infectious enthusiasm. "Why don't you tear it off?"

Have you ever tried to rip a good cashmere sweater to shreds? It can't be done, not with the bare hands, but you can have a ball trying. I was almost sorry when Amber at last solved everything by peeling it over her head.

She stood there, naked to the waist, jigging up and down to some tune inside her head, and her magnificent breasts trembled with newfound freedom, their coral tips offsetting the delicate expanse of ivory.

"You want to go for the big one now, hey, Al Wheeler?" she asked excitedly. "Or would you rather quit while you're ahead and take the cashmere home with you?"

"If they want me to go home they'll have to carry me out on a board!" I said hotly.

"That's my boy!" she said proudly and gave me a playful punch just under the heart which advanced any lurking coronary five years closer at least.

"You're going for the big one—I'll help get you started," she said generously. "Don't let anyone tell you this show is rigged!"

She ripped open the zipper which held the velvet pants tight across her hips, then fired an imaginary starting-pistol.

"From here on in, you're on your own, lover!" she said breathlessly, then followed up with a brutal judo chop across my kidneys to prove her point. I guess it was about then I had the first faint doubt in my mind about who needed the protection.

By the time I found out for sure it was me, I didn't care, of course.

10

Mavis Seidlitz

Mr. Bliss called another emergency conference for ten the next morning but he didn't ask me to take any notes this time and I was glad he didn't because that Al Wheeler still had my notebook and I couldn't find the pencil even. The only thing worrying me—apart from my big problem—was whether Mr. Bliss would let me sit in at the conference so I could spend the time looking at Jason Kemp, because that guy had definitely gotten under my skin—in a manner of speaking, I mean.

I knocked on the door of Mr. Bliss's trailer around ten minutes before the conference was due to start and heard him yell for me to come in which was maybe an encouraging sign. There are some days at the studio when he doesn't speak to anyone, not even to himself on the Dictaphone.

So I went on in and Mr. Bliss scowled at me absent-mindedly and it made my heart beat so fast I was real grateful to the manufacturers who made my bra out of that stuff that breathes right along with you all the time.

"What is it, Mavis?" Mr. Bliss said abruptly.

"Well," I stammered, "It's just that I've got a problem, sir."

"*You* got a problem?" He lifted his eyes and stared at the ceiling in a wonderful gesture of despair like a close-up shot right out of one of those wide-screen biblical epics. "What the hell do you think *I've* got?" he said bitterly.

"An ulcer?" I asked uncertainly.

"I have an—ah, never mind!" he snorted.

So if he didn't want to talk about his never-mind, I was grateful—but it didn't look like I'd made a good beginning. Still I figured I had to keep on going because this was probably my last chance to talk to him alone.

"Well," I said, "you remember you hired me to keep tab on Amber Lacy and see she didn't get into any trouble—man trouble, that is?"

"You think I'm a moron?" he said coldly. "Sure, I remember—so what?"

"I hate to say this," I said, confessing my big problem. "But now Lee Banning and Mel Parker are dead and Drew Fenelk's in jail—there's nobody left to protect her against, is there?"

Mr. Bliss scowled at me for a long moment, then ran his hands through his hair like he was impatient about something.

"We got another conference in five minutes from now, right?" he asked heavily.

"Right!" I said quickly.

"We had one yesterday morning—right?"

"Right!"

"What happened to Amber at that one?"

"Mr. Ivorsen clobbered her off her chair!" I said eagerly, to prove *my* memory was O.K. even if his was slipping a little.

"So you think he'll bring her roses this morning?" he snorted loudly.

"Well," I said thoughtfully because I could see he wasn't absolutely sure and that was why he asked my advice, "I don't know about roses, Mr. Bliss, because flowers are hard to get out here—maybe a cactus, huh, in a pot?"

"You lamebrained lunatic!" he screamed. "Once Kent Ivorsen's clobbered anybody—including Amber Lacy—he's only got one ambition and that's to keep on doing it until he's sure they stay clobbered!"

"No roses?" I queried.

"Mavis, honey!" He suddenly grabbed my arm and dragged me across the trailer to the nearest chair and sat me down forcibly.

"Don't make it tough all over by trying to think this thing out. I need you—Amber needs you—we all need you! Use your head only to stick it in between Amber and Ivorsen if he takes a slug at her! You're still on the payroll, Mavis, just so long as you stop any violence between the two of them, understand? We've got enough publicity out of two murders already without adding any more—and besides if Amber gets a black eye, it'll put the shooting schedule back to hell and gone!"

"Yes, sir, Mr. Bliss!" I said, and I felt real happy again because there's nothing like knowing you're wanted and I needed the money, too.

"O.K." he said, and took a deep breath like he'd just run a long race or something. "So sit there—and shut up!"

I did like he said and maybe five minutes after that, Amber walked into the trailer. She wore a heavy toweling shirt and a pair of ranch pants that looked O.K., I guess—but she walked stiffly like she was awful tired. I couldn't see her eyes because of the huge pair of sunglasses covering them, but her face looked awful pale and her lips had a kind of chewed-up look like she wasn't getting her vitamins or something.

"Lucian!" She sank into the nearest chair and glared balefully at Mr. Bliss. "Do you have to call these conferences in the middle of the night?"

"Emergency, honey," he said absently, "and you should know we've had enough of those lately!"

"Why don't you be smart and just give up?" she asked in a tired voice. "Then we could all go home and get some sleep!"

"Do me a big favor, Amber?" he pleaded. "Stay out of Kent Ivorsen's hair this morning—we got enough trouble already."

"That—" Amber tried hard but apparently she couldn't think of an adequate name to describe him. "I'm going to fix Mister Ivorsen, but good!"

"Not on my time, huh?" Mr. Bliss asked anxiously. "Save it until we've finished the shooting schedule?"

"Nobody ever hit me and got away with it yet!" Amber snarled. "And that includes him."

Maybe she went on talking some more but I didn't hear her because right then Jason Kemp came in and it was like the sun rose for the second time. I mean he was so handsome and everything, and now that we kind of knew each other real well I appreciated his masculine good looks even more.

"Good morning, Mavis," he said, giving me a wonderful smile, followed by a slow wink which just made me flip. Then he looked at Amber and he even smiled at her so I figured he must be in a real good mood this morning and maybe it was seeing me that did it.

"How're things?" he asked her real nice.

"Drop dead!" she told him nastily and it only went to show what a mean personality she was, after she'd been married to him once for four whole days—the lucky thing.

Right after that Mr. Ivorsen and Mr. Toro came in and sat themselves down.

"O.K.," Mr. Bliss said briskly. "I've been working on this nearly the whole night so you lucky people who've had some sleep—"

"Hah!" Amber interjected rudely.

"—listen hard because I don't want to have to say it twice," Mr. Bliss went on ignoring her rude interruption. "Mr. Ivorsen is in agreement with me that the logical thing to do now is have Jason take over the lead in the series."

"Well!" I turned and beamed at Jason. "Congratulations!"

"Thanks, Amber," he smiled back at me.

"Yeah," Amber said sharply. "Now you don't have to murder anyone else, Jason. Disappointed?"

"I don't like that kind of thing said even as a joke," Mr. Ivorsen said primly. "We all know the murderer, Fenelk, was arrested last night!"

"Don't kid yourself, little man!" Amber laughed harshly at him. "That Al Wheeler's a long way from being through with you yet!"

I saw the worried look in Mr. Bliss's eyes and I figured I'd better start earning the money he was still paying me, so I dug my elbow sharply into her ribs.

"What did you say?" Mr. Ivorsen asked sharply and started to get up off his chair.

"She didn't say anything, Mr. Ivorsen." I smiled sweetly at him while I took Amber's hand in mine and bent her little finger back sharply. "Did you, honey?" I asked in a friendly voice.

"Let go of—" Amber didn't finish the sentence because about halfway through she realized she had the choice of being nice or having her little finger in splints. She ground her teeth for a moment, then finally shook her head. "No!" she snarled. "I didn't say a goddamned word!"

"So you don't have anything to worry about, Mr. Ivorsen!" I gave him another big smile and felt awful glad when he sank back onto his chair again.

"Our research revealed that Shep Morrow had a cousin—Cal Morrow," Mr. Bliss went on, giving me a grateful smile and I gave Amber's little finger a gentle tweak just to remind her. "So we propose to introduce Jason—as Cal Morrow of course—in the first episode, seeking revenge against those who ambushed and murdered Shep and his sidekick. He finds too, that his cousin left his fabulous diamond ring to him and he swears an oath not to wear it until he's avenged his cousin's death."

Mr. Bliss paused for a moment and blinked hard. "It gets me," he said simply, pounding his chest, "right here! I think our writers have come up with a wonderfully powerful emotional situation—and of course we can't afford to let forty thousand dollars' worth of diamond ring go to waste just because we lost a couple of actors!"

"Sounds great," Jason said, "real great!"

"I'm getting Jorgens and Matt Blair out to play the villains," Mr. Bliss continued. "They come high, but I figure for this first show they're worth it. We have to establish Jason as a real tough boy to take Shep Morrow's place in the series, and using two real tough villains will help do it. They should be here by tonight, so we'll start shooting again tomorrow morning. But meantime we need some publicity pix, so this afternoon, Jason, I want you and Amber up at the deserted mineshaft for some stills. The photographer knows exactly what I want so get your time from him—O.K.?"

"O.K. Lucian," Jason said happily. "I'll be there."

"You'll need the ring, too," Mr. Bliss said. "He can collect it from you, Kent?"

"Before he leaves," Mr. Ivorsen said with a nod. "Don't forget to return it as soon as you get back, Mr. Kemp. This is the real thing this time, not a paste imitation!"

"I'll do that," Jason nodded.

"We'll want you in the dance-girl's costume, of course," Mr. Bliss said to Amber. "O.K.?"

Amber glared at me for a moment, then nodded slowly, "I'll be there."

"Fine." Mr. Bliss beamed. "That's all then, people!"

I kept tight hold of Amber's little finger until Mr. Ivorsen and Mr. Toro were safely out of the trailer, then let go of it. Jason was busy talking to Mr. Bliss and neither of them were paying any attention to us.

"Where did you learn a sneaky trick like that?" Amber hissed, while she rubbed her finger tenderly. "Some dime-a-dance joint, I'll bet!"

"Mr. Bliss is paying me to see you don't get your teeth knocked out by Mr. Ivorsen, honey," I explained. "And you should be grateful for the protection."

"I don't need protection from you, you female Tarzan!" she said coldly. "I've got all the protection I need from a guy named Wheeler."

"Al?" I smiled pityingly at her. "Honey, he's a good-looking man, sure, but he's a cop—he doesn't have time to play your kind of games."

She smiled in a superior kind of way. "That's all you know—he didn't spend three hours this morning in my trailer drinking coffee!"

For some reason I couldn't explain, she made me mad insinuating a guy like Al Wheeler would even think of making a pass at her.

"Maybe Mr. Ivorsen hit you too hard yesterday," I said sweetly. "You know—like you're still punch-drunk and dreamed up the whole thing?"

"That reminds me," she snapped. "That lipstick message was real cute—one of these nights I might write a note across your midriff, honey, but I'll use a nail file, not lipstick!"

"I'll walk you back to your trailer," I said tersely, "and make sure you don't bump into Mr. Ivorsen on the way and get your face pulped in like you deserve."

"Sure"—she grinned nastily—"and on the way I'll fill you in one some of the details, honey, I just know you'll be interested. That Al Wheeler is really a man!"

She got up and walked out of the trailer and I followed her, fighting hard against the temptation to give her a quick demonstration of the art called unarmed combat.

Keeping my hands off Amber Lacy for the rest of that morning was one of the hardest exercises in will power I've ever gone through in my whole life. I mean, I've met some real feline dames in my time, but she took first prize without even trying. All those nasty things she said about Al Wheeler which I didn't believe were true anyway—well, maybe a couple of things sounded like him—I couldn't help remembering the look in his eyes the night before when he'd seen me doing my hip exercises in my shortie pajamas. But, still and all, no man could be that energetic the way Amber claimed he was.

Finally, right after lunch, she was dressed up in the tattered saloon girl's outfit again and all ready for the publicity pictures and I was about worn out keeping my temper. We walked down to Jason's trailer and he was there with the photographer and a car and driver waiting.

Amber looked at me with a sneer on her face just before she got into the car. "There's one thing, honey," she said, looking at Jason as she said it. "You don't have to worry about your aging Romeo being alone with me all afternoon—he's safe!" Then she got into the car and slammed the door shut.

"She's been giving you a rough time, Mavis," Jason said as he came close—and being near him like that dazzled me almost as much as that glorious hunk of ice on his finger did. "Just ignore her," he went on, "she's sick in the head!"

"She doesn't worry me too much, Jason," I said, smiling at him bravely. "But the more I'm with her the more I sympathize with how Mr. Ivorsen must have felt yesterday when he hauled off and let her have it!"

"Tell you what," he said softly. "Why don't you and I relax tonight? After all that's happened, we've both earned a break."

"Sounds fine," I said warmly. "Where?"

"We'll get away from this dump for a while," he said. "Take a drive into Pine City and see some bright lights for a change, how about that?"

"Gosh!" I said breathlessly, "That sounds wonderful."

"It's a date then." Jason bent his head suddenly and kissed me and maybe it started out as just an affectionate peck but it wound up different. We kind of just merged together and I was way out on Cloud Nine when a harsh voice brought us back to reality.

"Can't it wait till you get back, Jason?" Amber leaned out of the car and asked loudly. "You don't have to worry about Mavis—she's a pushover any time! I'm not going to sit here, waiting while you work off your surplus energy!"

"I guess I'd better go," Jason said and let go of me reluctantly. "See you this evening, huh?"

"You bet!" I said fervently. Then he got into the car beside Amber and they sat in opposite corners of the back seat which made me feel a little better anyway, and the car drove off.

It had been a hectic morning being Amber's keeper, and now she'd gone for the afternoon I figured I could catch up on some rest, so I went back to my trailer and lay down on the bunk. I guess I must have dropped off to sleep almost right away and I was right in the middle of a beautiful dream where I was the Queen of the West and wearing

Amber's saloon girl dress and everybody was drinking my health and cheering when suddenly a man came in through the batwing doors with both guns blazing. He killed maybe a dozen cowpokes before I got a good look at him and then I saw it was Mr. Ivorsen and he looked at me with a horrible gloating look in his eyes and the next thing I knew he'd grabbed me up in his arms and was dragging me toward the doors. Then the doors swung open again and I heard a great blast of trumpets and in walked Jason in a silver cowboy's outfit with gold-plated guns in his holsters. He looked at me and I melted inside. Then he looked at Ivorsen and a deadly calm came over his face. "Draw!" he said quietly and just as—

"Hey, Mavis!" a voice said patiently. "Wake up!"

"Kill him, Jason!" I shouted excitedly. "Kill him!"

The hand patting my face grew more insistent until I opened my eyes reluctantly and saw Al Wheeler looking down at me.

"Go away!" I told him, but it wasn't any use.

"You were having a bloodthirsty dream there," he said interestedly. "Who did you want killed?"

"Never mind!" I said coldly, then sat up and took another look at him. His face had a drawn look about it and there were dark circles under his eyes. I felt sorry for him thinking how hard he must have been working ever since Lee Banning was murdered—then I remembered!

"Just what were you doing this morning, Al Wheeler?" I asked frigidly.

"Sleeping, mostly." He grinned at me. "Even a cop has to sleep here and there—in spite of what the County Sheriff thinks."

"I suppose that was after you left Amber Lacy's trailer?" I said nastily.

"I didn't know Amber was a girl who kissed and told," he said unconcernedly, "but I guess it figures."

"Well!" I said. "And you've got the nerve to come in here after you've been—"

"Relax," he said, "this is business, Mavis. Those notes of yours were a great help, by the way."

"I don't care what my notes—" I stopped suddenly because I saw the man standing behind him for the first time.

"What's that murderer doing loose in my trailer?" I gurgled nervously.

Al Wheeler turned his head casually and looked at Drew Fenelk for a moment, then back at me.

"He's no murderer," he said. "He was framed."

"That's what I tried to tell you last night!" Fenelk said acidly, "but you wouldn't listen. All the humiliation I had to endure, and the physical violence—including being beaten up by your sergeant! I will sue the county sheriff's office, Lieutenant, for false arrest, assault, damage to my professional reputation and—"

"Shut up!" Al said coldly. "Or I'll change my mind and take you right back—hold you as a material witness."

Drew Fenelk paled, then said stiffly, "May I ask your birth date, Lieutenant?"

"Eh?" Al looked at him blankly for a moment. "April 27—why?"

"I thought so," Fenelk said scathingly. "Taurus—the bull!"

Al ignored him and smiled at me warmly. I had to admit to myself even though I was mad at him about Amber, when he looked at me like that I couldn't help feeling a girlish flutter under my bra.

"Mavis," he said slowly. "How would you like to help catch a murderer?"

"I don't know," I said doubtfully. "I'm just a confidential consultant, and that doesn't usually include—"

"Look, honey," he said in a deep, kind of sincere voice. "You wouldn't want him to get away with a double murder, would you? If you hadn't given me those brilliant notes of yours, I'd never have guessed who it is anyway!"

He sat down easily on the bunk beside me and slid his arm around my waist like I was his girl or something.

"All you have to do is go talk with him for a little," he said softly. "Kind of mesmerize him with your beauty, you know?"

His hand started a gentle exploration of my hip and before I could gather the strength to fight it, I had the empty feeling inside back again and I was glad I was sitting down already because my knees were trembling, too.

"How about it, honey?" he asked gently. "Will you do it?—for me?"

"Well," I said weakly, "what would I have to do—exactly?"

"You go see Ivorsen," he said quickly, "and have a little talk with him—that's all there is to it."

"What do I say?"

"Ask him if that diamond ring is genuine and is it really worth forty thousand dollars," Al said.

He was the kind of explorer who never stays long in one place, that was for sure; already his hand had mapped out my hip, retraced its journey back over my waist, and now it was making a fast scouting trip into the hill country. It made it awful hard for me to concentrate on what he was saying, and of course that creep Fenelk was sitting there fidgeting, which didn't help either.

"Why would I ask him that?" I said faintly.

"Smart girl, Mavis!" he said approvingly. "That's what he'll ask you—why you want to know. Then you tell him you were worried because Lucian Bliss has promised he'll give it to you and you know he's broke so you figured maybe it was another paste imitation."

"You're crazy!" I said. "Ouch! Don't *do* that!" I looked at him angrily but I guess his hand didn't see it.

"Right then Ivorsen should get real interested and ask lots of questions," Al went on calmly. "Be a little reluctant to give the answers—don't be too eager—but then tell him you saw Bliss take the ring off Banning's finger right after he was shot and when you asked Bliss about it, he pleaded with you to keep quiet—promised he'd give you the ring right after he'd collected the insurance on it. He told you he was flat broke and he didn't dare tell Ivorsen what a financial mess he was in. Then you say you've been worried ever since you heard that ring was only paste—so you want to know for sure if the one Ivorsen has is real."

"That's an awful lot to remember, Al!" I said. "I don't think I can do it."

Then those darned fingers of his made a quick squeeze play and I just went limp and leaned my head on his shoulder.

"Sure you can do it, Mavis," he said confidently. "Maybe you won't even have to say that much—Ivorsen might leave in a hurry before you've finished!"

"O.K.," I said in a kind of dreamy sigh. "I'll do it, Al."

"That's my girl," he said happily and for a moment there, I wondered if his father was an octopus.

"I guess I'll have to act it out real good," I said thoughtfully. "I know! I've got a great idea—how about I play it dumb?"

"Fine!" Al said. "Be natural!"

He got up from the bunk suddenly and I nearly fell over, he let go of me so quick.

"So let's get the big scene rolling!" he said briskly. "Make it look real, Mavis! Good luck, honey!"

"Wait a minute," I said feebly, getting onto my feet slowly. "You mean I've got to do it now?"

"Right away, honey," he said. "We don't have much time."

While he was talking, he put his hand in back of my shoulders and pushed me gently toward the door, so by the time he'd finished, I was outside the trailer already.

"Al!" I said nervously. "Why don't we—"

"Best of luck, Mavis!" He smiled brilliantly at me for a moment, then closed the door firmly in my face. So there was nothing else I could do but walk along to Mr. Ivorsen's trailer and knock nervously on the door. Mr. Toro opened it a couple of seconds later and stared at me hard.

"Please," I stammered, "I'd like to see Mr. Ivorsen if he isn't busy?"

"Ugh!" Mr. Toro grunted then waved his hand for me to come in.

I guess I knew exactly how Red Riding Hood felt when she stepped inside her grandmother's cottage and saw the wolf drooling at her. Mr. Ivorsen was sitting in a comfortable chair, smoking a cigar, but as soon as he saw me, he jumped to his feet and came over.

"This is a pleasure, Miss Seidlitz," he said, giving me one of his rare, eighteen-karat smiles.

"I wanted your advice, Mr. Ivorsen," I gulped. "I've of a problem."

"Lovely girls like you shouldn't have problems," he said sadly. "But you can rely upon my considered advice."

His hand snaked out and patted my hip consolingly. "I consider it a duty, Miss Seidlitz, to aid a beauty in distress!"

"Well," I said, and had to gulp again, "that diamond ring, Mr. Ivorsen—could you tell me is it real?"

He smiled again while his hand beat out a heavier rhythm on my hip and I was glad I carried enough insulation not to bruise easy.

"Of course it's genuine!" he said. "Worth forty thousand—" The smile faded slowly from his face. "Why do you ask?"

"It's nothing really," I gabbled. "Only—well—I was worried that it might be another paste imitation, that's all."

"You must have a reason for worrying," he said. "A special reason, maybe?"

"Well,"—I laughed uncomfortably—"I wouldn't like to mention it really, Mr. Ivorsen—I mean, Mr. Bliss being such a good friend of yours and everything—it wouldn't be right!"

"Bliss!" His face set like granite. "What has Bliss got to do with this?"

"If he hadn't told me he was broke," I said awkwardly, "I wouldn't have worried. But you know how it is, Mr. Ivorsen, a guy—even a real nice guy like Mr. Bliss tells you he's broke and right afterward promises you a diamond ring. And when I heard about the other one being a phony, I got worried."

"He promised you the diamond ring," Ivorsen grated harshly. "After he'd told you he was broke?"

"I guess I shouldn't have said that," I murmured, trying to look embarrassed. "But I think you've got a right to know, Mr. Ivorsen—after all it's your money he's been spending, isn't it?"

"My money!" For an awful moment I thought he was going to choke to death in front of my very eyes. He closed his eyes for a couple of seconds and they were bloodshot when he opened them again.

"Why did he promise you the ring?" he said thickly.

"For keeping it a secret," I said. "For not telling anyone I saw him take the ring off Lee Banning's finger right after he was shot."

The look on his face while he just stared at me for maybe a full half-minute, nearly frightened me to death. Then suddenly he took a deep, shuddering breath and tried to smile, which made his face look more like a screaming skull than ever.

"You were very wise to ask my advice, Miss Seidlitz," he whispered. "Very wise. I think I should have a talk with Lucian first before I advise you definitely. Please excuse me." His fingers snapped violently. "Toro!"

"Ugh!" Mr. Toro grunted then lumbered toward the door.

"This may take a little time, Miss Seidlitz," Ivorsen snarled. "Don't wait—I'll contact you as soon as I know something definite."

I could see a brand-new thought hit him right then—his hand squeezed my hip with a thoughtful, probing deliberation.

"I don't know about that ring," he said almost to himself, "but if you're interested in jewelry, Miss Seidlitz, I feel sure we can come to some mutually agreeable arrangement!"

One final squeeze and then he followed Mr. Toro out of the trailer. I felt glad he was gone. I was beginning to feel like I was the iced cake at a birthday party—anyone wanted a piece they just helped themselves!

I waited a couple of minutes, then walked out of the trailer and looked around cautiously but couldn't see anybody else outside, so I guessed it was O.K. to go back to my own trailer. Along the way I checked my watch and saw it was nearly five o'clock which meant Jason would be back any minute so I kept on walking toward the end of the trailer line, to meet the car as soon as it got back.

I couldn't help grinning to myself as I walked, thinking how amazed Jason would be when I told him what had happened, and how proud he'd be of me for helping Lieutenant Al Wheeler catch a murderer!

11

Al Wheeler

After I'd slammed the trailer door shut in Mavis's face, I waited twenty seconds, then opened it again a couple of inches. I watched her walk toward Ivorsen's trailer slowly, and kept my fingers crossed she wouldn't chicken out at the last moment. But, bless her rounded curves, she kept on going and I saw her knock. Then somebody opened the door and she went inside.

I turned around and looked at Fenelk who still had a griped expression on his face like what the hell was he doing here anyway when he should be home studying a starlet's natal chart.

"Now it's your turn," I told him. "You know what to do—walk in on

Bliss and tell him I turned you loose with apologies. I told you I was sure your knife was stolen from your trailer and that paste imitation diamond ring was planted in your pocket. But make it fast—I want you out of there before Ivorsen arrives."

"You realize what you're asking, Lieutenant?" he said coldly. "Betray a friend!"

"You got the choice," I said equally coldly. "That—or back behind bars."

"I should have known something like this would happen," he muttered. "With Mars and Saturn in conjunction—"

"And Wheeler wheeling in orbit!" I snarled. "Get moving, Fenelk."

He went out of the trailer, still muttering to himself, and I followed maybe ten seconds later, in time to see him entering Bliss's trailer.

I walked down to where the Healey and the prowl car were parked and Polnik looked at me hopefully.

"How's it coming, Lieutenant?" he asked.

"I wouldn't know," I said. "Just keep your fingers crossed—and if you hear a scream for help, come running—it'll probably be me."

"Sure thing, Lieutenant!" he grinned. "You're always kidding—if anybody screams for help while you're around, it's a dame for sure, huh?"

"You should have been around here last night," I said morosely. "You could have been surprised!"

I leaned against the prowl car, lit a cigarette, and looked back down the line of trailers. Five long minutes went past, then Fenelk came out of Bliss's trailer and started walking toward me. Maybe a minute later, Ivorsen came out with the faithful Toro right behind him and the two of them hurried over to Bliss's trailer, then disappeared inside. It was like a game of chess and now it was my move—with any luck I'd wind up with a fool's mate.

Fenelk still had that gloomy look on his face when he stopped in front of us. He looked at Polnik for an instant and shuddered visibly before he turned his glance toward me.

"Is there anything else you require of me, Lieutenant?" he asked heavily.

"No," I said, "you're as free as the zodiac. How did Bliss react when he saw you?"

"I don't understand it," he said sadly. "I don't understand it at all! You would have thought he'd be pleased—excited, even—to see me a free man again. From the look on his face when I said the things you told me to say, he was disappointed!"

"I wouldn't worry," I said consolingly. "You can always predict the future for Amber Lacy if you need a new client—and for that you don't need her birthdate even."

His face brightened a little. "I wonder if she'd be interested—she'd make a fascinating subject!"

"You can say that again, pal!" Polnik said huskily.

"I figure it's about time I called on Bliss," I said, moving away from the prowl car. "It looks like his busy afternoon."

It took maybe a minute to reach the trailer. I opened the door and walked in without bothering to knock. Inside, the three of them froze momentarily into a fascinating tableau as they saw me come into the trailer.

Ivorsen was standing in the center of the floor with his feet spaced wide apart, his hands thrust deep into his pants pockets, a cigar clamped firmly between his teeth.

Bliss was backed up hard against the wall in one corner with both arms held up in front of his face, making a continuous whimpering noise, while blood trickled steadily down his face from the cut above his right eye. Toro looked relaxed as he stood facing Bliss and massaged the knuckles of his right hand in an absent-minded way, more like he was limbering them up.

"Financial conference?" I asked politely as I slammed the door shut behind me.

"This is a private matter, Lieutenant," Ivorsen said sadly. "I find I have been cheated by a man I trusted and it is not a pleasant feeling!"

"That's tough," I said sympathetically. "Don't let me interrupt—you go right ahead."

"Lieutenant!" Bliss said in a note of hysteria. "They'll kill me! You've got to stop them!"

"Like Mr. Ivorsen said"—I shrugged elaborately—"it's a private affair—nothing to do with me. But I'll stick around if you want and make sure they don't actually kill you."

Ivorsen stared at me suspiciously. "What do you mean by that?" he grated.

"I can understand a guy getting half killed when he's cheated somebody who trusted him out of a lot of money," I said carefully. "I'll stick around to make sure you don't get too enthusiastic, like stop him breathing permanently."

A slow smile spread across his face. "Thank you, Lieutenant," he whispered. "I am pleasantly surprised at your intelligent appraisal of the situation." He lifted one hand out of his pocket and snapped his fingers. "Toro!"

The man mountain grunted; a moment later his fist slammed through Bliss's ineffectual guard and landed on the cut above his right eye with a noise that made me wince. Bliss screamed thinly and sagged forward with both hands pressed against his face.

"No more—please, Kent!" he whimpered. "She lied to you, I swear it! I never promised her the ring—never!"

"You took it from Banning's hand after he was shot," Ivorsen grated. "As far as you knew it was the genuine article! Why?"

"It's a lie!" Bliss moaned. "A dirty lie!"

Ivorsen took the cigar from his mouth and studied it carefully for a moment, then sighed deeply. "Toro!"

"No!" Bliss yelled. "Not again!"

"Search your soul, Lucian," Ivorsen said earnestly. "Ask yourself, what better thing can I do than tell the truth?" He rammed the cigar back into his mouth again. "I want you to do this thing for me of your own free will, Lucian—it will pain me deeply if you lose the sight of that eye!" He waited a moment and when Bliss still didn't answer, sighed again. "Toro?"

"Ugh!" Toro raised his massive arm again, ready to drive it home into Bliss's face, and right then the producer cracked right open.

"O.K.!" he babbled desperately. "I'll tell you the truth—but tell this gorilla to stop!"

"He'll stop," Ivorsen said, "so long as you tell the truth—and the whole truth."

"I took the ring," Bliss said dully. "I was desperate—I'd been using some of the company money for my own needs. There was no chance I could replace it before your auditors made their quarterly check. The ring was insured for the full amount so I figured the insurance money would cover me until I could sell the ring, and then everything would be all right."

Ivorsen turned his head and looked at me sorrowfully. "You see, Lieutenant," he said in a somber voice, "I have been nursing a viper to my bosom!"

"Maybe it's a penalty for having such an honest face," I suggested. "How did you react to Banning's demand for a new contract?"

"New contract?" he repeated slowly. "Banning never asked for one!"

"How big a piece does Bliss have of *Dead Shot*?" I asked quickly.

"Fifteen per cent," he said. "Not enough for him, apparently, even though I found all the money to back him in the enterprise—a notoriously bad risk, too, you understand?"

"If Banning had asked you for a piece of the show—or else he'd quit—" I said, "how would you have reacted?"

"He was the show," Ivorsen said reflectively. "I'd have come to terms with him—maybe given him half Bliss's percentage if Banning insisted."

"He wanted twenty per cent," I said. "He gave Bliss a month to sign a new contract or he walked out—there was a week or so to go to the deadline when he died."

Ivorsen looked across reproachfully at the producer. "You didn't have confidence in me, Lucian, you kept all this to yourself! I am deeply hurt."

"Please!" Bliss whimpered. "Can I sit down?"

"But, of course," Ivorsen nodded. "I am not a sadist—Toro!"

There was the inevitable grunt, then the man mountain grabbed Bliss by the lapels of his coat and hurled him across the trailer toward the nearest chair. The producer cannoned into the chair a second later, knocking it out from under himself, then finished up prone on the floor.

"Toro," Ivorsen chided him gently, "please help Mr. Bliss into his chair."

Toro picked up the chair with one hand and slammed it down onto the floor, then picked up Bliss with the other hand and slammed him into the chair.

"There," Ivorsen said comfortably. "You see—now you can relax." He looked at me again. "You were saying, Lieutenant?"

"My guess is he never told you about Banning's demands because he knew what you'd do—cut his percentage to meet the actor's demands," I said. "But he thought up an alternative which would take care of the actor permanently, and let him steal the ring to take care of his financial troubles."

Ivorsen stared at me silently for a while. "It was Lucian who substituted the live bullet for one of the blanks?" he asked finally.

"I figure it was his idea," I said. "But that wasn't enough. However good Jason Kemp's reputation was as a dead shot, Bliss couldn't bank on Kemp aiming the gun at Banning—he couldn't be sure the shot would kill him, not merely wound him. He had to cover his bet."

Bliss lifted his head slowly and stared at me with his mouth hanging open. The blood still trickled down the side of his face in a steady stream and he had the look of a wounded animal trapped without hope of escape.

"Kemp is an actor who's been on the skids for the last three years," I said. "A man desperate for survival in a tough business who knew he didn't have a chance. So Bliss made him a proposition—he'd put the live bullet into the gun—all Kemp had to do was make sure when he fired it he aimed real good and shot to kill. That's right, Bliss, isn't it?"

The producer looked at me dully, his mouth working spasmodically as he fought for control.

"Answer the Lieutenant—truthfully, Lucian," Ivorsen snarled. "You don't want Toro to have to start over?"

"No!" Bliss said fearfully. His eyes dilated as he stared back at me again. "All right, damn you! I made a deal with Kemp! I substituted the bullet—all he had to do was aim it right!"

"And in return you promised him the lead in the series after Banning's death."

"Yes!"

"But it went bad," I said. "At the conference next morning, Ivorsen insisted that Mel Parker should have the lead, not Kemp. You tried to bulldoze him but he threatened to withdraw his financial backing and you couldn't risk that."

Bliss's head slumped forward wearily. "Kemp threatened me—said he'd go to the police and tell them my proposition, then say he'd refused to go along with it but I must have substituted the bullet anyway."

"So now you had to get rid of Parker, too?" I said.

"What about Fenelk?" Ivorsen demanded. "It was his knife—and the paste ring was in his pocket!"

"You made it pretty obvious at the conference you suspected Fenelk," I growled back at him. "You also made it pretty obvious that you'd be happy so long as one of the people actively concerned in producing the show wasn't involved in the murder, because if they were it would cost you money. Bliss saw the way you felt and picked on Fenelk as the ideal fall guy, knowing you'd back him up to the hilt."

I lit a cigarette and looked at Bliss distastefully. "It was easy to steal Fenelk's knife—the poor sucker trusted Bliss, figured he was the only friend he had around the place. And to make it look real good, Bliss even made a supreme sacrifice by planting the diamond ring in Fenelk's pocket. Afterwards when you proved it was paste, the shock was too much for him and he passed out—remember?"

"I remember," Ivorsen nodded. "After all the planning and conniving— all the risks he'd taken to get that ring and then have to sacrifice it again to alibi himself against murder—he found out it was worth maybe fifty dollars!" He chuckled softly. "I don't wonder he fainted."

"He even made sure he knifed Parker right outside Fenelk's trailer to clinch it," I said. "But he was an amateur with a shiv and he botched it up a little—he didn't kill him first go."

Bliss shuddered violently. "It was dreadful," he whispered. "Dreadful! I told him I wanted to see him secretly because I knew who killed Banning although I couldn't prove it, and I was afraid his life was in danger. I waited for him outside Drew's trailer...." His eyes shut tight against the memory. "When he came up to me I had the knife in my hand ready and once he was close enough I thrust it into his stomach."

He shook his head blindly. "Mel pulled away from me and the knife was torn out of my hand—I could see the hilt sticking out of his stomach—and he screamed. Ah, God! He screamed! I couldn't stand it—I ran back to my own trailer and threw myself down on the bunk, put my hands over my ears to stop the noise but I could still hear his screams—" His eyes opened again and he stared blindly across the room. "I guess I always will!"

"Did you fix a time with Kemp for when you'd kill Mel Parker?" I asked.

"Sure," he nodded. "Kemp insisted I make it a certain time so he could fix an unbreakable alibi—he figured you already had him lined up as a prime suspect. He'd made a date in his trailer with Mavis Seidlitz and she was going to be his alibi, but that got fouled up somehow."

"Peggy Banning fouled that up by coming in at the wrong moment all set to blow his brains out," I said. "I'm glad she didn't get around to killing him—now the State can do it for her!"

Ivorsen dropped his cigar butt to the floor and his foot ground it into shreds with slow deliberation.

"So that's the end of *Dead Shot*?" he said.

"That's one service Bliss performed for the community, anyway," I said. "All I've got to do now is round up Kemp on the way out, and it's all over."

"Wait a moment," Ivorsen snapped. "That story Mavis Seidlitz told me about Lucian promising her the ring—it wasn't true?"

"Not one word," I agreed.

"Then where did she get it from?"

"Me," I said modestly.

The color ebbed from his face slowly as he stared venomously at me.

"You mean you used me deliberately—knowing I'd force the truth from Lucian by methods you couldn't afford to adopt?"

"Something like that," I said.

"And that dumb blonde played me for a sucker!"

His mouth twitched suddenly. "You won't get away with it, Wheeler!" he hissed. "I'll even the score in my own good time—and neither will that dirty little—"

I backhanded him across the side of his face so the words were swallowed in his own pain.

"You have a bad habit of hitting women, little man," I told him earnestly. "You clobbered Amber Lacy yesterday and knocked her out cold. It's a bad habit—could get you into real trouble sometime."

"Toro!" He screamed the command and jumped at me a second later, his hands reaching for my throat.

Ivorsen was only a little guy and maybe I wouldn't have done it but I figured Amber was owed something. I slammed my right fist into his solar plexus, catching him in mid-air so he got the full impact, coming and going. He landed on his back when he hit the floor and lay there, spreadeagled, without moving.

I looked across at the man mountain and saw he hadn't moved a muscle even.

"Toro?" I said questioningly.

He nodded, then raised his right hand in front of him and snapped his fingers solemnly. I watched, mystified, as he walked over to where Ivorsen sprawled on the floor, and knelt down beside him. The massive fingers plucked a cigar from his top pocket and peeled off the wrapping gently. Then, with infinite solicitude, Toro rammed the cigar halfway down Ivorsen's throat, and carefully used the palm of his hand to crush what was left protruding from his boss's mouth into a pulpy mess which smeared all over his face.

Carefully the man mountain got onto his feet and looked at me gravely for another moment before he snapped his fingers again and shook with silent laughter.

12

Mavis Seidlitz

"Isn't it exciting, Jason?" I finished breathlessly. "Just imagine me helping trap a murderer!"

"Sure, honey," Jason said slowly, "just great!"

"You don't seem very interested!" I said, feeling real hurt he hadn't shown just a little enthusiasm. "I mean, it was a compliment really, Al Wheeler asking me to do it, don't you think?"

"Yeah—sure," he said. He didn't even look at me, he kept looking over my shoulder down the trailer line the whole time.

"You know where Ivorsen and Toro went right after they left you?"

"Sure," I said. "Straight across to Mr. Bliss's trailer—right after Drew Fenelk had just left."

"Fenelk?" Jason snapped. "What's he doing back here?"

"It's O.K.," I said. "He's not a fugitive or anything—he came with Al Wheeler, so I guess Al let him go when he was sure he wasn't the murderer."

"Yeah." Jason still kept on looking over my shoulder.

"If you can't stand to look at me, I'll go away so you're not bothered anymore!" I said tartly.

Then he did look at me and I could see by the look on his face that something was worrying him real bad.

"I'm sorry, Mavis!" He smiled at me and his eyes crinkled so I felt that wonderfully warm feeling inside again and then I knew that everything was O.K.

"It's all right, honey," I said snuggling closer against his wonderful chest. "What's eating you?"

"I just had a wonderful idea!" he said. "The hell with waiting around here—let's you and me head straight for Pine City and those bright lights right now—how about that, honey?"

"But, Jason!" I wailed. "I'm not dressed or anything!"

"You look fine to me, honey," he whispered, and held me tight. "If we leave now I figure we can stop along the way and watch the sun go down on the desert."

I guess that did it—I mean what red-blooded girl could resist an invitation like that?

"All right," I whispered. "You just talked me into it."

"Fine!"

He moved away from me so quickly, I nearly fell flat on my face. "My car's parked with the others—a blue Mercury—you get it will you, honey? The keys are in the ignition. Pick me up at my trailer. It'll give me time to get out of this cowboy suit."

"Whatever you say, lover," I said fondly.

"And—er—Mavis." He smiled again but this time his eyes didn't crinkle. "If you happen to see Wheeler on the way, don't tell him what we're doing—he'll probably stop us going because he wants statements from the both of us or something stupid like that."

"I won't," I promised.

"Great kid!" he said, and the next moment he just disappeared.

For a moment I was real worried. Then I figured he must have ducked around the back of the trailer line for some reason, so I started walking toward the area they'd established as a carpark the first day we arrived on location which was maybe a couple of a hundred yards back of the trailer camp itself.

It took me around ten minutes to get there and find Jason's blue Mercury. I hopped into the front seat and started the motor. Then I backed out and made a U-turn onto the main track which led straight through the camp. I stopped when I was outside Jason's trailer and honked loudly.

He came hurtling out of the door like a streak of blue lightning and I just had time to move over before he hurled a suitcase into the back and jumped into the driver's seat of the car. The next moment my neck almost snapped as Jason slammed his foot down on the gas pedal and the car leapt forward like we were making time at Indianapolis.

"Hey!" I yelped. "What are you trying to do?—kill me?"

"Don't want to be late for that sunset," he said grimly. "Take a look out the rear window, honey—tell me if you see anything."

I twisted around in the seat obediently and took a look.

"A couple of men just came out of Mr. Bliss's trailer," I told him excitedly. "One looks like Mr. Bliss and he's been hurt or something because his face is bleeding. Oh, and the other one's Al. Hey—what do you know?" I smiled happily. "He's waving—I bet he just knows we're sneaking out to watch the sun go down on the desert. Gosh! He looks real excited, Jason—he's waving both arms around like a maniac or something. He's even running now—can you beat that?"

Jason didn't answer—I guess because he was too busy driving flat out. The trailer camp started to shrink rapidly in the rear window but I could still see good old Al running like mad, even though he was about the size of a midget now.

"I think we should have stopped and spoken to him, Jason," I said anxiously, a moment later. "He must have wanted to talk to us real bad—he's getting into that little sports car of his right now."

He still didn't answer me, so I turned around to face the way the car was heading again and looked at him to see what was wrong. His face was set in a tight mask and for a horrible moment he looked like a complete stranger—someone I'd never even met before.

"What's the matter, honey?" I asked nervously.

"Nothing!" he snarled. "Keep watching the back window—tell me when you see his car!"

"O.K." I said coldly. "But if you ask me, this is just stupid—I mean, what are we doing? Having a race to see who gets to Pine City first or something?"

"Shut up!" he snarled. "Do as you're told, you dumb ox!"

The last thing I'd expected from Jason was that he'd insult me on the way to watch a sunset and all! I had to bite my lower lip hard to keep the tears away while I twisted around again to see out the rear window.

For maybe ten seconds I didn't see a thing in back of us, but then I saw a small cloud of dust in the distance and as I watched, it started slowly moving closer.

"I can see him now," I said dully.

"How close?" he rapped.

"Maybe half a mile—I wouldn't know," I said listlessly. "But he's gaining all the time."

"That does it!" Jason said savagely. "I can't lick that damned sports model—it takes a screwball cop like Wheeler to be driving one of those things!"

He turned the wheel suddenly and there was a scream from the tires as the car swung in a huge skid, then finally straightened out again heading at a right angle to the way we'd been going.

By the time I'd managed to straighten myself up in the seat, I could see the deserted mineshaft looming up in the windshield dead ahead. For one awful moment I figured Jason was going to drive straight on into it, but at the very last moment he wrenched the wheel to one side and brought the car to a screaming halt beside the deserted shack.

I heaved a sigh of relief when he killed the motor and figured that sunset must really be something if it meant that much to him to get there on time.

"Out!" he said crisply and leaned across me to open the door.

"Wait a minute!" I said coldly. "Who do you think I am, anyway? What's gotten into you?—"

He gave me a violent push which sent me out of the car, sprawling onto my hands and knees in the sand. By the time I'd gotten to my feet again, he was beside me with the suitcase held tightly in his right hand.

"Inside the shack!" he grated and gave me another push before I had a chance to argue.

The door swung open as I hit it, and I went stumbling into the center of the room. Jason was right behind me, and as soon as he was inside the shack, he dropped the suitcase on the floor, then spun around and slammed the door shut.

"You great big overgrown mannerless slob!" I said furiously. "Who do you think you are pushing me around like a sack of clams or something! I've a good mind to—"

"Shut up!" he snarled. "Or I'll ram your teeth down your throat!"

I stared at him, speechless with fury, while he dropped onto his hands and knees to open up the suitcase. As his hands moved there was a brilliant flash of multicolored light that dazzled me for the moment and I realized he was still wearing the fabulous diamond ring. He gave a satisfied grunt and pulled a gun out of the case and checked the magazine.

"Are you out of your mind?" I gaped at him. "What do you think you're doing?"

He didn't answer for a moment and I heard the high-pitched roar of Al Wheeler's sports car rapidly coming closer.

"A couple of things you'd better get straight, doll," Jason said suddenly. "Wheeler is after two murderers—not one. And the one he hasn't got is me—I killed Banning!"

I stared at him dumbly for a long moment because I couldn't believe it. Then I slowly realized that the Jason Kemp I'd fallen for was the stranger—the one I'd figured was a stranger in the car was the *real* Jason Kemp.

"Make sure you've got it right, Mavis!" he said coldly. "I don't want to kill you but I will if you make me—so do as you're told!"

The sound of the sports car was real close then, and Jason's mouth tightened into an ugly thin line. "The only thing between me and freedom is that stupid cop out there," he said. "You do anything to spoil my concentration, doll, and I'll let you have it! You understand?"

I licked my lips a couple of times before I could answer him.

"Sure, Jason." I said in a strangled voice. "Anything you say!"

"That's better," he said softly.

From outside there was a scream of tires as the sports car came to a skidding stop. Then the sound of the engine died and there was silence for a little while. Jason stood beside the window, the gun held ready in his hand.

"Hey, Kemp!" Al Wheeler's voice suddenly shouted. "You can't go any place from here. Why don't you play it smart and come out of there with your hands on your head?"

Jason snarled silently and edged the gun around until it pointed in the direction of Al's voice, then pulled the trigger twice. The shots sounded deafening inside the shack and my head rocked for a while after the noise had died away.

Slowly, Jason edged himself forward to take a look out the window and from outside another gun fired twice, making Jason dodge back frantically as the slugs buried themselves in the ceiling.

"Don't be a dope!" Al shouted. "There's no future in it, Kemp! You don't have the guts for this kind of fight—not when the other guy's got real bullets!"

I guess that really got Jason on the raw because his face went white with fury. He snarled a lot of rude names, then stood up at the window and fired four shots—one right after the other.

I heard a couple of them ricochet from the car and I kept my fingers crossed for Al that he'd managed to dodge the other two. I mean, not only because he was a cop and Jason was a murderer—besides that, I was coming to realize fast that I really liked the guy for himself.

For a long couple of minutes nothing else happened and I could see a faint grin start to spread across Jason's repulsive face as he figured he must have got Al. Then another shot came from outside and Jason's face dropped again.

"Face it, Kemp!" Al shouted, and he sounded almost cheerful. "You couldn't hit the Rockies with a sawed-off shotgun at five paces!"

Jason suddenly checked his gun again, then looked at me with a nasty glint in his eyes.

"I've got two left," he said slowly. "I guess you're going to have to get me out of here, Mavis!"

"What do you mean?" I asked cautiously.

"Take off your blouse and skirt!" he said curtly.

"What!" I glared at him.

"I don't have the time to argue," he snarled, coming toward me slowly. "Take them off or I'll tear them off—please yourself!"

"O.K." I said nervously when he got close. "I'll do it—but I think you're the—"

"Shut up!" he snapped. "I'm letting you off the hook easy—I could change my mind!"

I figured by the look on his face he meant every word of it so I kept quiet and slowly unbuttoned my blouse. There was a derelict chair which was the entire furnishing inside the shack, so I draped my blouse across it carefully and hoped I'd be back to retrieve it sometime. Then I unzipped my skirt and stepped out of it reluctantly and draped it on top of the blouse. That left me in a strapless bra and a pair of white briefs that were all too brief for the kind of situation I'd gotten myself involved in.

Jason stared at me, then grinned appreciatively. "That should really knock Wheeler's eye out!" he said. He turned his head away suddenly and shouted out, "Wheeler! You hear me?"

"I hear you," Al called back.

"I'm coming out," Jason yelled. "With Mavis—and she's going first. If you shoot you'll collect the dame—you got that, copper?"

There was a long pause, then Al shouted, "I heard you!" and somehow he didn't sound cheerful anymore.

"All right." Jason turned back toward me. "We go now, Mavis—you first. You'd better tell Wheeler to hold his fire once we're out this door or you'll die a premature death! Start moving, huh?"

I didn't have any choice so I walked toward the door with the emptiest feeling inside that I've ever had in my whole life before. I took a deep breath and pulled the door open wide and stepped out into the bright glare of the desert, and at the same moment Jason grabbed me with one arm around my waist, pulling me tight against his chest.

It didn't seem real then—like I'd seen it all before someplace. Then it jibed—of course I'd seen it all before when they rehearsed the first scene on the day Lee Banning was killed. Only it was Banning instead of Wheeler out there helpless—and it was Amber, the kidnaped saloon girl who Jason held as a shield—not me.

Al Wheeler lifted his head from behind the Mercury and stared across at us anxiously, the useless gun in his hand. Jason laughed gleefully in my ear and his free hand raised the gun to aim at the Lieutenant.

I didn't even have to think about it, I mean, because it was all there in the script anyway. I bent my head suddenly and opened my mouth wide—then sank my teed into Jason's hand with all the force I could. He yelled furiously and the next moment I went flying through the air and landed with an awful thump, face down in the sand.

There was the sound of two quick shots followed by third and then nothing. I scrambled up onto my hands and knees and rubbed my eyes frantically to get the sand out so I could see what the hell had happened.

From somewhere close to me I heard soft steps crunching in the sand and I thought I'd die from sheer terror ii I didn't clear my eyes and see who it was. The footsteps came closer still and in desperation I forced my eyes open, but my vision was too blurred and all I could see was the wavery outline of somebody standing in front of me.

"If that's what exercise does for you, honey," an awed voice said, "don't ever stop!"

I cried with pure relief then, and the hot tears took the rest of the sand out of my eyes so I could see again. Al Wheeler held out a handkerchief sympathetically and waited until I'd blown my nose a couple of times and wiped my eyes.

"That was a smart move, Mavis," he said cheerfully.

"For a while there we had a problem."

Instinctively I looked across to the door of the shack and saw Jason lying in a crumpled heap just in front of it.

"You got him?" I said happily.

"He was a lousy shot," Al said.

"How is he?"

A look of annoyance showed on his face for a moment. "He's dead, of course!" he said coldly. "You figure I'm another amateur or something—an actor yet!"

"I'm sorry," I apologized. "I'm all upset."

"Sure," he said. "Anyway, it's all finished now."

I scrambled up onto my feet and started to brush off the sand that clung to me everywhere. I must say Al was awful nice and insisted on helping me and I never saw a more conscientious guy—he wouldn't quit until the very last grain!

Then I walked back inside the shack and put on my blouse and skirt again, being careful on my way out not to look at Jason's body because I just knew it'd make me nervous again.

"Squeeze yourself into the Healey, honey," Al said.

"I won't be a moment."

I did like he said and squeezed was the word—I never knew a sports car could be so small before—they fit like a girdle. Then Al came back and got behind the wheel.

"Polnik can clean up the rest of it," he said idly, "but I figured I'd better take that ring along."

"Al," I said softly, "I've been an awful dope—fancy me ever feeling romantic about a louse like Jason Kemp!"

"Don't worry, honey," he said softly. "You can't trust your emotions all the time—and you don't have a brain to help out either."

"Gosh, thanks, Al!" I smiled brightly up at him. "And thanks for saving my life—you know that louse kidded he was bringing me out on the desert just to see the sunset!"

"We can take care of that for you, Mavis!" Al said firmly. "In around ten minutes from now—and I know just the spot to see it from. After that I figure I can clear things up at the Sheriff's office in not longer than an hour. And after that—"

He started the motor as he spoke and it made so much noise I couldn't hear what he was saying except for a few isolated words here and there like "apartment," "hi-fi," and "couch."

Then the noise level dropped suddenly and he grinned at me. "How does that sound, Mavis, honey?"

Well, you know how it is—I mean, I didn't want to look like a moron or something, so I smiled right back, and said, "That sounds great, Al. Like fabulous!"

"Fine," he said, beaming at me. "I know you'll be crazy about my breakfast specialty—eggs benedict."

Then he revved the motor again and the next moment I screamed suddenly.

"What's the matter?" he shouted anxiously.

"Don't *do* that!" I said coldly.

"Relax, Mavis!" He grinned again. "That's the gear shift—on the floor. I was just shifting."

"How many gears?" I yelped desperately.

The car zoomed forward and I couldn't hear whatever it was he shouted at me. So all I could do was just sit in the darned bug and hope for the best. But you can take it from me I'll never buy one of those little sports monsters—I'd never get the hang of it—eight gears yet!

THE END

The Stripper
- - - -
Carter Brown

1

The crowd on the other side of the street was thickening fast when I parked the Austin Healey outside the Starlight Hotel. It was a pleasant, lazy kind of afternoon—a hot sun in a cloudless azure sky, with a gentle breeze rolling in off the Pacific Ocean.

It was a time to laze on a beach with a bikini-unclad blonde, or sit in a shady bar and listen to the gentle clunk of ice cubes in a tall glass. A time for dreaming, when everyone felt good just to be alive—and maybe in the whole of Pine City there was only one exception. The girl stood out on a ledge fifteen stories high, getting ready to jump.

Inside the lobby a bunch of uniformed cops from the Sheriff's office kept the curious crowd clear of the elevators. I rode up to the fifteenth floor and found the right room with no trouble at all. Sergeant Polnik greeted me inside the door with a worried frown corrugating his sloping forehead.

"Lieutenant Wheeler," he said hopefully. "Cheez! I'm sure glad you got here! The Sheriff's going nuts hanging out the window and all—still trying to talk some sense into that screwball dame out there."

An agitated character with protruding eyes and a pencil line of twitching mustache thrust himself in front of the Sergeant.

"You have to stop her, Lieutenant!" he gabbled almost incoherently. "We can't have young women using our hotel for suicides—the publicity will be murder!"

"Why don't you make up your mind?" I suggested politely, then placed the flat of my hand against his chest and nudged him out of the way.

Sheriff Lavers was sitting on the sill of the open window, his back twisted painfully as he talked with the girl who stood outside on the ledge. The sight of his tight-stretched pants was tempting but I firmly resisted the impulse, out of a reluctant respect for authority and an even greater reluctance to lose the pay check I've grown used to at the end of every month.

"I guess if she didn't jump when she saw *his* face," I said loudly to nobody special, "we got nothing to worry about anymore."

The Sheriff's heels jarred onto the floor, then he turned toward me, his face a mottled color.

"So you finally got here, Wheeler," he grunted. "See if you can talk any sense into that girl out there—I can't!"

"She's a psycho?" I asked.

"Not like you'd figure," he said in a worried voice. "No hysterics, no nothing. The way she's acting, you'd figure the Girl Scouts were having their annual cookout, or something!"

"Did she give you a reason for wanting to jump?"

He shook his head. "Like I said, she just don't make any sense. Her name's Patty Keller and the only thing worrying her right now is what time you've got!"

"She's not worried about how much time she's got?" I queried.

"Either way I wouldn't know," Lavers said heavily. "See what you can do with her, Wheeler."

I sat on the sill he'd recently vacated and looked out, then down—and it was a big mistake. The massed crowd on the sidewalk was only a collection of pinheads; for a moment I watched the toy automobiles being pushed along the street by an invisible hand, then vertigo caught up with me fast. As I turned my head quickly, I saw the girl standing about six feet away with her back pressed against the outside wall. The ledge was no more than eighteen inches wide, and the gentle breeze off the ocean suddenly turned sinister as it plucked at the hem of her skirt.

She didn't look any more than twenty at most—a thin-featured face and mousey-colored hair—and she didn't look nervous even. Her blouse was kind of sloppy and the hem of her skirt a couple of inches too long. Maybe she was a misfit like her clothes, and this was her big problem that one step forward could resolve for all time.

"Hi," she said quickly in a bright, eager-to-please voice. "I'm Patty Keller. Who are you?"

"Al Wheeler," I told her. "You're wasting your time out there, Patty, the streetcars don't come this high."

"That's very funny," she said gravely. "You're a police officer, I guess?"

"A lieutenant," I admitted. "You got a big problem or something, Patty?"

"Or something," she agreed. "What time have you got, Lieutenant?"

I checked my watch. "Five of three—you expecting company?"

"Now I get it." She smiled wisely. "That sheriff tried the sympathetic bit—you know—'Tell Daddy all about it.' When that didn't work they sent you out here to try the comedy routine, right?"

"You're much too smart for me, Patty," I said sincerely. "But you got it wrong. I'm representing the street cleaners. They don't want the job of cleaning up what's left of you after you hit the sidewalk."

Her face paled a little. "That's—that's horrible!"

"Sure, it is," I agreed. "So do them a big favor and come back inside, huh?"

She shook her head determinedly. "I'm sorry, Al, this is something I have to work out for myself!"

"You sure I can't help?"

"There's nothing you can do to help!" she said in a voice so casual that it made the finality of rejection almost brutal.

"Then maybe I can get you something—a cigarette—a cup of coffee?" I sounded stupid to myself even, but "keep them talking" was the tested theory.

"No, thanks." She looked straight down for a moment. "I guess there's an awful lot of people down there, Al. I bet there's newspaper reporters and cameramen and everything—even a television camera, maybe?"

"Sure," I said. "And all of them want just one thing, Patty—for you to come back inside this window! You do that one little thing and you'll make thousands of people throughout the city feel good—make them feel life really is worth living after all!"

"What time is it?" she asked abruptly, and that did up the philosophy real neat.

"I just told you—it's almost three." I took another look at my watch. "Three on the button—and what the hell difference does it make anyway?"

It wasn't the kind of question that you expect an answer to, but for a moment she looked like ten thousand bucks and a vacation in Rio hung in the balance. Suddenly the frown of intense concentration cleared. She took a deep breath and for the first time smiled at me with genuine warmth.

"I guess you're right, Al," she said easily. "It would be stupid to disappoint all those people down there, wouldn't it? I'll come back inside now."

"It sure would," I said fervently. "Remember, you got all the time in the world—so just take it easy. Keep your back hard against the wall and kind of slide toward me, huh? One little step at a time will be plenty."

Patty Keller nodded, then slid her right leg toward me, keeping her back pressed taut against the wall. Her first step brought her maybe a foot closer to the window. I twisted my body around, straining toward her with my arm outstretched and that cut down the distance between us to four feet. In back of me, I felt the Sheriff's large hands clamp down onto my legs, and that made me feel a little better.

"You're doing just fine, Patty," I said. "A couple more steps and—"

She'd already taken one of them while I was talking, and was about to take the second. Her right leg slid forward again and her ankle was almost within reach of my hand—almost. Then she moaned softly and her left leg stayed right where it was.

"O.K.," I yelped frantically. "Take a rest, honey, you got all the time in—"

Her face suddenly contorted grotesquely. Her knees seemed to buckle, and she swayed forward, then bent in the middle like a jackknife, overbalanced, and plunged. I made a desperate grab for her ankle and missed by not more than six inches, losing my balance at the same time. It was only Lavers' iron grip around my knees that saved me from falling out the window.

Her drop to the sidewalk fifteen floors below couldn't have taken more than two or three seconds. For much longer I could hear ricocheting in my head the sound that accompanied it—half moan, half scream, like something out of the primeval forests before people were born.

I got into the office around nine-thirty the next morning, and Annabelle Jackson—the Sheriff's secretary and the most likely reason I'll lose my mind—lifted her blonde head and smiled happily like I'd just broken a leg or something.

"Doctor Murphy is with the Sheriff right now," she said in her soft southern accent. "They're both waiting for you, Lieutenant, and my guess is you should have an alibi ready!"

"It's real nice of you-all, honey chile, to tip me off," I said gratefully. "One of these days I'm going to do you a big favor, like picking out my very own burial plot ahead of time, so you can go spit on it whenever you feel inclined!"

"I know you're kidding, Lieutenant," she said sweetly. "I mean, who'd bury you?—except the city sanitation department, maybe?"

It was a sobering thought that held my attention all the way into the Sheriff's office, and then from the look on Lavers' face I obviously had other things to think about.

"Sit down, Wheeler," he growled. "This may take a little time!"

I sat in one of the visitor's chairs and looked at Doc Murphy and he looked right back at me, so to break the monotony I looked at the Sheriff and the same thing happened.

"What are we expecting?" I ventured finally. "Fallout?"

"Patty Keller," Lavers said, "the girl who jumped off that hotel ledge yesterday afternoon."

"She didn't jump—she fell," I corrected him. "She was on her way back inside when she got sick and—"

"You said that yesterday," he interrupted rudely, "I figured it was the usual Wheeler reaction. What female could possibly commit suicide when she was favored by a personal appearance of Nature's gift to her own sex—?"

"You're jealous, Sheriff!" I interrupted him with equal rudeness. "Just because you've gotten fat and—"

"All right!" He bit the end off a cigar, then shoved the black cylinder into his face. "That was yesterday—Doctor Murphy's finished his autopsy since then."

"She fell fifteen stories onto a concrete sidewalk and you need an autopsy to establish the cause of death?" I wondered out loud.

"Why don't you concentrate real hard, Lieutenant?" Murphy asked amiably. "See if you can come up with one intelligent answer. You said she got sick and that made her fall. Expand that a little, will you—as a personal favor?"

"Since when would I want to do the mortician's friend a personal favor?" I said. "She was edging her way back to the window when she suddenly groaned—her face was all screwed up like she was in agony. Then her knees buckled and she doubled up and over-balanced. That's about all there was to it."

Murphy looked at the Sheriff and nodded wisely. "It adds up, all right."

"You two are real cute," I said coldly. "So play secrets and see if I care!"

"She kept checking on what time it was—right?" Lavers prodded.

"Yeah," I muttered. "Like morning workouts at Santa Anita.... Hey, come to think of it, when I told her it was three o'clock, she suddenly changed her mind about staying out on the ledge—like that!" I snapped my fingers.

"Interesting," Murphy mumbled. "She was loaded with apomorphine."

"Apomorphine? Like morphine?" I said.

"No, not like morphine at all. It's a derivative, but it's not a narcotic. It's a powerful emetic. A mere trace of it can be used as an expectorant, and as little as a twelfth of a grain makes you toss up that arsenic your wife gave you in your oatmeal—but good! It produces acute nausea, vomiting, fainting, giddiness. It's hard to say how much she'd gotten, but it was enough to do the trick."

"But why in God's name would she drink something like that when she was about to take a dive off a building?" Lavers said.

"She didn't drink it—it was a hypo. Not that it matters much, except that the timing is different," Doc Murphy explained. "It's usually given that way—in the arm, not the stomach."

"Then it certainly looks like she had a little help," I said. "Most of us don't go around sticking needles in our own arms."

"*Plenty* of us do!" he corrected me. "It's a cinch—as any mainliner will tell you, plus a lot of other people who have had one reason or another to give themselves shots."

"So maybe she'd eaten a bad oyster," Lavers suggested gloomily, "and she wanted to get rid of it, and she took the stuff, and then decided she was tired of living anyway, oyster or no oyster, so she tippy-toed out on the ledge and mulled it over for a while trying to make up her mind, and then *blam!*" He snorted. "Nuts! It doesn't make sense!"

"How long after the shot would it take for the reaction to hit?" I asked the doc.

He scratched his head and screwed up his face. "Pretty hard to say, for me anyway—I haven't had any occasion to use it since I was a resident in the hospital on emergency call. About ten or fifteen minutes, maybe."

The Sheriff met my questioning look with a sour expression. "She called the desk and told them she was going to jump," he said bleakly. "They sent the house dick up there right away to see if it was a gag or not. I got there fast with Polnik—you took longer—" he gave me that one through clenched teeth "—I suppose the whole thing from the time she phoned the desk until she went down might have been fifteen minutes, give or take a couple."

"Was the hypodermic found in her room?" I asked him.

"No one was looking for it yesterday, and there's nothing there today. All she had was an empty overnight case with her—which figures, if you want to take a hotel room but plan to exit fast, by the express route!"

"When had she checked in?"

"Only a couple of hours earlier. No one with her, and no one called or went up to see her, as far as they know at the desk. She lived in a one-room apartment on the wrong side of Grenville Heights. Polnik should be checking it out right now. She only had one relative we can find so far—a cousin."

"Who's he?"

"It's a she," Lavers said morosely.

"If she's under sixty and under one-eighty pounds," Murphy said in a gleeful voice, "Wheeler will come back with a whole dossier, complete to the last birthmark—and you know where you mostly find that one?"

"You're just jealous, like the Sheriff," I told him disdainfully. "You Hippocratic hypocrite!"

Lavers encompassed both of us with a baleful glare. "The cousin's name is Dolores Keller—commonly known as *Deadpan Dolores*." He shook his head in a gesture of numb despair. "This has all the signs of a Wheeler case. I guess I should realize by now that nobody can fight Fate—right, Doctor?"

"Deadpan Dolores?" I gurgled. "How come?"

"She's billed as the girl who says it all from the neck down," he snarled. "She's a stripper in a burlesque club."

"There comes a time in every man's life," I said in an awestricken voice, "when he's given his just reward."

"I sure hope I'm around when you get yours, Wheeler," Murphy sneered. "I'll do the autopsy for free!"

"Before you start," Lavers said resignedly, "I want that Jefferson case report finished up. How soon will I have it?"

"Sometime late this afternoon, sir," I said promptly. "But don't worry about it, I'll get right onto this new case just as soon as I'm finished with the Jefferson report—even if it means working on my own time tonight. You know me, Sheriff," I added, smiling modestly at him, "I'm conscientious!"

"I know you from way back, Wheeler," he snarled, "and there just ain't no justice!"

2

When night has fallen over the city and the neon signs blink and glitter along the boulevards, I get a moment of nostalgia here and there for the time when the world was young, and Wheeler along with it. The time when I'd stop and look at a life-size poster framed in brilliant lights, depicting some gorgeous doll wearing not much at all, and hear the faint jazzy music coming from inside the joint. As I looked, my heart would skip a beat with the exciting but uncertain yearning for the day when some of the mysteries of the female sex would start unraveling for me. I guess you lose that feeling along with adolescence—and a little magic goes out of your life at the same time.

This neon spelled out *Club Extravaganza* and the life-size poster standing out front of the entrance was a portrait framed in brilliant lights of *Deadpan Dolores*—"the girl who says it all from the neck down." I got my moment of nostalgia looking at it, and a little extra besides. Shot from a three-quarter angle, Dolores was a tall, beautifully built blonde; her hands were cupped behind her head, and she wore the usual spangled bra-cups, known as "pasties" in the trade, and a rhinestone G-string.

But it was the face that made me take a second look, and for Wheeler this was strictly a new approach. Dolores was a strawberry blonde with her hair pulled tight back across her head, leaving a short, urchin-cut fringe, and knotted at the back in a twelve-inch pony tail. Her face was molded in broad planes; her overly generous mouth curved in a faintly cynical smile, while her dark eyes sparkled with about the last thing you'd look for in a stripper—intelligence. All this from one li'l ole poster, and I could hardly wait to get inside and see the real thing.

I checked my hat because I was definitely in no hurry, then walked on to be greeted by the maître d'. He was a hairy, musclebound character wearing a wrinkled tuxedo—and an alphabetical index of the world's dirtiest stories filed in back of his eyes.

"I want to see Dolores Keller," I told him.

"You come to the right place, friend!" He leered at me like we were both members of the same fantasy club. "The next show don't start for a half hour yet. You want a ringside table, maybe I can fix it?"

"You hire out binoculars for a small fee, too?" I snarled at him.

His eyes narrowed and maybe an ugly expression appeared on his face, but who could tell? "Hey, listen," he rasped in a gravelly voice, "I don't know what your angle is, but if you want trouble, you got the right guy for it, friend!"

"I guess it's no use asking you to do me a big favor and drop dead," I said regretfully. "So do me a small favor and stop calling me 'friend'—'Lieutenant' will do just fine!"

I took out my badge and shoved it under his nose; if he couldn't read I was all set to spell it out, but the sudden sick look on his face said he could read just fine.

"Cripes!" he gurgled. "I'm sorry, Lieutenant, I didn't know you was—"

"We all have our problems," I sympathized. "You got that repulsive face, and I got to see Dolores Keller."

"Sure, sure!" He turned and beckoned me to follow. "Right this way, Lieutenant."

We threaded our way through the tables, past the five-piece combo who were playing a cha-cha like they held a personal grudge against Latin America, through a curtained doorway, and down a corridor to the dressing rooms. The maître d' stopped outside the second door and knocked.

"Who is it?" a feminine voice asked from inside.

"Louis," he said. "There's a police lieutenant here wants to see you, Dolores."

"So send him in," the voice said coldly. "You don't expect a cop to pay the cover charge?"

I went inside the dressing room, closing the door on Louis behind me. Dolores was sitting at a dressing table, outlining the deep curve of her lower lip with a small lipstick brush. When she'd finished the expert job, she turned around to look at me. The robe which had made her look modest from a rear view was wide open—underneath she was dressed the same as in the poster out front. This time she was not only life-size but alive so the impact was that much greater. After a concentrated five-second study, I figured that poster just didn't do her justice.

"I'm Lieutenant Wheeler," I told her, "from the County Sheriff's office."

Her lips parted in a faint smile. "What did I do, Lieutenant?—one bump too many?"

"It's about your cousin—Patty."

There was a plaintive squeak from a box in the corner, which sounded like it needed oiling. Dolores sprang to her feet and rushed over to the box, then knelt down and lifted a small bundle of fur in her arms.

"Bobo!" she crooned reassuringly. "Poor little Bobo! Were you feeling all neglected down there? You know your big mommy loves you always!"

She came back to the dressing table and sat down again facing me, still holding the bundle protectively cradled in her arms. A small pointed head lifted above her forearm and the bright eyes of a pooch stared at me with insolent disdain.

Dolores smiled at me again. "Bobo hates being left out of anything—he gets awful jealous whenever I have company!" She hugged the pooch even tighter to her bare midriff. "Doesn't 'oo get jealous, 'oo naughty little Bobo, h'mm?"

The pooch gave a couple of sharp affirmative yelps, then was so exhausted it had to leave its pale pink tongue hanging out while it panted for breath.

"If the noise worries you, you can always have it stuffed," I suggested helpfully.

That revived the little monster long enough to let out a series of frantic yelps that had my nerve ends crawling for cover.

"You pay no attention to the wicked man, Bobo honey!" Dolores glared at me balefully. "He's just a horrible, cruel old policeman—and I bet *he's* jealous!"

"I was only trying to be helpful," I protested. "I figured you could get a couple of G-strings out of the pelt maybe, and it could make for a new gimmick."

She closed her eyes and shuddered violently and for a moment I figured the pooch's hair was about to stand on end.

"So forget it," I said apologetically. "You were going to tell me about Patty, remember?"

"Poor kid!" Her eyes were still cold as she looked at me. "She must have had some tough breaks to jump out of a hotel window like that!"

"You know any reason why she could've wanted to kill herself?"

Dolores shook her head. "I didn't know her real well, Lieutenant. She only came to Pine City about six months back, from back home in Indiana. Her folks got killed in an auto smashup and I guess I was about the only relative she had left. We didn't get along too well—she wanted to be a dramatic actress and she figured my job was degrading or something!"

"She didn't approve of you being a stripper?"

Her eyes grew even colder. "I don't care for that word, Lieutenant, I am an ecdysiast!"

"A—huh?"

"Ecdysiast! It comes from the Greek and translates as 'shedding skin'," she explained icily. "There's a world of difference between an exotic dancer and a mere clothes-peeler, Lieutenant!"

"I'm sure," I said humbly. "You figure Patty was maybe still emotionally disturbed about her parents' death?"

"No," she said confidently. "I think she was glad to be rid of them—they figured a girl's place was right there, down on the farm where she was born." Her eyes were reflective for a moment. "Maybe they were right?"

"How about her friends?"

"That's easy—she didn't have any."

"Nobody?"

"This may come as a big surprise to you, Lieutenant," she snapped, "but even in southern California, the lonely are legend!"

"That's a good phrase—I must remember it," I told her. "You mean she didn't have one friend?—not even a boyfriend?—there was no man in her life at all?"

"It's about a month since I last saw her," Dolores admitted, "but up to that time anyway, there was no boyfriend. Things had gotten so bad, she'd joined up with a lonely hearts club even. She was all excited about it—couldn't wait for her first blind date. It was real pathetic!"

From the security of her warm and intimate embrace, the pooch gave me one last stare of cynical confidence, then closed its eyes and went to sleep. The heavy sound of its breathing still persisted but at least it was longer between pants.

"You remember the name of the lonely hearts club?"

"Sure—the Arkright Happiness Club. I asked Patty if it was run by a guy called Noah Arkright because he'd be a real expert at pairing off—but she didn't think it was funny at all."

"Neither do I," I said honestly. "But I'll bet Bobo bust a gut laughing."

"You are a horrible man!" She clutched the pooch even tighter until it squealed reproachfully without waking.

"There's always something vicious about a man who doesn't like dogs," Dolores said darkly. "It's a sure giveaway."

"You call that a dog?" I asked in genuine amazement. "Honey, the only difference between your pooch and any other ego-projection is that Bobo comes fur-lined. It's not the dog I dislike, only what you've done to it."

"Why don't you get the hell out of here, Lieutenant," she asked tightly, "if you're all through with the questions?"

"I guess I am—for now," I said. "But most likely I'll be back."

I had the door half open when she spoke again, the curiosity overriding her dislike of me for a moment.

"Does it matter this much, Lieutenant? I mean, why Patty killed herself? There's nothing anybody can do about it now, is there?"

"The questions are routine," I said vaguely, then turned and looked at her. "You ever stop to think—you and your 'the lonely are legend' and all—that if you'd given her maybe one-tenth the affection you give that pooch, she might still be alive right now?"

The muscles in her face set rigid as she stared back at me; then the pooch came awake with a sudden frantic help and leaped out of her arms to avoid being squeezed to death.

"It's just a thought," I said politely, then closed the door on her frozen features before she got around to throwing something.

On the way out I collected my hat and gave the girl two bits to prove I was a big spender even though the night was a hell of a lot younger than she was. I stopped and had another look at the life-size poster under the red neon. I gave it a whole five seconds, but there wasn't even a twinge of nostalgia. Then I drove the Austin Healey back home and was inside the apartment by ten.

I put Sinatra's "In the Wee Small Hours" on the hi-fi and made myself a drink. Sitting in an armchair, listening to the greatest vocal interpretation of "Mood Indigo" I ever heard, the living room walls seemed to shrink a little. I got a sudden urge to push them back a couple of feet. My time was my own—I had a choice. I could sit and drink all night by myself or go to bed and sleep by myself—so what the hell was I feeling depressed about? Two drinks later I thought the hell with Deadpan Dolores—even if I was the latest recruit to join her legend—and went to bed.

Next morning, with bright sunlight streaming into the apartment, I felt no different at all. For a couple of seconds I considered going straight to the office but the thought of Sheriff Lavers' face when he read that Jefferson report decided me against it. A guy has to face facts and the fact was I felt lonely. A guy has to be logical and the logic was to do something about it. Don't sit around and mope, kiddo, get out there and make the real big try. Face it—if it's a lonely hearts joint you need, get out and find one.

I found the Arkright Happiness Club about an hour later on the thirteenth floor of a mid-city building—but maybe the floor was only coincidence. I knew a guy once who spent a week in Miami with his best friend's girlfriend strictly through coincidence—they just happened to book the same room in the same hotel at the same time. What happened to my ex-best friend could happen to the Arkright Happiness Club, could happen to a dog even—a pooch yet—and I was back to Dolores Keller again.

Inside the office I felt kind of disappointed because it looked about the same as any other office—no pink plaster Cupid aiming a dart at a delicate portion of someone's anatomy, not even a vase full of hearts and flowers yet. Then I got my first look at the receptionist in back of a big desk and all of a sudden my heart sang—a little off key maybe, but definitely sang!

She was brunette with a careless hairdo and a Tahitian suntan to match the sultry beauty of her face. When she looked at me I saw her eyes were alert with a kind of primitive warmth. It was no trick to close my own eyes for a moment and see her poised on the bow of a lugger, her naked body silhouetted momentarily against the magnificence of a tropical dawn—then she dived cleanly into six fathoms of crystal clear water to gather a few more priceless pearls for me, before breakfast.

"Good morning," she said, and the overtones of her vibrant, faintly husky voice had my fingers plucking for breadfruit already.

"Uh!" I managed, and it was some effort, at that.

"Please sit down," she said and made the words sound like a sarong of love. "I'm Sherry Rand—and you are Mr.—?"

I plunked heavily into the nearest chair and it sighed like the trade wind through the palm trees. "Wheeler," I muttered incoherently. "Al Wheeler."

She smiled and her teeth were all priceless pearls, and what the hell we were doing in an office instead of an outrigger canoe, I'd never know.

"Please don't be shy!" she implored me. "We have hundreds of people who come in here for the very same reason you did. They're nice people but they're lonely and they want to meet other nice people but they don't know how to go about it—so they come to us. What did you say your name was?—Mr. Whooper?"

"*Whooper?*" That took care of the tropical paradise in one swift sheet of flame. I glared at her nastily. "Wheeler! Do I look like the kind of guy who'd be a whooper at this time of the morning?"

"I'm sorry, Mr. Wheeler!" Her lower lip pouted slightly, and her stunning silk blouse did the same as she took a deep breath. "You were mumbling a little, Mr. Wheeler, but you seem to have gotten over your nervousness quite fast!"

"A morning wheeler can be a reasonable kind of guy just out bowling his hoop," I snarled. "But a morning whooper—"

"Well, now—" Her voice was still bright but the smile was getting a little limp around the edges. "Just how can we help you, Mr. Wheeler? I imagine you're looking for a nice girl with maybe a view to matrimony—and we're here to help you find the right one! Do you have any special preferences?"

"You mean I get to lay out the measurements like a mail order for a Sunday suit?" I asked interestedly.

"We don't guarantee to find the exact girl of your dreams, Mr. Wheeler," she said carefully, "but most times we can come pretty close."

I thought about it for a couple of delirious seconds, then said it out loud. "The girl I'm looking for is a peachy blonde," I admitted. "Not honey, or strawberry, or tomato, but—you know—peachy? With a face that's a kind of cross between Marilyn Monroe's and Elsie Blatt's—Elsie was the girl I sat next to in junior high—I mean I want she should look exotic but homey. I figure her vital statistics would be around 42-18-39—and I want she should be rich, a good cook, and wear jazzy underwear all the time."

For a long moment Sherry Rand stared at me in frozen wonder, then her face dissolved helplessly and her body shook with delightful laughter.

"Are you *sure* you're not a whooper?" she giggled.

Fun is fun but there comes a time to get down to business like the bridegroom said as he put away the Scrabble set on the first night of his honeymoon.

"I'm a cop," I said apologetically. "There's a lieutenant tag instead of a mister."

She stopped laughing and looked at me cautiously for a while, like maybe this was the best gag of all but she wasn't absolutely sure.

"You—a police officer?"

"I know it sounds kind of stupid," I admitted. "But all the best cops have gone to Hollywood to work in television, so right here in Pine City they have to get along as best they can with the dregs—like me."

"You really are a police lieutenant?"

"They gave me a badge even!" I tossed it on the desk in front of her and she stared down at it like it was a three-dollar bill.

"I don't understand, Lieutenant," she said finally, a bewildered look on her face. "This is a legitimate enterprise and we've never had any—"

"Well, there always has to be a first time," I said in a consoling voice. "I just want to make some inquiries about a former client of yours—Patty Keller."

"I guess you'd better talk with Mr. or Mrs. Arkright," she said doubtfully. "Excuse me."

I waited while she announced my presence and intentions in a hushed voice—the kind the morticians have copyrighted for when they're using the past tense—to whoever was listening on the other end of the phone.

Then she hung up and said both Mr. and Mrs. Arkright would see me right away and it was through that door on my left.

So I opened the door to my left and walked into a small but neat office. This time there was a vase—it sat on the desk and it contained a spray of faded carnations. The flowers matched the rest of the furnishings—the drapes, the carpet, the wall paint—they were all faded. In back of the desk Mr. and Mrs. Arkright were standing like a faded photo in the family album—I had an eerie feeling that if you tapped either of them sharply on the shoulder all you'd get would be a cloud of dust.

Mr. Arkright was a little, chubby-faced guy with rimless glasses and the remains of his hair combed thinly back over his pink scalp—held in close contact by a glossy hair tonic. He wore a slightly crumpled gray suit which was maybe real sharp around the time Herbert Hoover was inaugurated. His tie was like jazzy with the alternating stripes of gold, black, and red, and it was knotted absurdly tight and small against the high starched collar that left him no neck at all.

"Good morning, Lieutenant," he said in a rusty voice that squeaked a little like he hadn't been oiled in a long time. "My name is Arkright—Jacob Arkright—and this is my wife Sarah."

Sarah was tall and lean with it. Her face, all angles and hollows, was surmounted by thinning, frizzy hair that had been dyed a brilliant titian. She wore a shapeless black dress that hung on her gaunt frame like a dust cover carelessly tossed over a high-backed chair. Her eyes were a faded blue and kind of fuzzy around the edges. When she spoke, her voice had a sharp, brittle quality, like she was used to hearing evasive half-truths and she wasn't about to stand any nonsense from a police officer either.

"Sit down, Lieutenant." She pointed to a dusty chair. "Now—Sherry said you had some questions about one of our clients?"

I sat on faded cretonne, a little worn about the edges, and wondered how desperate you had to be for a little companionship to wind up in a dump like this. Sarah Arkright watched me for a moment, then resumed her own seat in back of the desk. Her husband still stood beside her, and his right hand dropped to her shoulder in a pose that put them even closer to that family album photo, circa 1927.

"Patty Keller," I said. "She was a client of yours, Mrs. Arkright."

"Patty Keller?" she repeated sharply. "I don't remember her, do you, Jacob?"

"I—think so." He cleared his throat apologetically. "A young girl who was very shy and wanted to be an actress—I do hope she hasn't gotten into any trouble, Lieutenant?"

"Didn't you read about it in the newspapers?" I asked him.

"We don't read newspapers!" Sarah snapped.

"Not in a long time." Jacob smiled at me, and with those over-white dentures, it was a mistake. "The standards of modern journalism, Lieutenant ..."

"She's dead," I said coldly. "Yesterday afternoon she walked out onto a hotel ledge fifteen floors up and—"

"Suicide?" The rimless glasses magnified a kind of watery compassion in his eyes. "How tragic!"

Sarah Arkright folded her hands in front of her and pursed her lips thinly in disapproval.

"They don't have any roots," she observed calmly. "None of them do, that's their trouble today. No aim in life—all the standards have gone!"

"And Patty Keller along with them," I grunted. "Do you keep a file on your clients?"

"Of course." Jacob looked shocked at the thought of anyone doubting their businesslike efficiency. "Excuse me a moment, Lieutenant, and I'll get it for you."

He walked out of the office with a springy step which reminded me of the little white ball that used to bounce over song lines in one of the six shorts accompanying the feature at a Saturday matinee when I was a kid. After he'd gone I got out a cigarette and was looking for a match when Sarah spoke her sharpest yet.

"Not in this office, if you don't mind, Lieutenant! One thing neither of us will tolerate in this office is the foul smell of tobacco!"

Jacob returned as I replaced the unlit cigarette in the pack. He handed me a white manila folder, then resumed his position behind his wife's chair. The folder contained a couple of neat, typewritten detail sheets. Under the heading, "Patty Keller," was listed her address, age, occupation, interests, likes and dislikes—and it looked like somebody had done a real job on them. Page 2 was even more interesting. It was headed "Desirable Companion," and then broken down into detail under various subheadings, such as age, occupation, and financial status—all classified as unimportant. Character and interests were the things that concerned Patty: "Should be a kindly, sensitive man, interested in the arts and live theater especially."

The harsh voice of Sarah Arkright interrupted my reading.

"As you can see, Lieutenant," she said almost smugly, "we take a great deal of time and trouble analyzing our client's wishes before we attempt to find them compatible companions. Because of this, our percentage of successful introductions is very high—more than sixty per cent of our clients finish up marrying someone they've met through our Happiness Club!"

"How many wind up dead on a sidewalk like Patty Keller?" I wondered out loud.

The last notation in the folder was of a meeting arranged between Patty and one Harvey Stern, and the date was three months back. I ignored the outraged snort from Sarah at my last crack, and looked at her husband.

"This meeting with Harvey Stern—" I prodded him. "How about that?"

"Is that the last notation on the detail sheet?" he asked, squeaking a little on the last word.

"That's right."

"Our system works this way," his wife cut in forcefully. "We study the detail sheets and if we think two clients are potentially compatible, then we arrange an introduction. We do nothing further until one—or both—of them reports back that the introduction wasn't satisfactory. In that case we then arrange a further introduction. If that's the last notation on the girl's sheet, she hadn't reported back to us at all."

"How about this Stern character?" I asked. "Did he report back?"

"I'll go get his file, Lieutenant," Jacob said quickly and bounced out of the room again.

Sarah glared at me in open hostility. "I don't see what this girl's demise has to do with us—or our club!" she grated. "I consider this an unwarranted invasion of privacy, Lieutenant!"

"That's your privilege," I said politely. "Maybe this Stern character was a sex maniac and the experience of her first date with him drove the girl to suicide?"

She was still making gabbling noises deep in her throat when Jacob materialized with a manila folder, a blue one this time.

"Blue for boys and white for girls?" I said.

He flashed those store teeth at me. "Blue and pink would have been even nicer," he said. "But we'd already started with white."

I shuddered slightly as I took the folder from his hand. "You use black for widows and gray for the divorced?"

Jacob made a faint incoherent squeak, then darted for the cover of his wife's chair. I took a quick look at the last entry on Harvey Stern's detail sheets and saw the last date he'd had through the club had been the one with Patty Keller, and the dates matched. Harvey must have been one of the foundation members or maybe he was just unlucky—that date had been about the fifteenth on his list.

"I'd like to have these files for a couple of days—if you don't mind?" I said.

"Lieutenant!" Sarah looked shocked. "Those files contain confidential information. We guarantee all of our clients privacy! We couldn't possibly—"

"They'll be marked 'Top Secret' and kept in the county sheriff's safe at his office." I smiled brightly at her, then got to my feet. "Thank you for your help, Mrs. Arkright—and you, too, Mr. Arkright. Anytime I feel lonely I'll know where to come."

Sarah's face was a color to match her dyed hair while she struggled to find the right words; the rimless glasses magnified the bewilderment in Jacob's eyes into complete confusion. I left them looking like a couple of disturbed personalities in a psychiatrist's casebook, wondering on my way out of the office how they'd look with their heads shrunken down to the size of the knot in Jacob's tie. Cute as buttons, I figured.

Back in the outer office I stopped for a moment in front of the receptionist's desk and sniffed the fragrance of frangipani. I closed my eyes and could hear the sibilant rustle of grass skirts as they weaved a frenzied pattern around hula hips.

"Is something the matter, Lieutenant?" Sherry Rand asked anxiously. "You feel sick?"

I opened my eyes reluctantly, but the reality was almost as good as the fantasy. "Honey," I confessed, "I'm real lonesome but I don't have the price of joining the Arkright Happiness Club, and I don't feel I could be happy here—not after meeting the owners. You figure you could help out somehow?"

The primitive warmth was still lurking there in her eyes as she looked at me closely for a moment.

"I'm not sure," she said cautiously. "What did you have in mind, exactly?"

"A kind of blue and white folder combination," I said. "Dinner—my hi-fi machine—"

"Is situated inside your apartment, for sure," she said sweetly. "It comes with the intimate lighting, loaded drinks, and free-form couch—right?"

I looked at her suspiciously. "Who blabbed?"

"It's all part of a general pattern," she said shrugging gracefully. "If—just once—some guy would come up with an original idea for a date!"

"How about a burlesque show?" I asked, with sudden inspiration.

She blinked a couple of times. "You know something, Lieutenant? I never did get to see a burlesque show—outside of Muscle Beach, anyway."

"It's a once-in-a-lifetime opportunity!" I urged. "See it now with an expert, on-the-spot commentator—a guy who can point up that vital fraction of a second when a grind changes direction and is about to become a bump."

"I never saw a burlesque show," she repeated slowly. "You can pick me up around eight."

"Give me the address," I panted, "like on which island do I beach my canoe?"

3

You could have told by the flowers every place that it was a florist's shop even if you hadn't looked at the fancy script on the shopfront outside. A girl with thick hornrims and lank hair came forward to greet me. She wore a lilac-colored smock and flat-heeled shoes, along with a dedicated look on her face like she personally supervised the bees pollinating all summer.

"Good morning." Her voice was precise. "A corsage for a lady?—a dozen red roses?"

"Just some talk with the owner, thanks," I explained. "You think maybe he'd like a corsage?"

"Mr. Stern is very busy at the moment," she said frigidly. "And he never sees salesmen on a Wednesday, anyway!"

"An unfortunate traumatic experience with some roughneck pushing fertilizer?" I sympathized. "I'm Lieutenant Wheeler from the county sheriff's office, and I'm interested in hearts—not flowers."

She walked away from me, weaving her way around the gigantic vases that cluttered the floor until she was finally lost from sight in a back room. I lit a cigarette in self-defense against the heavy mingled scents that hung in the shop, then saw the florid-faced guy with a pink carnation in his lapel hurrying toward me as fast as his short legs would carry him. His face was a little plump and unwrinkled, like it had a lot of massage and was well scrubbed at least three times a day.

"I'm Harvey Stern," he announced breathlessly as he stopped in front of me. "My assistant said you are from the county sheriff's office?" His voice had a bland quality to match the pink and white complexion. Cut off cleanly at the knees and standing in a pastel-colored vase, he'd blend happily with his surroundings, I figured, showing the hostess had good, if not exciting, taste in floral decoration.

"Lieutenant Wheeler," I told him. "I'd like to ask some questions about a girl called Patty Keller."

"I read about it." He shook his head sorrowfully, then removed an immaculate white pocket handkerchief and dabbed his forehead gently. "A shocking tragedy, Lieutenant! A young girl like that with everything ahead of her—why would she want to destroy herself?"

I sighed patiently. "It's a good question and I'm trying to find an answer, Mr. Stern. Maybe you can help me."

"Me?" The look of surprise showed up a little too late to be completely spontaneous, "Why me, Lieutenant?"

"The Arkright Happiness Club," I said. "That's how you met her, isn't it?"

"Oh—that?" Stern looked faintly embarrassed. "I wonder if we could discuss this in private, if you don't mind? My office is just down there."

I followed him past glass-fronted jungles of orchids, carnations, roses, gladiolas; past pails of greenery and pots of ivy; through a small greenhouse area with benches jammed with flowerpots, and even a bunch of dwarf trees which I guessed figured prominently in the dreams of a pooch called Bobo. Finally we made it into Stern's office and he closed the door while my sinuses gratefully noted that there wasn't a single cut flower in the room. He moved around in back of a kidney-shaped desk and invited me to sit down in one of the molded fiberglass chairs, cunningly shaped to anchor only those people blessed with pointed buttocks.

"I guess membership in a lonely hearts club isn't something you want talked about out loud in public, Lieutenant." Stern gave an embarrassed giggle. "A confession that you've flunked out in the school of human relationships!"

"The lonely are legend," I quoted happily. "Or that's the word from the burlesque set as I hear it. Anyway, I'm a cop, not an analyst, and it's Patty Keller who interests me."

"Of course," he said, nodding eagerly. "I can't tell you very much about her, Lieutenant, I'm afraid. You see, I only met her the one time. The club fixed up the date for us as usual—around three months back, as I remember—and that was the only time I met her."

"The date wasn't successful?"

"I'm afraid not." His head shook sadly, and I wished he'd stop using it for punctuation—another five minutes of it and I'd need a couple of tranquilizers.

"What kind of a girl was she?" I prodded.

"She wasn't very attractive—physically, I mean," he said carefully. "Not that I attach too much importance to looks, you understand. She just didn't know how to make the best of herself and her clothes were all wrong. But they weren't really important—only the external signs of conflict."

I gritted my teeth. "Then how about we get down to the essentials, Mr. Stern? I got my own fantasy of the perfect female and I'm willing to bet money she's no more unreal than yours, so why don't we stay with facts?"

"Yes, sir," he said and swallowed hard. "Of course, the essentials! Well, I'd say she was a maladjusted personality, Lieutenant—I guess that's about the size of it!"

"You mean like she was unhappy—goddam miserable, even?" I grated.

"That's it!" He smiled dubiously, then saw the look on my face and didn't push his facial muscles anymore. "She had a miserable home life, she said, then her parents died and she thought she'd be free to do what she always wanted—become an actress. But she wasn't getting any breaks and her money was running out fast." His head twitched again. "It was a depressing evening, Lieutenant, I can tell you!"

"Did she say anything about taking her own life?—maybe hint a little?"

His eyebrows knit together in a troubled line. "Now you mention it, I seem to recall she said she couldn't go on much longer like this—unless something happened soon, she'd have to end it all." He shrugged. "By that time I wasn't listening too good—all I wanted was out—and I figured she meant she'd go back to Pumpkin Creek or wherever it was she came from in the first place."

"She just wasn't your type?"

"That's for sure," he said fervently. "I'm the nervous type myself—kind of shy—I'm looking for an outgiving girl, Lieutenant, someone to boost my ego. One more night with that Keller dame and it could have been me stepping off that ledge!"

I felt a sudden draft on the back of my neck and turned my head in time to see a bunch of muscles breeze into the office without bothering to knock. A real big guy with overlong blond curly hair and the kind of good looks that go to make the Hollywood version of a Roman gladiator. He wore a skintight sweatshirt and polished cotton pants, along with dirty white sneakers. I figured he'd be in his late twenties and was maybe a beach beatnik, or the garbage collection was running late this week.

"Hi, Romeo!" Muscles said in a booming voice. "How's every little thing with the guy that can't resist?" He ignored Stern's murderous glare and grinned at me, real buddy-buddy.

"Old Harvey here," he confided in a loud voice, "he's about the biggest Casanova you ever did meet! All the dames fall for him in a big way—big ones, blonde ones, little ones, brunette ones, even the redheads and the fat ones. Maybe it's being around the flowers all the time that makes him smell so sweet, huh? Or maybe it's because he's a big spender with personality? Sometimes I figure I should scratch a hole in my sweatshirt and stick a carnation in it—you figure it's the buttonhole that does the trick?"

"Shut up, Steve!" Stern said venomously. "You aren't even funny! Can't you see the *lieutenant* isn't amused?"

"Lieutenant?" the giant repeated slowly, and for a moment his face fell apart. "You mean—like a cop?"

"Lieutenant Wheeler—from the county sheriff's office!" Stern snapped. "This is Steve Loomas, Lieutenant, a client of mine with a misguided sense of humor."

"Yeah," Loomas said weakly. "That's me—always working for the laughs. I guess I walked in at the wrong time, huh?"

"We were about all through," I told him. "Tell me something—what does a guy like you want with flowers?"

"Huh?" He looked at me like I was just out of Mars, with three heads all saying something different at the same time.

"Mr. Stern said you were a client," I explained patiently. "So—unless he's running a bordello in the back room—you buy flowers from him, right?"

"Oh—sure—flowers!" Loomas nodded vigorously. "Yeah—all the time."

"So what do you want with them?" I persisted.

"Well—" he gave me a sickly grin. "You know how it is, Lieutenant, a guy likes to keep his pad looking nice."

"Like you never know who's about to drop in for tea?" I suggested sweetly.

His mouth dropped open as he stared at me blankly for a moment, then he made an effort and clamped his jaw tight.

"Sure, sure, Lieutenant, that's about the size of it." He edged toward the door. "Well, I sure am sorry for interrupting you guys. See you later, Harv—see you around, Lieutenant!"

"I wouldn't be surprised," I said honestly.

The door closed with a soft click and without Loomas' bulk, the office expanded back to its former size.

"He's a nice guy but—" Stern tapped his forehead significantly "—an actor—an out-of-work actor, mostly—he doesn't have too much up here!"

"Maybe because he's got so much everywhere else?" I suggested brightly. "Just one more question, Mr. Stern. How do you get along with the Arkrights?"

"The Arkrights?" He looked genuinely bewildered for a moment. "Oh—the Happiness Club Arkrights—just fine, Lieutenant. Why do you ask?"

"They strike me as being a couple of odd-ball characters," I said. "I wondered what their effect is on a client. They just don't seem the type to be running a lonely hearts organization—I can't see them having the sympathetic approach."

"Maybe you're right," he said politely. "I met them the first time after I joined the club, but I don't think I've seen either of them since then. Most of the real work is done by their receptionist, I think."

The look in his eyes said he was remembering Sherry Rand, and I didn't blame him one bit, in fact I was right there with his memories, except he could stay the hell off my tropical island!

"Thanks for your time, Mr. Stern," I told him, and slid my non-pointed buttocks out of the uncomfortable chair.

"Not at all, Lieutenant." He escorted me to the door. "I wish I could help more—a young girl like that killing herself!" His head started wagging again. "A terrible tragedy—terrible!"

I had a steak sandwich in a diner after I left the florist, and got back to the office a little after two in the afternoon. Annabelle Jackson lifted her honey blonde head and looked at me like I was a hot news flash.

"How nice of you to stop by, Lieutenant!" She smiled sweetly. "The Sheriff's been waiting all morning—just hoping you might spare him a few minutes."

"It's one of my charity days," I explained modestly. "You know how it is—today I am dedicated to spreading sweetness and light. If I can bring a little sunshine into the Sheriff's sordid existence by sparing him a couple of minutes, who am I to deny him so much pleasure for such a little effort on my part?"

She tapped a pencil on the desktop thoughtfully while she considered. "I don't think he sees it quite that way," she said finally. "But why don't you go in and find out for yourself?"

"There's no hurry," I said hastily, and lit a cigarette to prove it. "I just got to thinking—how long is it since we had a date—even a small one?"

"Not long enough!" she said tartly. "I can still remember the unpleasant detail!"

"It was your own fault—if you hadn't screamed so loud, you wouldn't have bruised your larynx," I said reasonably. "I would have let you out of the apartment even if the janitor hadn't busted the door down. Did you figure me for a wolf, or something?"

"Girl-eating tiger, more like!" She brooded over her memories for a few seconds. "That was a real expensive dress and it's never looked the same since, in spite of the invisible mending!"

"An understandable mistake," I said with dignity. "The way I heard it, you said, 'Take it off,' not, 'Take it easy!' You should have spoken louder, honey chile."

"I was screaming at the top of my voice," she said coldly. "Those five loudspeakers of yours were all going at full volume, remember?"

"Why don't we start over?" I suggested. "How about tomorrow night?"

"Not tomorrow night or any night during the next thirty years, Al Wheeler!" she said decisively. "Once bitten by a girl-eating tiger—"

"Well—" I shrugged casually. "When you get real lonely, let me know, and I'll give you an introduction to an ace lonely hearts club that guarantees to find either the perfect mate or an adequate hotel window high enough above the sidewalk."

An ominous growl in back of me made me leap a couple of inches into the air. For a nasty moment I wondered if I was treed by a girl-eating-tiger-eater. Then I looked around quick and saw it was a lieutenant-eating sheriff—maybe it wasn't any improvement.

"I hate to disturb you, Lieutenant," Lavers growled nastily. "I know it's in bad taste to mention work while you're around. But would you mind very much stepping inside my office just for a moment—" the veins stood out on his neck as he shrieked the last word at the top of his voice—"now!"

"Yessir!" I skipped past him fast in case he decided to stab me with the hot end of his cigar while I was real close.

He slammed the door shut and while the whole office was still rocking, waddled around to his chair and plunked down into it wearily. I sat in the nearest visitor's chair with a look of polite attention on my face because when you get right down to it, I prefer being assigned on an indefinite basis to the Sheriff's office as an alternative to being returned to the homicide bureau, where so many guys outrank me, it makes for ulcers.

"That Jefferson report," Lavers said coldly. "I'd like to congratulate you on a masterly thesis, Wheeler. Your exposition of the psychoneurosis of a con man is fascinating."

"Thank you, sir," I said with appropriate modesty. "It was nothing."

"You're damned right it was nothing!" he snarled. "The one thing you didn't bother explaining was why Jefferson's still walking around a free man after he conned that finance company out of twenty thousand dollars!"

"I thought you knew that already, sir," I said respectfully. "We know he did it, but we can't prove it—there's not one single piece of evidence that would stand up in court."

"And you're prepared to let it go at that?"

"What do you suggest, sir?" I still kept it polite. "I should follow him to Mexico and stay right behind him until he passes one of those unmarked, small-denomination bills?"

"The deputy mayor owns some stock in that finance company!" Lavers grumbled.

"Leave us hope he doesn't own stock in the insurance company that covered the finance company!" I suggested cheerfully.

The Sheriff brooded for a few seconds, then shrugged his massive shoulders. "All right! How about this Keller girl?—or did you just stay in bed this morning?"

I gave him a rundown on what had happened up to now, and the only thing I left out was my coming date with Sherry Rand. Even a cop is entitled to some kind of private life. The Sheriff would accuse me of putting sex before duty, and as a matter of principle I hate ever admitting he's right.

"The way you tell it, it all adds up to suicide," Lavers said when I'd finished. "That's the way the cousin tells it—plus this Stern character she had a date with. Maybe we should leave it at that?"

"I'd like to kick it around some more," I told him. "It's got a kind of wrong feeling about it, Sheriff. The Arkrights would be more at home running a funeral parlor instead of a lonely hearts club. Harvey Stern could have cheerfully murdered Loomas when he made his pitch about him being the Casanova of the cut-flowers set and all."

"I guess you've been around enough women by now to develop some feminine intuition!" he said sourly. "You know how accurate that is?"

"Don't forget the apomorphine, Sheriff," I reminded him. "How do you explain that?"

"Pure coincidence," he snorted. "I see no connection between a bad oyster and suicide, no matter how you cut it. If you were considering knocking someone off, Wheeler, I ask you—would you give her something to make her throw *up?*" His voice rose to a pitch of frustration.

"If I knew she was going to be perched on a fifteen-story ledge I might," I commented. "Besides, we're not in a month with an *R* in it."

"With that keen sense of humor, you can laugh yourself down to a sergeant in no time at all," he said coldly. Then he folded his paws over his paunch, leaned back, and said indulgently, "All right, Wheeler, just how do you propose further investigating the case, if I may ask?"

"With your permission, sir," I said, ignoring his sarcasm, "I'd like us to solicit the help of Miss Jackson."

"Dammit, Wheeler!" he said hotly. "You leave that girl alone! She's the best secretary I've ever had and I'm not about to take a chance on losing her because—"

I figured it would take a little time and I was right. It took fifteen minutes before he called Annabelle into the office, and another ten to bring her up to date on the situation. My throat was running dry by the time I'd finished, and I could tell right away by the incredulous look on her face that I hadn't made a good job of it.

"You mean," she almost spluttered, "you want me to go and join this—this lonely hearts club?"

"Right on the button, honey chile," I said admiringly. "It's the only lead we've got so far and we need somebody on the inside."

Annabelle took a deep breath and smoothed the clinging sheath dress down over her hips, so that her generously rounded curves jutted prominently like landscaping in paradise.

"Me?" she repeated in a disbelieving voice. "Join a lonely hearts club? Most nights of the week I've got one already—right outside my apartment door!"

"I thought maybe we could fix that," I said humbly. "You could wear the wrong kind of clothes and no make-up—a pair of glasses with plain lenses maybe—comb your hair the wrong way—leave your girdle at home and—"

"I do not wear a girdle!" she snarled ferociously. "And furthermore, Al Wheeler, I do not—"

"You've been in Pine City for six months. You work as a stenographer in City Hall, but not for the Sheriff, of course! You don't know anybody here and you're real lonely. Your job bores you. What you really want is a glamorous career—an actress or a model—something like that. You don't care about a man's looks or his income bracket, only his soul. An intelligent, sensitive and refined gentleman is your ideal."

Annabelle looked at me hopelessly for a moment, then appealed to Lavers.

"Is he out of his mind, Sheriff?" she pleaded.

"That's always been my opinion," Lavers said smugly. "You can relate it to the phases of the moon mostly, I find."

"Then I don't have to do this crazy stunt he's babbling about?"

"It's entirely up to you, my dear," Lavers said easily. "I think it's a pretty irregular suggestion!"

"From Lieutenant Wheeler that's strictly routine!" she said coldly. "Thank you, Sheriff."

"Sure, you don't have to do it," I agreed. "Chances are this kid, Patty Keller, did really kill herself and wasn't murdered at all. It doesn't make any real difference whether we find out for sure or not—except I keep hoping that some other poor kid who's alone and desperate in a big city doesn't wind up the same way all because we didn't pursue—"

"Sheriff?" Annabelle bit her lower lip doubtfully. "Do you honestly think it would help if I did like he says?"

"You've got a lot of courage," he muttered, "asking a man holding political office to be honest! If I must—then the answer's yes, there's a slight chance it could help. But that's no reason for you to do it if you don't want."

"O.K.," Annabelle said dismally. "Then I'll do it!"

"That's what I like about the South," I said admiringly, "they've got courage and integrity!"

"I sure wish you-all had told me that the last time I was in your apartment, Lieutenant," Annabelle said bleakly. "I might have stayed!"

4

The repulsive grin of admiration on Louis' face when he greeted Sherry Rand died a sudden death when he saw me in back of her.

"Back again, Lieutenant?" he said hoarsely.

"Strictly for pleasure, friend," I said amiably. "Maybe you can find us a ringside table?"

"Sure, sure!" He nodded emphatically, "Anything you want, Lieutenant."

He gave us a table that was hard up against the raised dais, took our order for cocktails, then lumbered away. I took another look at Sherry Rand and thought happily of the long intimate hours ahead of us, depending on just how fast I could get her out of the Club Extravaganza and back to my apartment.

"This is fine," she said approvingly. "We should get a real good view from here."

"I've got one already," I said objectively.

She was the same sultry brunette with the careless hairdo I'd met in the Arkright Happiness Club, but maybe more so. The black sheath with its wedge-cutout top and flounced skirt showed a lot more of that Tahitian suntan than I'd seen before. The fragrance of her perfume was definitely primitive, made from equal parts of tropical sunset, crushed hibiscus leaves, and pagan love song.

An undersized waiter served the drinks while the five-piece combo played Gershwin like they didn't care who won. We ordered dinner and the food was lousy but who goes to a burlesque show to eat? Then the house lights dimmed as the combo hit a rousing discord; the emcee bounced into the center of the dais like a zombie who was getting his voodoo at cut rates. The gags rated even cheaper, but mercifully he only had a five-minute spot before the strippers took over.

Sherry Rand was completely absorbed as she watched a silver blonde work her way through a routine of bumps and grinds. She was still fascinated by the time a slightly overweight redhead and a too-lean, gray-streaked brunette had finished identical routines, and the emcee was back with a fast line of dialogue that made "Who was that lady I saw you with last night?" a joke for intellectuals.

I ordered fresh drinks and the waiter delivered them just in time—a second before the whole room was suddenly plunged into darkness. Five seconds later a single spotlight picked out Deadpan Dolores standing in the same spot where the emcee had been a few moments back, and it was one hell of an improvement.

She stood motionless in a graceful pose with her arms raised above her head. A long, flowing black robe covered her completely from neck to ankles. When the indignant muttering of the male patrons had risen to a mutinous roar, the house lights brightened slowly and the robe became completely transparent, revealing the gorgeous body underneath, clad in the same rhinestone minimum as the life-size poster out front.

I guess the routine basically wasn't much different from the others, but the sinuous movements became erotic when seen through the transparent black nylon. Some time later she stripped off the robe and the background music doubled in tempo and excitement as she performed a dance that was a mixture of hula and Egyptian belly dancing, and nobody would have believed so many things could go all ways at the one time.

The audience was still applauding frantically as she rested for a moment, her face still completely deadpan—not one facial muscle had twitched even since she first appeared. Then she walked leisurely toward our table. She stopped only when her thighs were almost touching the table edge and her face relaxed into a sizzling smile. "Hello—students!" she murmured loud enough for most of the audience to scream wildly in appreciation. Right then I began to realize that prodding Louis for a ringside table had been one big mistake.

Dolores straddled her legs slightly and cupped her hands behind her neck, while the combo slid into the steady, rhythmic beat of "Bolero." She bent forward slowly from the waist until the top half of her torso was not more than a foot from the tabletop. Her dark eyes sparkled wickedly at me for a moment, then her pectoral muscles rippled into action under the smooth skin and the bra cups began oscillating gently—and in opposite directions! "Bolero" suddenly increased its tempo, and Dolores went right along with it.

I was suddenly panic-stricken as I realized that if the tempo got any faster, and Dolores along with it, I was about to be hit in the face by one of those wildly gyrating curves; so I turned my head away quickly and heaved a thankful sigh of relief at having been smart enough to avoid the danger.

The music stopped abruptly and in the sudden silence, Dolores' voice rang loud and clear. "*Coward!*" she said scornfully and it brought the house down while I sat quick-frozen with embarrassment. I never knew how the rest of the show went—I was still sitting there numbly with my face burning real bright like a beacon.

A fresh drink was delivered, breaking the spell. I grabbed the glass and swallowed the contents in one long gulp, then looked up to see the amused glint in Sherry's eyes.

"I thought it was cute," she said easily. "I wonder if I can do it."

"Not here!" I pleaded frantically. "Try it any time you like—but any place but here, please?"

"Of course," she said, nodding coolly. "I don't think this dress would stand up to it, anyway."

My nerves wouldn't stand for very much more and I knew it. I signaled the waiter frantically and lit a cigarette, my fingers shaking as they held the match.

"I enjoyed it very much," Sherry said. "It was a wonderful idea, Lieutenant, and I'm very grateful."

"Yeah," I said hoarsely. "Real relaxing—and the name's Al."

"Hello!" Sherry smiled warmly at a spot a couple of feet over my head.

"We met already!" I said blankly.

"Hello," a voice said right over my head, and I leaped six inches out of my chair.

Dolores moved into my line of vision, wearing a silver sequined sheath that was supported by one finger-width shoulder strap. Her wide mouth was curved in a cynical grin as she sat down between us—the waiter having produced a chair from nowhere in two seconds flat.

"I hope I didn't embarrass you, Lieutenant?" she said, her voice dripping with mock sympathy. "But it was all Bobo's idea, really."

"That pooch is one of the real hot dogs," I said, coldly, "and my guess is he'll wind up hamburger like the rest of them!"

"I thought your act was terrific!" Sherry said quickly. "I was fascinated—I couldn't take my eyes off you."

"I guess having a petrified rabbit for my only competition made it easy," Dolores said and smiled warmly at her. "I never saw a man so downright nervous in my whole life before!"

They both laughed companionably while my teeth gritted together so hard they were almost worn down to the gums.

"How about a drink?" I snarled. "They serve a dog-catcher's daiquiri here—specialty of the house—over-proof pooch-hooch, with a twist of pelt!"

"Poor Bobo," Dolores said calmly. "I have a feeling you don't like him somehow, Lieutenant."

A burst of raucous laughter from a nearby table saved me from trying to think up a snappy answer. Sherry turned her head casually to see who was making the noise, then her face brightened with recognition.

"I know that man from somewhere, I'm sure!" she said determinedly. "Maybe he's a member of the club."

I looked across and saw a familiar carnation, flanked by the slightly overweight, redheaded stripper on one side, and the gray-streaked brunette on the other. The table in front of them was crowded with bottles and they looked like they were having a wow of a party. "He's having a ball," I commented.

"He always does," Dolores said in an amused voice. "He's the regular Don Juan of the joint—a real big spender, too. Harv, they call him—I don't know the rest of it."

"I guess I must be mistaken." Sherry giggled suddenly. "With the company he keeps, I couldn't have met him at our club!"

"He's here maybe four nights a week," Dolores said. "The two girls with him are building a nice collection of jewelry between them—but he thinks it's just his personality, of course."

Sherry stood up then, extricating her black clutch bag from our clutter of Scotch and ashtrays on the small table, and peered around the dim room. Reconnaissance successful, she said, "Don't go away, Dolores—I'm crazy to have a real talk with you," and made her way efficiently through the throng to the back of the room.

Left alone with Dolores, my embarrassment returned. I couldn't think of anything to say, and I concentrated harder than ever on Harvey's table. About then, two men walked up to it.

The first guy was medium height and a little heavy with it, wearing an immaculate dinner suit. His bald head gleamed as he leaned forward to speak with Stern, but I lost interest right there when I saw the second guy. It was strictly from Old Home Week—the other guy was Muscles, the beachcomber, now better dressed in sports clothes, but for sure the same Steve Loomas I'd met that morning in the florist's shop.

"The smaller one is Miles Rovak—the owner," Dolores said when I asked her. "That shows just how much dear old Harv rates. Rovak wouldn't be bothered talking to more than a couple of customers during the whole week!"

"Who's the blond character with him?" I asked casually.

"Steve something—Loomas—he works for Miles," she said. "I had to bat him down hard one time, and since then we don't talk much anymore."

"Excuse me a minute, Dolores," I said getting to my feet. "I'm sure Sherry will be back in a minute. Have a drink while you're waiting."

"My!" Dolores batted her eyelids up at me. "You sure are a free spender, Lieutenant! Is it all right if I have the good Scotch?"

I walked across to the most popular table in the whole room and smiled down at the florid-faced guy with the pink carnation in his lapel.

"Hello there, Harv," I said pleasantly. "Looks like you'll make that diploma yet in the school of human relationships!"

Stern looked up at me vaguely for a moment, then his face paled a little. "Good evening, Lieutenant," he said with no enthusiasm at all. "This is a surprise—seeing you here."

The redhead sitting on his left heaved a deep sigh that shook her whole magnificent balcony in a quivering movement.

"Hey!" she said in a too-loud voice. "I'm getting bored—how about some action, huh, Harv?"

"Speak gently to him, honey," I warned her. "He's the shy type. You want him to bust out crying or something?"

The gray-streaked brunette on his right looked at me curiously. "Get him!" she said coarsely. "Who is this creep, huh, Harv?"

I looked at her and shook my head sadly. "You just don't dig Harvey at all," I said regretfully. "Sure, he's looking for an outgiving girl O.K., and after watching your routine tonight, I'd say he'd gotten himself one—but you got to remember to boost his ego the whole time. Right, Harv?"

"A weirdo!" The brunette gaped at me for a couple of seconds. "A creep! Why don't you have Steve throw the bum out of here, Mr. Rovak?"

"Shut up!" Loomas said coldly. "You run off at the mouth too much, Lena—you should watch it!"

"You know this man, Harvey?" Rovak asked in a clipped voice.

"This is Lieutenant Wheeler—from the sheriff's office," Stern answered in a strangled voice. "We met this morning."

"It's nice," I said mildly, "meeting people again this way. How's the pad, Mr. Loomas? Smelling real sweet now, I'll bet?"

"Huh?" the beachnik said blankly.

"All those flowers you bought from Harvey's shop this morning," I reminded him. "Remember?"

"Oh—them!" He smiled bravely. "Yeah—the pad looks real great—sure smells sweet like you said."

Lena—the gray-streaked brunette—giggled suddenly. "You—with

flowers in your pad, Steve? Whatsa matter, you don't like girls anymore, or something?"

"I told you before to shut up," he said in a low voice. "The next time you'll wind up flat on your face—maybe it'll make for an improvement!"

A sudden pinched look showed on the brunette's face as she looked down studiously at the table, avoiding Loomas' cold look of fury. She didn't say another word.

"My name is Miles Rovak," the bald-headed guy said, obviously working hard at getting some warmth into his voice. "Nice to have you here, Lieutenant—I'm the owner of the club."

"Thanks," I said. "I liked the floor show fine. I guess I had about the best view in the house!"

"We do our best," he said absently. "You're here on pleasure, not business?"

"Right," I agreed. "I just wanted to say hello to Mr. Stern. Don't let me break up the party."

"Real nice meeting you," Rovak said, then snapped his fingers. "Louis!"

The ugly face of the head waiter appeared right beside him in two seconds flat. "Yeah, boss?" Louis asked anxiously.

"The Lieutenant's check," Rovak said easily. "I want you should tear it up."

"Yeah, boss." Louis had a pained expression on his face.

"That isn't necessary," I said.

"Real nice having you visit, Lieutenant," Rovak said. "I want you should be my guest any time."

"Well, thanks," I said sincerely. "Any time you're in the county jail I hope I can do the same for you!"

"Hey, listen!" Loomas objected loudly, then shut up suddenly as Rovak's elbow knifed into his solar plexus.

"It's a joke," the club owner said in a tired voice. "You know you don't have a brain, Steve—so why knock yourself out trying to use it, huh?"

I went back to my own table and found Sherry but no Dolores.

"What happened to Deadpan Dolores?" I asked.

"She had to get ready for her next number or something," Sherry said. "I like her. She gave me some good tips on how to—you know?"

The wedge-cutout top of her dress began to quiver alarmingly as I watched, bug-eyed.

"Sure, sure!" I said nervously. "I'll take your word for it, honey."

"I was only limbering up," she explained casually.

"I guess if Dolores is getting ready for her next number, that means we're about to witness another floor show," I said cautiously. "I don't think I could tolerate that comic a second time around. I couldn't tolerate that intimate, real close-up technique of Dolores', either. How about we fade the scene?"

"Why not?" Sherry agreed amiably. "You have any hot suggestions where next, Al?"

"I was just thinking of my apartment," I said vaguely. "You know—the hi-fi machine and all."

"That sounds just fine." She smiled warmly at me, while I gaped back in amazement. "I mean, I could practice there, couldn't I? You don't share the apartment with anybody else, do you, Al?"

"Not on a permanent basis," I assured her.

On the way out I stopped for a moment beside Stern's table and saw the party had shrunk a little. Rovak and Loomas had gone, so again there was just the florist with a stripper on either side of him. Right then I figured him for the star pupil of the lonely hearts club.

"We're just leaving," I said unnecessarily. "Thought I'd stop by and say good night, Harv."

"Real neighborly," he croaked. "Good night, Lieutenant!"

The gray-streaked brunette braced her body and gave me an out-of-focus stare through blurred eyes.

"You say he's a cop," she said loudly. "I say he's a creep!"

"Don't pay attention to Lena, Lieutenant," Stern said anxiously.

"I didn't pay any attention to her act," I said graciously. "Why should I start now?"

"Why, you—" The brunette started out of her seat, but Stern jerked her arm savagely and she bounced back again.

"Have fun, Harv," I told him. "That is, if you can unload Lena."

We got back to my apartment maybe a half hour later, and I left Sherry in the living room while I went through to the kitchen to get some ice. When I got back she was taking a close look at the hi-fi machine.

"You don't have a record of that 'Bolero,' Al?" she asked hopefully.

"Sorry," I apologized. "You want some rhythm, I can give you the Duke's 'Caravan'—and for that you don't need castanets!"

"Fine," she said with a bright smile. "Put it on, huh?"

I left the ice bucket on the table and sorted out the record, then put it on the hi-fi machine. Then back to the table and the serious concentration of making drinks. By the time they were ready, the number was maybe halfway through.

"Ellington—the master," I said. "If there hadn't been gypsies before he composed this, there sure would've been right after the first time he played it!"

"I—can't—talk—now!" Sherry's voice panted breathlessly from somewhere in back of me.

I turned around slowly, figuring that not even an Ellington record could have made her breathless in so short a time, and right away—in no time at all—I was breathless, too.

The black sheath—with its cute cutout top, flounced skirt and all—was draped carelessly over the back of the couch, and a sheer black nylon slip lay right beside it. Which left Sherry wearing a minute, strapless, black satin bra and matching bikini-size panties.

She had her hands clasped behind her head and her eyes closed, her body gyrating gently in time to the music. What the bumps and grinds lost in professionalism they sure made up in enthusiasm—and that Tahitian suntan did stretch as far as the eye could see, which was a hell of a long way.

"Hey!" I said hoarsely. "Aren't you scared you might catch cold?"

Sherry opened one eye and squinted at me dreamily. "Not a chance," she said thinly. "Not so long as I keep on the move." A violent bump punctuated the sentence. "I think this routine is wonderful," she murmured through an ecstatic sigh. "How else could a girl get so much exercise without even moving from one place?"

It was a good question and I wasn't about to spoil it with an obvious answer.

"I made you a drink," I told her. "You must be getting thirsty by now."

Slowly the wild gyrations simmered down into a fluid, rippling movement as she undulated across to the couch, then dropped onto it—in perfect time with the last chord of "Caravan." I walked the drinks across to the couch and sat down beside her.

"Thanks," she said, taking the glass and raising it to her lips. "I hope you're not one of the squalid guys who load a girl's drinks, Al?"

"Are you kidding?" I asked coldly. "With the going price for good Scotch being what it is these days?"

She drank a little, then relaxed, leaning back against the upholstery. "It tastes O.K.," she announced. "How did you like my routine?"

"It left me the same way it left you," I said honestly. "Breathless!"

"You're the first guy I ever met who had one original idea, anyway—taking me to the burlesque show," she said. "It's opened up a whole new life for me, Al. I may never be the same again!"

"The Arkright Happiness Club's loss will be the Club Extravaganza's gain!" I said solemnly. "I can see the time coming when I'll brag real hard that I once saw Sherry Rand's routine without having to pay the cover charge."

Sherry smiled dreamily. "That's nice! And talking of the Arkright Happiness Club—was that the reason you asked me for a date tonight?"

"Only the half of it," I admitted.

"O.K.," she said and sighed gently. "So start with the questions."

"They'll keep," I told her.

"Be smart, Al," she said coolly. "Business before pleasure—and it gives me time to cool off a little before I practice my routine again."

"The guy in the club tonight," I said. "The short one with the red face and the carnation, having himself a ball with the hired help. You were right—you had seen him at the Happiness Club. His name is Stern—Harvey Stern."

"I thought his face was familiar," she said comfortably. "But I don't remember anything else about him—if you're about to ask."

"I wasn't," I said. "Stern figures you do most of the real work around the place. Is that right?"

"Just the routine." She shrugged. "The Arkrights pay real well—so I have to earn my keep."

"Did they tell you why I was asking questions about Patty Keller?"

"She killed herself," Sherry said in a somber voice. "It sounded horrible."

"It was," I agreed. "I saw it happen. You remember Patty at all?"

"Vaguely."

"What happens when somebody walks into the Happiness Club, wanting to join up?"

"They see me first. I pass them on to one of the Arkrights, and after the interview's finished, whichever Arkright handled it gives me the details so I can make out the personal file on the new member. Then I cross check all the files and sort out the eligibles for one of the Arkrights to make the decision."

"Decision?" I queried.

"Who will be the new member's first date," Sherry explained patiently. "And that's about it—I handle the accounts, too."

"You remember whether it was Jacob or Sarah Arkright that made the decision on Patty Keller's first date?"

"No." She shook her head firmly. "Sorry, Al. Next question?"

"No more questions," I said. "You want to practice your routine some more while I make us another drink?"

"Sure," she said enthusiastically. "Play that record again for me, will you?"

I started the record going again, then moved over to the table and made fresh drinks. When I'd finished, I turned around and saw Sherry back in her original stance, her hands clasped behind her head, her body weaving gently. Only this time something new had been added—or more accurately, subtracted. The black satin bra and panties had joined the dress and slip on the back of the couch. And that Tahitian suntan did have a hundred per cent coverage. I put the drinks back on the table because I didn't want to spill good Scotch all over the carpet.

Sherry opened her eyes and looked at me lazily. The ceiling folded back and we were enclosed by a star-spangled, velvety tropical night. She came toward me slowly, her firm breasts jiggling a little as she walked, and her rounded hips moving in an exotic pagan rhythm of their own.

She stopped only when her lithe body was pressed hard up against me. A bright flame burned somewhere in back of her eyes, giving them a hot, melting warmth as they looked into mine. I slid my arms around her, my hands moving over the satin smoothness of her suntanned skin.

"I was right the first time, Al." She laughed huskily. "You are a whooper from way back!" Then her laughter changed suddenly into a shiver of ecstasy—and all the delights of my fantasied tropical paradise were suddenly real.

5

I was back again with that family album photo, circa 1927, and any time now I was going to say, "I love my wife—but, oh, you kid!" then put on my raccoon coat and get the hell out of there.

Sarah Arkright was seated in back of her desk, a look of frozen distaste on her face, while her ever-faithful spouse Jacob stood beside her, his hand on her shoulder. I couldn't make up my mind whether he was giving her physical support, or maybe he'd keel over sideways if he took his hand away.

"This is a most outrageous request, Lieutenant!" Sarah said harshly. "First you take two of our personal files away with you, and now you want to see another dozen or more! I can't possibly allow it."

"I can subpoena them," I said pleasantly. "You wouldn't want to put me to all that trouble would you, Mrs. Arkright?"

"I can't think of one good reason why not," she said acidly. "You may be a police officer, young man, but your manners are disgusting!"

"Now, now, Sarah!" Jacob smiled at me nervously and once again I figured the guy who'd made his teeth had a lot to answer for.

"Don't pay any mind to what Sarah says, Lieutenant," he went on quickly. "It's just her way—I guess you could say her bark is worse than her bite."

I shuddered at the sudden thought of Sarah about to bite, and reached for a cigarette to steady my nerves; then remembered I couldn't smoke in the office because the foul smell of tobacco was something else they didn't tolerate, along with lieutenants.

"Sure," I said to Arkright. "It's just that I'd like a little more cooperation from your wife. We're trying to nail down just why the Keller girl killed herself—and as she was one of your clients, I'd figure you'd be anxious to help."

"I don't see what searching through all our confidential files will accomplish," Sarah snapped. "A proper investigation is one thing, Lieutenant, while pandering to morbid curiosity is quite another!"

"The last date you organized for Patty Keller was with Harvey Stern," I said. "That makes us interested in Stern, naturally. His personal folder shows he's dated over a dozen girls since he's been a member of your club. We'd like to know a little more about these girls—how they made out with him. That's why I want to see their records."

Sarah primped her hideously red hair absently with one talon-like hand.

"I refuse!" Her brittle voice shook with anger. "I shall see our lawyers about this—this unwarrantable invasion of our privacy!"

"Now, now, Sarah!" Jacob repeated uncomfortably.

"Oh—shut up!" she snarled at him.

Behind the rimless glasses, his eyes swam with mortification. He took his hand away from her shoulder, let the fingers fiddle with the too-small knot of his tie for a few moments, then walked away from her stiffly, with all the bounce gone out of him.

"We have a duplicate of Harvey Stern's file," he said in a rusty voice. "I'll check the names of the girls from it, then get their files for you." He opened the door and stepped outside, closing the door behind him noiselessly.

"Well!" Sarah Arkright gobbled for a moment while that fuzzy look that was always around the edges, spread right across her eyes.

"It might be easier if I check those files in the outer office, Mrs. Arkright," I said politely, and stood up.

"Since my husband sees fit to ignore my opinions, I am powerless to stop you, Lieutenant," she said flatly. The hollows in her cheeks deepened, giving her raddled face an even gaunter look.

"But I shall still see our lawyers—it's quite obvious that only a lawsuit will teach you any appreciation of the rights of respectable people!"

I got to the door, then looked back at her for a moment.

"Mrs. Arkright?" My morbid curiosity got the better of me. "Do you Charleston?"

"What?" Her face was a dull scarlet.

Jacob Arkright and Sherry Rand were busy searching a row of filing cabinets when I came into the outer office. I lit the cigarette I'd been wanting for the last ten minutes, then walked over and joined them.

"Shouldn't keep you long," Arkright smiled at me. "Oh—this is Miss Rand—but you've probably met already?"

The ashes of a passionate fire burned briefly in Sherry's eyes as she looked at me, then her full lips curved into a faintly mocking smile.

"We've met, Mr. Arkright," she said politely. "As a matter of fact, we found we share a common interest."

"Really?" Jacob looked pleased at the thought that someone in his organization had made friends with the law. "What's that, Miss Rand?"

"Primitive dances," Sherry said innocently. "The Lieutenant is by way of being an expert on gypsy tangos—their inner meaning, stripped of all pretense and—" she fingered the front of her nylon blouse absently "—er—encumbrances."

"Fascinating!" Arkright said vaguely. He fished out a new file to add to the already impressive stack Sherry was holding. "There—I think that about does it, Lieutenant!"

"Thanks a lot," I told him. "You mind if I borrow them for a little while?"

"Certainly not." He beamed at me anxiously. "You will return them as soon as possible?"

"For sure," I agreed.

"Good. Now, if you'll excuse me, Lieutenant, I feel I should be getting back to my wife."

"Of course," I said gravely. "I think she's missing your helping hand right now."

He gulped and a wan look spread across his face as he went back to the explosion waiting for him behind the door. After he'd gone Sherry moved in and leaned her delightful weight against me.

"I haven't seen you since breakfast," she murmured. "Did you miss me so bad you just had to come around the office?"

"I hate to disappoint you, honey," I said sadly. "But it's not you. It's that Sarah Arkright I'm crazy for—twenty-three skidoo! We're about to run away together and open a speakeasy in Chi. I got a friend who makes first grade booze in a bathtub out of sour apples and the dregs from Sterno cans. We got it made, Sarah and me!"

"What?—the bathtub booze?" Sherry asked coldly.

Then she backed off smartly, leaving me with my arms full of personal files. I looked down at them hopefully, wondering if there was any Kinsey-type research hidden under all those cute white covers.

"I've got everything?" I asked her.

"*Nearly* everything," Sherry observed drily. "To some girls, that is. Personally, I go for a slightly different type myself.... Oh, you were talking about the folders? Yes, you've got them all."

"Thanks a whole heap," I said.

There was a sudden burst of sound from the Arkrights' office—her thin voice rising to a crescendo, followed by the sound of a shattering vase.

"Sounds like Jacob's not making out too well in there," I observed. "Who's the boss of the outfit, anyway, him or her?—or are they equal partners?"

"They share about fifty per cent of the club between them," Sherry said casually. "The other fifty per cent is owned by a silent partner. I've never even met him—he never comes into the office at all."

"A partner who's not only silent, but invisible!" I was impressed. "For sure he's not a politician!"

"I don't know what he is." Sherry yawned sensuously. "His name's Rovak."

I gave her the beady-eyed look usually reserved for finance company managers. Then I remembered she'd left our table when Dolores and I had seen him in the Extravaganza last night. "Rovak, huh? And his first name's Miles. I shouldn't be surprised."

"You do know him!" She looked mildly surprised. "What's he like, Al?"

"You're on the level?" I stared at her suspiciously. "His name is Miles Rovak?—for real?—and he owns half this lonely hearts bureau?"

There was another resounding crash from inside the Arkrights' office and once again Sarah's voice was raised in bitter vituperation.

"Cross my heart—hope to wear falsies before I'm thirty if I'm telling a lie!" Sherry swore solemnly. "Why all this nasty suspicious cop jazz, Al? Is it important?"

"I don't know, honey," I said honestly. "But it could be. I guess I'd better take these files down to the Sheriff's office before Sarah finishes with her husband and comes looking for me!"

"I hope she's not too tough on him," Sherry said. "Jacob's a nice little guy—mostly—and I like everything about him except for those gypsy hands that keep wandering the whole time." She made a face. "You know—*clammy!*"

"Cheez!" I said feelingly. "If I'd been married to Sarah for as long as he has, my hands would be clammy, too—along with my mind!"

"You don't have a mind, Al," she corrected me. "You're just one big bundle of desire with nerve ends like radar! I'm blacklisting you with all the lonely hearts clubs in California!"

"What for?" I protested.

"Just in case they maybe have a receptionist who could provide competition!" She smiled wickedly, placed her hands behind her head and oscillated her hips, straining the tight skirt to the limit of tensile strength. "See if you can get a record of that 'Bolero' thing, Al," she said dreamily. "I've got a whole new routine worked out in my mind already!"

I took the files down to the office and found the Sheriff was out visiting with the mayor at City Hall, which was a break. Sergeant Polnik ambled into the office with a worried look on his face.

"Lieutenant?" His forehead corrugated alarmingly and I gave him my full attention because I always have a nervous feeling that if he ever has three separate thoughts in one day, there'll be a whirring noise inside his head and everything will fall apart.

"What can I do for you, Sergeant?" I asked sympathetically.

"Well, the Sheriff says I'm assigned to help you on this suicide case." He brooded for a moment. "I don't know what we're looking for, Lieutenant, and it worries me." He hesitated for a moment to make sure his meaning came across crystal clear. "I mean, like I'd feel better if you told me to do something, Lieutenant. I've been sitting around waiting since yesterday morning, and now I'm worried the way the Sheriff keeps on looking at me every time he goes by!"

"Polnik," I said sorrowfully, "I've been neglecting you!"

I started in to rack my brains for something I could give him to do, when I had a sudden inspiration.

"See these?" I pointed to the heap of files on the desk.

"Sure, Lieutenant." His eyes lit up suddenly. "Hey! I get it—portology!"

"Poor *what?*"

"Dirty books," Polnik said with an air of smug superiority. "That's the proper name for them, Lieutenant—and that's why they all got those plain covers, huh?"

"Sergeant, this is your big chance!" I said desperately—any kind of explanation would be fatal and I knew it. "These are files from a lonely hearts club. Each one represents a dame, and I want you to question all of them!"

Polnik gaped at me for a few moments, his jaw hanging slack, then slowly a beatific smile spread across his face.

"I always knew it would happen," he said simply. "If I stayed around you, Lieutenant Wheeler, long enough, someday there'd be a case where I got all the beautiful dames for once! Cheez!" He took out a large handkerchief and blew his nose emotionally.

"All these dames have one thing in common," I told him. "They all had a date organized by the lonely hearts club with the same guy—Harvey Stern. Get them talking about Stern—I figure he could be the boy we're after. Use your technique, Polnik—get them to open up their little hearts to you—no secrets, huh?"

Polnik was glassy-eyed at the thought. "You can trust me, Lieutenant!"

he said emphatically. "By the time I get through with all those dames, they won't have one secret left to share between them!"

He stacked the files into an orderly pile with loving care, then carried them out of the office. I figured he had enough work to keep him busy for the next couple of days—just so long as he took time out to sleep. He has the same trouble I've got—when work means dames, he's dedicated.

I called the Club Extravaganza and asked to speak with Mr. Rovak. The dame who answered the call had a voice that sounded like a blunt file scraping over rusty tin.

"He ain't here," she said loudly. "Who wants him?"

"That's a good question," I told her and hung up.

The directory gave his home address as out on Ocean Beach, and I figured the ten-mile run down there wouldn't be wasted on a sunny afternoon right after lunch. In fact it would be good for my neuroses as well as the Austin Healey's spark plugs. I made one more call before I left the office, to Captain Johns in the homicide bureau, and asked him would he get somebody to run a check on Rovak, Loomas, and Stern, and see if they had any record. Johns said O.K., it was no trouble, and how was life in the Sheriff's office? I told him it was just fine if you happened to be a sheriff—and how was life in the bureau these days? It was my own fault for asking. By the time he'd finished detailing the major faults of the homicide bureau I could have been halfway to Ocean Beach already.

6

The road seemed to slide straight down the side of a cliff, and right at the bottom was Rovak's house. It was quite a place—white stucco and palm trees, and a high adobe wall in front to keep out the peasants. But the iron gates across the driveway were wide open, so I guessed Rovak wasn't figuring on a revolution this year.

I drove in and parked the Healey behind an aristocratic Mercedes—the snooty model with fuel injection—and got out. The house was flanked by a long concrete walk which led to a diamond-shaped pool. Beyond the pool, the Pacific Ocean sparkled in the afternoon sunlight, and a wooden jetty probed out far enough into deep water to accommodate the massive cabin cruiser secured at its head.

A couple of cane lounging chairs had a couple of people lounging on them beside the pool, and right away I knew it was something I should investigate—even at this distance you could see the people were female. I walked briskly toward them because that's the way I always react to females—real brisk. When I got close and they could hear my footsteps on the concrete, the nearest one raised her head a couple of inches and looked at me. A bundle of fur, supine across her bare midriff, yapped reprovingly at her sudden movement.

"Oh, my God!" a familiar voice said. "Somebody must be paying him to haunt us now, Bobo!"

"Well—as I live and gasp!" I said, eyeing her green satin two-piece swimsuit appreciatively. "If it isn't Deadpan Delores."

At the sound of my voice, the pooch whimpered the canine equivalent of "Take to the hills, men!"—then leaped from Dolores' midriff onto the concrete and skulked under the protection of the lounging chair.

The strawberry-blonde stripper regarded me with an expression of frank distaste on the broad planes of her face. "I don't mind it so much at the Club," she said coldly, "because I only work there. But what gives you the right to invade my privacy in my leisure time, Lieutenant?"

"Yeah!" a second voice joined the act. "How about that?"

I recognized the gray-streaked brunette as she got up off the lounging chair and stood there glaring at me. Lena, the girl who ran off at the mouth—the too-lean stripper, I'd tabbed her, but I guess everything's relative, and that overblown redhead who'd done the routine alongside her at the Extravaganza had thrown things all out of proportion—and I ain't kidding. Anyway, if she was a lean type, I was a soprano.

She wore a turquoise sharkskin swimsuit that had a V-opening all the way down the front to her waist, held together insecurely by fragile crisscross lacing. That front lacing revealed a disturbing symmetry of swelling curves that blossomed fully under the turquoise sharkskin—and the minimal phrase would be "well developed."

"Some guys have sure got their nerve!" Lena continued aggressively. "Coming busting in here like this when two ladies are relaxing in private! I said he was a creep the first time I saw him, honey, and was I right or was I right?"

"Why do you dye your hair, Lena?" I asked interestedly.

"A gray streak's fashionable, that's why!" she snapped.

"I wasn't talking about the streak—I mean the rest of it?" I said brightly. "It doesn't make you look any younger, honey, if you know what I mean?"

"Hey, listen!" She stuck her hands on her hips and planted her feet wide, all set to give me a generous rundown on my ancestry for free.

"I'd love to, honey, but I don't have the time," I said hastily. "I'm looking for Miles Rovak."

"He's down there"—Dolores pointed toward the jetty—"on the boat. Do us a favor and fall overboard will you?"

"I just can't figure out why you girls don't like me," I said sorrowfully. "It's not my fault I'm a cop, I had no choice—it was either that or work for a living."

"A cop and a comic!" Dolores rolled her eyes pleadingly skyward. "Anytime now he'll start on that 'A funny thing happened to me on my way to the mortuary tonight' routine!"

"He don't look like a cop to me—or a comic, either," Lena said thoughtfully. "More like one of those carnival geeks—eats live frogs or something horrible like that!"

"Dolores," I said, real dignified, "kindly ask your mother to refrain from making crude remarks about me. I'm sensitive."

"Mother?" Lena nearly choked. "Why you—you—I'll scratch your eyes out!"

She came at me like she'd just been catapulted from a Navy carrier, her fingers crooked into claws, the silver-coated talons reaching for my face. I let her face run into the palm of my outstretched hand, then pushed gently. The timing was right and she reversed suddenly without missing a step—one moment she was moving fast toward me and the next she was back-pedaling equally fast away from me. Her first five backward steps landed firmly on the hot concrete, the sixth in mid-air, and the seventh into the pool. She yelled once, her arms flailing helplessly as she lost her balance, then she disappeared beneath the surface, leaving only a faint trail of bubbles in everloving memory.

I heard a low, moaning noise beside me and looked down to see Dolores squirming on the lounging chair, helpless with laughter.

"I don't—know—if she can—swim!" she gurgled frantically.

"I wouldn't worry," I said soothingly. "We should know for sure at any time now."

Lena's head broke the surface a moment later. She grabbed the side of the pool with both hands, rested for a moment, then hauled herself out onto the concrete. Her hair was plastered tight across her scalp and her mascara had run, making an eccentric pattern of smudges across her face so she looked like a Sioux on the warpath—and maybe she was.

"Swimming!" I shook my head reproachfully. "Lena—at your age!"

Her face contorted with volcanic fury and she opened her mouth to blast me where I stood, but the only thing that came out was water. Lena caught on real fast—to speak, to shout, to scream, her first necessity was air. So she took a deep breath, about the deepest I'd ever seen, and I guess it wasn't her fault at all. How could she have known that swimsuit wasn't designed for getting wet?

The crisscross lacing tightened suddenly until it looked like it would finish up embedded in her flesh, but its tensile strength just couldn't match up to her lung capacity. There was a sharp snapping sound as the lace broke in about three separate places, and it altered the whole shape of the swimsuit real fast. Instead of that V-opening right down the front to her waist, there was now a generously scooped U-opening right down to her waist. My second guess was proved right—Lena was a very well-developed girl—and if I'd had some "pasties" in my pocket I would have loaned them to her right then and there.

"Lena—don't!" Dolores screamed hysterically, and collapsed onto her chair again. "You'll kill me!" Her whole body shook uncontrollably with gigantic spasms of laughter.

Lena took one horrified look down at the front of herself, then did the only possible thing a lady could do under the circumstances—she leaped back into the pool again.

"I don't like to mention it," I said to Dolores, "but you figure Lena seems kind of nervous about something?"

"Go away!" Dolores gurgled. "I'll bust out of mine too in a minute!"

It looked like a good time to go see Rovak, so I headed toward the jetty, studiously avoiding turning my head to see what was causing the frantic threshing sounds I could hear in back of me. I reached the end of the jetty about thirty seconds later and stepped onto the snow-white deck of the cruiser. A head of blond curls, long overdue for a cut, appeared out of the hatchway a few seconds later, and a look of surprise showed on Steve Loomas' face as he stared at me.

"Hell!" he croaked finally. "For a moment there, you had me wondering if you was real, Lieutenant!"

"Everybody's saying that," I said uncomfortably. "I'm beginning to get a complex."

He came out on the deck and flexed his muscles in an automatic reflex against the slight breeze coming in off the ocean. A pair of those knee-length, skintight pants that the Hawaiians have conned us into thinking are something new and not a rehash of the Gay Nineties, was the only clothing he wore. Close up, those king-size muscles were impressive, and he flexed them a little more, maybe not so much for my benefit as to make sure they didn't seize up on him suddenly.

"I'm looking for Miles Rovak," I told him. "Dolores said he was out here on board the boat."

"Yeah, he's here," Loomas said, nodding. "I'll get him for you." He stuck his head back down the hatchway and yelled, "Mr. Rovak—Lieutenant Wheeler's up here—wants to see you." Then he smiled at me uncertainly. "We keep on bumping into each other all over, don't we, Lieutenant?"

"Like they say, it's a small world," I agreed. "Put a couple of flower lovers into it and they're sure to keep meeting up together. You must show me your pad sometime, Steve."

Loomas was saved the trouble of worrying about an answer, by the arrival of Rovak on deck. His bald head was bright pink from a little overexposure to the sun; a gaudy shirt over a pair of Bermuda shorts two sizes too big for him, covered the thickness of his body. In that kind of getup he should have looked ridiculous but he didn't. Maybe it was the unconscious air of authority he had, or maybe it was the arrogant strength of will which showed in the harsh lines deep-etched into his face. Rovak just didn't have a sense of the absurd himself, I guessed, and therefore he would never look absurd.

"You wanted to see me, Lieutenant?" he asked brusquely.

"Some questions," I told him. "About a girl called Patty Keller."

"Patty Keller ..." He repeated the name a couple of times, then shook his head. "I don't think I ever heard the name before."

"She's dead," I explained. "Went off a hotel window ledge a couple of days back. We're trying to find out why."

Rovak shook his head slowly. "I can't help you, Lieutenant. I'm sure I never knew the poor kid. What makes you think I can help, anyway?"

"A string of coincidences so long you wouldn't believe them," I said amiably. "The only relative the Keller girl had in town was a cousin who turned out to be a stripper, Dolores, who works in your club. Patty belonged to a lonely hearts club and her last date there, was with a florist, Stern. While I'm talking to shy, introverted old Harv, who should breeze in but Loomas here?—calling Stern a Romeo and buying flowers for his pad!"

Out of the corner of my eye I saw Loomas wince visibly at the mention of flowers, then carefully avoid meeting Rovak's eye.

"Last night I was at your club," I continued, talking to Rovak. "And who do I meet but good old Harv having a ball with two of your sexiest strippers sitting in at his table! This guy needs a lonely hearts club? I asked myself. Somebody tells me he's a regular client at your club, Mr. Rovak—got the reputation of being a big spender and a wolf at the same time. So I went over to his table to say hello and who should be there but Steve Loomas again!"

"I'm sorry," Rovak said curtly. "But I don't dig all this. What's the significance, Wheeler?"

"Patty Keller's cousin works at your club," I said patiently. "Stern, her lonely hearts date, is a regular client at your club. Loomas, his pal who calls him Romeo, works for you. And then this morning I hit the biggest coincidence yet. I find out you don't just own the Extravaganza—you also own fifty per cent of the Arkright Happiness Club!"

"Is there some new law against legitimate investments?" he snapped.

"Not the last time I looked," I admitted. "I'm just curious to know when a coincidence stops being one—I figured you might be able to tell me."

Rovak took a cigar from his shirt pocket, bit off the end and spat it over the side, then rammed it between his teeth in an irritated gesture.

"I don't know from coincidence!" He found a match and lit the cigar, wreathing his face in fragrant smoke for a moment. "What little sense I can make out of your spiel, is that you're investigating the cause of some poor kid's suicide, right? So—for the second and last time—I never even heard of her until you told me her name. And a coincidence is just a goddamned coincidence!"

"Maybe if we come at it a different way, Mr. Rovak?" I suggested politely. "The way it's worked out, you're the hub of the whole thing—coincidentally. That makes things kind of convenient for me because you know everybody concerned. Like Harvey Stern, for example. Tell me about him."

"All I know about Stern you've said already," he grunted. "A fat little guy with a red face who must sell a hell of a lot of flowers if the dough he spends in my place is any indication!"

"Can you figure one good reason why a guy who's a big spender at your burlesque club would need to be a member of your lonely hearts club at the same time?"

Rovak grunted sourly, then shook his head. "No," he admitted, "I guess I can't at that."

"Now, maybe, you can begin to understand why I'm so fascinated by coincidence," I told him. "Especially where Harvey Stern is involved."

"You figure old Harv was the reason why this dame knocked herself off?" Steve Loomas asked incredulously.

"Don't knock yourself out thinking, Steve," I said kindly. "It must take most of your strength to keep those muscles working now."

"He's got a point," Rovak growled. "Is that what you think?"

"Maybe," I said.

"You seem to be going to a hell of a lot of trouble to establish why this kid killed herself." He looked at me curiously. "Is it that important, Wheeler? I mean, supposing you do prove she did it because of Stern—there's still nothing you can do about it, is there? Maybe it's a shame, but it's no crime to be the reason for somebody killing themselves, is it?"

"Not as long as Patty Keller *did* kill herself," I said softly.

Rovak puffed his cigar for a few moments, his hard eyes boring into mine. "There's some doubt about the matter?" he asked finally.

"There's a lot of doubt about the matter," I agreed with him. "And it keeps getting bigger all the time!"

Loomas had a grayish tinge under his deep suntan. "I read about it in the papers," he said hoarsely. "They said she jumped!"

"I was hanging out the window, trying to talk her into changing her mind," I said. "I was sure she had—she was on her way back inside when she swayed suddenly and fell. She never jumped."

"Well," Loomas said, shrugging his massive shoulder "even so, Lieutenant, that's not murder—is it?"

"The autopsy showed there was apomorphine in her blood stream," I said, and told him what that could do. "If we discover that someone else gave her that, then we'll have a pretty good idea of whether it was murder or not."

"*Now* who's talking about coincidences!" Loomas yapped in my face. "Who would give anybody something like *that* if they wanted to get rid of them? She probably took it herself for some reason!"

"Maybe," I snarled. "On the other hand, maybe old Harv is a good friend of yours or maybe he owes you money, huh?"

"Don't get me wrong, Lieutenant!" Muscles gulped. "I was only trying to point up the possibilities, that's all."

Rovak tossed the butt of his cigar over the guard rail and smiled apologetically at me.

"I'm glad you told us the significance of your investigation, Lieutenant," he said quietly. "I wish I knew more about this Stern guy, so I could help."

"Thanks," I told him. "You could tell me something—just to satisfy my own curiosity. How come a man like you owns fifty per cent of a lonely hearts club?"

He grinned frankly. "I guess it does sound kind of strange at that—after you've had a good look at the Extravaganza! But the answer's real simple, Lieutenant, it's a goddamned good investment. The Arkrights have been running that kind of service most of their lives and they're pretty expert at it by now. A couple of years back they came out here from the East with all the know-how but no capital. Somebody put them in touch with me, and I checked their record—it was impressive. So I put up the capital in return for a half-ownership. They run the whole deal, of course. I've never been inside the office, even."

"Like you said—there's no law against investment in a legitimate enterprise," I acknowledged.

The breeze got stronger, whipping up a sudden gust that made Loomis flex his muscles defensively.

"How's the acting racket these days, Steve?" I asked conversationally.

"Acting?" He blinked at me a couple of times. "How the hell would I know?"

"Isn't that your racket?"

"Somebody's been kidding you, Lieutenant!" He laughed. "Me—an actor! I work for Mr. Rovak, look after his boat—things like that."

"I must have a word with good old Harv," I said gently. "I'm a cop with no sense of humor when I'm working."

"It was him that told you I was an actor?" Loomas shook his head bewilderedly. "He must be losing his mind!"

"'A mostly out-of-work actor' were the actual words he used, as I remember," I said. "Maybe there's a simple answer—like he's a congenital liar?"

"Maybe it isn't as simple as that," Rovak said sharply. "I've been thinking—since you told me why you're so interested in that Keller girl's death—that I don't go for that long string of coincidence any more than you do, Lieutenant! The more I hear you talk, the more it sounds like Stern is the guy in back of all these coincidences!"

"You could be right," I nodded. "If I keep on plugging hard enough, I figure sooner or later I'm going to find out for sure."

"Is there anything I can do to help?" he volunteered.

"I don't think so," I said, "but thanks for suggesting it—and thanks for being patient with all my questions."

I stepped back onto the jetty, then headed toward the pool. When I got there, I saw Lena had disappeared, but Dolores was sprawled face down on her lounging chair. A wad of hair peered up at me from under the chair then vanished quickly, and a moment later I heard a whimpering noise that was definitely neurotic.

"You should buy that pooch of yours some analysis," I said to Dolores' shapely back. "He's developing a fixation about me!"

"Doesn't everybody?" she asked coldly.

I lit a cigarette, taking my time about it, while I admired the view on the lounging chair. Then Dolores rolled over slowly onto her back and glared up at me.

"You have eyes like red-hot rivets!" she snapped.

"Is it my fault you happen to be an exotic, ravishingly beautiful woman?" I asked heatedly. "Am I responsible for the long-stemmed loveliness of your legs?—the geometric perfection of the rest of your anatomy?—the hundred-per-cent-plus desirability quotient you have? Blame your mother and father if you must blame somebody, but not me—I'm strictly an innocent bystander!"

"Well!" Her eyes widened with surprise and maybe something else, I couldn't be sure. "I never knew a cop could be that poetic before!"

She sat up on the chair to take a closer look at me.

"It's not the kind of vocal appreciation I'm conditioned to, you understand?" she said in a wondering voice. "Up until now, most of my compliments have been at the top of the lungs—y'know?—in simple, homespun locker-room language."

"This could be the start of a whole new era," I said modestly.

"I have the uneasy feeling this could be the start of something," she said thoughtfully. "Kidding aside, Lieutenant, what does appeal to you most about me—if anything?"

"You really want to know?" I said soberly.

There was a shade of embarrassment in her eyes. "Even if you have to be a little earthy!"

"Your face," I told her.

"You're kidding!"

"The hell I'm kidding!" I said abruptly. "The first time I ever saw you was on that life-size billboard outside the club. Sure, you got a wonderful figure, but you wouldn't be a stripper if you didn't. But that face of yours stopped me dead in my tracks. It's not beautiful, you understand, but it's got personality and intelligence and they're both kind of rare in burlesque."

Her eyes filled almost to overflowing for a moment, then she blinked fiercely and turned her head away.

"My God!" she said in a muffled voice. "You'll have me going like some starry-eyed college kid in a minute!"

"Or like your cousin—Patty?" I suggested.

She looked back at me, the hurt showing on her face. "Did you have to spoil it that way?" she whispered.

"The feeling is—and it's getting stronger by the minute—that she didn't kill herself after all," I said briskly. "Now it looks like she was murdered. I thought you might like to know."

I started walking again, past the chair, toward the Healey on the driveway.

"Lieutenant!" Her voice was suddenly frantic. "Wait a minute ... Lieutenant? ... Hey, come back here!"

I kept going until I reached my car, then reversed it down the driveway out onto the road and pointed its bullet nose up toward Pine City again.

The top was down on the Healey and the sea breeze felt good against my face. I wondered if I was getting any place at all—or if Patty Keller had been murdered, even. All I had was that string of coincidences I'd detailed for Rovak—and maybe they meant nothing. Right then I couldn't see any alternative to the unoriginal squeeze play I'd been using all the time. If you don't watch it, it can get to be a little corny in spots. You keep seeing the same people over and over again, asking the same questions. You try to look wise and make vaguely ominous remarks—

and all the time you're hoping that somehow, someplace, you'll get some kind of result from somebody. For all you know, the guilty party is two jumps ahead of you the whole time and silently laughing his head off as he watches your fool antics.

It was a cheering thought to keep me company on the way back to the city. Later, I wondered why I'd gotten this strong feeling about the kid's death. Maybe because I was right there when it happened. That sounded like a reasonable answer and I'd have been happy to stay with it, only I knew it wasn't true. The real reason why it had gotten so deep under my skin was because a girl called Patty Keller had died suddenly and unpleasantly—and nobody in the whole wide world gave a goddamn about it. In back of my mind was the uneasy conviction that if it had happened to a guy named Wheeler instead of a girl named Keller, the reaction would have been about the same. So somebody had to worry about the girl and I was elected. Because if I didn't worry for her, who would worry for me?

It was about then I figured if Dolores sent Bobo to a headshrinker for analysis, maybe I should go along, too. We could share our fixations along with a couple of rubber bones on the headshrinker's doormat.

7

"Apomorphine?" Stern repeated. "I never heard of it before, Lieutenant! Is it something you can buy in a drugstore?"

"Not without a prescription," I said. "But I guess that wouldn't stop anybody if they wanted some bad enough."

The white carnation in his lapel seemed to wilt a little. I didn't blame it at all—the heavy, cloying atmosphere inside the florist's shop, choked with the scent of a hundred different flowers was enough to make even an orchid wilt.

Harvey Stern's pink and white complexion changed color rapidly, like a chameleon, alternating between the two colors but favoring white most of the time.

"Murder!" he said breathlessly. "It sounds so—so fantastic, Lieutenant! A harmless, pathetic girl like Patty! Who would want to kill her?"

"You—maybe?" I growled.

"Me?" His plump body quivered agitatedly. "You're joking, Lieutenant!"

"You both belonged to the same lonely hearts club," I said evenly. "You were the only date she ever had through that club. The last time I was in here you told me about it. You felt embarrassed belonging to such a club, you said, it was a confession that you'd flunked out in the school of human relationships. You were the nervous type, you told me, you needed somebody to boost your ego."

"I only told you the truth—as I see it at least," he said defensively.

"Then Loomas busted into your office and told me you were a real Romeo," I went on. "No dame could resist you. Last night I saw you in the Extravaganza, whooping it up a little with a couple of strippers for company. You didn't look the nervous type then, Harv, you looked like you were enjoying it just fine—until you saw me, anyway. They tell me you're one of their best clients—a wolf, but a free-spending wolf!"

He stuttered helplessly to a standstill.

"Your old buddy, Steve Loomas, just dropped around to buy some flowers," I snarled. "'He's an actor—a mostly out-of-work actor!' He works for Rovak who owns the burlesque club and you knew damned well he did!"

"I—I was upset—nervous," Stern babbled incoherently. "I didn't know what I was saying."

"I got your personal file from Jacob Arkright," I pounded him again. "Patty Keller was the last one of more than a dozen dates arranged for you through the Happiness Club. We took the files of every girl who ever had a date with you, Harv, and they're being checked right now. All we need to do is find another suicide—a sudden death, even—and you're in more trouble than you and a brace of good lawyers can handle!"

He covered his face with his hands, his body still shaking violently.

"Lieutenant," he pleaded in a quavering voice, "if that girl was murdered, I swear I didn't do it! I had no reason—no motive—this whole conception is a nightmare!"

"If you're a congenital liar, Harv, this kind of shock treatment could have therapeutic value," I said coldly. "But I don't think you are. My bet is you lied for good reason. Either you murdered the girl or you're trying to cover for somebody else. I'd think it over real hard because time's running out on you fast. Any minute now it's going to be too late to tell the truth because nobody will believe it—whatever it is!"

I turned away from him and walked out of the shop—not too fast in case he changed his mind right then and wanted to call me back. But he didn't. He just stood there with his hands still covering his face and his body twitching like he had palsy. If it was a severe traumatic reaction maybe it did him some good—but for sure it didn't do me any good at all.

It was around six when I got back to the Sheriff's office, and the breeze had gotten a lot more violent in the last hour, like it would be blowing up a storm before the night was through. I opened the office door to step inside and nearly cannoned into a dame on her way out.

"Sorry," I said, real polite, and stood to one side to let her go through.

She reminded me vaguely of Patty Keller, I thought absently as I glanced at her. The same straggly blonde hair, the face devoid of makeup; her clothes didn't fit so she looked shapeless, whether she really was or not. She gave me a filthy look as she drew level, and I figured that was typical of all the dames who could spend ten years on a desert island with a whole detachment of Marines and never get a second look even.

"Good night, Lieutenant!" she hissed at me suddenly. "Or don't you speak to your friends anymore?"

"Huh?" I croaked feebly. "We've met someplace before?"

"Al Wheeler!" Her fist suddenly beat a frantic tattoo against my chest and I figured she must have flipped her lid for sure. "You—you fiend!" The heel of her shoe ground against my shin with excruciating accuracy. "This is all your fault!"

"Lady," I whimpered, "either I got an identical twin I haven't even met yet—or you have a great big hole in your head! I don't know you from a crowd!"

"That's what makes me so mad!" she hissed, then clobbered me across the side of my face with her purse. "It was all your idea in the first place—I'd be a big help, you said! Join that lonely hearts club and—"

"Lonely hearts club" I peered closely into her face. "It is you?" I said feebly. "Annabelle?"

"On my way to my first date, courtesy the Arkright Happiness Club," she snarled. "And you don't even recognize me—that does up my ego real fine. Now I feel confident!"

"Annabelle, honey!" I said hastily. "You're a genius—it's a masterpiece no less! Nobody would recognize the real you—the glamorous, magnificently beautiful southern rose, with those proud generous curves jutting—"

I collected the purse on the other side of my face.

"Where they jut is none of your business, Al Wheeler!" Annabelle said fiercely. "And if I ever find out this is just your idea of a funny gag, I'll—" The purse crunched against the bridge of my nose with eye-watering emphasis. Then she marched off with a determined stride, leaving me to wonder whether Sherman would have ever made it to Savannah if he'd had Annabelle around to contend with.

Sheriff Lavers was sitting in his office, a pile of white file folders stacked on the desk in front of him. He was busy reading one of them and didn't notice me come in. I watched respectfully for a few seconds, then cleared my throat gently.

"Occupation: county sheriff," I murmured. "Desirable companion: young and blonde, sexy and immoral—with just the one hobby."

Lavers lifted his head and looked at me thoughtfully for a while, then shook his head slowly in open admiration. "How did you guess?"

"We all have the same dreams, Sheriff," I said modestly. "Sometimes it frightens me—millions of guys sharing the same dream every night, with the same girl. I bet she's scared to go to sleep nights!"

"If you're one of those millions, I understand her problem," he grunted. "Polnik told me about these—" he gestured toward the stack of folders. "He's still out checking on the women involved. There was a kind of glazed look in his eyes when he left, so I'm not too sure when we can expect him back—if ever!"

"That Polnik—" I sighed gently. "He gets all the breaks around here."

"Oh, sure!" Lavers grunted. "He gets the girls from the lonely hearts club, while you're stuck with the strippers from the burlesque club! I can arrange a swap if you like, Lieutenant."

"Thank you, sir, but no," I said quickly. "I think a good law enforcement officer should stick with the assignment given him, rough as it may be!"

The Sheriff's eyes rolled toward the ceiling in mute appeal, but for once the luck of the Wheelers held good, and no bolt of lightning descended upon my head.

He tapped the stack of personal files with one finger. "Did you take a good look at these, Wheeler?"

"Not yet, Sheriff."

"A couple of interesting points," he rumbled. "They can keep for the moment. What progress have you made today if any? I know I'm an incurable optimist but I'm presuming you did do a little work for this office sometime—a half hour maybe—sandwiched in between a redhead and a blonde?"

"Gosh, Sheriff!" I said admiringly. "I wish I could afford the writers you got—I'd have every case wrapped up before lunchtime yet."

The telltale purple started to flood across his cheeks.

"Progress, sir?" I started in real fast on a summary of the day's events before the smoke started to whistle out of his ears. He'd calmed down again by the time I'd finished and it made me feel a little easier in my mind. One of these days Lavers is going to explode into little pieces and stay that way—and I don't want to be the guy who lit the fuse, then let it burn too long.

"That reminds me," the Sheriff said when I was all through, "Johns called you back this afternoon. No record on Rovak or Stern, but Loomas did two years in San Quentin for a mugging rap—got out around eighteen months back."

"It's interesting but it doesn't prove anything," I said glumly.

"Let's get back to the personal files for a moment," Lavers said. "These represent every date Stern's had through the Arkright Happiness

Club?"

"That's right," I said. "But we won't know much about the women concerned until Polnik gets back and tells us something about them—or the ones he's gotten to contact so far, anyway."

The Sheriff had that nasty, smug look on his face he always gets when he's about to pull a fast one.

"We got—" he ran his finger down the spines of the folders as he counted "—fourteen files equaling fourteen females, and the one thing they got in common is they all dated Stern through the lonely hearts bureau—right?"

"Right," I said cautiously.

He shook his head triumphantly. "Only half right, Wheeler. There's another factor, common to nine of them. Those nine have also dated a guy named George Crocker."

"But not Patty Keller," I said. "She only had the one date and that was with Harvey Stern."

Lavers fumbled in his top pocket for a cigar, then changed his mind and took out his pipe and tobacco pouch from the top drawer of his desk instead. I didn't like that—the pipe meant he was getting to feel mellow and that nearly always means he's outsmarted me already.

"Maybe," he suggested as his pipe bowl burrowed into the pouch.

"What do you mean, maybe?" I said coldly. "It's an established fact."

"Only if you're sure you can trust the records," he said, with a damn site too much logic for my liking. "Only if these files are always kept completely up to date by the Arkrights. Maybe Patty Keller did have a date with this Crocker—after the one she had with Stern—but for some good reason it wasn't noted on her file."

"Could be," I said glumly. "Why don't we take a look at Crocker's file and check if there's a lead in it someplace?"

"I sent a patrol car around there especially to pick it up," Lavers growled. "I called Arkright and told him my men would be there to collect Crocker's file, and he put on a big act how his wife was going to sue for a piddling little ten million dollars or something—invasion of privacy, some crap like that. I told him it was up to him—either he turned it over voluntarily, or we'd get a court order."

The Sheriff grinned fiendishly. "I also told him if he made me go to the trouble of getting a judge's signature for one little file, I'd make sure a posse of reporters came with me when I arrived to search his premises!"

"You're a real cagey sheriff, Sheriff," I said coldly, "So where is the file on George Crocker now?"

"That's a good question," he growled. "It's disappeared from the filing cabinet."

"Who said?"

"Arkright, for a start. He had hysterics all over the office, so the boys told me. They didn't believe him, naturally, and he told them to go ahead and search the whole office. They made a real job of it but they didn't find any folder with the name of George Crocker on it."

"You figure Arkright's either hidden or destroyed it?"

Lavers shrugged his wide shoulders. "Arkright—his wife—the receptionist—an unknown quantity called X—your guess is as good as mine, Wheeler."

A cloud of dense smoke from his pipe drifted my way and one sniff confirmed my worst suspicions. "Why don't you try tobacco in that thing sometime?" I said and nearly choked. "Make a break from that stuff the city sanitation department keeps unloading on you."

The phone rang and Lavers had a look of vague disappointment on his face as he picked it up—maybe he'd had a red-hot answer all ready for me.

"County Sheriff," he said, then grunted sourly, "Yeah, he's here."

He passed the phone across to me. I hauled myself out of the chair to get it, then said, "Wheeler," into the mouthpiece.

"Lieutenant, this is Harvey Stern," an agitated voice announced in my ear. "I've—I've been thinking over you said earlier. I think maybe you're right!"

"About what?"

"About me telling the truth before it's too late for anyone to believe it," he gabbled. "I'm still in the shop. Do you think you could come out and see me right away? It's difficult to talk over the phone—it's all very involved and—"

"Sure," I told him. "I'll be right out, Harv. You wait there for me."

"I'll most certainly do that, Lieutenant." He sounded almost grateful as he hung up.

I handed the phone back to the Sheriff, and he looked at me inquiringly.

"That was Harvey Stern," I explained. "He's ready to talk—wants me to go out to his shop right away."

"All right," he grunted. "Don't forget to ask him about George Crocker—and you'd better call me when you're through talking to him. I'll be home most likely—even a county sheriff has to eat."

"Looking at you, Sheriff, nobody would ever guess!" I said admiringly, then got out of there fast.

Around thirty minutes later I parked the Healey outside the shop and climbed out. The neon sign was lit, announcing brightly to the world that one Harvey Stern, Florist, dwelt within the portals beneath; but the front door was closed and nobody answered the bell. If Harv had changed his mind about talking to me, I figured he sure had picked a lousy time to do it. After I'd hit the bell a half-dozen times, I tried the door and found it wasn't locked. Sometimes there are advantages to being a simple-minded character like me.

Inside the shop, the overpowering mingled scents of a hundred different flowers hit my sinuses with a triumphant tenacity as I closed the door and fumbled for the light switch. A couple of seconds later when I flooded the interior with light, I saw that the shop was empty except for the flowers. I called out Stern's name a couple of times and didn't get any answer, so I walked through toward the office in back with the faint hope he was waiting there for me and he'd suddenly gotten stone deaf at the same time.

I opened the office door, stepped inside, and switched on the light. Stern was there O.K., sitting in back of his desk, but he wasn't waiting for me. He wasn't waiting for anything anymore, except Judgment Day maybe. His body was slumped forward across the desk and a trail of blood had seeped from the hole in the side of his head, down one side of his face, to form a dark pool on the desktop.

There was a gun still clutched in his right hand and close to it an envelope with my name written across the front. I picked it up and opened it, extracting the note from inside. Stern's signature was at the bottom; his typing was very neat and his prose was to the point, almost terse:

> *You were right, Lieutenant—it was my fault Patty killed herself. I took her out a few times and I guess I kidded her along a little so she figured we were going to be married. Then she started getting on my nerves so I told her it was all over and we were through. She got hysterical and told me she was pregnant and if I didn't marry her, she'd kill herself. I thought she was pulling the old routine on me, so I told her fine, go ahead and kill yourself, it'll save us both a whole lot of trouble. I never dreamed she was serious about it. I guess I've been half out of my mind ever since. I don't think I can face the truth coming out. This way out is the best for me. This way I don't have to see the look on my friends' faces after they know the truth.*

I dropped the note back onto the desktop beside a tall, slender vase of calla lilies. They seemed kind of appropriate and I wondered if Harv had thought of that before he pulled the trigger—and I had my doubts on both scores.

8

"The minister, the doctor, and the florist," Doc Murphy said happily. "We're all mostly concerned with births, marriages, and deaths. The happy and unhappy triumvirate!"

"A man blows his brains out, and the doctor gives us philosophy yet!" Sheriff Lavers said disgustedly. "You have a perverted sense of timing, Doctor!"

"You should remember, Sheriff," Murphy said gleefully, "that it's mostly death that gives both of us a living!"

"You don't really believe Stern blew his brains out, Sheriff?" I asked incredulously.

Lavers looked at me coldly for a couple of seconds, then sighed heavily. "Here we go again!" he snarled. "The man who can't tolerate any simple and logical explanation for anything! They must have a word for people like him in psychiatry, Doctor!"

"Sure," Murphy said promptly. "I could have given it to you a long time back—'nuts!'"

"When the two of you are through with the song-and-dance routine," I said patiently, "maybe we can talk a little logic?"

"The man shot himself," Lavers snorted. "That's self-evident! He left a signed note giving his reasons—that's also self-evident. What more do you want?—a repeat confession from beyond the grave on a Ouija board?"

Two white-faced guys in white coats loaded the corpse onto a stretcher and wheeled it out of the office on its first stage of the trip to the morgue. I lit a cigarette to take the suffocating onslaught of flower scent out of my nostrils and tried to keep from blowing my stack.

"I think it's all a little too neat," I said mildly. "It all adds up a little too easy—like somebody laid it out real careful."

"This may come as a surprise to you, Wheeler," Lavers said heavily, "but sometimes things really work out that way—real neat!"

"Doc," I appealed to Murphy, "Patty Keller wasn't pregnant, was she?"

"No, sir," Murphy said confidently. "She wasn't."

"It doesn't prove anything," Lavers said quickly. "She probably told Stern that, trying to force him to marry her, and when he wouldn't—when she threatened to kill herself and he said it was a great idea—that was the last straw. She was a lonely girl with nobody to turn to for help, and Stern treating her the way he did was enough to knock her right off balance. What do you think, Doctor?"

Murphy's satanic face sobered down a little as he thought about it for a moment. "It's possible," he conceded finally. "It was a pretty terrible—and total—rejection, at that!"

"Anything else, Wheeler?" the Sheriff asked triumphantly.

"How about the apomorphine?"

"How about it?" he said irritably. He turned to Murphy. "Doc, have you considered the possibility that she meant to use it as a cough medicine? Didn't you say it had that use too?"

"Yes—but that's very unlikely. No one would give themselves a big shot of it for that purpose."

"She had no medical training," Lavers snorted. "Look at all the people who take five times the normal dose of something because they think it will do them five times the good! It happens all the time."

"When I came into the shop, it was in darkness," I persisted. "I switched on the lights and walked through to the office. When I got in here, this room was also in darkness."

"So?" Lavers grated.

"So Stern called me and said he was ready to talk and for me to come right out," I said. "Then what happened? He sat at his desk and thought about it—decided he couldn't face the truth getting out and he'd rather die first. So he types a note, explaining all the reasons, seals it an envelope and addresses it to me. Takes a gun out of the drawer or wherever it was, then switches out the light—goes back and sits down behind his desk and shoots himself? If you were in his place, would you bother about the light?"

"Maybe," Lavers said. "Who knows what a guy will bother about when he's in a frame of mind to kill himself?"

"Oh, brother!" I said feelingly. "Then how about the mysterious George Crocker you discovered in those files? How about the odd coincidence that when you look for his file in the lonely hearts office, it's suddenly disappeared?"

"Could be coincidence," he said stoutly. "Could be there's some scandal attached to Crocker that the Arkrights don't want made public."

"Could be the county sheriff's got rocks in his head," I said disgustedly. "How about *that?*"

"Like I told you before, Wheeler," he grunted, "you just can't take a simple explanation for anything. I sincerely think you should consult the doctor here about seeing a good psychiatrist and having some analysis. It's getting to be a fetish with you—you have to complicate the most uncomplicated issues!"

"If I need a headshrinker, so do you," I said icily. "But at least I don't need a body-shrinker, too!" I stormed out of the office, hearing Murphy's raucous cackle rising to a crescendo in back of me.

It took a couple of hours, a couple of drinks in a midtown bar, and a rare steak in a restaurant way over my income bracket, before I'd cooled off enough to think about the Sheriff without lighting a magnesium flare inside my head. By that time the evening was all shot anyway, and there was nothing left to do but go home to bed.

It was after eleven-thirty when I walked into my apartment and found I had company. At first glance I figured somebody had stolen a Far East sunset and dumped it on my couch. At second glance the sunset resolved itself into a strawberry blonde, wearing a silk blouse printed with all the warm-glow colors of the spectrum and a pair of tight, ankle-length pants, the color of a sun-kissed orange. Two jade bangles nestled on her right wrist, matching the pendant earrings that shivered ecstatically when she moved her head.

"Don't you ever come home, Al Wheeler?" she asked softly. "We've been sitting around all evening real lonesome, haven't be, Bobo?"

The mound of fur sprawled in her lap moved economically, and from somewhere inside there came a small, plaintive yapping sound.

"Dolores Keller," I said. "As I live and my dreams come true! How the hell did you get in here?"

She smiled lazily. "I told the janitor I was your cousin, just got into town unexpectedly from Monotonous, Montana, and he let me in. He also said you've got more cousins—"

Bobo raised his head suddenly and gave out with a growl that sounded almost doglike.

"You figure 'cousins' is a dirty word in dog language?" I asked interestedly.

"Like it is in janitor's language?" Dolores smiled sweetly. "Anyway—you finally made it. Aren't you going to offer me a drink or something?"

"Sure," I said. "Take your choice. Scotch on the rocks, with a dash of soda—the way I like it—or Scotch on the rocks?"

"Don't confuse me with detail," she said. "You make it—I'll drink it."

I got ice cubes and glasses from the kitchen, then made the drinks and took them over to the couch.

"I don't like asking personal questions," I said as I sat down beside her, "but that pooch—is he house trained?"

"Don't listen to his insults, honey boy!" Dolores crooned apologetically to the bundle of fur. "He can't recognize a gentleman when he sees one!"

She got up and carried Bobo over to the nearest armchair and lowered him into it gently. He whined reproachfully for a full five seconds, then relapsed into sleep again.

"You ever wonder if he got bitten by a tsetse fly sometime?" I queried.

"He can't adjust to night club hours, poor darling," she said as she sat down beside me again.

"Talking of night clubs—how come you're not working at the Extravaganza tonight?"

"Even a stripper gets a night off sometime," she said. "And here I've wasted it sitting around waiting for you."

"If I'd known you were coming I'd have been home early—and primed the hi-fi machine," I told her. "How come I'm so honored, so unexpectedly?"

"You were in a mad rush this afternoon out at Rovak's place, Al," she said wistfully. "All those beautiful things you said about me, and I didn't get to hear half enough!"

"You're kidding!" I said accusingly.

"Maybe—just a little."

She turned toward me, and the broad planes of her face were set in a suddenly serious mold, while her dark eyes watched me intently.

"The rest of it is something you said about Patty—that she was murdered?"

"That was the firm opinion of the sheriff's office this afternoon," I said gloomily. "But now I'm the only guy who still subscribes to the same theory."

"What happened to change everyone else's mind?" she asked curiously.

I told her about Stern, the note he'd left for me, and how Lavers figured that tied up everything nice and neat. Her face tautened as she listened, and there was a somber look in her eyes when I'd finished.

"I don't believe it—Patty saying she was pregnant and threatening to kill herself if he didn't marry her," she said in a low voice. "She wasn't like that. She didn't have the kind of self-centered determination to play it that way. She was just a naïve kid who'd lived in the sticks all her life until she came to Pine City. He was lying, Al!"

"That's how I figure it, too," I agreed. "The only reason Harv had for writing that note was because somebody had a gun at his head while he wrote it. But I got to prove it—and that's the hard part, gorgeous!"

"I'll help you!" she said eagerly.

I looked at her doubtfully. "How come you suddenly got a big change of heart about the country cousin?" I asked. "The first time I saw you, it was one big joke—the lonely hearts club and all. You got a whole barrel-load of laughs out of it."

"I guess I was just trying to keep it that way," she whispered. "I was scared to let it get close enough to hurt me, Al. You can understand that?"

"Maybe," I said. "How do you figure on helping me?"

"I'll do anything you say," she said eagerly, "anything all!"

"Don't tempt me!" I told her. "An ecdysiast who's built the way you're built shouldn't say things like that, or you'll find yourself shedding skin in no time at all!"

"Seriously, Al!" she said. "Tell me what I can do to help."

"Right now, I wouldn't even know," I confessed. "You could tell me about Rovak maybe? Did you know he's got fifty per cent of the Arkright Happiness Club?"

Dolores's eyes widened. "No, I didn't," she said flatly. "You think he had anything to do with Patty's death?"

"Not directly," I said truthfully. "But my guess is he knows a lot more than he's telling. There's something phony about that lonely hearts club, and Rovak being a half-owner, he must know what it is."

"I can't see any connection between the two of them—a lonely hearts club and a burlesque club?" Dolores said blankly. "Can you?"

"I can't see anything and that's the main reason I'm steadily losing my mind," I growled. "You ever hear of a guy called George Crocker?"

"No, not that I recall." She shook her head. "Where does he figure in this?"

"That's something else I don't know," I said. "What do you know about Loomas?"

"No more than I did the first time you asked me. He works for Rovak—looks after his boat—comes into the club a lot." She shrugged gracefully. "That's about all."

"Was he an actor one time, do you know?"

"If he was, I never heard about it," she said. "I don't like him at all, not even one little bit of him. He's a woman-chaser but that only makes him a man. There's something else again, though—underneath all that bronzed muscle is a nasty, vicious streak of violence."

"He did a couple of years in San Quentin for mugging," I said. "You wouldn't figure a guy like that would know a boat from a bathtub. Does Rovak ever use it much?—or is it just tied up to that jetty the whole time, looking real pretty?"

"He uses it O.K.," Dolores said firmly. "He's away for a couple of days at a time about once a month—real deep-sea stuff, I think."

"I guess it's no crime for Loomas to be a real sailor," I said sourly. "Maybe I should go back to the Arkrights and start over." I climbed onto my feet wearily. "About here, we need another drink."

Back on the couch with fresh drinks, the line of questioning didn't look any more promising than before. I sat in silence, thinking but for a savage quirk of fate I could have been born with a kilt, and have spent a short blissful life blending Scotch for home consumption instead of export to the bluidy Yanks.

"What you need is a change of pace, Al Wheeler," Dolores said suddenly in a brisk voice. "Think about something else for a while. How are you making out with that sultry sexpot you had with you at the club?"

"Sherry?" I said obviously. "She's got ambitions to become a stripper."

"My God!" Dolores croaked. "She needs help!"

"Not much," I said complacently. "She has all the right equipment. Last night she practiced a little up here for a while—one try and she's almost a professional!"

"It needs a pro to pick a pro!" Her voice was frozen around the edges. "I can understand you being dazzled at close-up range in your own apartment, naturally! You'd drool at the sight of anything female taking off her clothes in your own living room, of course!"

"I would not," I said, matching her quick-frozen voice with an iceberg quality in my own. "I also happen to be a pro—not in the same line of business of course," I added hastily, "but I definitely have an eye for that kind of thing."

"Oh, sure!" she said and laughed shortly. "Two eyes—both popping!"

"She made a pretty good job of all your routines." I sighed and slowly shook my head. "And this was her first time out, so to speak. But then I guess you pros get into a routine—and the routine gets kind of rigid as time goes by?"

"*Rigid!*" She leaped from the couch like she'd just been goosed by a gander. "I'll show you from rigid! You got some music?—any music?"

I made the hi-fi machine in one convulsive leap. "Anything at all," I told her airily. "How about the 'William Tell Overture'? —that'll shake any stiffness out of your points."

"Just put a record on the machine," she snarled, "and keep your fingers pressed tight against your eyeballs!"

In the middle of the rack was a long-playing record of a honky-tonk piano, strictly barrel-house style, and I suddenly realized I'd been saving it all these years for just this occasion. I put it on the machine carefully, lit a cigarette, then turned to watch Dolores go into action. For the first time in my life I knew exactly how a sultan felt the moment before he snapped his fingers.

Dolores took off her golden-thonged sandals and placed them neatly in front of the couch; unbuttoned her shirt almost absentmindedly, as she listened to the honky-tonk rhythm with deep concentration. Then the shirt fluttered onto the couch as gracefully as a matador's cape, and was followed a moment later by her bra. She wriggled sinuously out of the skintight pants, tossed them carelessly on top of the small heap, then moved to the center of the carpet.

She stood motionless, her arms raised above her head with her fingers entwined, the overhead light giving a satin sheen to the flowing curves of her gorgeous body—naked except for a pair of white silk briefs. I slid onto the couch and sat waiting for the pro demonstration, with all that excited, uncertain yearning of adolescence right back with me—in spades.

Suddenly Dolores burst into action in a volcanic eruption of energy, her torso weaving and gyrating in a fantastic symmetry of motion that always kept in perfect time with the beat of the piano.

The forgotten cigarette burned down between my fingers as I watched spellbound. Her eyes were half closed and there was a look of something close to rapture on her downcast face, as her body performed the incredible, the unbelievable, and the impossible.

Straight burlesque is for the sex-starved and lonely—a succession of erotic bumps and grinds that range from the bawdy to the obscene—and finish up plain monotonous. But this was something I'd never seen before—a dance without the movements of a dancer, a paean of frank and sensual delight, the proud display of a perfectly molded torso controlled by an iron discipline. Maybe this was how they danced in a pagan temple under the cruel and implacable eyes of their stone idols when the world was fresh.

Then—finally—the record ran out of music and Dolores' rippling curves gradually subsided until she stood motionless, poised like a pagan goddess hewn from thin-veined marble. Her arms dropped slowly to her sides and she shook her head suddenly as if she'd just awaked from a dream.

"I could use another drink after all that, Al Wheeler," she said conversationally, "and watch you don't tread on your eyeballs when you stand up!"

I tottered to my feet and walked rubber-legged across the room to where the Scotch and the rest of it stood on the table. Dolores was on the couch again when I returned with a glass in each hand, the only sign of any exertion being the steady rise and fall of her high, full breasts as she breathed deeply and rhythmically.

"Thanks." She took the nearest glass out of my hand and drained the contents in one long swallow, returned the empty glass, then took the second drink out of my other hand and dispatched the contents in the same minimum of time.

"Be my guest!" I said bitterly, then tossed the empty glasses over the back of the couch in a gesture more designed to leave me both hands free than to have dramatic impact in the old hat Russian style.

"How does your little sexpot rate now?" Dolores asked in a sleek, pantherish voice.

"Strictly an amateur," I said truthfully. "That was magnificent! Why don't you do that instead of your usual routine in the club?—it would knock, 'em dead!"

"Isn't there some brand-new tag about not casting pearls before swine?" she asked easily. "The average ringside customer at the Extravaganza pays his money with just one thing in mind—and that's what he gets."

"I guess you're right," I conceded. "Would you like a couple more drinks?—or maybe I could bring the bottle this time?"

"No more drinks, Al," she said softly. "I'd like some more poetry—like that stuff you gave me this afternoon Remember?"

"I remember," I told her. "Like you happen to be an exotic, ravishingly beautiful woman, with legs that are a sonnet of long-stemmed loveliness only to be compared with the geometric perfection of the rest of your delightful anatomy—which all adds up to a hundred-per-cent-plus desirability quotient—that kind of poetry?"

"That kind of poetry!" she whispered softly.

Her hands found mine and guided them gently until they cupped the heavy curves of her breasts. Her fingers squeezed suddenly, and the long nails dug painfully into the backs of my hands.

"You ever play charades, Al?" she asked in a low husky voice. "Like somebody thinks of a word and somebody else has to act it out?"

"I guess so," I admitted. "I've played all kinds of games. This one sounds like a hangover from the kindergarten set."

"Not the way we're going to play it!" Her voice rippled with laughter. "I'm going to think of a word and you have to act it—O.K.?"

"There's nobody left to guess the answer," I protested.

"Who cares?" Her nails dug still deeper into the backs of my hands. "Right. You all set now, Al?"

"I guess there's a little kook in all of us," I said, sighing resignedly. "Sure—go ahead. What do I have to act?"

"That cute word you used the polite way—only this time let's take the alternative," she murmured. "Ravishing!"

"You mean you're going to put up a fight?" I objected.

"Only for a little while—you coward!" She pouted her full lower lip at me. "I tire very easily!"

It was a lie—well, a half-truth, anyway. Sure, she didn't put up much of a fight, but that jazz about her tiring easily—oh, brother!

9

Maybe every family has a private affliction, but they don't talk about it outside their own four walls, and the Wheelers are no exception. One member of the family in every third generation inherits the curse of the Wheelers, and in this one it had to be me. It's nothing real serious—just an occasional, sudden stabbing pain in the solar plexus which hits when it's least expected. I got it the next morning the moment I stepped into the outer office of the Arkright Happiness Club. The attacks have grown rarer as I get older and lately I'd figured maybe I'd outgrown it—a guy like me still having twinges of conscience—it's ridiculous.

But the twinge hit me the same moment I saw the welcoming smile on Sherry Rand's face, and heard the reproachful beat of native drums inside my head at the same time.

"Hello, Al honey," she said in that hibiscus-fragrant voice. "Where were you last night? I kind of figured you might call me."

For a moment I was tempted to tell her the truth, but what the hell? Dames are funny that way—I just knew she'd never understand that charades was just a game the way I played it with Dolores.

"I got involved, honey," I told her, which was nothing but the truth.

"I read about it in the morning papers." She shuddered faintly "He was that fat little man with a carnation you spoke with at the burlesque club the other night, wasn't he?"

"That's right," I said. "Harvey Stern—one of life's little tragedies and all that jazz. Are the Arkrights busy dispensing happiness right now?"

"I'll tell them you're here," Sherry said. She lifted the phone, and a few seconds later told me I could go right on in. "Last night wasn't entirely wasted," she said enthusiastically. "I spent nearly three hours practicing my routines. I'd like for you to see the improvement, Al."

I could feel the dark circles under my eyes widen as she spoke.

"That sounds great, Sherry, real great," I said hoarsely. "I'll call you, huh?"

"Oh, sure!" she said coldly. "This don't-call-me-I'll-call-you, Wheeler, is a sudden change, isn't it? Or am I just another trophy pinned on your living room wall now?"

"It's just all this wet weather," I mumbled as I headed toward the Arkrights' office. "It kind of numbs my vitality."

"It hasn't rained in a week!" she snapped.

"But that's only on the West Coast," I croaked, and escaped into the temporary sanctuary of the inner office.

Sarah Arkright was sitting stiffly in back of the desk, and Jacob Arkright was standing slightly behind her, his hand resting gently on her shoulder. Right then I began to wonder if they were real people at all. They could be wax dummies, wired internally with sound tapes, and each morning Sherry would dust them off first thing and they'd be all set for another day.

Jacob wore a different suit—a crumpled brown this time, and another jazzy tie with a pattern of pink dots against a purple background—and the small, tight knot looked more than ever like an angry boil on his high starched collar. He smiled nervously at me while his rimless glasses glittered with a high-polished benevolence.

"Good morning, Lieutenant," he said rustily. "We read about Harvey Stern—"

"In the morning papers?" I reproved him. "I trust you're not contaminated by the standards of modern journalism?"

Sarah's angular face got a pinched look as she glared at me coldly. She'd changed the shapeless black dress for a shapeless blue dress and it was no improvement. I figured she sat the whole time because if she moved you'd hear the bones grating together, and that would be something nobody would want to hear before lunch, anyway.

"Now that the whole sad story of Patty Keller is finished," she said sharply, "perhaps you'll be good enough to return all the files you have that belong to this office, Lieutenant?"

"Sure," I nodded. "I'll have them sent around today—if the Sheriff hasn't sent them already. I was just wondering—did that George Crocker file turn up yet?"

"No," she said flatly, "it hasn't."

"I can't understand it, Lieutenant." Jacob shook his head bewilderedly. "I can't understand it at all. It's most irregular."

"More to the point," Sarah asked in that brittle voice, "is it of any further importance now?"

"I think so," I said easily. "But then I don't think either Patty Keller or Harvey Stern killed themselves."

Her faded blue eyes got a little more fuzzy around the edges as she stared at me. "Are you out of your mind?" she asked, and it sounded like a genuine question.

"But the papers said—they quoted Sheriff Lavers—" Jacob protested weakly. "I find this most confusing, Lieutenant."

"You and me both!" I agreed fervently. "But that's my theory and I'm about to prove it. My guess now is that George Crocker's the key to the whole mystery—find him and I've found all the answers. I'd like you to tell me all you remember about him, please."

They looked at each other helplessly, then back at me.

"Was he tall or short? thin or fat?" I said patiently.

"Thin," Jacob said firmly.

"Fat!" Sarah snorted.

"Tall," Jacob said.

"Short!" Sarah snapped.

"Let's try it another way," I pleaded. "Which one of you first interviewed him?"

They glared at each other for a long moment, then announced, "I did!" simultaneously.

"Maybe it was your silent partner who handled George Crocker for the club—Miles Rovak?" I suggested.

"That's absurd, he's never even been inside the office," Sarah said.

"I'd like to believe that, Mrs. Arkright," I said pleasantly, "but somehow I just can't bring myself to have explicit faith in your memory—or your husband's either."

"You have been both rude and objectionable on each occasion you've been inside this office, Lieutenant!" She leaned toward me, her bony fist gently pounding the desktop. "We will not tolerate it any longer. If you wish to speak to either of us again, at any time in the future, we shall insist on having our lawyer present. Good day, Lieutenant!"

"Sarah?" Jacob's voice quavered a little. "I don't think—"

"Exactly!" she snarled. "And you never have in the thirty-five years we've been married!"

The phone rang and she snatched the instrument up from the desk. "What is it?" She listened for a few seconds and the hollows in her cheeks were shaded a pallid blue color. "The stupid fool!" she said softly. "Why didn't he—? Never mind! Yes, I think you are right, it's the only thing you can do—increase the consignment by one. I'm busy right now so I'll have to call you back later."

She hung up and raised her tufted eyebrows a fraction. "Are you still here, Lieutenant?"

"One more question and I'm gone," I said. "Are you frightened of Rovak? Is that why your memory suddenly fails when I ask questions about George Crocker?"

She smiled thinly. "Your rudeness is equaled by your imagination, Lieutenant. That is ridiculous!"

I retraced my steps into the outer office. Sherry had her head bent over some papers and she didn't look up as I went past. It was a bleak, unfriendly world and if I hadn't been so goddamned tired, maybe I would have done something about it.

From the Arkright Happiness Club, I drove to the Lavers Lair for

Lovelorn Lieutenants, but he wasn't in his office, and neither was Annabelle Jackson. I sat in a chair and smoked a couple of cigarettes; then a living monolithic slab shuffled in, a look of intense gloom set deep on its crudely chiseled face.

"A lousy morning, huh, Lieutenant?" Sergeant Polnik said dolefully. "All that work wasted. It ain't right—there ought to be a law against some bum knocking himself off and leaving a note that does honest, hard-working cops like us out of a job!"

"Without doubt there are thousands of honest, hard-working cops throughout the country," I observed coldly. "I don't think they include us, Sergeant."

"It was just a figment of speech, Lieutenant," he murmured. "I got hell from my old lady for being in so late last night and she wouldn't believe I was working the whole time." He scratched his head with an aggrieved finger. "Then when I get in here this morning the Sheriff tells me it's all over and he don't even want to hear my report. He was shouting and waving his arms around like one of them Navy guys on a sinking ship or something—"

"Semaphoring?" I suggested.

"Some are—some ain't," Polnik said. "I always figure a guy is entitled to his own private life, Lieutenant! Like I was saying, the Sheriff's real mad. Says I'm just as bad as that no-good Lieutenant—you should forgive the expression, Lieutenant—wasting his time and the taxpayer's dough on a wild booze chase, he says!"

"Goose chase?"

"What the hell difference?" Polnik asked moodily. "I waste all day and half the night working my feet into an early grave and all I get is a bawling out from my old lady and the Sheriff!"

"Things is tough all over, Sergeant," I sympathized. Then I suddenly remembered. "Hey! Wait a minute, you were checking all the dames listed on Harvey Stern's file, right?"

"For what good it done me!" he grunted.

"Sit down, Sergeant," I said briskly, pushing him into a chair. "Tell me all about it—don't miss a thing. No detail is too trivial."

"Lieutenant," Polnik said, peering at me dubiously, "you're ribbing me again?"

"Cross my heart!"

A slow smile spread across his repulsive face. "You really mean it? Cheez!" He gulped emotionally. "Thanks a million, Lieutenant. Well, the first dame on the list is a Gladys Vlotnik, and she lives out on Casey Street, but when I get there—"

I had no place else to go and nothing to do but listen to him, and that was just as well, because Polnik was the conscientious type cop. If he walked down a street just once, he could tell you the exact color of the curtains in all the windows—and insisted on telling.

He'd drawn a blank on the first four names from the list—none of them were living at the same addresses any more. They'd all moved, leaving no forwarding addresses. The fifth had been a middle-aged schoolteacher who'd had hysterics at the first mention of the Arkright Happiness Club and the name of Harvey Stern, then had driven Polnik out of her apartment with the sharp end of an umbrella.

"I figured she was a little—you know, Lieutenant?" Polnik tapped the side of his head significantly, and the sound it made was reminiscent of the homing call of a woodpecker. "Anyways, the next one was a real dish—Lola Lundy. She's a hoofer in one of the downtown night clubs and she was sleeping when I pushed the buzzer. I guess she just got straight out of bed and opened the door." Polnik blushed at the happy memory. "She was wearing one of them chemises like spun glass, you know? One look and you got the dame tabbed right down to her birthmarks. And a funny thing about that dame—talking of birthmarks—"

"Leave us not discuss the more delicate secrets of Lola's anatomy, Sergeant!" I pleaded. "Did she tell you anything interesting about the lonely hearts club?"

"Yeah, a whole lot," he said feelingly. "It was around three in the afternoon when I got there, but she hadn't had breakfast yet, what with her working such late hours and all. So she opened a bottle of Canadian Club and—"

"For breakfast?"

"She said it helped keep up her strength," he said defensively. "Then she invited me to join her, and after that we got to talking and before I knew it, the bottle was empty, it was dark outside and she was still talking." The light faded regretfully from his eyes. "I never did get that dame to stop goddamn well talking!"

"What did she say!" I grated.

"Say? Oh, yeah—the Arkright Happiness Club? Well, she'd just gotten into town—this was six months back—and she was all alone and she wanted some guys to take her out and show her a good time. So she joined up with the club."

"Maybe she had her back teeth filled at the dentist's, too?" I snarled. "I want to know about Harvey Stern and that's all—you understand, Sergeant?"

"Well, O.K. But you said not to leave nothing out, never mind how stupid, Lieutenant! Yeah—Stern? She figured he was a creep with wandering hands worse than—" Polnik blinked rapidly. "—well, wandering hands. And he kept on wanting to find out if she had any dough in the bank the whole time, so after the second date with him, she gives him the bum's rush."

"And that's all about Stern?"

"That's all about Stern," he agreed placidly.

"Maybe we can save ourselves a little time here," I said slowly. "Did any of the others say anything more about Stern than Lola did?"

"No, Lieutenant. A couple more said about the same. He seemed like he was more interested in any dough they might have than he was in them."

"Well, thanks, anyway." I bared my teeth at him, and hoped it would pass for a smile, but the way he reared back said it didn't.

"There was one dame who's dead now," he volunteered hopefully. "She got married—some guy she met through the club, the old bat who owned the apartments told me—and she was killed in an auto accident in New Mexico three weeks later."

"What was her name?"

"I got it right here, Lieutenant." He thumbed laboriously through his notebook until he found the right entry. "Yeah—Joan Penton."

"Was that her married name?"

"I guess not—the old bat never did find out the name of the little fat guy she married."

"Little fat guy?" I prodded him. "Did the old bat say anything else about him?"

"She didn't like the look of him at all." Polnik shook his head sadly. "Dressed too neat for an honest man, she said, with that carnation in his buttonhole and all."

"None of the others either married or dead?"

"Not the ones I talked to. But I guess the first four I never got to see could be either married, or dead, or both, huh?"

"I guess they could, at that," I said. "Thanks, Sergeant. Nobody mentioned a guy called Crocker—George Crocker—by any chance?"

"Crocker? Oh, sure—Lola talked about him all the time. She figured she was crazy for the guy until one night he tried to talk her into going for a weekend cruise on his boat, and then got real nasty when she refused. The way she tells it, he tossed her into his car and said she was going anyway, but he had to stop for a red light about a mile out of town and she dived out the car and ran. She never saw him again after that, she said, and didn't want to, either. Is this Crocker important, Lieutenant?"

"The way I figure it, he is," I said. "What else did you get on him from Lola?"

"Nothing much," he admitted. "She was too busy drinking all the time and telling me to keep my big hands—anyway, she didn't talk much about Crocker after telling me how he turned nasty in the car that last time."

"She must have said something more than that!" I growled desperately. "What was this Crocker, he had a boat for weekend cruising? A millionaire yachtsman?—a fisherman?—what?"

"That's right!" Polnik slapped his forehead, and I watched expectantly to see his hand splinter, but it didn't. "He was a great big handsome hunk of man, she said, and he was an actor."

"Thanks, Sergeant," I said gratefully. "You've been a big help!"

"I have?" His forehead corrugated alarmingly as he tried to figure out why. "Cheez! I'm sure glad all that time wasn't wasted, Lieutenant."

"Sure," I said. "Have you seen Miss Jackson this morning?"

"No," he said, shaking his head. "The Sheriff figured she was just late getting in. He had to leave by nine-thirty and get over to City Hall for a special meeting or something."

I reached for the phone and dialed the number of Annabelle's apartment, then listened to the phone ring for a couple of minutes without anyone answering. A sudden painful twinge in my solar plexus reminded me Annabelle had gone out on her first date organized by the lonely hearts club the night before—courtesy, Al Wheeler.

"Drop over to her apartment and see if she's sick or something," I told Polnik, and gave him the address. "If she's not home, check with the janitor or anybody around and find out if anyone's seen her this morning."

"Sure," he said and started to get out of his chair when the phone rang. I lifted it and said, "Sheriff's office," into the mouthpiece.

"I'd like to talk with Miss Annabelle Jackson, please?" a crisp feminine voice said.

"She's not in today," I told the voice.

"Oh?" She hesitated for a moment. "Then connect me with Lieutenant Wheeler, please!"

"This is Wheeler speaking."

"I'm Jenny Carter," the voice said heatedly, "Annabelle's roommate—and I'd like to know just what you've done with her, Lieutenant!"

"I haven't done a thing with her, Jenny," I said, "and I never knew she had a roommate."

"Since a couple of months back." She chuckled briefly. "That's after your time, I think, Lieutenant."

"I guess that's right," I said. "Annabelle doesn't seem to trust me anymore for some peculiar reason."

"For five distinctly sound reasons," she said briskly. "She told me them—one by one. But seriously, I'm worried about her—she didn't come home at all last night. What have you done with her, Lieutenant?"

"I haven't done anything with her, Jenny!" I protested. "Believe me—I was about to send a sergeant nut to the apartment to check if she was there or not."

"But she was out working for you last night!" she said accusingly. "She told me something about it—some crazy idea of yours that she should join this lonely hearts club. She went out on her first blind date from the club last night and she never came back. And now you say you don't even know what's happened to her?"

"Take it easy," I told her. "We'll find out all right. There's probably some logical explanation—"

"—Like she's been murdered!" Jenny Carter screamed hysterically.

"Like she met some wonderful guy and they went to Reno and got married," I yelled. "You stop worrying. We'll call you just as soon as we've got a line on Annabelle." Then I hung up on her quickly before I got some more hysterics.

Polnik looked at me inquiringly. "Was that about Miss Jackson, Lieutenant?"

"Her roommate," I said shortly. "Annabelle hasn't been home all night. There's no need for you to go out to the apartment now, but there's something else you can do for me."

"You name it, Lieutenant," he said dutifully.

"Go around to the Arkright Happiness Club right away," I told him. "Tell them your name is Jackson, and you're Annabelle's older brother. Last night she went out on her first date from the club and she hasn't been home since, and unless they find out what's happened to her right away, you're going to the police."

"Me—a cop—go to the police?" Polnik said feebly.

"You aren't supposed to be a cop!" I snarled. "You're just her older brother—you can be a telegraph linesman if you want!"

"Cheez! You figure I could be a railroad engineer?" he asked hopefully.

"Why not?" I said hopelessly.

"Thanks, Lieutenant!" Polnik's chest swelled with pride. "That's what I always wanted to be when I was a kid. If only Mom could see me now!"

10

Polnik got back to the office around three in the afternoon, with a look of misery on his face.

"It was no good, Lieutenant," he said apologetically. "I did like you said and the receptionist—Cheez! what a dame that one is!—took me right in to the Arkrights, I gave them the spiel and banged the desk a couple of times to make it look good, but they swore I must have the wrong happiness club, they didn't know from any Annabelle Jackson. We argued for maybe a half hour with me saying I knew for sure this was the right club, and them saying I had to be wrong. They offered to let me search their files and I did—but there was nothing there with Miss Jackson's name on it." He shrugged his gorilla shoulders. "So then I didn't know what the hell to do so I came back here." He looked at me with sublime faith. "I figured you'd tell me what to do next."

"I wish I knew," I said bitterly. "You did all you could down there—it's no fault of yours, Sergeant. Pleading no knowledge of Annabelle was the obvious out for them."

"Does the Sheriff know yet?" he asked.

"He hasn't been back," I said. "I guess that meeting's going to take all day."

"He's over in City Hall," Polnik said eagerly. "You want me to go over there right now and tell him, Lieutenant?"

"No!" I said sharply. I remembered how Lavers had reacted to my idea of getting Annabelle to join the lonely hearts club in the first place. Now that he was convinced the case was sewn up tight by Stern's confession, his reaction to the news of Annabelle's disappearance would be violent. I didn't see how he could help, anyway, and I had enough problems without adding the County Sheriff to them.

"So what do we do now, Lieutenant?" Polnik's rasping voice broke my train of thought. "You was just kidding when you said you didn't know, huh?"

I wondered fleetingly if a jury would bring in justifiable homicide if I shot him where he stood. "I'm thinking, Sergeant," I muttered hoarsely. "Even for a Wheeler, it takes a little time."

The phone rang and I grabbed it.

"Lieutenant Wheeler?" a husky feminine voice asked.

"That's me," I snarled, and thought if this was Jenny Carter I'd find out where she was, then go around there and throttle her with my bare hands.

"Al!" The voice was so faint I could only just hear it. "This is Dolores."

"Hi," I said bleakly. "I can hardly hear you."

"I'm calling from the Extravaganza," she said. "I can't speak any louder in case somebody hears me. Al, you remember our talk last night?" She gurgled throatily. "We *did* talk for a while, remember? And I asked how I could help?"

"Sure, I remember," I said.

"Well, I don't know if this means anything or not, but I heard Rovak talking with Loomas—and they're definitely taking out the boat tonight and they expect to be gone for a couple of days. Rovak said something about being sure to have the consignment ready for loading by ten tonight. Is it important, Al?"

"I think so," I said. "Very important."

"This is rehearsal day down here," she said. "That's why I'm at the club all afternoon. But I could get away around five and meet you. I know Rovak's house pretty well, Al. If you want, I think I could smuggle you in so you can see what goes on."

"I'd like that very much, Dolores," I said sincerely. "Where will I meet you?"

"There's a bar two blocks south of the Extravaganza called the Bird of Paradise. I'll be there at five, or a little after."

"O.K.," I said. "And thanks a million, honey."

"See you in the Bird of Paradise," she said, a hung up.

I put the phone down and looked at Polnik. "I just got a lead, I think," I told him. "It's going to take a while to follow through. Meantime I want you to run a check on the dame who married Harvey Stern and then got killed in an auto accident. What was her name?"

"Joan Penton?"

"If it was Stern, it's likely he didn't use his real name, and they probably got married in Nevada," I said. "Sweat on it, Sergeant—this may be the first concrete piece of evidence we can get. I want to know where they were married, and under what name—the details of the auto accident—and whether the girl left any money and who got it—and was she insured and if so, who collected that?"

"O.K., Lieutenant," Polnik said and nodded ponderously. "I'll get onto it right now."

"I'll be gone I don't know how long," I said. "When the Sheriff gets back you'd better tell him what's happened."

"What will I say when he asked where the—where you are, Lieutenant?"

"Tell him I went out," I said. "But if he doesn't hear from me by midnight to contact the Coast Guard and have them look for a forty-foot cabin cruiser, registered under the name of Miles Rovak."

The Sergeant scribbled frantically in his notebook, then looked at me blankly. "What if they find this boat and you ain't on it, Lieutenant?"

"Don't say things like that!" I shuddered. "Every time I get to feeling a dedicated cop, somebody always has to louse it up for me real good! If I'm not on board that boat, it's likely I'll be gone for around three weeks—then the chances are I'll get washed up on a beach someplace."

"Just so long as you're coming back, Lieutenant," Polnik said heartily. "I wouldn't like to feel you was leaving us for good."

I parked the Healey a little way down from the Bird of Paradise, in the first available space, then walked back to the bar. Inside it was one of those dimly lit, elegant bars that cater to the boss-secretary and different husband-different wife combinations. I felt like a blind man until my eyes got used to the gloom, then I threaded my way around some empty tables to a corner booth. A waiter who looked like he was working his way through the morgue so he could sleep nights in the graveyard without the other vampires sneering at him, took my order, then padded silently away—on cloven hooves, maybe.

I lit a cigarette and checked my watch. It was five after five, but Dolores had said she might be a little late. The waiter served my drink and then I saw her come into the bar, so I told him to bring a couple more of the same.

The waiter's eyebrows shot up and he gave me a look that penetrated right to my cirrhosis of the liver. It was a damn shame I was jackknifed behind the table. It kept him from taking my full measure—for the brass-handled box.

"Make them double," I said. "I'm feeling a little faint."

Just then Dolores arrived at the table, and the waiter turned his penetrating look on her. She was wearing an apricot-colored dirndl with a billowing skirt and a tight bodice that molded her full breasts with close attention to detail. The measurements our zombie was taking were not vertical this time, I noted, and he couldn't have cared less whether the inventory included a liver or not as long as everything else was accounted for.

"Run along, sonny," I said to him. "You're out of bounds."

"Two doubles?" he said.

"In spades," I answered, and I detected the shadow of a smirk on his gray face. He double-checked her blouse size, re-echoed my order in a murmur of sheer disbelief, and managed to stumble his way back to the bar.

"What's with him?" Dolores said as she slid onto the leatherette seat beside me.

"That's the trouble—nobody." I smiled at her and she smiled back warmly.

"It's nice to see you again so soon, honey," she murmured. "I washed the dishes after you'd gone this morning—so your apartment's real neat and tidy."

"It's always been my dream," I said in a hushed voice. "A passionate affair with a girl who was real domesticated. A dame who could look sexy in an apron, with her hair in curlers and—"

The waiter served the drinks, putting one glass in front of Dolores, then hesitating for a moment as he saw the untouched first drink still in front of me. He looked back and forth between us, and then just back and forth between Dolores until I wondered if he was considering her cleavage as a likely spot to deposit the Scotch. Finally he placed the glass about an eighth of an inch in front of her, as a kind of oblation.

Dolores shoved it over to my side. "What's the matter with that guy anyway? He gives me the creeps—he must be a kook or something," she said.

"You meet all kinds," I shrugged away the problem. "Tell me some more about this boat ride that's scheduled for tonight."

"I don't know much more than I told you over the phone, Al," she said. "I was passing Rovak's office—the door wasn't all the way shut and I heard their voices, so I stopped to listen. Like I told you, Rovak told Loomas to have the boat ready to leave tonight and be sure to have the consignment loaded by ten—and they'd be gone a couple of days. 'The usual run,' he said. Whatever that is."

"Anything else?"

"Let me think." She tapped one finger against her cheek absently. "Yes, there was something else. Rovak said this would be the last consignment they'd be running for a while, until things cooled down again."

"How do you figure on smuggling me into the house?"

"At the end of rehearsal I pretended to faint," she said. "Then I said I felt sick, and Rovak told me to go home and not bother about coming back to the club, so I won't be missed. If I arrive at his house tonight, tell him I figured the sea air would do me good and I knew he wouldn't mind me staying the night, I don't see how he can argue about it, do you?"

"I guess not," I agreed. "But he'll argue for sure if he sees me right beside you."

"I thought about that," Dolores said confidently. "If we take my car, you can keep out of sight on the floor of the back seat when I drive in. I'll park on his driveway and get out fast, so nobody will come close to the car. You wait in there until I get a chance to come back and take you into the house. How about that?"

"I don't have any better ideas," I said.

"Are you going to have Rovak's house surrounded by police officers with Tommy guns and tear gas and all?" she asked breathlessly. "You know—the way they do it on television?"

"I'd look awful stupid if I did and Rovak's consignment turned out to be fishing bait!" I shuddered at the thought. "This is strictly a one-man—and a one-woman—operation, honey. I'm trying to find some proof that Rovak's mixed up in a racket which somehow involved your cousin Patty. And what we're about to do is strictly illegal for anybody, but goes double for a cop! Nobody knows anything about this—not even the Sheriff—except you and me."

Dolores tasted her drink, her eyes bubbling with excitement.

"It's real exciting!" she said enthusiastically. "I feel like I'm a secret agent or something!"

"You have a time schedule worked out, X-9?" I grunted.

"Sure! I figure we don't want to get out there too early. For one thing we want to be sure Rovak's already there—and he might get suspicious about my sudden recovery, too. I thought after we've had a couple of drinks here we could get a meal, then leave around eight. That would get us out there around eight-thirty, in plenty of time before the boat leaves."

"That makes sense," I agreed. "Maybe you really are X-9, and that X denotes the only female operative in the whole counterespionage network, authorized to carry a blowpipe for lethal purposes! You think we'll need a password and countersign?—something like 'Take it off!' as the password, with the countersign, 'Cheez! Put it back!'?"

"Al Wheeler!" she said giggling helplessly. "You're the craziest guy I ever met, and I don't believe you're a cop for one moment! You're a retired vaudeville comic, practicing some new routines for your comeback!"

We followed Dolores' timetable pretty close—a couple more drinks in the bar, then a steak in the chophouse around the corner. It was near enough to eight o'clock when we got into her four-year-old hardtop and started out.

A half-hour later we came over the crest of the road that seemed to drop almost perpendicularly down the side of a cliff to where Rovak's house nestled right at the bottom. Dolores braked the car to a stop on the crest, then turned and smiled at me nervously.

"Now I get butterflies," she said throatily. "You think maybe now is the time for you to disappear into the back seat, Al? We'll be there in a couple of minutes."

"Sure," I said. "But we made good time and there's no real hurry, so why don't we talk for a few minutes first? Cigarette?"

"Thanks." She switched off the motor, then slid a cigarette out of the pack I offered her. I lit it, and one for myself, then leaned back against the upholstery. I put my free arm around her shoulders, letting my fingers brush gently against the taut curve of her left breast under the cotton dirndl. She sighed gently and snuggled closer to me.

"It's a beautiful night," I said. "But no moon—I guess maybe that's why Rovak picked it."

"So he's got less chance of being seen?" Dolores murmured against my shoulder. "That doesn't sound like his boat trip is very legal does it?"

"I was wondering," I said lazily, "just how Miles has it figured—the iron gates left open so you can drive right in and park well down on the driveway close to the house. Rovak and Loomas waiting in the shadows on either side, so when you stop the car they each open one of the back doors and ram a gun into my face. After that I join Annabelle Jackson as extra loading for the consignment, and the boat takes off on schedule. Then sometime in the early hours of the morning they dump us into the ocean, and the operation's a complete success."

Her body stiffened suddenly. "Al—what are you talking about? Have you gone out of your mind?"

"It was a nice try, honey," I said. "You wait around my apartment last night until I get home with a double-barreled excuse—one, you've had a change of heart and now you're grieving for your cousin Patty real bad and you want to help justice—and two, you're just crazy about Wheeler, anyway. What you really wanted to know was had I swallowed Stern's fake suicide and the note he'd written tidying up everything so nicely."

"You can't mean that, Al?" she said in a choked voice. "After all I've done to—"

"I don't know how Annabelle suddenly got to be a problem," I went on, "but she obviously did. And you had one other problem, too—that was me. So the smart thing was to take care of both at the same time. That meant getting me onto the boat with no fuss—and no county sheriff hot on my trail. When you heard my sergeant had been around to the lonely hearts club, making like he's Annabelle's brother and not getting anyplace, you gave him time to report back to me. Then you called at the psychological moment and gave me a lead which would bring me right out to Rovak's boat of my own free will."

"I don't know how you can even think such things, Al Wheeler!" she said in a muffled voice. "It's all lies—dreadful lies!"

"I told you once, Dolores honey, that it was your intelligence that appealed to me most of all about you," I reminded her. "You should have remembered that then maybe you wouldn't have played it so awful dumb the way you did in the bar tonight. All that little girl jazz about cops with Tommy guns and tear gas surrounding the house—it was a clumsy way of handling it. But then, of course, you could've figured I was as dumb as I look?"

"I need a handkerchief!" she said in a muffled voice, and picked up her purse from the seat beside her.

She had the gun halfway out before I clamped my hand over her fingers and squeezed until she whimpered with pain and relaxed her grip so the gun slid back inside the purse.

"Too bad," I said respectfully. "A natural reaction. Any dame that's crying needs a handkerchief—and you didn't rush it, either."

"Oh, shut up!" she snarled. "And take your stinking paws off of me!"

I took my arm from around her shoulders, lifted her purse and the car keys in one hand, and opened the car door on her side with the other.

"Out!" I told her, and gave her a shove of encouragement.

She turned and looked at me contemptuously when we were both standing beside the car.

"What now?" she sneered. "We wait for reinforcements?"

"Take off your shoes," I told her. She hesitated for a moment, then did as she was told. "Now the dress and the slip," I said.

"Wait a minute!" she said angrily. "I'm not—"

"If you don't, I'll rip them off," I said casually. "Come to think of it, it could be more fun that way!"

Dolores had the dress pulled over her head almost before I'd finished talking. Then the slip followed and that left her in a strapless bra and a pair of briefs. She shivered suddenly in the slight breeze that came in off the ocean as I tossed her clothes and shoes into the back of the car.

"And there it is, nature girl," I told her as I got back into the car. "Here's your big chance to run barefoot in the breeze, over turf and glen!"

"You dirty sonovabitch!" she said from between clenched teeth.

"Dolores—honey!" I said reproachfully as I started the motor again. "You always said you were crazy about poetry!"

I let the car roll down the hill slowly in second, while I eased the thirty-eight out of its belt holster and put it on the seat beside me. As the car neared the bottom of the hill, I flicked the headlight beams on high, and their brilliant light showed that the iron gates across the driveway were wide open. I drove slowly into the driveway and saw the Mercedes parked about thirty feet ahead. If Rovak and Loomas were where I figured they had to be—one on either side of the driveway—the headlights would blind them enough so they couldn't distinguish who was driving the car. So I was safe until I stopped and that gave me a whole three or four seconds. Just enough time to ease the car door open a little, and pick up the thirty-eight.

I braked the car to a stop a few feet in back of the Mercedes, then flung the door wide open and jumped out as I heard the sudden flurry of footsteps on either side of the car. Both the back doors were wrenched open and I heard Rovak's harsh voice growl, "O.K., cop! Come out nice and easy or—"

By that time I'd straightened up and could see the massive bulk of Steve Loomas, hunched forward as he leaned into the back of the car.

"Hey, boss!" he yelped frantically. "There's nobody here!"

"You're so right, George!" I said as I rammed the barrel of the thirty-eight against the side of his head. "Tell Rovak to drop his gun or I'll splatter your brains over the upholstery!"

"Boss!" Loomas stuttered wildly. "Don't—"

The sudden explosion of Rovak's gun was shatteringly loud inside the confines of the car. I'd taken the obvious precaution of standing right in back of Loomas, and Rovak had no way of getting at me except through that massive-muscled body, but that wasn't about to deter him. He fired three shots from his side of the car, and Loomas' whole body quivered as each slug slammed into his chest. Then he toppled forward slowly into the back seat, and as his bulk fell away from me, Rovak's silhouetted head suddenly appeared in my line of vision. I guess he saw me at the same time because he fired another shot, making the mistake of not elevating his gun quickly enough, so the slug took Loomas neatly between the eyes—but you can only kill a man once and Loomas was already dead before that slug hit.

I lifted the thirty-eight carefully and squeezed the trigger twice. Rovak screamed thinly and spun around, then disappeared out of my line of sight. I heard the clatter as his gun dropped on the driveway, and raced around the back of the car toward him.

When I got there he was down on his hands and knees, and there was a steady splashing sound as an ever-widening pool appeared on the concrete beneath his bowed head. His gun lay a few feet away, and I kicked it into the bushes lining the driveway, then put my hand on his shoulder.

"Rovak?" I said. "Where are you hit?"

He pulled his shoulder away from my hand violently, then suddenly his arms splayed sideways and he pitched forward onto his face and lay still. I knelt down and turned him over gently; he was already dead, and there was nothing recognizable left of his face below the forehead.

I got to my feet and raced toward the front door of the house and found it was slightly open when I got there. I slammed it wide open with my foot and yelled, "Outside, you guys, and fast! Rovak's got trouble!" Then I flattened myself against the wall beside the open door and waited.

Heavy footsteps clumped down the hallway, and a moment later a hairy, muscle-bound gorilla lumbered out of the doorway and past me, heading toward the car. I caught up with him in a couple of paces and slammed the gun barrel down across the back of his head. He got tired of running all at once and collapsed to the ground. I got back beside the open door again and waited another thirty seconds but nobody else came out.

A closer inspection revealed the unconscious gorilla was my old buddy, Louis, the maître d' of the Extravaganza, and it got to be like old home week. He didn't look like he was going to wake up for a long time, so I left him while I searched inside. The whole place was deserted, and it made me feel better, being sure there had only been the three of them in the house. When I got back to the driveway again, Louis was grunting painfully as he struggled up into a sitting position. I nudged his left ear with the thirty-eight and he stopped grunting right away.

"Rovak and Loomas are dead," I said conversationally. "I'd as soon have you dead, too, because it would be neater that way. So do an old buddy a favor and try something, huh, so I'll have an excuse?"

He squinted up at me, his head wobbling nervously on the short, squat neck, his eyes pleading.

"Don't kill me, Lieutenant!" he quavered. "I'll do anything you say—anything!"

"Get up on your feet and we'll go take a look at the boat," I said. "The consignment's already loaded, right?"

"I don't know what you're talking about," he mumbled as he staggered to his feet.

"That does it!" I said happily.

"*Wait!*" he screamed. "Sure, sure—you're right! The consignment's already loaded just like you said, Lieutenant!"

"So let's go unload it," I prodded his spine with the gun to emphasize the point.

We walked down the jetty, then climbed on board the cruiser's immaculate white deck.

"Where are they?" I asked.

"Down below—locked in the cabin," Louis mumbled.

"You got a key?"

"Yeah—right here." He pulled a key chain out of his pocket and handed it to me.

"That's good, Louis," I said approvingly. "You keep going this way and you could live another whole ten minutes yet!"

I made him go first down the ladder that led to the cabin, and followed behind, but not too close. When we got there I gave him back the key, let him unlock the door and lead the way inside. The consignment had been loaded all right. Directly opposite us, with their backs pressed hard against the bulkhead, were three cowering girls—and the one in the middle was Annabelle Jackson.

She saw the gun in my hand and made a rapid recovery.

"Well," she sniffed, "if it isn't Al Wheeler! You sure took your time about getting here."

"I would've made it a lot sooner," I said apologetically, "but your roommate was so upset the way you just disappeared, I had to comfort her."

"Jenny?" Annabelle said suspiciously.

"There we were," I said nostalgically, "sitting in your apartment with me busy comforting Jenny—and Jenny busy being comforted. The hours just flew!"

"Jenny?" she snarled.

"Tell me something, honey chile," I asked. "How come they picked you for a phony so fast?"

"A little elementary psychology, Lieutenant," she said coldly, "which you apparently overlooked. Every girl tries to make the best of her looks—so if one girl deliberately tries to make the worst of them, she obviously must have a good reason. After they grabbed me, they checked at City Hall and found out who I worked for. So then that dreadful man—Rovak—said I could be useful two ways."

"You'd fetch a good price as part of this consignment," I said, "and he could use you as bait for me."

Annabelle looked annoyed. "How did you know?"

"Elementary psychology, honey chile," I said easily. "Just one more question before we go back to the house and call up the posse. Who did you see when you registered with the lonely hearts club? The receptionist—Sherry Rand?"

"No," Annabelle shook her head. "She was out to lunch when I got there—so Mrs. Arkright interviewed me, then organized the first date with that muscle-bound beast, George Crocker!"

"Alias Steve Loomas," I said brightly, "and speak softly of the dead."

"You killed him?" Her eyes widened as she stared at me in horror.

"What's the fun in being a hero if you can't leave a few dead villains lying around?" I said reasonably. "I'm glad Sherry Rand isn't involved in this."

"Another of your conquests—hero?" she asked icily.

"Only one on this case, honey chile." I smiled sweetly at her. "Being so busy with Jenny didn't leave me much time."

11

It had gotten to be a real late night what with the explanations to the County Sheriff and the sheer bliss of watching the changing expressions on his face while he listened. He almost took the two corpses in his stride after that, but they never really worried me because I knew ballistics would prove Rovak had killed Loomas and not me. The best of it was watching Laver's face when we stopped at the top of the hill on the way back to town and picked up a gorgeous strawberry blonde whose lusty curves were hardly concealed by a small bra and miniature briefs. She was huddled on the side of the road, shivering violently and blue with cold when we stopped. The Sheriff's eyes had popped out of his head when she climbed into the car and snuggled up against him for some warmth. Finally he'd gotten his voice back and glared at me wildly, then asked huskily just how many more near-nude females had I left scattered around the countryside.

So, even if I was tired, it was still a bright and sunny morning after the long night when I stepped once again into the offices of the Arkright Happiness Club. Sherry Rand's face was stony when she looked up and saw me, and I didn't even hear one faint twang of a Hawaiian guitar in the background.

"Lieutenant Wheeler," she said icily, "you know, I was stupid enough to think you might really call me last night—that shows just how naïve I can get, doesn't it?"

"I was busy, honey," I said regretfully. "Real busy!"

"Funny thing," she said through a yawn. "I didn't read about it in the morning papers."

"But you will," I said cheerfully. "Are the Arkrights at home?"

"Sure," she said. "I'll tell them you're here."

"This time you don't need to bother, Sherry honey," I told her. "I'll announce myself."

I opened the door of the private office and stepped inside. Sarah Arkright was sitting in back of her desk as ever, but Jacob had pulled a switch on me. He was perched beside her—in a smaller chair naturally—and they looked like they were going over the monthly accounts.

Sarah's eyes widened for a moment when she first saw me, then the fuzziness spread quickly from the outer edges across her pupils, leaving two opaque masks to hide her thoughts.

"This is beyond all tolerance!" she snapped. "Don't you even have the decency to wait until you're invited into a private office before you walk in, Lieutenant!"

"I must say," Jacob put in his squeaky two bits, "this is hardly a civilized attitude, Lieutenant!"

"You might as well get used to uncivilized attitudes," I said easily. "Where you're going, you'll run up against them all the time."

I pulled a chair away from the wall and sat down facing them, then lit a cigarette.

"Put that disgusting thing out immediately!" Sarah's gaunt cheeks flamed a violent red. "How dare you! How dare—"

"The consignment never got away last night," I said conversationally. "Rovak killed Loomas—and I killed Rovak. Louis and Dolores Keller are under arrest and they spent most of the night talking their heads off in the D.A.'s office downtown. You mind if I smoke?"

Jacob's skin turned a dirty gray color as he stared at me. His mouth dropped open so wide that the dime-store teeth that had given him such faithful service these last thirty or so years suddenly gave up trying, and the top plate collapsed onto the bottom with an uneasy clacking sound.

Sarah stiffened her back into an even more upright position in her chair, if that were possible. Her bony fingers intertwined, then locked solid with a brittle sound.

"We shall consult our lawyer—of course!" she said firmly, then looked at her husband for approval for the first time in her life; but he didn't even notice—he was too busy with one hand shielding his mouth, making frantic gobbling noises as he tried to juggle that top plate back into position again.

"A nice racket you had going here for a while," I said, "making it all ways—even legitimately. Miles Rovak had a hot connection with the Latin American bordello trade, and they were always willing to pay big money for girls who were young and preferably blonde. With Loomas, or George Crocker—whatever name you prefer—dazzling the girls with his muscles and finally persuading them to come cruising on his boat, that side of the deal was sewn up real fine."

"Not a word," Sarah said in a cracked voice. "Not a word until we consult with our lawyer!"

"Sure," I said and nodded politely. "Then you had Stern working the older clients—the middle-aged spinsters who were getting even more lonely and more foolish. If he couldn't con them out of their hard-earned money any other way, he'd even marry them. Of course afterwards he'd take some insurance on their lives, and if they were unfortunate enough to sustain a fatal accident on their honeymoon—well, that's life, kids, ain't it?

"We got the detail on Joan Penton—the late Joan Penton, I should say. It wasn't really so tough for Stern that Rovak forced him to write that note to me, then killed him, because Stern couldn't have lived very much longer anyway. And a bullet's preferable to the gas chamber, I always say. What do you say, Mrs. Arkright—Mr. Arkright?"

Sarah licked her lips which were white around the edges and said nothing; Jacob still struggled with his teeth and moaned softly to himself the whole time—but not about the teeth, I guessed.

"Dolores told us all about Patty—her country cousin from the sticks who got under her feet the whole time," I went on amiably. "How the fool kid would stick her nose into other people's business. How she was stage-struck and wanted to be a great actress. How she sneaked up close to a door that wasn't properly closed one night when she was staying in Dolores' apartment, and overheard a confidential conversation between Dolores and Rovak concerning the Latin American trade."

I shook my head admiringly. "That Patty! Whatever else you can say about her, you have to admit she was single-minded. She offered a trade—her silence in return for the organization making her into a big star! I guess you have to be just out of the sticks to offer that kind of deal!"

My cigarette had burned down to a stub and there wasn't an ash tray in the room, so I walked across to the desk and dropped the butt into the vase of withered carnations. It made a faint, squelching hiss as it hit the water and it sounded an adequate requiem for good old Harv—the guy who always had a carnation in his buttonhole.

"When she was standing out on that hotel ledge, I talked with her through the window," I said. "She didn't look like she was going to jump at all. The only thing that interested her was the time—she kept on asking what time it was every few minutes. When it got around to three o'clock, she said she'd come back in. She started toward me, then the nausea hit her and she lost her balance and fell. The autopsy revealed the shot of apomorphine—you know that?"

"Not a word without consulting our ..." Sarah's voice shook so much she couldn't finish the sentence.

"When Dolores told us about Patty's deal—that she'd keep quiet about your white slave trade as long as you made her a big star—" I shrugged "then it hit me. She was just a naïve country kid who didn't know from nothing. It would be easy—real easy—to con her into thinking a fake suicide attempt would land her on the front pages of all the newspapers and launch her into a successful acting career. Once she was convinced that all she had to do was stand on a narrow ledge for a certain length of time and then climb back into the window again, it would be just as easy to convince her she ought to have an injection before she went out there—to steady her nerves."

"My guess is," I went on, "that you told her it would take, say, a good solid half hour on that ledge to make a real impression on the public—it didn't matter much what precise length of time you advised as long as it allowed more than enough time for the injection to take effect. But when she got out there, five minutes seemed like about five years to her, and when she saw the crowd that had collected, she figured she could cut short the time and come back in sooner. I was there and saw her make that decision—but she made it about ten seconds too late."

I put my hands on the edge of the desk and leaned on them.

"Which one of you sold the idea to Patty Keller?" I asked softly. "Which one was it who pushed the needle into her arm and deliberately gave her the apomorphine, knowing that the violent reaction was bound to send her over the edge?"

Jacob dropped his head, showing the gleaming whiteness of his skull, with the heavy hair tonic plastering the last remnants of his hair tight against it.

"It was wrong," he mumbled, and tears trickled down his cheeks in a token of remorse that was too late by one hell of a large margin. "Wrong! I never really did agree to getting rid of that child in that way, Sarah, you know it!"

"Oh—stop sniveling!" Sarah said contemptuously. The bones in her hands cracked as she unlocked the fingers. "Yes, Lieutenant, everything you've said is true. It was my idea to persuade that stupid girl to get out onto the ledge—and it was I who gave her that injection!"

"You sound like you're proud of it," I said wonderingly.

"You don't understand!" she said fiercely. "You're like the rest of them, hidebound with a stupid, sentimental morality that divorces human beings from any real contact with one another. In every city throughout the whole world, there are millions of desperate, pathetic people, cut off completely from any real contact with any other human. The lonely, Lieutenant—"

"—are legend!" I finished it for her. "I should have known that wasn't one of Dolores' original phrases!"

"That was why we started out Happiness Club in the first place," she said proudly. "To help the lonely, the lost and afraid little people of the earth! What could a stupid little moron like Patty Keller hope for in her life—nothing! I did her a kindness—a great and wonderful kindness.

She went from the ecstasy of seeing her dreams start to come true—as she thought—into almost instant and peaceful oblivion.

"The girls who took our cruise, Lieutenant? All of them were lonely and afraid—why else would they come to us in the first place? None of them would find a decent husband—there are not enough men to go around, let alone decent men! We sent them where they would enjoy contact with more men than they'd ever dreamed of in their wildest moments. We sent them where they could work for their pleasure and enjoy the most intimate of human contacts incessantly until—" Her voice had been rising steadily as she spoke, until it finally broke into a high-pitched scream.

"Sarah!" Jacob gripped her arm imploringly, with a vigor that was a far cry from the family photo album, circa 1927. "Sarah, dear—please, don't do that!"

She stared down with incredulous horror at his hand for a moment, as if she had never seen it before. Then she thrust it violently away from her.

"Don't you dare touch me!" she screamed at him. "You filthy, vile creature! Don't you dare touch me! In the thirty-five years of our married life, I've never allowed you to touch me! So don't you dare think that—"

Her eyes dulled suddenly and she slumped back into the chair, just as Lavers and a uniformed cop came charging into the room.

"What the hell goes on in here, Wheeler?" the Sheriff asked quickly. "We could hear her screaming—"

"She's only fainted," I said. "She confessed to the Keller girl's murder. She sold her the idea that standing out on a ledge, pretending to be about to throw herself over, would make a wonderful publicity story for an aspiring young actress—and she gave her the shot of apomorphine. But I don't think we'll ever get a conviction, Sheriff." I turned to Polnik, "Call an ambulance," I told him, "And tell them they'll probably need a restrainer along, too."

"Poor Sarah—the excitement's been too much for her!" Jacob cackled suddenly. "Maybe I'm the strong one, after all!"

I walked out of the office and closed the door behind me. I took time out to light a cigarette before I went over to Sherry's desk.

"Honey doll," I said, grinning warmly at her. "Tonight is definitely and irrevocably a free night for Wheeler. How about dropping over to my apartment and showing me some of those wonderful routines you've been practicing?"

"Drop dead!" she said, and she didn't even bother to look at me while she said it.

So around ten that night I was sitting in my lonely apartment, listening to lonely music from my lonely hi-fi machine while I drank a lonely drink. The world was bleak and had shrunk into four lonely walls and I couldn't make up my mind whether to go out and get drunk or stay home and get drunk. Then the buzzer sounded.

I opened the door cautiously because who knows whose husband carries a long grudge? A pocket-sized Venus, with soft black hair that curled lovingly around her shoulders, looked up at me with a brilliant smile on her lovely face.

"Lieutenant Wheeler?" she asked in a soft, melodious drawl.

"That's me," I gurgled.

"I'm so glad I found you," she said calmly and pushed past me inside the apartment.

By the time I got back into the living room, she was sitting on the couch, her legs crossed carelessly so I could see their shapeliness a long way past the arbitrary hemline.

"I'm Jenny Carter," she said calmly, and took a deep breath that made her expensive cashmere sweater about twice as interesting as anything they got in the Extravaganza. "Annabelle won't believe me anyway when I tell her it didn't happen—so I figured I might just as well come over to your place and have it happen."

"Huh?" I gulped and stared down at her bug-eyed.

She reached out a casual hand and jerked me off balance so I collapsed on the couch beside her. Then she moved easily onto my lap and draped her arms firmly around my neck.

"Comfort me, Al Wheeler!" she said seriously. "I think I'm going to enjoy it!"

THE END

Alan Geoffrey Yates Bibliography (1923-1985)

**As Carter Brown/
Peter Carter Brown**

Series:

Al Wheeler (no U.S. edition unless otherwise stated through to *Chorine Makes a Killing*)

The Wench is Wicked (1955)
Blonde Verdict (1956; revised for the U.S. as The Brazen, 1960)
Delilah Was Deadly (1956)
No Harp for My Angel (1956)
Booty for a Babe (1956)
Eve, It's Extortion (1957; revised as Walk Softly Witch!, 1959, and further revised for the U.S. as The Victim, 1959)
No Law Against Angels (1957; revised for the U.S. as The Body, 1958; 1st U.S. Wheeler)
Doll for the Big House (1957; revised for the U.S. as The Bombshell, 1960)
Chorine Makes a Killing (1957)
The Unorthodox Corpse (1957; revised for the U.S., 1961)
Death on the Downbeat (1958; revised for the U.S. as The Corpse, 1958)
The Blonde (1958; reprinted in the U.S., 1958)
The Lover (1958)
The Mistress (1959)
The Passionate (1959)
The Wanton (1959)
The Dame (1959)
The Desired (1959)
The Temptress (1960)
Lament for a Lousy Lover (1960) [includes Mavis Seidlitz]
The Stripper (1961)
The Tigress (1961; reprinted in the UK as Wildcat, 1962)
The Exotic (1961)
Angel! (1962)
The Hellcat (1962)
The Lady Is Transparent (1962)
The Dumdum Murder (1962)
Girl in a Shroud (1963)
The Sinners (1963; reprinted in U.S. as The Girl Who Was Possessed, 1963)
The Lady Is Not Available (1963; reprinted in U.S. as The Lady Is Available, 1963)
The Dance of Death (1964)
The Vixen (1964; reprinted in the U.S. as The Velvet Vixen, 1964)
A Corpse for Christmas (1965)
The Hammer of Thor (1965)
Target for Their Dark Desire (1966)
The Plush-Lined Coffin (1967)
Until Temptation Do Us Part (1967)
The Deep Cold Green (1968)
The Up-Tight Blonde (1969)
Burden of Guilt (1970)
The Creative Murders (1971)
W.H.O.R.E. (1971)
The Clown (1972)
The Aseptic Murders (1972)
The Born Loser (1973)
Night Wheeler (1974)
Wheeler Fortune (1974)
Wheeler, Dealer! (1975)
The Dream Merchant (1976)
Busted Wheeler (1979)
The Spanking Girls (1979)
Model for Murder (1980)
The Wicked Widow (1981)
Stab in the Dark (1984; Australia only)

Larry Baker

Charlie Sent Me (1965; revised from Swan Song for a Siren, 1955)
No Blonde Is an Island (1965)
So What Killed the Vampire? (1966)
Had I But Groaned (1968; reprinted in the UK as The Witches, 1969)

True Son of the Beast (1970)
The Iron Maiden (1975)

Barney Blain (no U.S. editions)

Madam, You're Mayhem (1957)
Ice Cold in Ermine (1958)

Danny Boyd

Tempt a Tigress (1958; no U.S.)
So Deadly, Sinner! (1959; reprinted
  in the U.S. as Walk Softly, Witch,
  1959, 1st U.S. Boyd; different
  version of the Wheeler title)
Suddenly by Violence (1959)
Terror Comes Creeping (1959)
The Wayward Wahine (1960;
  published in Australia as The
  Wayward, 1962)
The Dream Is Deadly (1960)
Graves, I Dig (1960; revised from
  Cutie Wins a Corpse (1957)
The Myopic Mermaid (1961, revised
  from A Siren Sounds Off, 1958)
The Ever-Loving Blues (1961;
  revised from Death of a Doll, 1956)
The Seductress (1961; published in
  the U.S. as The Sad-Eyed
  Seductress, 1961)
The Savage Salome (1961; revised
  from Murder is My Mistress, 1954)
The Ice-Cold Nude (1962)
Lover Don't Come Back (1962)
Nymph to the Slaughter (1963)
Passionate Pagan (1963)
Silken Nightmare (1963)
Catch Me a Phoenix! (1965)
The Sometime Wife (1965)
The Black Lace Hangover (1966)
House of Sorcery (1967)
The Mini-Murders (1968)
Murder Is the Message (1969)
Only the Very Rich (1969)
The Coffin Bird (1970)
The Sex Clinic (1971)
Angry Amazons (1972) [includes
  Randy Roberts]
Manhattan Cowboy (1973)
So Move the Body (1973)

The Early Boyd (1975)
The Savage Sisters (1976)
The Pipes Are Calling (1976)
The Rip Off (1979)
The Strawberry-Blonde Jungle
  (1979)
Death to a Downbeat (1980)
Kiss Michelle Goodbye (1981)
The Real Boyd (1984; Australia only)

Paul Donavan

Donavan (1974)
Donavan's Day (1975)
Chinese Donavan (1976)
Donavan's Delight (1979)

Max Dumas (no U.S. editions)

Goddess Gone Bad (1958)
Luck Was No Lady (1958)
Deadly Miss (1958)

Mike Farrel

The Million Dollar Babe (1961;
  revised from Cutie Cashed His
  Chips, 1955)
The Scarlet Flush (1963; revised
  from Ten Grand Tallulah and
  Temptation, 1957)

Rick Holman

Zelda (1961; 1st U.S. Holman)
Murder in the Harem Club, 1962;
  reprinted in the U.S. as Murder in
  the Key Club, 1962)
The Murderer Among Us (1962)
Blonde on the Rocks (1963)
The Jade-Eyed Jinx (1963; reprinted
  in the U.S. as The Jade-Eyed
  Jungle, 1964)
The Ballad of Loving Jenny (1963;
  reprinted in the U.S. as The White
  Bikini, 1963)
The Wind-Up Doll (1963)
The Never-Was Girl (1964)
Murder Is a Package Deal (1964)
Who Killed Doctor Sex? (1964)

Nude—with a View (1965)
The Girl from Outer Space (1965)
Blonde on a Broomstick (1966)
Play Now... Kill Later (1966)
No Tears from the Widow (1966)
The Deadly Kitten (1967)
Long Time No Leola (1967)
Die Anytime, After Tuesday! (1969)
The Flagellator (1969)
The Streaked-Blond Slave (1969)
A Good Year for Dwarfs? (1970)
The Hang-up Kid (1970)
Where Did Charity Go? (1970)
The Coven (1971)
The Invisible Flamini (1971)
The Pornbroker (1972)
The Master (1973)
Phreak-Out! (1973)
Negative in Blue (1974)
The Star-Crossed Lover (1974)
Ride the Roller Coaster (1975)
Remember Maybelle? (1976)
See It Again, Sam (1979)
The Phantom Lady (1980)
The Swingers (1980)

Andy Kane

The Hong Kong Caper (1962; revised from Blonde, Bad and Beautiful, 1957)
The Guilt-edged Cage (1963; revised from That's Piracy, My Pet, 1957; published in Australia as Bird in a Guilt-Edged Cage)

Ivor MacCallum (no U.S. editions)

Sweetheart You Slay Me (1952)
Blackmail Beauty (1953)

Randy Roberts

Murder in the Family Way (1971)
The Seven Sirens (1972)
Murder on High (1973)
Sex Trap (1975)

Mavis Seidlitz

Honey, Here's Your Hearse (1955; no U.S.)
The Killer is Kissable (1955; no U.S.)
A Bullet For My Baby (1955; no U.S.)
Good Morning, Mavis! (1957; no U.S.)
Murder Wears a Mantilla (1957; revised for U.S. as same title, 1962)
The Loving and the Dead (1959; 1st U.S. Seidlitz)
None But the Lethal Heart (1959; reprinted as The Fabulous, 1961)
Tomorrow Is Murder (1960)
Lament for a Lousy Lover (1960) [includes Al Wheeler]
The Bump and Grind Murders (1964)
Seidlitz and the Super Spy (1967; published in the UK as The Super-Spy, 1968)
Murder Is So Nostalgic (1972)
And the Undead Sing (1974)

Unrelated Novels/Novelettes (all non-U.S. unless otherwise noted)

Death Date for Dolores (1951)
Designed to Deceive (1951)
Duchess Double X (1951)
Forever Forbidden (1951)
The Lady Is Murder (1951; reprinted as Lady is a Killer with Murder by Miss Take, 1958)
Three Men, One Love (1951)
Uncertain Heart (1951)
Your Alibi Is Showing (1951)
Alias a Lady (1952)
Blackmail for a Brunette (1952)
Blondes Prefer Bullets (1952)
Hands Off the Lady (1952)
Kiss Life Goodbye (1952)
Larceny Was Lovely (1952)
Meet Miss Mayhem (1952)
Murder Sweet Murder (1952)
She Wore No Shroud (1952)
Sssh! She's a Killer (1952)
Chill on Chili/Butterfly Nett (1953)

Cyanide Sweetheart (1953)
Dead Dolls Don't Cry (1953)
Dimples Died De-Luxe (1953)
Judgement of a Jane (1953)
Kidnapper Wears Curves (1953)
The Lady Wore Nylon (1953)
The Lady's Alive (1953)
Lethal in Love (1953; reprinted as The Minx is Murder, 1956)
Madame You're Morgue-Bound (1953)
Meet a Body (1953)
The Mermaid Murmurs Murder (1953)
Model for Murder (1953; different from 1980 Al Wheeler title)
Moonshine Momma (1953)
Murder is a Broad (1953)
Penthouse Pass-Out (1953; reprinted as Hot Seat for a Honey, 1956)
Rope for a Redhead (1953; revised as Model of No Virtue, 1956)
Slightly Dead (1953)
Stripper You're Stuck (1953)
Widow is Willing (1953)
The Black Widow Weeps (1954)
Felon Angel (1954)
Floozie Out of Focus (1954; reprinted with A Bullet for My Baby, 1958)
The Frame is Beautiful (1954)
Fraulein is Feline (1954; reprinted with Moonshine Momma & Slaughter in Satin, 1955)
Good-Knife Sweetheart (1954)
Honky Tonk Homicide (1954; reprinted with Chill on Chili & Butterfly Nett, 1955)
Homicide Harem (1954; reprinted with Good-Knife Sweetheart & Poison Ivy, 1955; with Felon Angel, 1965)
The Lady is Chased (1954; reprinted as Trouble is a Dame, 1957)
A Morgue Amour (1954)
Murder—Paris Fashion (1954)
Murder! She Says (1954)
Nemesis Wore Nylons (1954)
Pagan Perilous (1954)
Perfumed Poison (1954)
Poison Ivy (1954)
Shady Lady (1954)
Sinsation Sadie (1954)
Slaughter in Satin (1954)
Strip Without Tease (1954; reprinted as Stripper, You've Sinned, 1959)
Trouble is a Dame (1954)
Wreath for Rebecca (1954)
Venus Unarmed (1954)
Yogi Shrouds Yolande (1954; reprinted with Poison Ivy, 1965)
Curtains for a Chorine (1955)
Curves for a Coroner (1955)
Cutie Cashed His Chips (1955; revised for U.S. as The Million Dollar Babe, 1961, as Farrel series)
Homicide Hoyden (1955)
Kiss and Kill (1955; reprinted with Cyanide Sweetie, 1958)
Kiss Me Deadly (1955; reprinted as Lipstick Larceny, 1958)
Lead Astray (1955)
Lipstick Larceny (1955)
Maid for Murder (1955)
Miss Called Murder (1955)
Shamus, Your Slip Is Showing (1955; reprinted with A Morgue Amour, 1957)
Shroud for My Sugar (1955)
Sob-Sister Cries Murder (1955)
The Two Timing Blonde (1955; reprinted with Honey, Here's Your Hearse, 1957)
Baby, You're Guilt-Edged (1956; reprinted with Pagan Perilous, 1959)
Bid the Babe Bye-Bye (1956)
Blonde, Beautiful, and – Blam! (1956)
The Bribe Was Beautiful (1956)
Caress Before Killing (1956)
Darling You're Doomed (1956)
Donna Died Laughing (1956)
The Eve of His Dying (1956)
Hi-Jack for Jill (1956)
The Hoodlum Was a Honey (1956)
The Lady Has No Convictions (1956; reprinted with Slightly Dead, 1959)
Meet Murder, My Angel (1956)
Murder By Miss-Demeanour (1956)

My Darling Is Deadpan (1956)
No Halo For Hedy (1956)
Strictly for Felony (1956)
Sweetheart, This is Homicide (1956)
Bella Donna Was Poison (1957)
Cutie Wins a Corpse (1957; revised for U.S. as Graves, I Dig!, 1960, as Boyd series)
Last Note for a Lovely (1957)
Lethal in Love (1957; different than 1953 title)
Sinner, You Slay Me (1957)
Ten Grand Tallulah and Temptation (1957; revised as The Scarlet Flush, 1963, Farrel series)
That's Piracy, My Pet (1957; revised as Bird in a Guilt-Edged Cage, 1963, as Kane series)
Wreath for a Redhead (1957)
The Charmer Chased (1958)
Cutie Takes the Count (1958)
Deadly Miss (1958)
Hi-Fi Fadeout (1958)
High Fashion in Homicide (1958)
No Body She Knows (1958; with Slaughter in Satin, 1960)
No Future Fair Lady (1958)
Sinfully Yours (1958)
A Siren Signs Off (1958; with Moonshine Momma; revised for U.S. as The Myopic Mermaid, 1961, as Boyd series)
So Lovely She Lies (1958)
Widow Bewitched (1958)
The Blonde Avalanche (1984)

As Tod Conway (western stories)

As Caroline Farr (house name shared with Richard Wilkes-Hunter and Lee Pattinson)

The Intruder (1962)
House of Tombs (1966)
Mansion of Evil (1966)
Villa of Shadows (1966)
Web of Horror (1966; reprinted in the U.S. as A Castle in Spain, 1978)
Granite Folly (1967)

The Secret of the Chateau (1967)
Witch's Hammer (1967)
So Near and Yet... (1968)
House of Destiny (1969)
The Castle on the Lake (1970)
The Secret of Castle Ferrara (1970)
Terror on Duncan Island (1971)
The Towers of Fear (1972)
A Castle in Canada (1972)
House of Dark Illusions (1973)
House of Secrets (1973)
Dark Mansion (1974)
Mansion Malevolent (1974)
The House on the Cliffs (1974)
Dark Citadel (1975)
Mansion of Peril (1975)
Castle of Terror (1975)
The Scream in the Storm (1975)
Chateau of Wolves (1976)
Mansion of Menace (1976)
Brecon Castle (1976)
The House of Landsdown (1977)
House of Treachery (1977)
Ravensnest (1977)
The House at Lansdowne (1977)
Sinister House (1978)
House of Valhalla (1978)
Heiress Of Fear (1978)
Room Of Secrets (1979)
Island of Evil (1979)
A Castle on the Rhine (1979)
The Castle on the Loch (1979)
The Secret at Ravenswood (1980)

As Raymond Glenning (stories)

Ghosts Don't Kill (1951)
Seven for Murder (1951)

As Sinclair Mackellar

Prompt for Murder (1981)

As Dennis Sinclair

Temple Dogs Guard My Fate (1968)
Third Force (1976)
The Friends of Lucifer (1977)
Blood Brothers (1977)

As Paul Valdez
(stories & novelettes)

Hypnotic Death (1949)
The Fatal Focus (1950)
Outcasts of Planet J (1950)
Jetbees from Planet J (1951)
Escape to Paradise (1951)
Fugitives from the Flame World (1951)
Kidnapped in Chaos (1951)
Killer by Night (1951)
Suicide Satellite (1951)
The Time Thief (1951)
Flight Into Horror (1951)
Murder Gives Notice (1951)
The Corpse Sat Up (1951)
The Maniac Murders (1951)
Satan's Sabbath (1951)
You Can't Keep Murder Out (1951)
Kill Him Gently (1951)
Feline Frame-Up (1951)
Celluloid Suicide? (1951)
The Murder I Don't Remember (1952)
Kidnapped in Space (1952)
There's No Future in Murder (1952)
The Crook Who Wasn't There (1952)
Maniac Murders (1952)
The Mad Meteor (1952)
Operation Satellite (1952)

As A. G. Yates

The Cold Dark Hours (1958)

As Alan Yates

Novel:

Coriolanus, the Chariot (1978)

Stories & Novelettes:

Client for Murder (*Leisure Detective* #7, 195?)
The Corpse on the Carpet (*Leisure Detective* #8, 195?)
Farewell, My Lady of Shalott! (*Action Detective Magazine* #6, 1952)
Hush-a-Buy Homicide (*Leisure Detective* #9, 195?)
Margie (*Action Detective Magazine* #5, 1952)
Merger with Death (*Leisure Detective* #12, 195?)
Murder in the Family (*Leisure Detective* #11, 195?)
Murder Needs Education (*Action Detective Magazine* #2, 1952)
Murder! She Says (*Detective Monthly* #2, 195?)
My Love Lies Murdered (*Action Detective Magazine* #7, 1952)
Nemesis for a Nude! (*Leisure Detective* #10, 195?)

Genie from Jupiter (*Thrills Incorporated* #14, 1951)
Goddess of Space (*Thrills Incorporated* #20, 1952)
No Pixies on Pluto (*Thrills Incorporated* #22, 1952)
Planet of the Lost (*Thrills Incorporated* #17, 1951)
A Space Ship Is Missing (*Thrills Incorporated* #16, 1951)
Spacemen Spoofed (*Thrills Incorporated* #23, 1952)

Autobiography

Ready when you are, C.B.!: The autobiography of Alan Yates alias Carter Brown (1983)

www.ingramcontent.com/pod-product-compliance
Lightning Source LLC
LaVergne TN
LVHW021801060526
838201LV00058B/3196